Praise for Adam Baker

'There's no denying the strength of Baker's prose. It's violent and blokey . . . but also intelligent. The first 100 pages, especially, are rich with harrowing detail about the last days of Saddam's regime . . . *Juggernaut* is a rewarding read.'
SFX Magazine

'Great characters, an amazing level of detail, an insane yet wholly believable plot - *Juggernaut* is an excellent read, full of grotesque images and unexpected revelations.'
David Moody

'It had me on the edge of my seat from page one.'
Stephen Leather

'[A] squad of mercenaries looking for Saddam's looted gold finds instead a bioweapon that turns healthy humans into psychotic undead monsters. The virus is apparently of extraterrestrial origin, and Baker depicts its gory, fantastical mutagenic effects with relish . . . and with clipped sentences and whipcrack paragraphs he maintains a relentless pace . . . *Juggernaut* is hugely entertaining and as unstoppable as its namesake.'
Financial Times

'*Three Kings* meets *The Walking Dead*, with enough intelligence and panache to make what could've been predictable a great page turner.'
SFFworld.com

'Adam Baker's style is very reminiscent of a combination of Matthew Reilly and James Patterson, and like both of those authors, he uses it to tell a punchy story that keeps you engrossed from start to finish.'
Sci-fi Bulletin

'While ramping up the tension and confusion, Adam Baker also ramps up the action and despite the limited canvas of the Arctic landscape, manages to devise an impressive variety of situations for the characters.'
British Fantasy Society

About the Author

Before writing his debut novel *Outpost*, Adam Baker worked as a gravedigger and a film projectionist. *Juggernaut* is his second novel.

www.facebook.com/adambakerauthor
www.darkoutpost.com
Find Adam on Twitter: @AdamBakerAuthor

JUGGERNAUT

ADAM BAKER

HODDER

First published in Great Britain in 2012 by Hodder & Stoughton
An Hachette UK company

First published as a paperback in 2012

A CIP catalogue record for this title is available from the British Library.

Paperback ISBN 978 1 444 70908 7
Ebook ISBN 978 1 444 70909 4

Typeset by Palimpsest Book Production Limited, Falkirk, Stirlingshire
Printed and bound in Great Britain by Clays Ltd, St Ives plc

Hodder & Stoughton Ltd
338 Euston Road
London NW1 3BH

www.hodder.co.uk

For Emily

Central Intelligence Agency
Near East Division TO: 12MF-3-57-8U

RESTRICTED **DOS—01**
SPEKTR - 12 GROUP OPERATION DOSSIER

PROJECT TO LOCATE AND ACQUIRE SPEKTR VEHICLE

TOP SECRET/SPEKTR GROUP EYES ONLY

WARNING! This is a TOP SECRET – SPEKTR GROUP EYES ONLY document containing compartmentalised information essential to the national security of the United States. EYES ONLY ACCESS to the material herein is strictly limited to personnel possessing SPEKTR – 12 CLEARANCE LEVEL. Examination or use by unauthorised personnel is strictly forbidden and is punishable by federal law.

SPEKTR – 12 GROUP　　　　Oct 2005

TOP SECRET **SPECIAL HANDLING** NO FORM

Central Intelligence Agency

Directorate of Operations, Near East Division

Doc ID: 575JD1
Page 01/1

08/25/05

MEMORANDUM TO: Project Lead, D.Ops
SUBJECT: Spektr

Colonel,

We conducted a Predator overflight of the contamination zone at first light this morning, and I am forced to conclude that our attempts to contain the infection have failed.

Analysis of 11th Recon surveillance images confirm a fire-fight of considerable ferocity has taken place. Scorch marks and cratering suggest grenade detonations. Some of the ancient temple buildings have suffered significant blast damage. Both helicopters have been destroyed.

We have been unable to make contact with the incursion team for twenty-four hours. Their last transmission suggested exploration of the valley was proceeding as planned. We then received a series of unintelligible communications we attributed to damaged sat-com equipment.

We must conclude that the incursion team is lost. Any further attempts to retrieve the virus flask are beyond our current back-channel resources, and risk exposing agency involvement in the Spektr project.

I respectfully suggest we initiate CLEANSWEEP.

R. Koell
Field Officer
CA Special Proj, Baghdad

TOP SECRET SPECIAL HANDLING NO FORM

Central Intelligence Agency

Directorate of Operations, Near East Division

Doc ID: 575JD10
Page 01/1

08/25/05

MEMORANDUM TO: Project Lead, D.Ops
SUBJECT: Spektr

Colonel,

Our pilot reports successful detonation of the Sentinel device over Valley 403 at 09:57.

Joint Special Operations Command has been informed that the explosion near the Syrian border was an operational matter and no further investigation is required.

The incursion team were mercenaries. A multinational squad of second tier special forces. They were not affiliated with any of the major security contractors currently operating in this sector. They had no agency connection and were unaware of the true purpose of their mission. We do not expect their disappearance to attract undue attention.

R. Koell
Field Officer
CA Special Proj, Baghdad Station

Central Intelligence Agency

Directorate of Operations, Near East Division

FLASH CABLE - READ AND DESTROY

TO: Project Lead, D.Ops
FROM: R. Koell

08/25/05
14:46 AST

Colonel,

I have just received a bulletin from Joint Special Operations Command, Qatar. They say they have detected movement within the contamination zone. They report a locomotive heading out of the blast area along an old mine track.

JSOC have personnel in the Western Desert as part of Delta operations targeting foreign mujahedeen along the Syrian border. They have re-routed an air patrol from 160th Special Ops to intercept the locomotive.

We have made Operational Command aware of our wish to debrief the occupants of the vehicle and we are assured of their cooperation. We are currently monitoring radio traffic to determine if a member of the incursion team has survived.

IRAQ

August 25th 2005

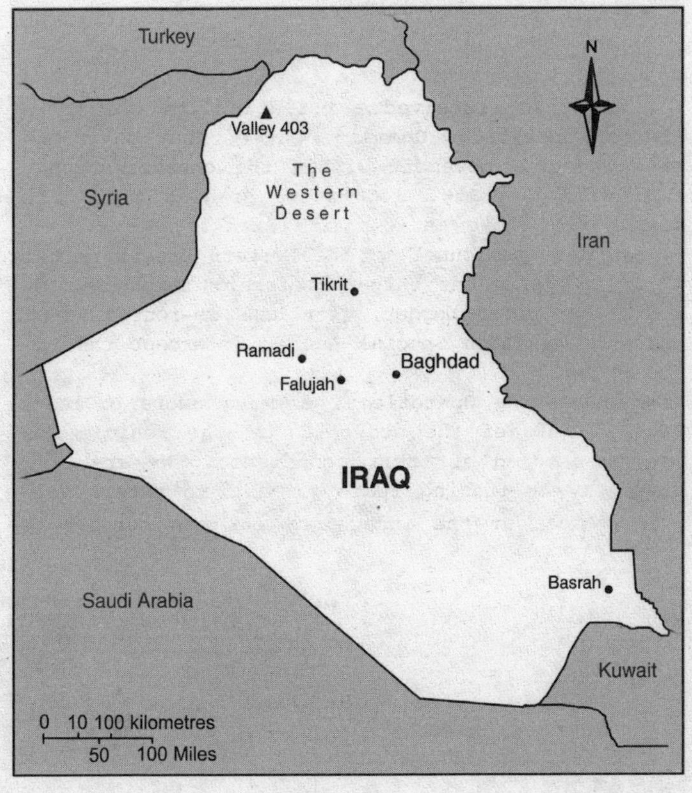

Ghost Train

The Western Desert
The Contamination Zone

The locomotive roared headlong through a rippling, caramel sandscape. A dust-streaked behemoth jetting black diesel fumes. A plough welded to the forward buffer bar scoured the dune-choked rails in a series of sand-bursts, like a speed-boat smacking through chop.

The engine looked like it tore out of hell. A shattered cyclopean nose lamp. Bodywork pitted, scarred, scorched black. Maintenance panels ripped away. Cables trailed and sparked.

The windshield was smashed. The cab was empty. The throttle was jammed at full power and lashed with rope. Rev needles at max. A tool box wedged the trip-brake pedal open. Every surface dusted in sand: the console, the driver's bar-stool seat, the plate floor.

The track ahead was blocked by a high fence half submerged in sand. Rusted chain-link propped up by metal stakes. The barrier stretched to vanishing point north and south.

Corroded stencil signs. Alternate English/Arabic. A warning to coalition troops and camel-driving Bedouin:

DANGER
TOXIC HAZARD

KEEP OUT

USE OF DEADLY FORCE AUTHORISED
IN ACCORDANCE WITH PA DIRECTIVE 84–4643

The locomotive punched through the barrier. It wrenched fence stakes from the sand. The plough blade sheering through chain-link like it was paper.

The Blackhawk flew low over dunes, chasing its shadow. It drew parallel with the locomotive.

Captain Flores held the chopper steady. She lifted her visor and surveyed the cab. Smashed windows. An empty driver's chair. She adjusted her helmet mike.

'*The bridge at Anah is out. That thing is going to drop into the fucking ravine.*'

Sergeant Tate sat in the cargo compartment. He had a goatee, and a big tattoo on his forearm: the Pegasus insignia of the 160th SOAR. *Night Stalkers Don't Quit.*

He tossed his rifle to Frost, the combat medic. He unbuckled his harness. He pulled on sand goggles and adjusted the earpiece of his radio.

'*Put me down on the roof.*'

The Blackhawk banked and hovered over the five-hundred-ton juggernaut. Flores adjusted airspeed, lowered the collective and nudged the cyclic forward.

The starboard tyre of the chopper gently touched down on the locomotive roof. Tate stepped onto the blackened, wind-scoured metal and the chopper pulled back. He crouched, lashed by downwash.

Tate crawled on his hands and knees along the cambered cowling. He climbed over louvered intake grilles and belching exhaust stacks.

He reached the roof of the cab. He climbed down onto the nose, holding the smashed air horn for support. He spat sand, crouched and peered through the broken windshield.

'*Anything?*'

'*Ghost train.*'

He swung his legs through the windshield. He slid across the engineer console into the cab.

Suede desert boots crunched on broken glass. He crouched and inspected debris that littered the floor. He examined Glock pistol clips and US STANAG magazines. He scooped up a handful of brass cartridge cases and let them spill through gloved fingers.

'*Spent rounds. Plenty of them. AK. Nine mil. Muzzle burn round each window. Fucking war zone.*'

'*Better cut the power. Few more miles you are going to run out of track.*'

Tate pulled off his goggles. He examined the lashed controls. He reached for the combat knife strapped to his webbing. Then he noticed the door ajar at the back of the cab. An access hatch with a big voltage zag. The engine compartment. He drew the Sig from his quick-release chest holster. He flicked the safety and chambered the pistol.

He kicked open the metal hatch. Deafening machine-howl from the cramped engine bay. A huge turbo-charged twelve-cylinder generator. Massive alternators and rectifiers. Pounding motive power.

He let his eyes adjust to the gloom. Sunlight shafted through roof vents. Fan blades projected swirling cartwheel shadows.

'*Hold on. I've found something.*'

A dusty boot protruding from behind the power plant. Tate edged along the wall of the tight engine compartment. A crouched shuffle.

Two figures in combat fatigues slumped in the corner, positioned beneath the down-draft of an overhead vent.

Ripped, ragged clothes. Blood spatters and sweat salt.

'*What can you see?*'

'*Couple of bodies.*'

Tate leant forward. He pulled aside the lapel of a prairie coat and examined dog tags.

S9346448
WHYTE
LUCY
NON AFF
O POS
MAR

He brushed black hair aside.

Lucy opened her eyes. Blue, like ice chips.

'You all right?' asked Tate. She snatched the knife from his chest rig. He caught her hand as she slammed the blade at his throat.

*

The locomotive at a standstill. Tate carried Lucy in his arms. He kicked open the slide door and jumped from the cab.

The Blackhawk performed a steep combat landing and set down among the dunes. Tyres settled in soft sand. Lucy and Tate were engulfed in a cyclone of rotor-wash.

Lucy turned her head. She wondered if the helicopter was a vivid hallucination. A vision of deliverance. Earlier that day, as temperatures peaked and she took shelter in the fan-blasted cool of the engine compartment, she succumbed to a lucid dream in which she explored the paths and arbours of a perfumed garden. She picked invisible flowers and wore them in her hair.

The main rotor slowed to a standstill. The sandstorm began to subside.

The side door of the chopper slid open. Three Delta jumped out, faces masked by sand goggles and scarves.

'There's another girl in the engine compartment,' said Tate. 'I think she's alive.'

He laid Lucy on the ground. A medic crouched beside her. He checked her pupils, checked the pulse in her neck.

'Severe dehydration. Bad heatstroke. Let's get her on a drip.'

He unfolded a litter. They lifted Lucy onto the stretcher and laid her in the cramped cabin of the Blackhawk.

They brought a second girl from the locomotive. Blonde. Unconscious. They strapped her to a litter and laid her next to Lucy.

Tate checked dog tags.

'Amanda Greenwald.'

The medic examined Amanda's bandaged leg. He pulled away crusted dressings.

'Shot in the thigh. Looks infected. Crack me some gauze and a suture kit.'

The Delta guys climbed aboard and sat looking down at the women.

Dust-off. Escalating engine whine. Rotor spinning up to full speed. A tornado of sand.

Lucy turned her head. A doorman in a full-face visor. She looked beyond the long barrel-drum of his Dillon Gatling gun, the fuel pods and Hellfire rockets. She watched the dunes fall away beneath her, the locomotive lost in a desert so vast she could almost see the curvature of the Earth.

The medic pulled a trauma trunk from beneath a canvas bench. IV equipment packed in Ziploc backs. He drove a large-bore fourteen-gauge needle into the back of Lucy's hand and taped it down. He uncoiled tube and plugged a bag of saline solution into her hand. He hooked the bag to overhead webbing.

The medic shouted to be heard above wind noise and rotor roar. 'Drink.'

He held a bottle to her mouth. She gulped and coughed. He poured water on her face and washed away grime.

'Look at me. Can you talk? How many fingers am I holding up?'

She tried to speak. Her cracked lips formed words but she couldn't make a sound.

She tried to reach out to the stretcher beside her and take Amanda's hand, but her arm was blocked by the centre stanchion.

'Don't worry. She's alive. You'll both be in Baghdad in no time.'

He gave Lucy more water. She gripped the bottle like it was life itself.

IBN Sina Hospital, Baghdad.

Lucy lay on a gurney. She was in some kind of triage room.

She struggled to focus. Cracked ceiling plaster. A broken light socket.

She turned her head. A smashed window. Glass on the floor. Streaks of arterial spray across the white-tiled wall, blood dried black.

A couple of Iraqi guys walked into the room. White coats, stethoscopes hung round their necks. Cheap sneakers crunched on grit and glass. They murmured in Arabic. They checked her pulse. They checked her eyes. One of them leaned into her field of vision, and switched to English. His voice was clear, educated, like he studied abroad.

'Lucy?' said the doctor. He looked like he hadn't slept for a week. 'Lucy, can you hear me?'

She wanted to reply, but she couldn't turn thought to speech.

'You're in hospital. We'll look after you, Lucy. You're safe now.'

He helped her sip water from a china cup. He helped her lie back.

They cut off her clothes. They sliced her laces with a knife and peeled off her boots. They released the press-studs of her Osprey body armour. They cut off her knee pads. They cut through her trousers and belt with trauma shears. They cut through her Union flag T-shirt. They let her keep her Nike sports bra and briefs.

They tried to remove her watch and pull the gold band from her wedding finger but she snatched her hand away.

They draped her with a sheet.

'Get some sleep.'

Lucy lay on a hospital bed halfway between life and death. A bare room. Iron bed-frame. Iron chair.

Sometimes she was alone. Sometimes Sergeant Miller sat on the chair beside her.

Come on, Sergeant Miller would tell her. *Keep fighting. You're not done yet.*

But Miller died two years ago in Afghanistan. He got fragged by a mortar round as his patrol entered a Helmand village on a meet-and-greet. Bled out from a gut wound as he lay in a ditch waiting for a medevac Chinook that took six hours to show up. Clutching his belly, panting and screaming. His coffin offloaded at RAF Lyneham, walked down the cargo ramp of a Hercules with a Union flag draped over the lid, then a slow cortège through Wootton Bassett. The battalion held a service at Camp Bastion. They laid a poppy wreath in front of the memorial wall. The padre led prayers in his sash and fatigues, until a rocket alert sent everyone running for the bunker.

'What's it like? Being dead?'

'*It's not so bad.*' Miller squeezed her hand. '*It's peaceful. A long sleep.*'

'Sounds nice.'

He shrugged.

'*No wife. No kids. I had nothing to leave behind. How about you? Do you have a reason to live?*'

She woke. She sat up. She sat on the edge of the bed. An old mattress mottled with piss- and bloodstains.

The ceiling fan revolved, gently stirring the air. Must be one of the brief periods each day when Baghdad enjoyed electrical power.

There was a needle taped to the back of her hand. A clear tube ran to an empty bag of saline hung from a rusted drip stand.

'Hello?'

She peeled tape and pulled the wide-bore needle from her hand.

'Hey. Anyone?'

Street noise from an open window. Car horns, the heavy throb of twin-rotor Chinooks.

Distant gunfire. Might be fire-fight. Sunni militia and the Mahdi Army duking it out. Or it might be a wedding party.

Crackling speakers. The noonday call to prayer. Muedhin summoned the faithful.

'*Allahu Akbar . . . Allahu Akbar . . .*'

Mournful. Alien.

There was an insectocutor on the wall. Two glowing ultraviolet bars. Lucy watched bugs spit and crackle as they were drawn into the lethal light.

A washstand. The faucet gulped and spat. She scooped water in cupped hands and drank.

A sliver of broken mirror screwed to the wall. Cracked lips. Sunken eyes. Peeling, sun-blasted skin. A living corpse. A thirty-three-year-old woman reduced to a desiccated hag.

She pulled shredded mosquito netting aside and looked out the window.

Bullet-pocked houses. Minarets. Saddam mural with his face scratched out. Everything the colour of dust.

Donkey carts. Fucked-up scooters. Diesel rickshaws.

She was outside the Green Zone. A Western security contractor lying in an unguarded hospital bed. She and Amanda could be snatched any moment. Sold out by medical staff, held for ransom by Ba'ath Fedayeen gangsters.

A Czech TV crew had been carjacked the previous month. Two guys shot by the roadside. Two women gang-raped and beheaded, star attraction in the latest al-Qaeda VHS sold in the souk.

She had to make it back to the Western sector.

Lucy bit down hard on her thumb, let a shot of pain and adrenalin shock her fully awake.

She stepped into the corridor.

'Hello? Anyone speak English?'

A distant doorway. A boy lay on a rusted, blood-streaked trolley. His right leg had been amputated above the knee. His neck was held rigid in a C-collar. Bandage like a blindfold. He counted prayer beads and whispered verses from the Koran.

She could hear a woman crying nearby. Deep grief.

Shuddering sobs and babbling despair, rising and falling like waves breaking against the shore.

'Hello?' Her voice echoed down the passageway. 'Mandy?'

The distant corridor junction was suddenly blocked by two figures in white biohazard suits.

The figures advanced towards her.

She turned and ran. Her legs failed and she fell against the corridor wall.

Gloved hands took her arms and carried her back to the room. They pushed her onto the bed.

The suited figures stood over her. She could hear the electric hum of backpack respirators. Air sucked through charcoal virus filters. Their gauntlet and boot cuffs were secured with gasket locks, and sealed with silver tape. Tyvek suit fabric creaked and squeaked.

White hoods. She could see faces behind Lexan visors. A lean, grey-haired guy. He looked military. And a young man. He looked well groomed, collegiate.

'Give her a shot,' said the kid. 'Chill her out.'

The older guy laid a case on a side table. He flipped latches. He loaded a hypo, slow and clumsy with rubber-gloved fingers. Amytal. He flicked bubbles from the syringe. He held her wrist. She was too weak to resist. She watched the needle prick her skin.

The college kid leant into her field of vision. 'Hi, Lucy.'

'You won't get anything out of her for a while, Koell.'

'They didn't change her drip?'

'Lucky she got a single bag. Looters stripped this place bare a couple of years back. They even took doorknobs. I brought an interpreter here last month. Got in a fire-fight. Lost his thumb. They tore his shirt and used it for bandage. Then they gave him aspirin. Charged me fifty bucks. Said they were running low on aspirin.'

The kid waved his gloved hand in front of Lucy's face and tried to click rubber fingers. 'Can you hear me, Lucy?'

Lucy decided to hide behind the drug and act stupefied. She ignored the men and stared into the cold blue glow of the insectocutor. She didn't blink.

'What's that on her wrist?' asked Koell. 'A Rolex?'

'An orderly tried to steal it while she slept. He got his eye gouged.'

Koell pulled back Lucy's eyelid. He flagged a penlight in front of her face and monitored dilation. 'She's weak, sedated. I don't think she can hear us. Where's the other girl?'

'Next door. Shot in the leg.'

'Blotches? Lesions?'

'Both clear.'

'Pity. We'll collect tissue samples anyway.'

The colonel kicked a pile of ripped clothes in the corner. 'Didn't have much equipment. Couple of radios. Binoculars. Empty canteen. The blonde had a machete tucked in her belt. Looked like it had plenty of use.'

'Nothing in their pockets?'

The colonel pointed to a crumpled photograph on the table next to the bed. 'Just a sorry-ass gang photo.'

Five soldiers. Lucy and her crew in a bar, laughing, toasting the camera.

Koell looked around. A sprig of cable where a light switch used to be. A tattered Koran.

'Not exactly Walter Reed.'

'Maybe we should take her back to The Zone,' said the colonel. 'This place is a shithole.'

'I was down at the twenty-eighth CASH this morning. They were overrun. Some Sunni fuck blew himself to pieces in the Al-Shorja Market. A flatbed with a bunch of artillery shells hidden under potatoes. Fucker lit them up and took out a foot patrol. Hell of a mess. Three KIA, two more expectant. Bunch of T-1 evacs with shrapnel, third degree burns. Fuck this bitch.'

'Even so.'

'Let's keep this shit compartmentalised. Let's keep them outside the wire. Every mercenary the world over has converged on this city. Ex-cons. Transients. Some of these creeps were running Salvadorian death squads. Most of them are hiding behind fake ID. Nobody will give a damn if a couple of privateers drop off the map. Nobody will notice they've gone.'

The colonel checked a clipboard. 'Lucy White. Thirty-three. British citizen. Fourteen Intelligence Company. Target reconnaissance. Honourable discharge.'

'She's nothing special. My driver is ex-Delta.'

The colonel flipped pages.

'No listed next of kin, no home address. Runs her own crew. "Vanguard Risk Consultants". Dummy corporation registered out of Uruguay. Plays mother hen to a bunch of Tier Two operators. Quality trigger-time. Three US citizens and a guy from Pretoria.'

'Good for them.'

'Seems a pretty low-rent outfit. Nickel-and-dime. Did some stuff in Honduras. They aren't connected. They're out of the loop. No State Department deals. Losing work to the big contractors. Mostly been pulling taxi runs. Hauled kitchen equipment for the new Halliburton chow halls. Shipped foreign currency to the Interior Ministry. Provided close protection for a couple of Exxon engineers.'

'Then she'll be just another KIA. Both of them. No need to complicate matters. They won't be missed. Let's tie up loose ends. Triple shot of phenol. Quick and painless. Finish them both, and get the fuck out of here.'

Koell took a pneumatic injector gun from the case and loaded a vial of clear liquid.

'Hold on,' said the colonel. 'This was your call. You found these guys. You sent them out to the valley. What the fuck happened out there? Don't you want to know?'

The colonel crouched beside Lucy. He waved a hand in front of her unfocused eyes.

'Can you hear me, Lucy? I want you to concentrate. I want you to tell me what happened.'

No response.

He sat in the chair next to the bed. He took Lucy's hand.

'Can you hear me? Can you understand what I'm saying? We've got a little something to help you sleep. But first I need to know. What did you find out there in the desert?'

No response.

The colonel examined the gang photo. The faded, smiling faces. He held the picture so Lucy could see.

'You have to tell me, Lucy. What happened to you? What happened to your team?'

FIVE DAYS EARLIER

The Score

Camp Victory. The US army compound at Baghdad International Airport.

Lucy and her crew sat on crates and watched marines transfer money from a bomb-proof Peli case to a black canvas holdall.

The soldiers had locked themselves in a caged section of the warehouse. Four men stood around a trestle table. Two to count and re-count, two to bear witness. They stacked bricks of hundred-dollar bills in vacuum-sealed plastic.

'Got to be three, four million at least,' said Lucy.

Lucy and her team were wearing full body armour. Lucy had a cheery Sheraton conference badge pinned to her flak jacket. 'Hello, my name is . . . FUCK YOU.'

'That shit is straight from the Federal Reserve,' said Toon. African-American. Black Power fist scribbled on the breast plate of his vest. Bald head. 'Consecutive serial numbers. You could steal it, but you couldn't spend it.'

'Bet some oily Swiss fucker would give you thirty cents on the dollar. Still a cool million.'

'Split five ways? Wouldn't go far.'

Lucy shrugged.

'I've been broke so long, I wouldn't know how to spend it.'

'Look at those clowns,' said Toon. 'Cherry motherfuckers. Green as grass. They've been in-country five minutes. We could take them out anywhere between here and the Interior Ministry. Wouldn't even put up a fight.'

'No. Make the drop. Cash the cheque.'

'Fuck that shit. Five hundred dollars a day. Is that how much your life is worth? Five hundred bucks is nothing.'

Lucy shook her head.

'My motto? "Live to spend it." No use being rich and dead.'

'No one would give a damn,' said Toon. 'Victimless crime. Not like this stuff is going to feed starving orphans. They're just greasing some Provisional chieftain for a bunch more reconstruction contracts. Only a sucker would stay honest in the middle of this shitstorm.'

Lucy watched a rat scurry along a roof girder high above them. She rubbed her eyes.

'All right, boss?'

'Yeah,' said Lucy. 'Just tired.'

Huang entered the warehouse by a side door. A combat medic and a good driver. He rejoined the crew and sat on a crate.

'What did you get?' asked Amanda. A Californian rich girl gone bad. She had blond hair, a nose ring and a meth habit. She had found redemption in the meditative breath control and serene focus of an airforce rifle range.

'The orderly is a cool guy. Happy to see a bottle of Jim Beam. He broke out a bunch of Percocet. A few Vicodin. Smoother ride than guzzling fucking NyQuil.'

Amanda and Huang bumped fists.

'You got to score some more Oxy. Pure, sweet buzz.'

'Fucking pill freaks.' Voss. Tall, lean, early forties. He had a thick South African accent. 'You think you're dealing with combat stress. You'll just rot your fucking brain, bokkie.'

'A person has to relax.'

'So cook up a spoonful of smack. Do the job right.'

The crew adjusted their scopes, their buckles, their laces. A series of pre-mission survival rituals. They checked mags and chambered. Green tip tungsten carbide penetrators.

Lucy bit the cap from a Sharpie. They wrote call-signs, grids and frequencies on their forearms.

'Radio check,' said Lucy.

They each wore a short-wave TASC headset. The radio was clipped to their webbing. Five-hundred-metre range. The mike was a Velcro throat-strap. The earpiece was a constant open channel.

Lucy stepped away from the group. She thumbed the pressel switch on her chest rig.

'Check, check, check.'

Affirmative ten-fours.

'Ladies. Gentlemen.'

An uptight CO. Hard to tell rank. Most marines removed insignia and ditched the salute when they moved in-country. Overt signs of seniority might attract a sniper's bullet.

The buzz cut surveyed Lucy's team with contempt. Mercenaries. Long hair and tattoos. All kinds of trophy jewellery and charms: sharks' teeth, rosaries, bullet pendants. They wore their sidearms at the hip instead of the chest plate snap-holster favoured by regular army.

Soldiers of fortune. No code. No honour.

They signed for manila packets. They tore open envelopes and counted cash. They tucked money in the map pocket of their vests next to sweetheart photos, goodbye letters and power-of-attorney.

'Time to move out,' said the CO.

The team stood and headed for the trucks. Voss had FUCK THE ARMY scrawled on the back of his vest.

A three-car convoy. Marines up front in a Humvee with a .50 cal mounted on the roof. Two black, twelve-cylinder GMC Suburbans behind. The GMCs were ghetto-rigged with heavy ram bars, ballistic windows and Kevlar panels.

They climbed into the first Suburban. A marine private took the wheel. Lucy rode shotgun. Amanda and Toon took the back seat. A young marine sat between them, hugging the padlocked money bag, trying to hide his fear.

Huang took the wheel of the third vehicle. Voss was rear gunner. He took a fire position at the tailgate.

Lucy watched the crew of the lead Humvee form a huddle and butt helmets.

'These fucking kids are going to get us killed,' muttered Lucy. She turned in her seat. 'Weapons very free, all right? Don't wait for an order.'

'Fuckin' A,' muttered Toon, adjusting his grip on his carbine.

Amanda cracked her knuckles.

'Wire-tight and good to go.'

The marine kissed a St Michael medallion and tucked it into his ballistic vest.

'Don't feel ashamed, kid,' said Amanda. 'Only a fool wouldn't be scared.'

Engine roar echoed through the vaulted warehouse. High-beams shafted through broiling diesel fumes.

A marine private hauled back the hangar door and the convoy rolled out into torrential rain.

They drove parallel to a row of warehouses. They sped through a field of Conex shipping containers and headed for the perimeter wire.

The compound gatehouse was a narrow breach in a HESCO sand barrier with twin machine-gun sangars either side.

They got waved through. They sped down a fresh strip of asphalt laid across desert to the expressway. Route Irish. The twelve-kilometre thunder run between the airport and the Green Zone. They passed bullet-pocked signs for Fallujah and Ramadi.

They drove fast and tight. Rain lashed the windshield. Wipers swept-double time.

Adrenalin high. Lucy stroked the rubber custom grip of her rifle. Every smell, every texture, hitting with the heightened clarity of dreams.

A few other cars on the road. A white Toyota pulled close

behind the convoy. An old man and his son. Windshield decked out with prayer beads and a gold fringe. Voss waved them back. They didn't respond. He shouldered his assault rifle and put a shot through the front grille. The Toyota swerved across the median and hit a ditch jetting steam.

'Salaam Alaikum, motherfucker.'

They raced past checkpoints, blast barriers and concertina wire.

Baghdad up ahead.

Ministry buildings split open by Tomahawks. Homeless families bivouacked in burned-out offices. Campfires flickered in upper floors throughout the night.

The 'Mother of All Battles' mosque. Each minaret shaped like a SCUD.

The skyline veiled in rain.

A tight side street. Slum housing. Crumbling concrete apartment blocks flanked a dirt road with a sewer trench either side. Lean dogs pawed garbage. A few locals in dishdashas sheltered in doorways.

Lucy pulled a map from the sun-visor pocket.

'What's he doing? Your CO. Why the detour?'

'JTAC says a truck flipped outside the old college. It's going to take them an hour to clear the road.'

'Not many people around,' said Toon. 'I don't like the atmospherics.'

Lucy slapped the driver on the shoulder.

'Tell your boss right in two hundred metres. We have to get out of these side roads.'

Burned-out cars. A rat-run alley blocked by oil drums full of rubble.

'They pay for a kill,' said Amanda. 'You know that, right? Sunni militia. Plant a bomb, kill a white skin. There's a bounty.'

'How much are we worth?'

'About three hundred dollars. Lot of money round here.'

'It's the rain,' said the driver. 'Everyone is hiding from the rain.'

'Your command vehicle. It's got electronic countermeasures, right? For roadside?'

'No.'

'I don't like it.' Toon craned to look up. Balconies and snarled phone cable. 'Classic choke point. Sitting ducks.' He turned in his seat and addressed the marine beside him.

'What's your name?'

'Rubin.'

'Tell your boss to speed up.'

The young marine hesitated, then spoke into his radio.

'India One, this is India Two. Come in, over.'

'*Go ahead India Two.*'

'Contract suggests we move a little faster, over.'

'*India Two, maintain radio silence, over.*'

'Roger that.'

'Tell him to keep out of the road ruts,' said Lucy. 'Perfect place for a pressure plate. Seriously. Tell him.'

'India One, this is India Two, over.'

'*Maintain silence, India Two.*'

'Contract suggests we keep out of ruts in the road.'

'*Tell her to fuck herself, over.*'

'Roger that.'

'Your CO is a fucking idiot,' said Toon.

'That's Lance-Corporal Cortez. You call him Sir.'

The lead Humvee stopped.

'What's the deal?' demanded Lucy. 'What the fuck is going on?'

Cortez kicked open the side door of the Humvee and got out.

'Fuck,' muttered Lucy. She extended the butt-stock of her assault rifle. She flicked the safety to Off, selector to Burst. She popped the door of the Suburban, ran across the street and threw herself against a cinder-block wall. Rifle to her shoulder. She scanned windows, parapets and balconies. No movement.

Voss in her earpiece:

'*Fuck is going on, boss? Fucking dead meat out here.*'

'Hold on.'

She wiped rain from her eyes and looked down the street. A Fiat Tempra station wagon parked by the roadside fifty yards ahead. The vehicle was empty. It sat low on the rear axle. Might be stacked with artillery shells. Might be a bunch of twenty-litre palm oil drums filed with a bath-tub brew of ammonium nitrate and aluminium filings.

Cortez slowly walked towards the Fiat. He stopped seventy-five yards out. He checked for disturbed earth. He scanned the ground for secondaries or a command wire. He checked balconies and windows, tried to gauge probable line-of-sight for a trigger man crouched with a cellphone detonator and a video camera.

'Hey. Cortez,' shouted Lucy. 'Let's back up, all right? We'll turn round. Get out of here.'

The corporal peered through the Fiat window. An empty back seat. An empty trunk. He relaxed. He jogged back towards the Humvee.

'Okay,' he shouted. 'Let's go.'

Slow motion:

Guy steps out of a doorway and shoulders an RPG. Flash. Billowing back-blast. Streaking projectile. Lucy screaming '*Get Down!*' Cortez looking at her like '*What the fuck?*' The grenade hits him between the shoulder blades and suddenly there is nothing left of the CO but pink mist.

It rained meat.

RPG guy stepped from the doorway again. He hurriedly clipped a fresh sabot into the smoking barrel and shouldered the weapon. A young, bearded guy in baggy trousers and white shirt. Lucy shot him through the left eye and blew out the back of his skull. He was thrown clean out of his flip-flops.

A compadre ducked out of the doorway and snatched up the RPG.

The driver got out of the Humvee and looked at scraps of wet muscle draped over the hood and windshield. Shock. Paralysis.

Lucy ran across the street. She grabbed him by the collar of his tac vest. His name patch said DANVER.

'Specialist. Did you radio it in?'

'No. Yes.'

'You have to get it together. Every mobbed-up Sunni in this quarter of the city will be heading this way.'

'We can't leave the Corp.'

Lucy glanced around. Scorched flak jacket and ribs beneath the Humvee. Arms and legs in the street. The corporal's head lay in the sewer trench, still wearing a K-pot helmet. Pooled blood and rainwater.

'We do not have the time to police this shit up.'

Crack of AK fire. Muzzle flash from a high window. Dirt kicked up around their feet. They took shelter behind the Humvee.

'Contact,' screamed Danver. 'Fire for effect.'

A marine squirmed through the roof hatch of the Humvee, racked the .50 cal and swept walls and windows with heavy fire. The vehicle rocked on its suspension. Jackhammer roar. The weapon ejected a stream of smoking brass. He pulverised balconies and blew craters in cinder block.

Toon and Amanda joined Lucy behind the Humvee and fired full auto up the street. Four-second burst. Reload. Rally shout:

'Like it?'

'Love it.'

A kid ducked out of a doorway and spray-fired his AK, so green he closed his eyes and looked away as the weapon bucked in his hands. Amanda dropped him double-tap: efficient centre-of-mass kill shots that shook him like hammer blows.

Another kid jumped from an alleyway. Distant shout:

'*Allahu Akbar . . .*'

Toon stepped out from behind the Humvee. Bullets spitting dirt at his feet. He selected full auto and ripped the kid's chest open. The kid fell dead. Toon dropped the spent mag and wedged a fresh clip in the receiver. Full auto. He made the dead kid dance.

Lucy dragged Toon to cover.

'You fucking idiot. Trying to get killed?'

Huang and Voss took flanking positions in doorways and guarded the rear.

'How many we got?' shouted Toon. 'How many shooters?'

'Two. Three. End of the street.'

Two shooters at a window seventy yards down the street. Amateurs. Spray-fire. She waited for a reload lull. Lucy popped single shots, blowing chunks out of the windowsill. Suppressive fire. She felt calm. A flow state. This was where she belonged.

The last two rounds in each mag were red-tip tracer to alert she was running low. She ejected the clip, pulled a fresh thirty-round STANAG mag from a vest pouch and slapped it into the receiver.

Danver dragged a backpack from the cab. He crouched behind the Humvee and worked the radio.

'Tell them we are by the old telephone exchange,' shouted Lucy.

'All call signs, this is India One, heavy contact, taking RPG and sustained fire. Grid: niner, six, two, five . . .'

The windshield took hits but didn't break. Spider web cracks in the ballistic glass.

Bullets splashed mud and rainwater.

'JTAC says stay put and dig in. The Quick Reaction Force are staging at Camp Freedom. We should have air cover in ten minutes. Mechanised exfil in twenty.'

'This is nuts. We have to pull the fuck back, get out of this enfilade.'

'RPG,' screamed Amanda.

The guy stepped out of an alley. Amanda shot him in the gut as he pulled the trigger. Flash. Billowing blast of rocket efflux. Streaking projectile.

The grenade punched through the windshield and blew out the command Humvee. Lucy threw herself down and lay in the mud. She hid her face from the scalding pressure wave, the supersonic corona of metal and glass.

She struggled to her feet like a boxer trying to beat the count. Concussed. Deafened. She tongued a tooth. She had lost a filling. She wiped blood from her nose with a gloved hand.

She grabbed Danver by his tac-vest and pulled him upright.

Debris imbedded in the road. Jagged shards of metal dug into walls, coiling smoke. Acrid stench of cordite.

The gunner rolled off the roof, legs and hair on fire. Lucy slapped out the flames, seized his collar and dragged him across the street.

A volley of AK fire. Bullets blew rock chips from a nearby wall.

Lucy kicked open a door and pulled the injured man inside, Danver on her heels. Toon and Amanda followed closely behind her, laying down fire.

A shuttered hair salon. Big mirrors. Beautician chairs. Wigs and hair extensions hung from the wall like scalps.

'Go firm,' she shouted into her radio. 'Huang, we need you.'

They lay cover fire as Huang sprinted down the street.

Huang unzipped his trauma kit. He cut away the guy's tattered pants and wriggled on Nitrile gloves. He swabbed the wounds with Betadine and pressed burn gel dressings on weeping flesh. He checked the kid over, patted him down for wounds.

'Fucker's veins are collapsing. Shrapnel. Must be an internal haemorrhage somewhere.'

The gunner fumbled at his groin.

'Don't worry,' said Huang. 'You haven't lost your dick.'

Huang pulled his bayonet from a belt sheath and sawed at the injured man's clothes.

The soldier trembled and arched his back. Grand mal.

'Can't you give him something?'

'Blood pressure is too low for morphine. You. Danver. Help me find the bleed.'

Voss ran through the doorway, slammed against a wall and slid to the floor. He was panting. He dropped a spent magazine and slapped a fresh clip into the receiver.

'More of them by the minute. We can't stay here, boss.'

Crackle of gunfire. Lucy crouched in the doorway. She gulped from her canteen. The Humvee was ablaze. Ammunition cooking off. Pistol rounds popped like corn. .50 cal rounds discharged with a heavy thud. The street filled with the sour stench of ignition.

'Were there phosphor grenades in that thing?'

'A few,' said Danver.

'The SUVs are starting to burn.'

'Where's the money?'

'Fuck the money.'

'We should throw a strobe.'

'No need,' said Lucy. 'Choppers will see the smoke.'

Bright arterial blood bubbling from a hole in the injured man's belly.

'Smells like shit,' said Danver.

'Gut wound,' said Huang. 'Intestinal bleed. The guy is pretty messed up. We need those fucking Bradleys.'

Lucy glimpsed movement in the lead Suburban. Private Rubin, frozen with fear, money bag in his lap.

'Ah fuck.'

The hood of the SUV was enveloped in flame. The tyres were ablaze. Burning oil and brake fluid trickled into the gutter. Rubin was starting to nod on the back seat, overcome by fumes.

Lucy gripped her rifle and prepared to sprint to the SUV. The wooden doorframe beside her exploded. She fell backward into the salon and rolled for cover. She pulled a shard of wood out of her cheek.

'Sniper. He's on the roof directly across the street. Mandy, lay suppressing fire. Brass him up. Toon, get Rubin out the car.'

'And you?'

'I'm going to take this fucker down.'

Three-count.

Amanda ducked out the doorway and directed burst-fire at the parapet across the street.

Toon ran to the SUV. He shouldered the money bag and pulled Rubin clear.

Lucy ran across the street and kicked in a door. Some kind of trashy boutique. She toppled mannequins as she ran for the stairs. Three flights. A ladder to a roof hatch. Lucy paused to catch her breath. A sudden wave of too-old-for-this-shit. Her hands were shaking.

She shook out cramps and climbed the ladder. She prodded the hatch open with the muzzle of her rifle.

She lunged up and out. She rolled clear and lay prone.

A wide, flat roof slick with rain. A rusting satellite dish. A couple of air-con units. A water tank. Thick smoke from burning vehicles in the street below. The bitter stink of melting plastic.

Lucy got to her feet dripping rain. She walked along the parapet. A young kid wrestling to reload a massive Dragnov rifle. He looked twelve, thirteen years old.

A gap between buildings. A thirty-foot drop into a garbage-strewn alley. She ran, and vaulted the chasm.

Lucy's boot clinked spent shell cases. The kid looked round. They stared at each other.

'Drop it,' shouted Lucy.

It broke the spell. The kid struggled to work the rifle bolt.

'Drop the fucking gun.'

The kid chambered the weapon and raised it. Lucy shot him in the chest. A tracer round pierced straight through him like a streak of laser light.

He lay on his back. He wiped rain from his eyes.

She could hear the thrum of incoming choppers. AH-6 Little Bird gun ships ready to lay suppressing fire at six thousand rounds a minute.

She knelt beside the kid. She examined the scorched wound.

'Can you hear me? Can you understand English?'

The kid smiled. Blood bubbled between his teeth.

'Fucking whore. Fucking American whore. You bad luck. You die soon.'

She grabbed the kid by his shirt and pulled him to his feet. He drooled blood and saliva. He pulled burnt dollars from the ripped chest-pocket of Lucy's flak jacket.

He held up the money.

'My god is greater than your god.'

Lucy threw him over the parapet. He fell three storeys into the wreckage of the burning Humvee, and was lost in flame.

She crouched on the roof and picked wet dollars from rainwater puddles.

Midnight. The Al-Rasheed Hotel.

Lucy and her crew in their suite. The room was furnished with leather armchairs and lawn furniture stolen from the Scheherazade Bar on the roof. Stars and stripes nailed to the wall with a couple of bayonets.

A mortar attack had blown the power. A random shell fired over the Zone's seventeen-foot blast wall had taken out a pylon. The room was lit by candlelight.

The team had stripped down to T-shirts and shorts.

'Hey,' said Amanda. 'I saw this marine sniper on TV the

other night. Reporter asked what he felt each time he killed a guy.'

'What did he say?'

'Recoil.'

Lucy smiled.

'Wish I could sleep,' said Lucy.

'I got Ambien. Might have some Motrin.'

Amanda fanned herself with a magazine. Her good looks uglified by heavy tattoos and a nose stud.

'I popped three bombers,' said Lucy. 'And NyQuil. Tripping my arse off. Too humid. Just can't sleep in this heat.'

'Hear that?'

The distant sound of guys bellowing 'Living on a Prayer'.

'Bechtel guys making their own fun until the power's back on.'

Lucy pulled a fresh Michelob from an ice bucket and ran the cold bottle across her forehead.

Huang, Toon and Voss were asleep on the floor, weapons and flak jackets propped against the wall.

Lucy and Amanda sat in facing armchairs. Money and pills on the table. Half-eaten flatbread and lamb kebab.

Rain lashed the window.

'Did you see Toon?' asked Lucy. 'Did you see him walk into line-of-fire?'

Amanda shrugged. She swigged vodka. 'We're coming apart. All of us. My ears arc shot. Ringing. It never stops.'

'I think we've used up our luck,' said Lucy. 'Playing Russian roulette each time we roll out Assassin's Gate.'

'I've been broke. I don't want to be broke any more.'

Amanda's dad kicked her out when she was seventeen. She slept in a car for a year. Summer. Winter. Parked each night in the lot of a Holiday Inn.

'Tell me about the guy.'

'It was a prisoner transport,' said Amanda. 'An old guy. Ex-Republican Guard. He told me about a convoy. A bunch of military vehicles escorting an armoured truck. A shipment of stuff taken from the vaults beneath the National Museum days before Baghdad got hammered by Tomahawks and looted to shit. Said they took the truck way out into the desert. Said it was still there.'

'What was in the truck?'

'Gold. Lots of gold.'

'Where is this guy?'

'Abu Ghraib.'

'Do you trust him?'

'I don't trust anybody.'

A table lamp flickered on and glowed steady.

'Hey.'

The room powered up. The rising hum of air-con. A beep from the wall phone. A click as the TV returned to standby.

'Let's talk to the guy,' said Lucy. 'Hear what he has to say.'

She closed her eyes and basked in the breeze as the ceiling fan stirred the air.

TOP SECRET SPECIAL HANDLING NO FORM

Central Intelligence Agency

Directorate of Operations, Near East Division

Doc ID: 575JJUFG
Page 01/1

08/21/05

MEMORANDUM TO: Project Lead, D.Ops
SUBJECT: Spektr

Colonel,

JABRIL JAMADI has been separated from former regime elements currently interned at JSOC's temporary HUMIT screening facility at Balad, and is now held in solitary confinement at Abu Ghraib, Tier Four. I believe, sooner or later, he will inadvertently reveal the precise location of our objective at the SPEKTR site.

We will continue covert electronic surveillance of his cell. We have a listening device with an independent power source wired into the light fitting. We monitor visitation requests. We have resources available to track his movements following the authorisation of his release. I feel this subterfuge is likely to prove more efficacious than rendition to our black sites in Egypt or Syria. JAMADI has so far proved impervious to standard interrogation techniques. I suggest we allow him to make contact with confederates outside the prison. We should look for an opportunity to turn him loose without arousing his suspicions. I am confident he will lead us to our objective.

R. Koell
Field Officer
CA Special Proj, Baghdad

Jabril

Abu Ghraib detention facility, twenty miles west of Baghdad.

'The Place of Ravens'. Saddam's grim Lubianka. Site of torture and summary execution.

The site was divided into three zones:

'The Hard Site'. The prison itself. A square mile of bleak cell blocks and courtyards. A concrete perimeter wall, high as a cliff face. Pylon floodlights and panopticon watch-towers at each corner. Cells used by coalition forces to isolate high-value detainees for interrogation by military intelligence and the CIA.

Camp Ganci. An adjacent tent city surrounded by razor wire and wooden guard towers. Home to prisoners accused of Iraqi-on-Iraqi crimes such as car theft, rape and looting.

Camp Vigilant. Home to ex-Ba'ath party officials and prisoners accused of attacking coalition forces. Holding pen for those likely to be tried for crimes against humanity and profiteering.

Lucy slowed the bullet-scarred GMC as she approached the blockhouse. Multiple checkpoints and blast barriers. Coils of concertina wire.

She lowered the side window and got a face full of rain. She flashed her provisional authority pass at an MP in a poncho. A hick reservist with a German shepherd on a leash. He checked his rain-sodden clipboard. He ticked Lucy and Amanda, then signalled the main gate.

★

The reception hall. Empty holding cells lined with wooden benches. Manacle rings set in the concrete floor.

Lucy shook rain from her prairie coat. Amanda slapped rain from her hat.

They badged a guard behind ballistic bank-teller glass and signed the log book. They cleared their weapons and passed them across the counter. They were patted down and scanned with a detector wand. They handed over their phones.

A big sign on the wall:

STRICTLY NO PHOTOGRAPHY

They clipped visitor tags to their lapels.

A young MP introduced himself.

'Staff Sergeant Castillo.'

His rank and name strip were blanked out with duct tape in case prisoners used ex-pat contacts in the US to target family members for blackmail or reprisal.

They handed Castillo a form. Justice Ministry. Permission to interrogate a detainee. Cost them a box of Dominican Cohibas to get it stamped.

He consulted a clipboard.

'Jabril Jamadi. A weird one. Guy walked out of the desert half dead. Picked up by a foot patrol. They held him at Balad for a while. Speaks very good English. We call him Jeeves. We've been holding him at the hard site while we enquired into his background.'

'Can we talk to him?'

'If he were an intel target, absolutely not. But his dossier is totally empty. He's got prints, a mugshot and a magistrate number. We've got nothing on him. He's a non-person. MI say they have a feeling he's senior Ba'ath. He matters. He's a player. But they can't place him anywhere in the party power structure. Sooner or later we'll have to hand him to the locals. Maybe they can beat something out of him.'

Castillo turned a key and pulled back a barred gate.

'The lights are out, I'm afraid. Rain. Something blew.'

Castillo led them through the prison. They each held yellow cyalume above their heads.

Dank corridors. Papers scattered on the floor. Pervading odour of sewage.

A woman shouted through the food hatch of a cell door.

'Heh-dee, bitch,' yelled Castillo, as they passed. 'Shut your noise.'

'You hold women?'

'Whores. We don't put them in the main camp.'

Flashing light from the tier above them. Echoing rock music. 'Welcome to the Jungle'. Strobes and a CD player hooked up to a car battery.

'What's that?'

'Nothing and no one.'

Ghost detainees. Softened for interrogation by a few days of sleep deprivation.

Castillo unlocked a cell.

'I'll wait outside.'

Jabril was lying on a bare bunk. Lean, fifties, white beard. He wore an orange jumpsuit and sandals. He had an ID tag clipped round his left wrist. His right hand was missing.

Jabril shielded his eyes from the sickly amber glow of the cyalume sticks.

He looked Lucy and Amanda up and down. He checked out high-end tactical gear. Expensive boots, slick drop holsters, clean Kestrel armour.

'*Salaam alaikum*,' said Lucy.

'*Alaikum salaam*. You're not with Intelligence.'

'No. We're civilian contractors.'

'British?'

'Long ago.'

'I'm surprised they let you in.'

'You might be disappointed to learn you are no longer

classed as a high-value detainee. They've downgraded your status. You'll soon be joining car thieves and pickpockets.'

Jabril crouched by the wall. He let Lucy and Amanda sit on the bunk.

'You speak good English,' said Lucy.

'I was schooled by Jesuit priests from Boston.'

The cyalume sticks threw long shadows.

Lucy gave Jabril a pack of Parliament cigarettes and a matchbook. He smiled at the matchbook. Printed by PsyOps and distributed in every major city the previous year. A portrait of Saddam next to gold coins stacked like casino chips. *REWARD. YOU DELIVER. WE PAY.*

Jabril used his stump to hold the cigarette packet against his knee. He extracted a cigarette and lit one-handed.

'They want to transfer you to Ganci,' said Lucy. 'The tent city. They say it's a bear pit.'

'I'll survive.'

'You've got no kin, no chance to buy your way out. Once you are transferred to the Provisional Authority, you're screwed. Those tattoo dots on the back of your hand. You're from Tikrit. Saddam's home town. Everything about you screams party elite. Your manner, your accent. Once they put you in the main prison population only a matter of time before someone cuts your throat.'

'That's my concern. Saddam. Did they hang him?'

'Not yet. They will.'

'I haven't spoken to anyone for weeks. The soldiers bring food. They empty my bucket. They never talk.'

'We could be your ticket out of here.'

'Is that right?'

'You spoke to a friend of mine. During the transfer from Balad. You've got a story to share. Let's hear it.'

'What do you want to know?'

'Tell me how you lost your hand.'

Jabril took a long drag on his cigarette.

'It's not about the money. I want to make that clear from the outset. It's not about the gold. It's about restitution.'

Lucy waited for the man to continue.

'I was a member of the Republican Guard, years ago. One of Saddam's elite troops. This is a tribal culture. I was born in Tikrit. I've led a privileged life since the day I was born.

'I was seconded to the retinue of Uday Hussein, Saddam's oldest son. I was head of his personal security. It was my job to arrange round-the-clock protection. I arranged decoy motorcades each time he left his home. I even had to arrange plastic surgery in Switzerland for his body-double, Latif. Accompanied the poor man to Zurich with a portfolio of reference photographs. Instructed the surgeon to widen Latif's nose, stretch his eyelids, reshape his earlobes.

'Uday was a maniac. You have no idea. Loud. Vulgar. Some nights he would cruise the streets in a blacked-out Corniche. He would pick a girl from the sidewalk. It didn't matter who she was. A young mother with her children. A wife with her husband. No one could protest. He would order the car pulled to the kerb. He would kick open the door and beckon. Sometimes he flashed a machete. He would take them to a hotel. He would clear a floor, order everyone from their rooms. I stood in the corridor, listening to muffled screams.

'I cleaned up the girls. That was my job. I gave them money, sometimes took them to hospital. The man was impotent. He blamed the girls. Each assignation ended in blood, recriminations, smashed furniture. It was horrible, but what could I do?

'Anyone who incurred Uday's rage would be seized in the night by the Mukhabarat and brought here, to Abu Ghraib. His enemies would be tortured until they confessed to imaginary crimes. Inmates would be forced to chose from a list of torments. An actual menu. Decide if they wished to be lowered into boiling water or have a cigarette stubbed out on their eye. Get raped with a Coke bottle or suffer endless electric shocks from a hand-cranked field telephone. Some were eventually released. Many were killed and dissolved in acid.

'They tell me some of the cell floors in this prison are indelibly stained with blood. Many have inscriptions scratched on the wall. "*Tomorrow I die. God have mercy.*"'

'Uday became increasingly unstable. He developed an irrational hatred of Kamel, Saddam's food taster. I don't know why. The argument came to a head at a party in honour of President's Mubarak's wife. Uday bludgeoned the man unconscious with a heavy cane. The Egyptian delegation had to stand and watch while Uday cut off the man's head with a carving knife right there on the dance floor. I had to usher screaming guests to an adjacent room and make apologies. It was clear, from that day forward, that Uday had fallen out of favour. He was too impulsive, too easily provoked to lead the country. Saddam began to favour Qusay, his younger son, for succession.

'One night we were at a private club. A discotheque on the roof of the Al-Mansour Melia Hotel. He danced, so we all danced. He cracked bad jokes and we laughed.

'Uday played blackjack. He was drunk. He snorted poppers. The croupier was a young girl. She was terrified. Her hands shook so much she couldn't deal cards. He slapped her around. He kicked her.

'He told me to take over. I dealt cards. He lost. He kept losing. He spat. He swore. There was nothing I could do. I couldn't control the cards. Each time he drew bust he threw cards in my face. He told me to stop laughing. I wasn't laughing. He said he would rape my mother. He would gut my father. He described how he would do it. Fresh detail each time he drew a bad card.

'He kept drinking. He kept losing. He needed five or less. He drew ten. He finished the bottle and smashed it over my head. He kicked over the table. I was on the floor. He stood over me with his machete. I raised my arm to protect myself. I don't remember much after that.'

'At least the fucker is dead.'

Lucy had watched the endgame play out on Al-Jazeera. Uday and Qusay fled Baghdad after the invasion and hid in a mansion in Mosul. Someone ratted them out. 101st Airborne surrounded the villa. The brothers refused to surrender. An A10 airstrike quickly reduced the building to rubble. Their bodies were shown on TV. Bloated, bruised faces.

'They had been sheltered by Nawaf az-Zaydan. Supposedly a loyal comrade. But, years earlier, Uday had ordered the execution of Nawaf's brother. Nawaf saw his chance for revenge.'

'And the chance to claim a twenty-million-dollar bounty,' said Lucy. 'They say Nawaf moved to California.'

Jabril shrugged.

'The man had a family. He gave them a new life.'

He coughed long and hard.

'I got a job as a guard at The National Museum. An old man with one arm. What else could I do? It was a fine job. The museum received few visitors. I patrolled empty rooms each day. Browsed cases of Babylonian pottery and Sumerian tablets. Relics from the reign of Nebuchadnezzar. For the first time in years I was at peace. I was safe from party intrigues, the regular random purges of Uday's entourage. Looking back, those were the happiest days of my life.'

Jabril lit a fresh cigarette.

'We knew the Americans were coming. State television broadcast nothing but propaganda and dreadful Egyptian soap operas, but anyone with a radio could listen to the BBC World Service. We knew Bush was determined to invade. The city was ready for war. Sandbags in the streets. Anti-aircraft batteries on the rooftops. Windows taped up. Baghdad became a ghost town. Most shops, most restaurants closed.

Anyone who had family outside the city packed their possessions in a car and fled.

'I thought I was safe at the museum. I thought the conflict would pass me by. Too old to fight. I had no intention of joining a futile war.

'We received a list. Artefacts to be retrieved from the museum basement ready to be shipped west. I assumed some effort would be made to preserve Iraq's history. I assumed the list would include the delicate Mesopotamian sculptures and pottery that drew tourists and academics from all over the world. But the only materials scheduled for preservation were plastic bank boxes hidden in a locked basement room.'

'Gold?'

'Saddam's personal wealth. Some of it. His private hoard. Had it been part of Iraq's official reserve it would have been held in the vaults of the central bank.'

'You saw gold? With your own eyes?

'The cases were sealed, but one of them fell and split as we loaded it onto a pallet truck.'

'How much in total?'

'The consignment weighed approximately two and a half tons.'

'Jesus,' said Amanda. 'That would be nearly two hundred million dollars' worth of bullion.'

'You need to understand the importance of gold in this part of the world. The Middle East is constantly swept by war and revolution. Paper currency has a habit of becoming worthless. And many people would rather trust their local hawala exchange than a big city bank. Saddam hoarded gold. That's how he kept the country together. He bought the loyalty of tribal warlords. He could bestow unimaginable wealth or order arbitrary executions. He played on their terror and greed.'

'So what happened next? You loaded the gold. Then what?'

'We were assigned a battalion of Republican Guards to

protect our convoy. The battalion was known as the Army of Sacrifice. It ran at half strength. Two hundred men. Praetorian troops. Each man underwent a strange initiation when he joined the battalion. He had to stand before his new commanding officer, drag a knife across his bare chest and swear to die for Saddam.

'The troops should have been guarding the southern frontier. Madness to waste able men supervising a consignment of gold. But I think they were secretly glad to flee the battle zone. They could survive the war with honour.

'We were given an armoured bank truck. Our instructions were vague. Seal the gold in the truck and leave Baghdad.

'We consulted a map. Where would be the best place to hide a Pharaoh's treasure? We needed a site so remote, so godforsaken, the gold would be hidden forever unless someone could guide you to the precise spot. We chose the Western Desert.

'We left Baghdad the night of the first airstrike. As I say, we were glad to be gone. Every soldier, no matter how old or infirm, had been sent to fight the Americans in the southern oil fields. But we had been spared. Our orders would allow us to flee west and avoid battle. You see, we knew the Americans would win. The deputy prime minister appeared on Al-Iraqiya, the national TV channel, waving a pistol. Parliament declared they were ready for martyrdom, swore to give their blood and their souls. But we wanted only to survive. Our mission would allow us to hide in the desert for the duration of the war, then emerge to rejoin our families.

'We left the museum in the early hours of the morning. We drove in a convoy of forty vehicles. Troop carriers, supply trucks, civilian cars. We crossed the Tigris just as air-raid sirens began to wail. Anti-aircraft fire streaked from rooftop gun emplacements. Then bombs began to fall. The sky lit up like sunrise. Volcanic eruptions of fire. Tomahawk cruise missiles slammed into the presidential palace, the foreign ministry and the main television stations. We drove through streets half choked with flames and rubble. Saddam broadcast a radio message. He promised victory. He said the Americans would endure a bitter defeat. We fled the burning city as fast as we could.'

'So what happened? An entire battalion drove into the desert. Weeks later, you walk out.'

'Gold. Gold can drive men to do terrible things.

'We built a camp deep in the desert. We listened to the radio each night. One by one we heard cities fall. Central command ordered us to join the fight, but we ignored the order. Eventually Baghdad ceased to respond and we knew that the regime had been swept away. We were on our own.

'We agreed to share the treasure. The gold belonged to Saddam but Saddam was gone.

'It should have been easy. But greed and distrust swept through our ranks like some kind of contagion. We split into armed factions. Each man became fearful of his brother. Pre-emptive betrayal. Fights became battles. A horrible exchange of fire. The details are unimportant. These were decent young men living in impossibly corrupt times. Let them rest.'

'So the only person to walk away from this bloodbath was you?'

Jabril held up his stump.

'I am an old cripple. I was happy to be overlooked.'

'How did you survive? You must have covered two-, three-hundred miles of desert. The average person couldn't last a day in that heat.'

'It is a matter of will. Put a man in a fiercely hostile environment like the desert or leave him marooned in Arctic wastes and you'll soon see what lies in his heart.'

Lucy unfolded a map.

'Give me a rough location.'

'There.' Jabril pointed to blank terrain. 'Al-Qa'im district, near the Syrian border. But you'll never find the gold. Not unless I lead you to the exact place.'

'Anything else we need to know?'

'The gold is still locked in the truck. That's the only problem. The door is secured by two combination locks. My colleague knew the combinations and I watched him die. You would have to cut your way into the armoured car.'

'Not an issue.'

'And I have to warn you. That section of desert is poisoned ground. There are toxins in the sand.'

'Like what?'

'Anthrax spores, sheltered in crevices and shadows. The odds of infection are low, but the consequences could be severe. Pulmonary collapse. Maybe worse. Intramuscular shots of antibiotic would give you some protection. But the real concern is botulinum residue. A strong neuro-toxin. It could paralyse your whole respiratory tract, kill you in minutes.'

'Bio-weapons? Chemical munitions?'

'Saddam's legacy. An attempt to suppress internal dissent. The airstrikes were methodically documented, although the files have long since been destroyed. It was an open secret. A deliberate attempt to obliterate the tribal population, instil terror and obedience.'

'What exactly happened?'

'It was early evening. The best time of day to release a chemical weapon. Diminishing sunlight. A blanket of rapidly cooling air hung over the desert. Perfect conditions for the dissemination of aerosol particles. They used an adapted L-29 Delfin trainer. Czech. A light jet with three-hundred-litre storage tanks slung below each wing. They flew at two thousand feet. Made a slow pass over every hamlet and farmstead in the western sector. Released their payload like a crop-duster laying down pesticide. A steady stream of vapour.

'Families were sitting down to dinner. Sheep and goats in their pens.'

'Why? Why did he do it?'

'September, ninety-eight. Saddam wanted to consolidate his power. He wanted to punish the northern Kurds for supporting Peshmerga rebels. Crush the tribal system. He wiped out Shabaks, Yazidis, Turkoman. There were deportations, mass executions. He released anthrax spores to kill cattle and poison the land. But it wasn't enough. He wanted a final solution. Operation Panther. To this day, no one knows exactly what they used. Some kind of binary nerve agent. Maybe VX. Maybe hydrogen cyanide. Something truly satanic.

'The plane flew overhead. Minutes later animals convulsed and dropped dead. Dogs. Cattle. They say some people coughed blood, and others died laughing. There were terrible lesions and skin turned blue. The ground remains tainted to this day. When some tribesmen returned to the area they soon suffered respiratory problems, birth abnormalities and high rates of cancer. Saddam's cousin organised the attack. Ali Hassan al-Majid. People will dance in the street the day he is hung.'

'Christ.'

'I was part of the regime. We all knew. We all heard. We all share responsibility. I'm not proud of the things I've seen and done. I'm not a good man. Each night I pray to God to spare me his terrible judgement and hell.'

'Your battalion spent weeks out there, camped in the contamination zone.'

'Yes.'

'And none of them got sick?'

'None of them got Anthrax.'

Lucy sat back.

'A fortune in gold, sitting in the desert, waiting to be found. Can you prove any of this story?'

'What is your instinct?' asked Jabril. 'Am I lying?'

'Yeah. I think you're lying through your arse. I don't know what happened out there in the desert, but you know what? I don't care. Tell me straight. Is there gold? Is that much true?'

'Yes.'

'If my crew go searching for the gold, if we travel to Al-Qa'im and find nothing but sand, I think you know what will happen. The boys won't be in a forgiving mood. It won't be pretty.'

Jabril nodded and lit another cigarette.

'Here's the deal,' said Lucy. 'Military Intelligence are done with you. A few days from now you'll be transferred to local jurisdiction and shipped out. They won't take you to Ganci right away. They'll take you for processing at the Central Station. Throw you in a holding cell. You'll be surrounded by fifty Sunni fucks wanting payback for a lifetime of hurt. You'll spend every waking moment trying to stay alive. You won't dare sleep. But there is an alternative. We could arrange your freedom.'

'In return for the gold.'

'We'd treat you fair. You'd get a cut.'

'How many of you are there?' asked Jabril.

'A team of five.'

'Do you trust them?'

'With my life.'

'Wait until your friends lay eyes on a mountain of gold. You will soon see how much their trust is worth.'

Lucy and Amanda rode the expressway towards Baghdad. Suffocating humidity. Rain blattered against the cracked windshield.

Amanda scrunched her Abu Ghraib visitor pass and tossed it from the window. She turned the air-con dial, put her hand over a dash vent until she felt a blast of chill air.

'Western Desert,' said Amanda. 'Tough terrain. Bandit

country. Peshmergas. Jihadi guerrillas. Fuckheads of every stripe.'

'Think it's all right?' said Lucy. 'Taking the gold?'

'It's dirty money. It's not going to build a hospital. It's going to end up in some asshole's Swiss bank account. Might as well be ours, right?'

'Yeah.'

Amanda kicked at bullets rolling in the foot well. The Suburban got shot to hell in the previous day's ambush. AK rounds had penetrated the Kevlar door panels. Gleaming silver mushrooms littered the carpet and seats.

She took an envelope from the glove box. Two new passports. Big gold crest. *Canada. Passport/Passeport.*

'We risk our lives every day,' said Amanda. 'Sooner or later, our luck will run dry. You keep saying you're sick of the life, you want to start over. Well, this is it. This is our shot. We could be home free.'

'Three tons of gold. Can't be hauled over sand dunes. We need choppers.'

'Gaunt has a couple of Hueys.'

'I don't want to involve Gaunt,' said Lucy. 'The guy is bad news.'

'Who else can we hire? A job like this has to be off the meter.'

'I guess.'

'This is our last war,' said Amanda. 'We need a retirement plan. We owe it to the guys. We can't them send them home broke.'

'Okay,' said Lucy. 'Let's roll the dice.'

TOP SECRET SPECIAL HANDLING NO FORM

Central Intelligence Agency

Directorate of Operations, Near East Division

Doc ID: 575JD3
Page 01/1

08/21/05

MEMORANDUM TO: Project Lead, D.Ops
SUBJECT: Spektr

Colonel,

JABRIL JAMADI has made contact with a team of security contractors operating under the name VANGUARD RISK CONSULTANTS. We believe they are unaware of the SPEKTR project. They are currently seeking helicopter transport to carry them to the Western Desert. This presents an excellent opportunity to secure our objectives at the SPEKTR site. The region of desert between Al Qa'im and Al Hadr is remote and hostile terrain favoured by foreign Jihadists attempting to establish smuggling routes in-country for mortars and surface-to-air missiles. We have yet to determine the level of risk presented by the contamination zone itself. It would be preferable to utilise a deniable back-channel proxy squad, rather than dispatch an Agency fire team.

I respect your reservations regarding the scope of the SPEKTR project, but I would draw your attention to Presidential Directive 39 which instructs the agency to undertake 'an aggressive programme of foreign intelligence collection, analysis and covert actions' in our efforts to combat terrorism. The offensive potential of the SPEKTR battle-strain is incontrovertible, and gives us a firm legal mandate in our steps to secure the virus on behalf of the United States.

R. Koell
Field Officer
CA Special Proj, Baghdad Station

Gaunt

Jim Gaunt pulled back the hangar door. Open for business. No different from a neighbourhood grocer hosing down the sidewalk and laying out fruit boxes and flowers.

He sipped from a silver thermal mug with Marine wings.

Dawn. Reveille. A plaintive bugle call crackling from loud-speakers. The rain had cleared. Sky bluer than he'd ever known. Wet asphalt would soon burn dry.

The morning delivery. Raphael drove down the airstrip service road. He pulled up in a five-ton flatbed. Russian RGD-5 grenades under tarp.

Gaunt checked his clipboard. Three hundred crates, twenty-four grenades per case. Surplus ordinance shipped from Johannesburg, via the Emirates.

'*Como estas*, baby?'

Raphael. Gaunt's partner. Each night he slept on a canvas cot at the back of the hangar, shotgun by his side. Hair tied back into a ponytail. Thick moustache. Leather waist-coat. Torso covered in jailhouse tattoos faded lavender with age. He ripped the cellophane from a king-size Balmoral and lit up.

'Absolutely fucking peachy,' said Gaunt.

Raphael kept a Rottweiler chained by the door. Sasha. She sat with her blanket and bowl. He teased her with a hunk of jerky. She slavered. She snapped and lunged, pulled against her heavy neck-chain.

Baghdad International Airport.

Bullet-pocked terminal buildings. 86th Airwing bivouacked

in a departure lounge, *To Dare Mighty Things* shield-banner draped to mask a Bollywood mural of Saddam leading his men into battle on a white stallion.

Thirteen-thousand-foot landing strip cratered by cluster bombs. Steady traffic from massive C141 *Starlifters*. The planes threw tight corkscrew turns as they descended towards the runway, popping starburst flares and chaff in case a ground-fired SA-7 locked on their heat-trail.

Fuel trucks pumped gas.

Loadmasters supervised forklift crews as they removed pallet cargo from vaulted holds. Generators. Water purification equipment. White goods. DHL de-planed sacks of mail and courier packages.

The planes were reloaded with metal coffins and wounded, and dispatched to Ramstein Airbase, Germany.

Gaunt was exiled to the far end of the runway. A low-rent private carrier. His hangar part-blocked by an abandoned twin-prop *Sherpa* turning to rust on the slipway, like the ghost of old wars.

Gaunt turned his face to the morning sun and breathed the sweet scent of aviation fuel.

'They revoked our pass, Ese,' said Raphael.

'The chit?'

'Expired. They won't renew.'

The Provisional Authority had been superseded by the Interim Governing Council. All private contractors had to renegotiate terms.

'They want us out, Ese. End of the month. Vacate and give them the keys.'

'I'll talk to the main office,' said Gaunt. 'Try to buy us more time.'

'I heard there's a vacant warehouse near the Central Station. We could rent space. Bid for police contracts.'

'A few helmets, a few flaks. Pocket change. Go down that route and we'll end up bartering AKs for cows. No. All the big deals are happening here. This is the hub. This is the action.'

'Ten months, bro. Been here ten months.'

'Just got to hold our nerve. Everyone else is making out hand over fist. Why not us?'

'You said we'd get Agency work. You said they were desperate for guys.'

Gaunt had approached an intel analyst at the Al-Rasheed two months ago. The basement sports bar favoured by Central Intelligence document recovery teams sent to scour bombed-out ministry buildings for paperwork and hard drives. The analyst was sitting alone, sipping scotch. Only guy in a shirt and tie. Gaunt took a stool next to him, begged for work, begged for a way in. The guy drained his glass and walked away without saying a word.

'Like I say. Just got to hold our nerve.'

Gaunt and Raphael unloaded the truck.

Engine revs. An SUV with a damaged muffler. They watched it approach up the service road. An armoured Suburban with heavy ram bars. Scorched, bubbled paint work. Body pocked with bullet strikes. Cracked windshield.

Lucy and Amanda.

Lucy got out the car. She raised her Oakleys and tucked them in her hair like an Alice band. She approached Gaunt and held out her hand.

'How've you been?' she asked.

'Fuck you.'

Amanda hung back and kept a hand on the butt of her sidearm.

Lucy checked out the interior of the hangar.

Stacked crates. Boxes of cheap boots. Blue Iraqi police uniforms still sheathed in plastic. MRE food pouches.

Gaunt's desk, cluttered with manifests, transit papers and end-user certificates. There was a framed photograph on the desk. Young Gaunt and his father, both in dress blues.

Amanda looked Gaunt up and down. Young guy. Crucifix round his neck. An old burn on his forearm, skin like melted wax. He wore a big skull ring on one hand, a West Point graduation ring on the other.

'What the fuck are you doing here, Lucy?' asked Gaunt.

'We need a ride. Three-day charter. We heard you might be looking for business.'

'You're kidding me, right? Take your shit-heap car and get out of here.'

Amanda lifted the lid of a green wooden crate labelled 'engine parts'. An ancient Russian machine gun. Bipod. Chipped wooden stock. Drum magazine.

'Where did you get this stuff?' she asked. 'A yard sale?'

'No market for American carbines,' said Raphael. 'Not round here. Fancy scopes and laser sights. Not interested. They want AKs. They trust them. They can get the spares, they can get the ammo.'

Amanda worked the slide and aimed at Raphael's dog. She pulled the trigger. Clack of an empty chamber. The dog barked and jerked its chain.

'Where does all this shit end up?' asked Amanda.

'Burqan oil fields, mostly,' said Raphael.

She laid the weapon back in its newspaper bed.

Lucy opened a crate and examined grenades. Russian. Green baseball grenades with a long aluminium fuse. Gaunt took a grenade from Lucy's hand. He pulled the pin. The safety lever flipped, and clinked on concrete. He tossed the grenade. Lucy caught it, unconcerned.

'Doubt you're dumb enough to pack them fused.'

She put the grenade on Gaunt's desk. It rolled among paperwork.

'Get out,' said Gaunt. 'I'm not going to tell you again.'

'Thousand dollars a day,' said Lucy. 'Plus a cut of the haul.'

Gaunt spat on her boot.

'Seriously,' she said. 'I got some work for you.'

Gaunt leant on his desk, hands planted either side of a Colt pistol resting on paperwork.

'Guess I'm not making myself clear.'

Amanda popped the restraining strap of her side-holster.

Raphael stepped between them.

'They got money, Ese. I want to hear what they have to say.'

Raphael led them between stacked crates of 7.62mm ammunition. African import stamps on the crates. Kinshasa. One battle zone to another. Half the rounds would probably misfire.

There were two Huey choppers at the back of the hangar. Vietnam-era war-birds. *Bad Moon* and *Talon.*

'These things actually fly?' asked Lucy.

'I bet my life on these girls,' said Raphael.

'Mind if we check them out?'

'Go ahead.'

Lucy and Amanda circled the choppers. Crude avionics. Old-time gauges and altimeters. Leather seats patched with duct tape.

'These things are older than my grandpa,' said Amanda. 'We're wasting our time.'

'Gaunt is just running his mouth. Look around you. He needs money. Needs it badly.'

'What about tattoo guy? The barrio gangbanger? What do you know about him?'

'Raphael? I asked around. Shitload of combat flight hours. Flown everywhere. Night recon. Kyrgystan, Uzbekistan, Tajikistan. Any stan you care to mention.'

Gaunt and Raphael watched them inspect the Hueys.

'The two chicks are wearing rings,' said Raphael. 'What's the deal with that?'

'What do you think?'

'We need the bucks, Ese. We need to eat.'

'I don't care if I fucking starve.'

'We ought to hear what she has to say. Thousand dollars a day, Ese. We can't turn it down.'

Lucy ducked beneath the tail-boom. She approached Gaunt and Raphael.

'How much can these things haul?' asked Lucy

'Sling-load, or cabin?'

'Cabin.'

'Three tons each, give or take,' said Raphael. 'We can take out the bench seats, easy enough.'

'Can they handle desert?'

'They've got filters.'

'So what do you say?'

Raphael relit his cigar.

'I'm wondering why you're talking to us and not military liaison.'

'Those grenades. Where did you guys pick them up? Pretoria? Liberia? They've got to be twenty years old. Corroded to hell. Sell those to some warlord down south and you've got a real problem. They'll crack open a box for training and find they don't go bang. They'll snatch you off the street. Cut you up slow.'

'That's my concern,' said Gaunt.

Lucy smoothed out a map, spread it like a tablecloth over a couple of grenade crates. Raphael fetched Dr Pepper from a refrigerator and cracked cans. Gaunt hung back, arms folded.

Iraq. All the major cities clustered east in the fertile alluvial plains of the Tigris and Euphrates. Irrigated vineyards. Pomegranate and date groves. Oil money down south near the gulf.

Lucy pointed west. Al Anbar. The Western Desert. Terra incognita. A here-be-monsters blank. No towns, no cities.

'Here,' she said.

'Middle of the desert.'

'Yeah.'

'Nothing out there,' said Raphael. 'Sand and scorpions. Might meet a few Bedouin. A few Talib. Slit your throat given a chance.'

'Those choppers. Could they make the trip?'

'Edge of their range but yeah, they could make it.'

'It's a salvage run. Stuff from the war. We find it. We load it. We bring it back.'

'Munitions?'

'No. Totally inert cargo.'

'Weight?'

'Approximately two tons.'

'Coke? Heroin?'

'No. Nothing like that.'

'Why us?'

'Like I say. Salvage. Less people involved the better.'

'Grand a day?'

'Up front. Guaranteed. After that: partners. A cut of whatever we find.'

'And how much is that likely to be?'

'Tens, maybe hundreds of thousands.'

Lucy uncapped a pen and wrote her cellphone number across the cover of an old *Stars and Stripes*, digits scrawled across Saddam's forehead.

'I'll give you guys some space to think it over. Call me, all right? Let's make some money.'

Gaunt and Raphael watched them leave.

'Fucking bitch.'

'But three thousand bucks, Ese. We're hurting. Everyone is getting rich but us.'

'You can leave anytime you want,' said Gaunt. 'You don't like the way I run things, you don't like the calls, then walk out the door.'

Lucy headed for Baghdad. The city viewed through a spider web crack in the windshield.

Amanda killed country tunes from Freedom 107FM and slotted Cypress Hill into the dash. 'Ain't Going Out Like That'. She turned up the volume. Lucy turned it down.

Lucy checked the rear-view. Locals kept clear. They pulled back, swerved to let the GMC pass. Provisional Order Seventeen. Paul Bremner's decree. Civilian security contractors were immune from prosecution. A licence to kill.

'Who next?' asked Amanda.

'No one,' said Lucy. 'We take the Hueys.'

'Did I miss something? Gaunt told us to fuck off.'

'He's desperate. I could smell it. Three thousand dollars. Sooner or later, he'll swallow his pride and call.'

'What's the story with you and him?'

'Fallujah. Couple of years back. Woman runs in front of our Warrior. Nearly got crushed flat. Babbling something about her family. Said a squad of US marines kicked down the door of her house, went berserk. I had to testify at the tribunal. They're doing a long stretch at Miramar Brig.'

'Gaunt?'

'He had a good lawyer.'

Gaunt fetched food from the terminal commissary, last in the queue as the canteen closed for the night. Enchiladas boxed in styrofoam. He walked back along the service road. The moonlit airfield was silent and still. Curfew. No flights until sunrise.

He entered the hangar side door. Darkness.

'Hey. Raph. Chow time.'

His voice echoed through the vaulted storeroom.

He walked to a pool of light. Stacked crates for a table. A bottle of bourbon and a checkers board.

'Raph?'

One of Raphael's shitty Balmoral cigars lay smouldering on the concrete floor.

Gaunt put the food on the table, drew his Colt and quickly backed into shadow.

He slid along the hangar wall. He took a Maglite from his pocket.

The guard dog was dead. Sasha. Head on a paw like she had fallen asleep. Right eye blown out. Someone threw jerky and shot her in the face as she chewed.

He slid back along the wall and found the side door. Closed and padlocked. Someone shut him in.

Gaunt crouched. An entire battalion quarter of a mile away in the terminal building. Must be some way to raise the alarm.

He fired four shots at the roof. Metallic roar. Muzzle-flash lit the hangar like lightning.

He stood panting in the dark. Let it be gangsters. Some militia come to rip-off his stock.

His old commanding officer always said: 'Don't let religious fucks take you hostage.' He showed the platoon execution footage. An al-Qaeda video. Shitty jihadi music. Mujahideen council logo. Guys wearing bandoliers and hoods. They stood behind some poor bastard in an orange jumpsuit. He looked drugged, emaciated. '*Allahu Akbar*.' One of the captors unsheathed a knife, gripped the man's head and sawed through his neck. The dying man squealed like a pig. 'Fucking Abdul motherfuckers. Fucking savages. Go down fighting, gentlemen. Do not let this happen to you.'

Gaunt looked across the hangar. His desk. The lamp cast a small cone of light. His phone lay on top of a *Playboy*.

He crept towards the desk. He snatched the phone and ran into shadow. He crouched against crates. The laminate security pass round his neck had the guardhouse number printed on the reverse. He thumbed the keypad.

He held the phone to his ear. Dial tone. Someone jammed a stun baton in the small of his back and shocked him paralytic.

*

They tied him to folding chair with plastic tuff-ties. Two buzz-cut goons and a young guy in a blazer.

'Where's Raphael?' asked Gaunt.

'I believe one of my colleagues is keeping him company.'

The guy examined a pallet of boxes. He lifted a cardboard flap. A novelty alarm clock. A white plastic mosque. He pressed a minaret. A squeak of tinny Arabian music. He threw the clock aside without comment.

The guy sat on a crate. Preppy. Slicked hair, polished loafers. Thin, precise, reptilian. He read one of Gaunt's pamphlets.

'*Falcon Logistics. A leading international logistics corporation with extensive experience assisting government and non-government agencies with the supply of defence matériel.* Is this the scope of your ambition? Scratching a living, war zone to war zone, selling bullets by the handful to child soldiers, cartels, Shi'ite death squads?'

'Building contacts.'

The guy held up Gaunt's academy ring. Fourteen-carat gold. Fire agate.

'You must be a little frustrated at your current situation.'

'I wanted to work for myself.'

'Fallujah. Operation Vigilante Resolve.'

'I was innocent.'

'You were acquitted of the rape charge. The summary court martial found you guilty of maltreatment towards detainees and dereliction of duty. You lost two ranks and four months' pay. You received an administrative discharge soon after.'

Gaunt didn't reply.

'I understand. You dedicated your life to the Corps. You expected some kind of affirmation, some kind of reward. Instead, here you are, orphaned and alone.'

'I'm doing okay.'

Gaunt's parents thought he was still in the Marines. They

sent letters. They watched for him on TV. Said they were proud of the way he and his boys were confronting America's enemies overseas.

'My name is Koell. Have you seen me before?'

'Once. At the Rasheed.'

'Then you know who I am.'

Gaunt and Raphael had been sipping umbrella drinks in the Scheherazade Bar.

'Who's the kid with the phone?' asked Gaunt.

Koell was sitting alone by the pool, talking into a sat phone, shielding his mouth in case someone read his lips.

'Black ops.'

'Yeah?'

'I've seen his kind before. I was out in Liberia. This was years back. Good times. We had a workshop at the edge of Monrovia. Gangs would bring fucked up Landcruisers. We would weld a heavy weapons mount, turn them into battle-wagons. They paid us in uncut diamonds.

'One day this kid from a missionary station drops by and tells me he has something to sell. Said it came down in a mangrove swamp one night. A falling star. Lit up the sky. Manmade. Some kind of engine pod. A spherical fuel tank with isolator valves. Thing was half melted. I told him I would swing by in a few days.

'The station was in Grand Bassa. Rainforest. Shitty roads. I was delivering a truckload of .50 cal to some local warlord. You know the type. Mirror shades. Pimp jewellery. All swagger. Fucking idiot.

'I drove to the missionary station on the way back. I liked the kid. I liked the nuns. I heard a bunch of them had fallen ill. I was going to take them cigarettes from the city. Good currency. They could use them to trade.

'Call it a sixth sense. I got halfway up the hill road then pulled over. Something not right. Too quiet. No birds.

'I headed up the road on foot. Watched from the jungle. I don't know what happened up there but it was major. The station was hidden beneath a geodesic dome. Choppers parked in the compound. There were guys in white biohazard suits.

'I got the hell out of there and drove back to town. I asked around. Nobody wanted to talk about the mission station. Bad hoodoo. But I found a French consulate official with a taste for liquor and loosened his tongue.

'There were these guys. White guys. They turned up in bad times. Kenya, during a Marburg outbreak; Burundi, during a bunch of Ebola cases. They spoke pretty good English but Pierre thought they were Russian. They used to show up during the sixties and seventies posing as tourists, journalists, Médecins Sans Frontières. But they were from Vektor. The weapons acquisition arm of Biopreparat, the Soviet biological warfare programme. Anytime there was an outbreak of an emergent disease, something new and lethal gestating in deep jungle, these guys showed up like the horsemen of the apocalypse. Procurement teams masquerading as humanitarian aid. Moving through jungle hospitals like ministering angels, collecting biopsy swabs and spinal fluid samples for delivery to Moscow in a diplomatic pouch.

'After the collapse of communism half these guys were out of a job. Highly skilled bio-weapon experts. PhDs in pharmacology. Spent their lives developing lethal psychotropic and neurotropic agents. Reduced to driving taxis and selling flowers in the street. These guys were party elite. They lived in the secret cities of the Soviet rustbelt. They were used to luxury dachas and Zil limousines. One by one they disappeared. Showed up in Libya, Syria, trying to sell VX neurotoxin. A gang of them got busted cooking methamphetamine in Mexico. The cream of the crop got picked up by the US. Given new names, a fuck-ton of cash, and sent to work at Fort Detrick.

'That's the scary part. They're still out there. Vektor. The men, the infrastructure. Cut loose. Sometimes freelance. They work for the Agency or private biotech, chasing their own agenda. Heard they showed up in Kosovo looking for body parts. Kidneys for rich fucks on dialysis. Used the POW camps as an organ bank. Hang around any of these shithole countries long enough you'll see the same planes time and again. Black charters. Antonovs. Ilyushins. They change livery and tail numbers, but it's always the same crews.

'I went out to the missionary station a few months later. It was gone. Burned and bulldozed. No sign of the kids, no sign of the nuns. Caterpillar tracks. No top soil. Someone dug a big pit and filled it in.

Later, I heard locals wouldn't go near the place. They say the jungle grew strange. They said it glowed at night. Said there were genetic abnormalities. Giant insects. Weird flowers.

'A shitstorm like Iraq? Wouldn't surprise me if those fuckers turned up on their own little death trip. Blood, gunsmoke. They'd smell opportunity. I wouldn't mess with them for a single second.'

Koell flicked open a lock knife. The metallic snap echoed through the vaulted hangar. He cut Gaunt free.

'Gesture of trust.'

'Fuck you.'

'Work for us. You need a cause. You're lost. You're broke. We need good men.'

Gaunt rubbed his wrists.

'The people you saw today. They want to head into the Western Desert. Take them where they want to go.'

'Why would I do that?' asked Gaunt.

Koell took a roll of bills from his pocket. Fresh notes bound by a rubber band. He threw the bills on the desk.

'Fuck your money.'

'You want to be part of the shadow world. You need a way in. Well, this is it. Go ahead. Step through the looking-glass.'

'Just fly the choppers?'

Koell took a folded photograph from his pocket. He smoothed it on his knee and passed it to Gaunt. A satellite shot. Rocky, lunar terrain.

'The National Reconnaissance Office designate it Valley 403. A limestone canyon. Locals call it The Valley of Tears. The Western Desert, near the Syrian border. Those security contractors believe there is gold hidden in the hills.'

'Gold?'

'You're welcome to whatever you find. Take your cut. Take it all. I don't care.'

Koell gave the nod. One of his goons put a MOLLE backpack at Gaunt's feet.

Gaunt popped the clips.

A chunky Thuraya XT sat phone.

Maps and aerial photographs.

A 9mm Sig Sauer automatic with a screw-thread barrel and a long, black titanium suppressor.

A box of tungsten-nytrilium hollow-points. Each bullet spiked like a molar. Designed to fragment and rip a wound like a shotgun blast.

A tube of caulk explosive and green box of e-cell detonators.

'There are items hidden in those hills. Items we wish you to find, and return to us.'

'Don't you have your own guys for this kind of thing? Agency teams?'

'I won't bore you with the politics of covert action. A man in my position must make ingenious use of finite resources. A deniable, back-channel asset is always our preferred means of operation. These mercenaries are entirely expendable. They could vanish from the face of the earth and no one would realise they were gone.'

Gaunt examined the pistol.

'Nothing more?'

'You're an ambitious man. You don't want to be small-time all your life. Those deadbeat mercs, they want money. But you have bigger ambitions. You want to matter. You want to make things happen. So impress me. Show me what you can do.'

Ambush

They came for Jabril at dawn. They kicked him awake and pulled him from his bunk. Full strip search. They had him bend, spread his ass cheeks and cough. They ran fingers through his hair. They checked his mouth with a flashlight. Then they threw him a fresh jumpsuit and told him to dress.

They returned his prosthetic hook. He twisted the hollow plastic cup on to the stump of his wrist.

They locked him in a wire holding pen with eight other men. Rough guys. Lean. Scarred faces.

Marines stood guard and told them to crouch on the cold concrete floor.

'Don't speak. Don't move.'

One of the prisoners stared Jabril down. He radiated violence and hatred. A big guy with one eye. He had seen the three tattoo dots on the back of Jabril's hand. Tikriti. Ex-Ba'ath. Marked for death.

Iraqi police showed up. They cross-checked charge sheets and magistrate numbers.

Rapists. Car-jackers. Mahdi militia.

They signed for the prisoners. Marines knew half the police employed by the Interior Ministry moonlighted as Shi'ite death squads. The convicts would be dead in a ditch by sundown.

The prisoners were shackled at the ankle, waist and wrist. Jabril's good hand was cuffed to his belt chain.

The men stood single-file, hoods over their heads. They were led to a loading bay. A young cop jabbed their legs and shoulders with the barrel of his AK to keep them moving.

They shuffled aboard a minivan. Jabril sat patiently in hooded darkness. Door slam. Engine start. He heard cops light cigarettes, the scratch of four matchbooks struck simultaneously.

The van left Abu Ghraib. It got waved through traffic control points and Hesco blast barriers. It joined the expressway and headed for Baghdad.

The prisoners sat in rows. Two guards at the front, two at the back.

The driver was called Ali. The guy riding shotgun was Najjar. The two kids on the back seat looked barely old enough to shave.

'There's a car,' said Ali, checking the rear-view. 'A shot-up Suburban. It's been tailing us since we left the prison.'

Najjar turned in his seat. He could see the Suburban fifty yards back. Bullet holes, scorched paintwork, heavy ram bars. No plates. The 4x4 accelerated and sped past. Tinted windows.

Backstreets. Ali checked his map. Designated route to the Central Station marked in red.

'Forget the map.' said Najjar. 'Head for the dump.'

'The dump?'

'The captain wants us to send a message. Leave these scum with the rest of the city garbage.'

Ali took his hands from the wheel and lit a fresh cigarette.

'Don't worry,' said Najjar, sensing his friend's discomfort. 'Those boys will pull the trigger. They volunteered. They want their first blood.'

Ali surveyed street traffic. The old quarter. A placid vibe. Kids playing at the kerb. Feral dogs rooting in the gutter. Old guys sat at a table smoking narghile pipes, sipping tea, playing dominoes, watching the world go by.

'Check the prisoners,' said Ali.

Najjar climbed into the passenger compartment. He tugged cuffs, tugged ankle chains. The big guy snarled and tugged back. He got an AK butt to the jaw to chill him out.

Ali glanced at the rear-view. 'It's back. The Suburban.'

'How did it get behind us?'

'I don't know.'

'Speed up.'

They didn't have time to react. The Suburban revved and roared past them.

The tailgate flipped up. A soldier in a gas mask and Stetson crouched in the rear. Small feet, small hands. A woman.

The soldier raised an assault rifle and fired a grenade launcher. A streak of smoke. Catastrophic detonation as the nose of the van blew out.

The front axle sheered. The van gouged asphalt and came to a shuddering halt.

Ali wiped blood and glass from his face. Ear-whining concussion. He tried to clear his head. The engine block was destroyed. The van was full of smoke. The hooded prisoners were screaming and thrashing in their seats.

Soldiers jumped from the Suburban. Irregulars. Mercenaries. They each wore gas masks. They threw smoke grenades and enveloped the vehicle in purple smog.

Ali shook Najjar. His friend was out cold, head on the dash.

Ali reached for his radio. He fumbled and dropped it into the foot well. He kicked at the side door. It was jammed.

He unholstered his pistol. He climbed into the passenger compartment. He fell into the narrow aisle between the prisoners.

He shouted to the guards at the rear of the van.

'Are you all right?'

Farm boys with rifles. They were uninjured, but sat stupefied with shock.

A baton round punched through a side window and bounced to the floor, jetting CS. Ali snatched up the canister and threw it back out the window.

A second baton round. Ali threw down his jacket and tried to smother the gas plume. His eyes streamed tears. He drooled snot.

He kicked open the rear doors. They tumbled into the road. More purple smoke.

Ali knelt and squinted through tears. Figures in the smoke. Pig-snout gas masks looming out of purple haze like monstrous, hybrid creatures.

He choked. He vomited. He raised his pistol and fired blind. The weapon was snatched from his hand. A punch to the jaw put him on his back.

He was dragged to the kerb. His hands were cuffed behind his back with plastic tuff-ties.

He spat. He blinked away tears. The street was deserted. The locals had fled inside and locked their doors. He could see the soldiers at work inside the van. They cut the prisoners loose. They bit through ankle chain with bolt cutters. They dragged hooded prisoners from the van.

The big guy made a run for it. He sprinted down the street, hands still chained behind his back.

One of the mercs, a tall man with hair tied in a ponytail, casually shouldered a pump action shotgun. He took aim and blew off the prisoner's foot. The injured man collapsed and lay screaming.

They lined the prisoners along the kerb and pulled off their hoods. Terrified men blinked at sudden sunlight.

A merc walked the line and checked faces. Short and slight. A woman. Her comrades deferred to her, like she was boss.

Her voice muffled by a gas mask:

'Him.'

They unshackled Jabril and dragged him to the Suburban. They drove away.

Ali sat by the side of the road, dumb with shock. The street was still fogged with purple vapour. He could hear sirens get closer.

Najjar climbed through the shattered windshield. He fell into the street.

'Hey,' shouted Ali. 'Over here.'

Najjar got up. His head was bleeding. He walked to the kerb, opened a penknife and cut Ali free.

He fetched a discarded AK from the back of the van. He checked it was loaded. He handed it to one of the boys.

'Finish it, before we have company.'

The kid looked down at the assault rifle in his hand, and the prisoners sat at the kerb. The convicts sobbed and begged for mercy.

'They are trash,' advised Najjar. 'Worse than dogs. You know what has to be done.'

The kid shouldered the rifle, closed his eyes and opened fire.

The Suburban sped down the expressway. They left Baghdad. Lucy and her crew peeled off gas masks. They opened the windows and cranked up Cypress Hill.

Voss drove the 4x4. Lucy sat on the back seat with Jabril, released his shackles with a universal key. She told him to hold his head back while she flushed his eyes with mineral water.

'Thank you,' said Jabril. 'You saved my life.'

Lucy tapped his forehead with the muzzle of her pistol.

'You're not free yet, Jabril. Consider this parole.'

Into The Desert

Two choppers flew out of a golden dawn.

Raphael flew *Talon*. The webbed bench seats had been removed. The cargo compartment was stacked with equipment. The payload was draped with tarp, lashed with rope.

Gaunt flew *Bad Moon*. Lucy and her team were strapped in the rear.

They watched sunrise over Baghdad. Traders heading to market, skirting acres of airstrike rubble. Horse carts, wheeled fruit stalls, painted trucks. The morning haze would soon burn off and be replaced by a brilliant blue sky.

'Got to make the journey before the noonday heat,' said Gaunt. 'Hotter the air, the lower our lift. We'll burn a heck of a lot more fuel.'

The metal-planked floor of the Huey was lagged with sandbags. Coalition choppers regularly took AK hits as they flew downtown. Crew listened for the tick of bullets striking the airframe. Sometimes RPGs streaked from rooftops, militia hoping to knock out a tail rotor. Most Blackhawks were reinforced with Kevlar. Pilots knew to fly high, fly fast, vary their route. Gaunt had to improvise.

They passed the city limits. Cinder-block dwellings and tin-roof shanties replaced by scrubland.

Lucy breathed slow and steady, tried to get her heart rate under control. Adrenalin rush. 'Don't worry,' Jabril had assured her. 'It will be a short trip. You won't see another living soul.'

She checked the 40mm grenade launcher bolted to the

barrel-rail of her assault rifle, made sure it was locked tight.

Gaunt broadcast a final clearance request to the Regional Air Movement Control Centre in Qatar.

'*Roger that, Q-TAC. Confirm your last: we are clear all sectors north. You have our heading November, echo, echo, six three . . .*'

They had filed a flight plan north to Mosul. They told Air Command they were shipping medical supplies.

Gaunt checked the laminated map-pocket on the leg of his flight suit. He nudged the cyclic. The helos banked west in tight formation.

They dropped off radar and skimmed the desert parallel to the Fallujah Expressway, a ragged ribbon of blacktop bisecting a boundless vista of dust. They flew fifty metres above the deck, skimmed the dunes at a hundred knots. They left Baghdad city limits and passed into the unmanaged airspace of Al Anbar Governate.

Lucy passed round a packet of salt tablets. They knocked them back with a swig of mineral water.

She took a tube of high-factor sun cream from her pack and smoothed lotion on her face and neck. She threw the tube to Toon. He squeezed a white worm of cream down each arm and massaged it into tattooed skin.

Toon had tattoos down both arms, Yakuza-style. Lucy asked him about it one night as they sat drinking in the Riviera Bar.

'Momento mori,' explained Toon, pointing at his arm. 'The lion. Leo Fowler. Blackhawk developed gear trouble over Kuwait City. He was the only guy to walk away. Dropped dead of an embolism three months later. The thistle. Jimmy McDougal. Immigrant from Scotland. His wife left him. Locked himself in a barrack toilet cubicle and blew his brains out. My personal memorial wall. Nobody else remembers these guys. They aren't listed among the fallen. But they were my friends.'

Lucy had no friends, no family, beyond the team. Better that way. During her days in Special Recon, she spent tense pre-mission hours slamming her knife into a dartboard while other squad members filled out next-of-kin and wrote goodbye letters to wives and kids. Every soldier she met could tell the story of some Dear John suicide, some beloved buddy that ate a bullet or drove into an abutment. She knew one guy with 'Linda Forever' tattooed on his forearm. Linda ran off with his brother so one night he sat in the barracks, poured caustic soda on his arm and sweated through the pain as flesh blistered and burned.

Better to travel light.

The Riv.

A low-ceiling dive favoured by security contractors. Part of the old presidential palace. A social club for the secret police converted to a coalition drinking den as a big Fuck You to the Ba'ath Party.

Blackwater guys considered themselves elite and stayed at the Rasheed, content to drink malted Astra near-beer with CPA staffers and Agency analysts. Everyone else, mercenaries from Fiji, Indonesia, El Salvador, the rootless Ronin of the world's war zones, found their way to the Riv.

Jukebox. Constant cigar fug. A guy with a biker beard manned the doorway metal detector.

There was usually grief.

Toon rolled down his sleeves and hid his tattoos. Amanda fed coins into the jukebox. Sheryl Crow. She and Lucy slow-danced while barstool drunks threw insults and beer caps.

A couple of Air Cav officers entered the club. They shouldered a space at the bar and ordered orange juice. The barman served them, looking doubtful, wondering if they were trouble. No reason regular troops should hang out at the Riv unless they wanted to pick a fight.

The soldiers smacked gum and stared down any privateer that looked their way.

'Cruising for a bruising,' muttered Voss.

They tripped a six-six contractor with Maori tattoos as he walked to the bar. He took a swing. Friends grabbed his arms and pulled him away. The Maori sat in the corner, sipping Blue Ribbon, waiting for Air Cav to step outside.

One of the officers tried to block Amanda as she headed to the bathroom.

'Hey, babe.'

She squirmed past him.

The guy sat at the bar and ordered triple bourbon. The barman said something as he poured. The officer told him to shut the fuck up. He threw dollars, snatched the bottle and headed for an empty table.

Toon headed to the bar for a fresh round of beers. Lucy and Amanda sat in a booth with the rest of her crew. The girls sat with arms round each other's shoulders.

Air Cav and his buddy kept looking at the girls. He kept drinking. Lucy watched him in the periphery of her vision.

Air Cav made his move at midnight. He slid off his chair. He swayed like the dance floor was the tilting deck of storm-tossed ship.

'Fucking bitch.'

Lucy stood to meet him. He took a swing. She ducked the blow. He staggered, balance thrown, and fell across a table shattering beer bottles.

'Motherfucker.'

He sat on the floor and pulled green bottle glass from his bleeding hand. His buddy crouched by his side and helped bandage the wound with napkins.

They staggered out the bar and into the street.

Three big Maori waiting, cracking their knuckles.

Back in the bar, Amanda drank chardonnay and got maudlin. This was their last war. Voss was thirty-eight. Toon was forty-three. Old-timers.

Amanda took out her phone and asked the barman to take

a group shot. They clustered round the portrait of Saddam that hung at the back of the bar near the jukebox. Beret, shades, big rip down his face. An inscription in English: '*Saddam Hussein al-Tikriti, the Anointed One, the Glorious Leader, direct descendant of the Prophet, president of Iraq, chairman of the revolutionary Command Council, field marshal of its armies, doctor of its laws, and great uncle to all its peoples.*' Someone had taped a newsprint picture to the portrait to obscure the man's sash and braids: Saddam in his underpants in an interrogation cell looking haggard and frightened.

Lucy and her crew grinned and threw gang signs. They toasted the camera. They shouted 'money' as the bartender pressed the shutter release.

Pop. Flash. A frozen moment.

Lucy watched dunes blur beneath them.

Toon drained his mineral water dry. He turned in his seat, unzipped and pissed in the bottle. He tossed the bottle out the open side door.

'All right there, Kaffir?' said Voss.' Trouble with your prostate?'

'Burnt any good crosses lately, Nazi motherfucker?'

Jabril watched the men, unsure if they were joking around.

Voss took a packet of biltong from his pocket. He threw it across the compartment. Toon folded a strip into his mouth.

Lucy tugged Jabril's sleeve. They had dressed him in combat gear. Coyote tan. Boots and field jacket from the Victory PX. She helped him with shirt buttons. He didn't object to US uniform. 'I'm a pragmatist. That's how I survive.'

She pointed at the desert ahead.

'What's that?'

Something in the sand. A long black line, cutting through the dunes.

'The fence.' Jabril shouted to be heard over rotor noise. 'Two hundred miles long.' He pointed with the metal hook at the end of his right arm. 'Skull and crossbones. Warns off Bedouin. It means we are entering the contamination zone.'

Amber cabin light. Twenty minutes from target. Cue to suit up.

They checked laces, checked belts and knee-pads, tightened the straps of their ballistic vests.

They checked mag pockets. Each of them carried eight clips of green-tip tungsten carbide penetrators.

They unholstered Glock 17s and press-checked for brass.

They pulled their rifles from vinyl dust sleeves. The barrel and muzzle vents of each weapon were patched with duct tape to seal them from sand. They slapped home STANAG magazines and chambered a round.

They each carried two M67 frag grenades hooked to their webbing, rings taped down.

They each wore a quart canteen on their belt and a three-litre Camelbak hydration bladder strapped to their backs.

Voss slotted shells into his shotgun.

Toon hefted a SAW from the floor and held it in his lap. Squad Automatic Weapon: a compact belt-feed machine gun. He attached a two-hundred-round box magazine. He fed the belt into the receiver and slapped it closed.

They strapped on sand goggles.

Lucy leant close to Jabril. She held out a Glock.

'You should carry a pistol,' she shouted. 'Just in case.'

Jabril shook his head.

Red light. One minute.

A quick descent.

Gaunt lowered the collective and eased the cyclic forward.

Combat landing. They came in fast. Heavy touchdown. Rotor-wash kicked up a dust storm.

Smooth deployment. The team jumped clear of the helos, ran through a blustering typhoon of sand and grit.

Defensive quadrant, guns trained on empty terrain. They each scanned their designated sector of fire.

Rotors decelerated and engine noise dwindled to silence.

'Clear.'

'Clear and covering.'

'All clear, boss.'

'All right. Stand easy.'

Middle of the Western Desert. Silence. Desolation. A faint breeze blew dust from the crest of each dune like a wisp of smoke.

Lucy took compact Barska binoculars from her chest rig. Three-sixty scan of the horizon. Brilliant blue sky. Rolling sand.

'Let's get the choppers under cover.'

Gaunt and Raphael unlaced bundles of desert camouflage netting and threw them over each chopper. They tented the nets with poles. The fabric coat masked thermal infra-red and absorbed radar. It protected the choppers from detection by ISTAR: Intelligence, Surveillance, Target Acquisition and Reconnaissance. The satellite network monitoring the Middle East battle zone. It would pick up nothing but sand.

Gaunt climbed the fuselage of each bird. He shook dust from filters. He stretched canvas covers over intakes and exhaust fairings.

Lucy looked up. She shielded her eyes. The sun was high. Morning haze had burned away. She could feel heat radiating from the sand around her. It would soon be too hot for the choppers to fly. Low air density. They were grounded until noonday oven heat diminished and evening cool gave them sufficient lift to get airborne.

'Hey. Jabril. Over here.'

She and Jabril climbed a high dune. They stared into the desert.

Lucy took a compass bearing. She pulled a laminate map envelope from a vest pocket.

'Why did we land so far from the valley?' asked Jabril.

'I want to approach on foot. We'll call in the choppers once the objective site is secure.'

Jabril pointed to a ridge of arid peaks in the far distance.

'There. That's where we need to go.'

Lucy checked her map. She surveyed the western horizon through binoculars.

'Those hills. What are they called?' she asked.

'Ancients called them The Mountains of the Dead.'

'You got to be kidding.'

'They are well named. Desolate peaks and canyons. No wind, no water. Just merciless heat.'

Lucy returned to the choppers.

She pulled on her prairie coat and turned up the collar. She wrapped a shemagh scarf round her head like a loose hood.

She helped strap Jabril into body armour.

'There's no one out here,' protested Jabril as she tightened clips and Velcro. 'The guns. The defensive drills. None of it is necessary. This is poisoned land. Taliban and Peshmergas stay away. They know better than to approach this area. We should fly direct to the valley.'

'I wouldn't last too long in my line of work if I relied on luck. It's always the routine jobs that get you killed. Assume heavy opposition every step of the way, and hope to be pleasantly surprised. Sure you don't want a gun?'

He held up his hook.

'My skills as a marksman have diminished since I lost my right hand.'

Toon tied a black do-rag round his head and draped a sweat towel round his shoulders to pad the SAW sling. He carried a heavy backpack full of box ammunition on his back.

Huang strapped on a medipac and unfurled a boonie hat.

Amanda shouldered her sniper rifle case and adjusted her straw Stetson. She dipped her fingers in a tub of zinc cream and painted the bridge of her nose and her cheekbones.

Gaunt sat in the shade of the *Bad Moon* cargo compartment. He watched Lucy put her foot on the door-lip and tie her boot.

'Assholes. All of them.'

'What the fuck do you know about soldiering?' said Lucy. 'Most of your combat hours were logged on a fucking PlayStation.'

'Bunch of losers. I asked around. Your girl spent her last tour amped on meth. Lucky to get detox instead of jail time. Voss did a long stretch for assault in Krugersdorp Prison. Another stretch at Zonderwater for robbery. Looks like you found your level.'

'They're good people. They just need someone to believe in them.'

'Toon. Got to be mid-forties. In the regular army he would be flying a desk. He wouldn't be front line.'

'Saved my arse more times than I can count. Laugh all you want, but one day soon you'll be old and begging for a break. Happens to us all.'

Lucy approached Voss.

'Hey, boss.'

'Stay here with Gaunt and Raphael, all right?' said Lucy. 'Keep a bead on them. I trust these guys about as far as I can spit.'

'You got it.'

'Seriously. Keep them alive. We need a ride home. But on a short leash. If they give you any shit, fuck them up.'

'Be a pleasure.'

Lucy stood with Amanda and surveyed the vista of sand ahead of them, the distant ridgeline rippling in mirage heat.

Lucy buttoned her prairie coat. Amanda adjusted the brim of her Stetson.

'Like it?'

'Love it.'

The team set off.

The Gatekeepers

They waded across dunes. They left a winding trail of footprints through the virgin sand. Their boots sunk ankle-deep.

The sun got high. The hills rose out of shimmering thermal distortion.

'Don't walk too fast,' advised Lucy. 'First rule of desert travel. Conserve sweat, not water. Guard against heat exhaustion.'

Amanda glanced back. The chopper netting merged with the landscape. They were alone in vast nothing.

Lucy strode ahead. She lifted her tinted goggles for a moment to wipe perspiration from her eyes. Blinding sun. Sand reflecting heat and light like a polished mirror. A decade spent in Middle East battlefields had left her skin tanned rich mahogany. She wished she brought moisturiser, then smiled to be worrying about her complexion while traversing one of Earth's hell zones.

Huang tripped and stumbled. A metal tube. A tank barrel protruding from a dune. They kept walking.

Toon stubbed his toe on a section of armour plate.

Amanda found a length of caterpillar track snaking across the sand like the interlocked vertebrae of an ox that succumbed to drought.

Broken vehicles beneath the dunes. Corroded Soviet hulks. T62 turrets. Artillery pieces. APCs. Jeeps. Trucks. All of them sunk in sand.

A pale scorpion basked on a turret hatch. Lucy stabbed

the creature with her bayonet. She watched the impaled creature wriggle and curl.

'What's all this junk?' she asked.

'There is an army beneath our feet. The second Al-Masina Armoured Division. They were massed in the desert during the first Gulf War, ready to defend Baghdad if the Americans decided to invade. The formation was picked up by a surveillance satellite. A series of B52 sorties pounded vehicles to scrap iron. "Whispering Death", they called it. Five-hundred-pound bombs dropped from high altitude. The concussions were so intense Turkish seismologists recorded the impacts as a massive earthquake. The bones, the wreckage, have been smothered by dunes.'

'Jesus.'

'This desert has been a battleground since the dawn of humanity. A fault line between east and west. Countless kings have led men into the wilderness, chasing imperial dreams. Legions swallowed without trace.'

'Sound like you love the place.'

'Once you have experienced absolute desolation, it never leaves your soul.'

Gaunt and Voss stood beneath the dappled shade of the camouflage nets.

Voss took off his baseball cap and wiped his brow.

'Soon be fifty in the shade.'

Gaunt looked out across the dunes.

'All those armies. One empire after another, fighting over dust.'

'The mercenary life,' said Voss. 'One pointless shitstorm after another. Better get used to it.'

'I'm not a merc. I'm a businessman.'

'Whatever you say,' said Voss.

'A man should have a code. Some kind of honour.'

'I'm older than you, kid,' said Voss. 'I've seen plenty of

friends die for nothing. Patriots, idealists. No one remembers their names.'

'I don't know why you're here,' said Gaunt. 'You and your friends. Whatever you find, whatever the big score, you'll head to the nearest casino and piss it away. Problem with you guys? You got nothing in your lives beyond money. No cause. Deadbeat privateers. This is all you will ever be.'

'Been more places, been more alive, than most guys dragging their brats round the mall on a weekend.' Voss pointed at Raphael. 'What's his story?'

'You are two of a kind. He's from some stinking LA slum. War is his home.'

Raphael had unzipped his flight suit and tied the arms round his waist. A big Virgin Mary tattoo etched across his back.

Voss cleaned his nails with a knife.

Gaunt returned to *Bad Moon* and grabbed his daypack from beneath the pilot's seat.

'I'm going to take a shit.'

He headed into the desert.

Voss watched Raphael place a mineral water bottle at the crest of a dune and take shots with his Colt. Puffs of sand each time he missed.

Voss unholstered his Glock. Quick aim/fire. The bottle burst. Water soaked into the sand and dried in moments.

Raphael mouthed, 'Fuck you.'

Gaunt walked a hundred yards into the desert and knelt on the lee side of a dune.

He looked up. Something circling in the far distance. A dove-grey fleck, wheeling like a vulture. He took binoculars from his pocket. A drone. They were under constant surveillance. The UAV's Ratheon sensor suite relaying real-time footage to Koell in Baghdad. The guy must have knocked heads and called in a lifetime of favours.

He checked his watch, unzipped the side pocket of his daypack and took out the sat phone. He keyed a four-digit code. Transmission scrambled through a Citadel algorithm.

He dialled.

'Brimstone to Carnival, over.'

Koell's voice:

'*Authenticate.*'

'Authentication is Oscar, Sierra, Yankee, Bravo.'

'*Go ahead, Brimstone.*'

'We are at the drop zone, approximately seven kilometres from the target. The advance team are proceeding to the objective site. Nothing hinky. Next sitrep at eighteen hundred, over.'

'*Ten-four. Roger and out.*'

A farmstead. Five sun-blasted hovels. Concrete and cinder block. Two-room dwellings. Sand-choked doorways. Nothing inside each house but scattered cooking pots and a few smashed sticks of furniture.

The team crouched and ran. Cover/fire formation. They hooked left and right. They took blocking positions.

'Clear.'

'Clear. Go.'

They kicked in doors.

Lucy had worked sweep-and-search operations in villages surrounding Kandahar, Afghanistan. Special Recon patrols. Two roofless Land Rovers with a .50 cal mounted in the rear. A snatch squad taking down intel targets. She led the breaching team. Gave the nod and was first in the door. Iron gates blasted open with shok-lok rounds. Quick room-to-room. Tables kicked over, beds upturned. A zip-cuff and head-bag for villagers scared paralytic by stun grenades.

Jabril and Huang sheltered behind a dirt culvert while the team searched each house.

Lucy's voice over the short-range TASC comms:

'*Okay. We're done.*'

They met at the patch of dirt that served as a village square. Empty windows, empty doorways. Ghost-town desolation.

'The place is dead.'

'Must we waste time playing soldiers?' asked Jabril.

'The day we get sloppy is the day we get killed,' said Lucy. 'Let's make use of the shade. Rest stop. Meet back here in fifteen.'

Lucy climbed a ladder and stood on a flat roof. She looked north and surveyed the hills through binos. Boulders and crags. Barren as the moon.

A slight breeze. The tails of her prairie coat billowed around her.

Jabril climbed and stood by her side.

'Not far,' said Lucy.

'No,' said Jabril. 'Not long now.'

He took a pack of Salems from the chest pocket of his flak jacket. He struck a match, lit a cigarette and savoured it.

He offered the pack to Lucy. She took a cigarette. She smoked half, stubbed and tucked the unsmoked butt in her pocket.

'Poor-girl habit,' she explained. 'Can't abide waste.'

She looked around.

'Why the fuck would anyone try to scratch a living out here?'

'Because it's all they have ever known,' said Jabril.

'What do locals call this stretch of desert?'

'Something dramatic. I forget. What do Americans call it?'

'The Motherfucker.'

Jabril smiled and shook his head.

'And yet they think we are the barbarian culture.'

'No point acting all sly and superior,' said Lucy. 'Those dumb yanks kicked your arse. That whole contest-of-civilisations thing didn't exactly work out for you.'

*

Toon picked up a rock and dropped it down a well. Brief clatter. No splash.

Amanda sipped warm water from the shoulder pipe of her hydration pack.

Scattered shoes and clothing.

'Must be nice,' said Amanda. 'A simple life. No bullshit. Straightforward.'

She fanned herself with her Stetson.

'Easy for you to say. Little Miss Trust Fund. Little Miss Finishing School. I was born poor. Nothing romantic about poverty. I used to work as a grill man. Flipped eggs for truck drivers and construction workers. Had to ask permission for bathroom breaks. Fuck that shit. And I was living like a king compared to these guys.'

'Hey. I worked. I had summer jobs. I wore a name badge.'

'Answer me this. When did Daddy buy your first car?'

'Just before he broke two of my ribs and kicked me out the house. That was the last parental dollar I ever saw.'

Toon looked around.

'Imagine playing out your whole life in a place like this. Poor bastards. Sitting in dirt watching their teeth fall out. No wonder they need God and the promise of something better.'

They pushed open a door.

Bare rooms. No plumbing. No electricity. A couple of beds. Some cushions and rugs. Everything dusted in sand fine as flour.

A back room. Scattered shoes. Broken tea glasses. An old, black bloodstain on the carpet. Cushions stuffed in the windows.

'Looks like a bunch of them died in here,' said Amanda. 'They tried to block the windows, keep out the gas. Plug every gap. Didn't do them much good.'

'Might have been best if they stepped outside and took a deep breath.'

She picked up a playing card from the sand-dusted floor.

She blew it clean. Ace of spades. Saddam's portrait on the back.

'Death card,' said Toon. 'The clean-up crew. I'm guessing they sent in a bunch of guys in NBC suits to take pictures and police up the bodies. They left a message in case any camel jockeys tried to resettle the place.'

'How does a guy do that? Saddam. How can he sit at his desk and sign the order? Live his life? Kick off his shoes, eat a meal, laugh at the TV, while all this shit goes down in his name?'

Toon shrugged.

'I've lost count of the men I've killed. I can't say they haunt my dreams.'

'But mothers? Children?'

'Never killed a woman.'

'Guy must be a psychopath. A proper, strap-him-down, throw-the-switch psychopath.'

'Evil. Some people are just plain evil.'

Huang was asleep by a wall. Lucy kicked him awake.

'All set?'

The team headed into the desert. They climbed dunes.

'Hold on,' said Amanda.

Something beneath her boot. Something white.

Lucy crouched.

'Sheep skull.'

'Take a look at this,' said Amanda.

A skeletal human hand. Amanda brushed away more sand. A child's skull.

'The villagers,' said Lucy. 'A mass grave. Poor bastards.'

Amanda dug out the skull. Sand poured from empty eye sockets. She brushed dust from the cracked cranium with a gloved hand.

'Part burned. They doused them in gasoline. Humans and cattle, piled together.'

Lucy kicked sand to cover the remains.

'Leave them be. That's the best we can do for them.'

Amanda scooped sand and reburied the skull.

'Sorry, kid.'

They headed north.

They entered the shade of the hills. A ridge of jagged crags high above them, like the ramparts of an impenetrable fortress.

Lucy uncapped her compass and checked the azimuth.

'Sure there's no one up there?' asked Lucy. 'Feels like we are being watched.'

'No one,' said Jabril. 'Kurdish militia might have used some caves for munitions storage, years ago. But they are long gone. Nobody dares come here now.'

Lucy spat grit. Toon pulled off his do-rag and dabbed sweat from his neck and face.

'People got no business living in a country like this.'

They watched a serpentine dust devil dance across the dunes ahead of them. A mini tornado riding the thermals where shadow met the sun.

'Not far now.'

They kept walking. The team adopted full combat formation. They spread out and kept three-sixty coverage of the terrain.

'Stay loose, all right? No bunching.'

Lucy took point.

Amanda held their left flank. She scanned the high valley walls above them.

Huang buddied with Jabril and checked dunes to their right.

Toon brought up the rear. He turned round every ten paces and walked backwards for a couple of steps, surveying the dunes behind them, SAW at the ready.

Railroad tracks half covered in sand.

'Follow the tracks,' said Jabril. 'They will take us to our destination.'

'Everyone all right?' asked Lucy, checking her team. 'Keep sipping water, yeah? Shout if you feel light-headed.'

They strode parallel with the tracks. Jabril walked beside Lucy.

'Why did you leave the army, may I ask?'

'I got tired of guys staring at my tits. Seriously. Eyes on me all the time. Another day, another butt-grabbing jackass. It wears you down. They have a saying: "Every chick in a war zone is a perfect ten." Even the guys with rings on their fingers consider themselves operationally single. A woman has two options when she puts on a uniform. She can either be a bitch or a whore. I don't want to be either. I'd rather be me.'

'Indeed.'

'Fucking military. Suck you dry and spit you out.'

Jabril pointed to an outcrop ahead of them.

'We are almost at the entrance. It is on the other side of this escarpment.'

'The valley?'

'A tunnel. Formed by natural erosion. Possibly an ancient underground stream. It was widened to accommodate the railroad track.'

The team came to a sudden halt.

'Holy shit,' said Toon.

'Whoa,' said Huang.

They stood looking at the cliff high above them.

The crude tunnel mouth was flanked by two colossal statues carved out of the rock face. Bearded men with the bodies of bulls and the wings of eagles. Blank eyes. Mouths set in a sneer of cold command. They stared, Sphinx-like, across miles of empty desert.

'Got to be three hundred feet,' murmured Toon. 'Maybe more.'

'Must have taken generations to carve,' said Amanda.

'Who are they? asked Lucy.

'Gatekeepers of the underworld,' said Jabril. 'No one knows their names.'

'Jesus.'

Lucy took an involuntary step backwards. She was daunted by the scale of the rock carvings, overwhelmed by a sudden rush of time-vertigo as she struggled to comprehend the antiquity of the gargantuan statues.

'Some suppose they are a twin image of Sargon, greatest of the Akkadian warrior-chieftans. King of the Southern Cities and Northern Plains, The Fist of God.'

'What's that inscription round the pedestal?'

Chiselled hieroglyphs taller than a man, deeper than an arm's length.

'A lost language.'

They looked into the impenetrable shadow of the tunnel mouth. Lucy stepped forward and stood at the threshold. She half-expected the light and wind-rush of an oncoming subway train. Sudden chill made her skin prickle.

'It's cold as a meat locker in here.'

Her breath fogged the air.

'Hell of a welcome mat,' murmured Toon, looking up at the gargantuan effigies.

'It's not a welcome,' said Jabril. 'It's a warning to travellers to turn back.'

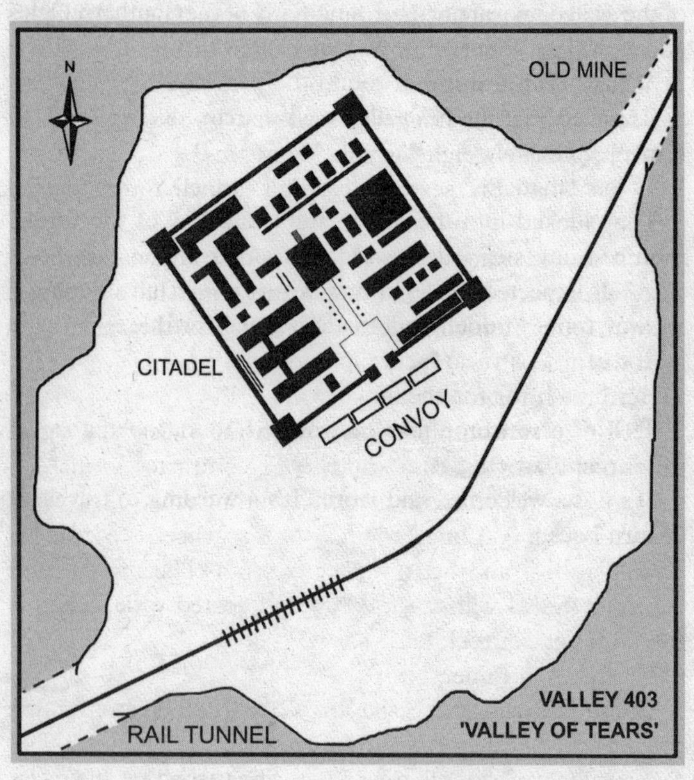
N
OLD MINE
CITADEL
CONVOY
RAIL TUNNEL
VALLEY 403
'VALLEY OF TEARS'

The Valley

They walked through the tunnel darkness. Their flashlights lit an arched, concrete roof. The crunch of boots on ballast echoed from the walls.

'How long is this thing?' asked Lucy.

'Approximately eight or nine kilometres.'

'What's that? Six, seven miles? This tunnel? You're fucking kidding me.'

'It's an old water course. An underground stream, cut through limestone sediment. Ancients must have explored the tunnel by torchlight, discovered it was the route to a secluded valley.'

'Why widen it for a railroad?'

'There were phosphate deposits in the valley. A Belgian mining company called Clyberta were contracted to develop the site. They drove a boring machine through this passageway. A massive thing. A huge, rotating cutting wheel. Slave labour cleared rubble and helped truck it south. The tunnel walls were reinforced with steel arches and coated with shotcrete to guard against rock falls.'

'So there's a mine?'

'Some tunnels and galleries. Clyberta abandoned the project when Saddam invaded Kuwait.'

'Freezing my arse off,' said Lucy. She turned up the collar of her prairie coat. 'This is crazy shit. I'm going to die of hypothermia in the middle of a desert.'

'It can happen,' said Jabril. 'There is a dramatic drop in temperature after sundown. The night wind can be lethal.'

'I don't intend to stay that long.'

They trudged in silence.

'Hold it,' said Toon. 'I got to stop a while.'

'In this cold?'

'I got to rest my knee.'

'All right,' said Lucy. 'Take five.'

They sat with their backs to the tunnel wall. Jabril lit a cigarette. His match flared in darkness.

'You know,' said Lucy, 'I've got a sister back in England. Christine. Lives in Oxford. Each time we meet I can't think of a fucking thing to say to her. Childcare, decor, gardening. Shit, I've watched cities burn.'

'Yeah,' said Huang. 'I was back in Clarksville last year. Everyone was so damn fat. Big Gulps and fried chicken. Made me want to puke.'

'I don't like it,' said Toon. 'This tunnel. Perfect place for an IED. Couple of old artillery shells. Pressure plate under the shingle. Anybody wanted to fuck us up, we'd walk right into it.'

Basic training, Fort Leonardwood, Missouri. Instructors hard-schooled by Vietnamese jungle terrain. Their advice: collude with the landscape. String tripwires across easy routes. Natural paths, forest clearings, river banks. Help your enemy betray themselves out of habit and lethargy.

'Quit whining,' said Huang.

'Fuck that. Regular army wouldn't set foot in this fucking place until a bomb crew gave the all-clear. They'd send robots, they'd do a mine sweep.'

'Why do you think we are all walking behind you?'

Lucy got to her feet.

'Okay. Let's get going.'

Toon walked next to Jabril.

'Hey. Jabril. How come we never see you pray to Mecca? Not the religious type?'

'I don't think God wants to hear from me.'

'What's that?' asked Amanda.

Something on the ground up ahead. A skeletal figure face down on the railroad track.

Lucy crouched over the body.

'Western clothes. Lowa boots. Fresh tread. A year's wages for a guy round here. How about it, Jabril? This guy sure as shit isn't Republican Guard.'

'I've no idea who he might be.'

'Couple of bullet holes in his jacket. Old blood. Walking wounded. And no flashlight. He stumbled through this tunnel in pitch dark then bled out. Poor fucker.'

A shrivelled scalp. Skin like leather. Mummified fingers dug into sleeper ballast.

'Jesus,' muttered Toon. 'This whole desert is an ocean of bone. Anyone comes out here gets eaten up.'

Lucy rolled the corpse. The body was a dried husk. Empty eye sockets. Rictus grin.

'Miserable place to croak,' she said.

'Does it make a difference?' asked Jabril. 'When the time comes?'

'I want to die in a bed,' said Toon. 'I want the last thing I see to be a smiling face. I don't want to die screaming in the dark.'

Lucy searched the man's pockets.

'Give me some light.'

Toon stood over her with a torch.

She found a crumpled pack of cigarettes. Sobranie. Premium Russian. She found a cheap lighter.

'No phone. No wallet.'

She took a black automatic pistol from the dead man's jacket pocket.

'Makarov.'

She ejected a cartridge. She held it in the beam of the flashlight and examined the stamp.

7.62
9X39US

'That's a Spetsnaz round. Russian black ops. US. "Umenshennaya Skorost". Low velocity. Silenced for wetwork. Sure you don't know anything about this, Jabril? Looks like we're not the first bunch of contractors to make the trip.'

'No.'

'My gut is telling me to turn tail right now. What's a Tier One Muscovite doing out here? This guy is a long way from home.'

Toon crouched by the cadaver.

'A dead Russian doesn't bother me.'

'No?'

'I'm more concerned about the thing he was running from.' Toon examined the Makarov pistol. He examined the corpse. 'Look at his hands. See those tattoos? This goon has been through the fucking gulags. You know what these Russian mobsters are like. Hardcore. Meanest motherfuckers on God's green earth. So why was he running in terror?'

'Fuck it,' said Lucy. She got to her feet. 'We're badder than anything we are likely to meet. Let's keep going.'

A pinprick of daylight in the far distance. Lucy switched off her flashlight and blinked. A glimmer like a distant star.

'Have we reached the end of the tunnel?' asked Amanda.

'Feels like we've been walking forever,' said Toon. 'There better be gold at the end of this fucking rainbow, Jabril. Don't put me through this for nothing.'

They kept walking. The tunnel mouth. Dazzling light.

'This is it, said Jabril. 'Our destination. We've reached the valley.'

They walked out of darkness into fierce sunlight. Cool tunnel air suddenly replaced by intense oven heat.

They shielded their eyes from the sudden glare.

*

Voss lazed in the doorway of *Talon*. He pulled down the brim of his cap and lay the shotgun across his lap.

Gaunt and Raphael sat in the doorway of *Bad Moon*. They had stripped out of Nomex flight suits and dressed in camo gear. They sipped lukewarm bottled water.

'Reckon he's sleeping?' asked Gaunt.

'No. He's wide awake. He's watching us. Been watching the whole time.'

Gaunt fanned himself with his boonie hat. He dabbed sweat from his face with a handkerchief.

Raphael swilled and spat.

'The man is a stone killer,' said Raphael. 'I can see it in his face. See that shotgun? See that big-ass knife? He's a farm boy. Used to gutting. Used to slaughter. Butcher you up real good. Wouldn't think twice.'

'He won't be a problem,' said Gaunt. 'Just have to pick our moment.'

'You okay with this? You were in the corps. But did you ever whack a guy? Do it up close and for real?'

'Don't worry about me. My hand is steady.'

'So how do you want to work this?'

'Might as well wait for them to find the gold,' said Gaunt. 'Do the grunt work. Locate the truck and crack it open. Then we hit them fast. Don't give them time to react.'

'How do you know Koell won't pull the same shit soon as we get back to Baghdad? Pop a cap in our ass soon as we deliver the goods?'

'He jumped us once. I'm not going to let him jump us again. Next time we meet, he'll be the fuck with a gun pressed to his balls.'

'Damn,' said Lucy.

Toon crossed himself.

'The Valley of Tears,' said Jabril.

A natural amphitheatre a mile wide. A bowl, like a vast

lunar crater. An alien landscape. Wind had shaped the sandstone outcrops of the high valley walls into sinister ossiferous lips and knuckles.

A squat citadel dominated the valley floor.

Stillness and sun-blasted silence.

'What the fuck are we looking at? A fortress?'

'A necropolis. A sacred city dedicated to the worship of the dead.'

High ramparts surrounded a maze of temple precincts. Forecourts, toppled colonnades and crumbled cloisters. At the centre of the labyrinth of half-tumbled masonry stood a huge, pillared edifice resembling the Parthenon. The entrance to the temple complex was a breach in the perimeter wall flanked by two high guard towers.

'What's that big building at the centre?'

'Some say it is the Temple of Marduk. A powerful Babylonian deity. God of gods. Creator of the universe.'

'How old is this place?'

'The temple might have been built in the reign of the Akkadian kings five thousand years ago.'

'How come I've never seen pictures of this place?' asked Lucy.

'This desert has been a war zone since time began. It doesn't attract many tourists. Maybe one day there will be toilets and a gift shop. Somehow I doubt it. Something about this place. Something oppressive. People will always stay away.'

'So where's the bullion?'

Jabril pointed towards the citadel. The hulks of innumerable military supply vehicles lay in front of the temple gateway. Trucks, Jeeps, APCs and civilian sedans. They were smashed and carbonised, buckled and burned black.

'The bank truck was part of that convoy.'

Lucy refocused her binoculars.

'Got to be two, three acres of scrap. Burned to a fucking crisp. What the hell happened?'

'As I told you. The battalion was ordered to return to Baghdad and join the fight against the Americans. Some officers were anxious to obey. Patriots and party zealots. Others were less eager to die for a lost cause. They wanted to wait out the war. And they wanted the gold. They intended to sit by their radios, wait until they heard news of surrender and armistice, then emerge from the canyon. They could each return to their families rich men. There was a mutiny. People quickly took sides. Some swore to honour their oath of allegiance. Some tore up their party cards and stamped them in the dust. A civil war ensued.'

'Looks like those trucks got hit by fucking napalm. Sure there wasn't an air strike?'

'The gun battle must have punctured fuel tanks and ignited gasoline. Tight-packed vehicles engulfed by a violent firestorm. Don't worry. The gold will be safe inside the cash truck. Protected from the flames by thick armour plate.'

Lucy slung her rifle over her shoulder.

'All right, then. Let's go get rich.'

TOP SECRET SPECIAL HANDLING NO FORM

Central Intelligence Agency

Directorate of Operations, Near East Division

Doc ID: 575JD5
Page 01/1

08/23/05

MEMORANDUM TO: Project Lead, D.Ops
SUBJECT: Spektr

Colonel,

We have received word that the incursion team have reached the SPEKTR site. The advance party entered Valley 403 at 15:00.

11th Recon Squad will provide Predator overwatch of the valley. We have eyes-on-target until nightfall. We should shortly have our first site assessment from our man on the ground.

I appreciate your concerns with regard to the possible spread of infection. Steps have been taken to ensure the virus does not escape the contamination zone. We are currently liaising with Technical Services and our flight crew at the clandestine logistics base in Sharjah. I am confident we have sufficient assets on standby to initiate the CLEANSWEEP protocol should radical containment measures be required.

I shall keep you fully informed, as per your orders.

R. Koell
Field Officer
CA Special Proj, Baghdad Station

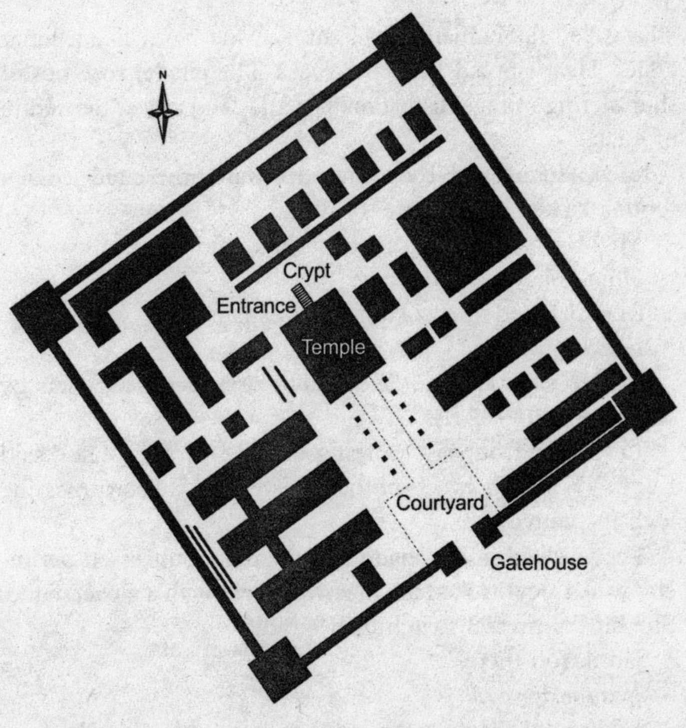
N
Crypt
Entrance
Temple
Courtyard
Gatehouse

The Temple

The valley floor. Fierce sunlight. A wide basin like a lunar crater. Heat rippled from the rocks. The citadel rose out of shimmering mirage distortion, like an island city at the centre of a lake.

Lucy, Huang and Toon walked towards the citadel. Each footfall kicked up a plume of dust.

'Might as well wave a fucking flag,' said Toon.

'Doing okay?' asked Lucy.

Toon dripped sweat. He looked exhausted.

'Fucking peachy.'

'Smile,' said Huang. 'We could be kiss-my-ass rich by sundown.'

'Let's spend our last working day like professionals,' said Lucy. 'Thorough sweep of the ruins before we start messing with the convoy.'

They walked in the shadow of the high, buttressed perimeter wall. Lucy stroked the massive blocks with a gloved hand. She hit the pressel switch of her radio.

'Jabril. You there?'

'*I can hear you.*'

'Where did they get the stone to build this place?'

'*The only archaeological survey of this site was done in eighteen ninety-one by a German Assyriologist called HV Hilprecht. There's a chapter in his* Exploration of Bible Lands. *The temple is granite. If it had been constructed from local limestone, it would have crumbled to powder centuries ago. Hilprecht says the stones were quarried five hundred miles south near Jalibah. It's hard to comprehend the time and manpower involved.*'

They stood at the threshold of the dead city, dwarfed by twin guard towers. They surveyed the column of vehicles parked in front of the towers, buckled and black like junkyard scrap.

'Better ignore the trucks for now,' said Lucy. 'We're probably alone out here, but let's not get sloppy. Full sweep of the citadel. Then we look for the gold.'

Lucy turned to Toon.

'Get up high. Give us some coverage, all right?'

'Sure, boss.'

Toon approached one of the gate towers. An arched doorway. Stone steps. He adjusted his grip on the SAW. He crept inside, and was swallowed by shadow.

Lucy and Huang contemplated the compound ahead of them. An extinct city. Flagstone courtyards. Tumbled pillars. Roofless buildings. A labyrinth of jumbled masonry, dusted in sand.

A long, ramped processional causeway led to the facade of the main temple structure. A wide gateway flanked by monstrous bull colossi.

'This is some spooky shit,' muttered Huang.

Amanda and Jabril climbed the steep valley wall. Amanda jumped from boulder to boulder. Jabril scrambled across scree, wheezing for breath.

They found a ledge.

Jabril released the Velcro straps of his body armour and pulled it over his head. He wiped sweat from his brow.

Amanda swigged from her canteen. She adjusted her TASC earpiece. She sat cross-legged. She pulled a long plastic Hardigg case from her backpack. Lid sticker: '*Silent souls inflict 308 holes.*' She flipped latches. A disassembled Remington M40, lying in a foam bed. A sleek, simple, bolt-action rifle with a scope.

She snapped and screwed each component together in a series of quick, precise movements. Receiver. Barrel. Scope. Bipod.

'Do you enjoy killing?' asked Jabril.

'I'm a professional.'

Amanda slotted match-grade Winchester bullets into a five-round magazine, and slapped it home. She unfolded a vinyl mat. She lay prone, tipped back her hat, and positioned the rifle.

She put the butt to her shoulder and pressed her cheek to the fibreglass stock. She uncapped the dayscope. She focused eight hundred yards distant on the far valley wall. Crosshairs centred on a small stone resting on top of a boulder.

'Be advised, firing for centre.'

'*Ten-four.*'

She fired. Puff of rock dust. Missed by a foot.

She re-calibrated the Leupold scope. She fired. Off by two inches.

Minor realignment. She fired. The little stone exploded in a shower of rock shards.

'Can I ask you something?' said Jabril.

'Sure.'

'You and Lucy. The rings on your fingers.'

'You Arabs think the West is one big orgy. Everyone getting laid but you.'

'I don't mean to judge.'

She shifted position and adjusted focus. She surveyed the citadel. She watched through the sniper scope as Lucy and Huang entered the precincts. She kept her crosshairs centred on the dirt between them. Lucy looked resolute. Huang looked jumpy.

Lucy's voice:

'*How's it going, Mandy?*'

'Don't worry. I got you.'

*

Toon took a Maglite from his pocket. The beam lit ancient steps worn treacherously smooth. The tight spiral passage amplified his laboured breathing. He had to squeeze and crouch. He battled claustrophobia.

He emerged into sunlight. The guard tower was capped by a stone platform surrounded by a high rampart.

He unclipped his backpack and laid out three boxes of link ammunition.

He snapped open the SAW bipod. He checked a two-hundred-round chain was clipped firmly into the receiver.

He pulled the towel from his neck and dabbed sweat from his face. He sipped from his canteen. He examined the stone slab beneath his weapon. A crude daemonic face etched in stone. He looked around. The rampart walls were inscribed with strange glyphs. Each stone block etched with runes and symbols. The floor of the platform was a giant cosmological chart. Deep grooves plotted astral orbits. The sun. The moon. Five planets. Earth at the centre.

He suppressed a shiver as he contemplated the awful antiquity of the building. Robed priests and acolytes must have stood on this platform and chanted in veneration of their tyrannical god.

'Was this some kind of fucking death cult?'

Jabril's voice:

'*Hilprecht attributes the temple to the worship of Marduk. But Marduk was a benevolent creator god. Whatever devotional rites took place here seem dedicated to an older, darker deity. Hieroglyphs throughout the complex show scenes from an imminent apocalypse, and demonstrate a preoccupation with the movement of the planets, specifically Jupiter.*'

Lucy's voice:

'*You got to remember, they didn't have TV.*'

Lucy and Huang explored the ruined necropolis. A succession of courtyards filled with tumbled blocks of rubble. Broken arches. Toppled colonnades.

‘Place is a fucking maze,’ murmured Huang.

Empty storerooms. Lucy switched on the barrel lamp of her rifle and scanned darkened interiors. Sand-choked doorways. Stone debris. Empty wall niches.

She checked dusty flagstones for signs of recent disturbance. She examined each entrance, looking for the needle-fine gossamer thread of a monofilament tripwire.

Kandahar. A whitewashed farmhouse. Home to a known bomb maker. Paid informants suggested the man kept a stockpile of old tank shells buried under his chicken coop. He gave local kids 1.5v batteries and improvised firing circuits. Twenty dollars a pop to lay IEDs along the nearby airport highway. Three of Lucy's Special Recon platoon were killed when a pressure-plate mine reduced their Snatch to whirling shrapnel in a millisecond pulse of white light.

‘Got to watch ourselves, all right?’ said Lucy's commanding officer. ‘This guy's a fanatic. He knows, sooner or later, he is going to get taken down. He'll lay on a surprise, take a bunch of us with him, if he can.’

They kicked in the door. The guy was eating dinner. He was sitting at his table, spoon in hand. Lucy shot him in the face and he nodded head-first into his stew.

She pulled back a curtain door. A side room. She saw rugs and cushions.

A wad of papers in the middle of the floor. Possible intel. Lucy moved to enter room but the CO shouted ‘Stop.’

She moved aside. The CO took a can of party shop Silly String from a mag pouch. He shook it. He sprayed. The can spat webs of yellow foam string at head height. The string drifted to the floor. A single tendril hung suspended at knee level. They crouched. Fine fishing line stretched taut across the doorway.

‘Shit,’ said Lucy.

‘Everyone out,’ shouted the CO.

They retreated two hundred yards into a poppy field and fired a couple of shoulder-launched LASM rockets into the farmhouse. Walls collapsed and a series of secondary explosions reduced the place to dust.

Lucy and Huang picked their way across a rubble-strewn chamber. Sunlight shafted through a hole in the domed roof.

'Any idea what these buildings used to be?'

Jabril's voice:

'*Part of the temple economy. Storerooms, perhaps. Built to contain grain, dried fruits, spices. There are no settlements or farms nearby. This was not a self-sustaining community. Someone with god-like authority picked this site, ordered the construction of a temple out here in the hinterland and kept it supplied with food and water. Despite the arid location, there are ceremonial pools, baths and fountains within the complex. A demonstration of unimaginable wealth and power.*

'*Can you picture how this site must have looked, thousands of years ago? Elaborate frescos painted on every wall. Rugs, silks, brass, perfumes. Yet the citadel is too remote to be erected for earthly prestige. It is a secret priest city. Lifelong home of soothsayers and astrologers. They would chant their incantations and sacrifice ritual offerings. They would study forbidden texts, transcribe opium dreams, dance themselves to a delirium. This was a serious place. A power-house of daemonic energy. The inner sanctum of the temple approached with the same trepidation as the plutonium core of a nuclear reactor. A great warlord wanted to draw down the power of the gods and blast his foes. When armies met on the sand he wanted his cavalry to sweep through barbarian ranks and lay them waste like a cyclone. Maybe he got his wish. Who knows?*'

Toon's voice:

'*This place scares the shit out of me, boss. Sooner we get going, the better.*'

'Everyone chill the fuck out,' said Lucy. 'It's just a bunch of rocks, all right? This isn't a vacation. We are here to work.'

They crossed a cloistered courtyard. They navigated tight avenues strewn with rubble.

'How long were you here, Jabril? You and your men?'

'*Two months.*'

'I haven't seen a single sign of disturbance. Not a footprint, not a cigarette butt. This place is pristine.'

'*Most of our troops wouldn't enter the citadel walls. The youngsters were superstitious and easily scared. Some of the night-watch said they saw ghosts. Figures moving on the ramparts in moonlight. We decided to camp further up the valley.*'

Huang turned to Lucy.

'What about bodies? Jabril said there was a big-ass gun battle. Place-should be a corpse-field.'

'Plenty of guys died out here,' said Lucy. 'I can feel it. And I'm willing to bet Jabril played his part. As long as he leads us to gold, I don't give a shit.'

They explored the dark recesses of a shrine built against the perimeter wall of the citadel.

Six internal pillars held up a low roof. A crude altar ready to receive votive gifts: libations and burnt offerings to win the favour of a minor deity.

'Whoa,' murmured Huang. 'Check it out.'

The room was carpeted with spent shell cases and discarded AK magazines. Each footstep clinked and chimed. The walls were cracked and cratered, brickwork blackened by muzzle-flare.

Lucy unsheathed her knife and dug a bullet from splintered granite brickwork. The bullet had mushroomed on impact. A misshapen, steel and copper coin.

'Hell of a fire-fight,' said Huang. 'Seriously heavy contact. Look at this. Emptied a full clip at the same spot in the wall. Damn near drilled right through it.'

Shell cases piled in the centre of the room. Empty magazines, up-turned ammo boxes.

Lucy brushed cartridge cases aside with her boot and stood at the epicentre of the debris.

'Two stacks of empty mags. I reckon two guys holed up in this room. Brought all the ammunition they could carry. Threw their shit down and let rip. Their last stand. Their fucking Alamo. Looks like they stood back to back. Fired about a thousand rounds. Fired in all directions. Look at that. Shooting way up the wall. Must have blown their eardrums. Must have melted their gun barrels. So much smoke they couldn't see a hand in front of their face.'

She scooped shell cases from the floor. Fresh bullets among scorched brass.

'They ejected a bunch of rounds. Misfires. Weapons overheated and jammed.'

'But who would try to overrun a couple of guys armed with AKs? What kind of maniac runs into that shitstorm? Even Taliban would hang back.'

'Maybe they went nuts. Heatstroke. Cabin fever. Started shooting at thin air.'

'Two guys? A shared madness?'

'It happens.'

'Want to ask Jabril? See what he has to say?'

'He's full of shit.'

Lucy raked her fingers through spent cartridges. She could almost hear it, smell it. The ghost of battle. Gunsmoke and stuttering muzzle flame. Men crazed with terror, frantically struggling to free the bolts of malfunctioning weapons.

'The more I see of this place, the less I like it,' said Lucy. 'Every instinct tells me to forget the gold and get the hell out of here.'

'We need this, boss. We got old. All of us. This is our last war. It's time to cash out.'

*

Toon unclipped his earpiece and let it hang. He didn't want to hear any more of Jabril's ghost stories. He sat with his back to the rampart wall. He wiped sweat from his eyes. Couldn't get used to the heat.

He looked up. Brilliant azure.

Years ago, back in Tennessee, he and his buddies stole a bottle of Dickel whisky from a liquor store. They told the young cashier someone was messing with his car. They snatched booze as he looked out the back door.

They got drunk in a field. They lay looking at the night sky. Toon was mesmerised by the stars. It was a hot night, but he felt a chill. Gazing up at a trillion miles of black nothing. He thought about it the next day. It was like an anti-heaven. A horrible, celestial absence. Beyond the blue skies of summer lay eternal cold and endless night.

He drank whisky a lot these days. Sat in the Riv until they threw him out and locked the doors. He got fucked up and hoped he wouldn't dream.

Intolerable heat. He wiped his face with his sweat towel and draped it over his head like a keffiyeh.

He hooked his earpiece back in place.

'How's it going, guys? Are we done, or what?'

Lucy and Huang walked up the central avenue: a wide, paved boulevard that swept from the citadel gate to the doorway of the main temple building.

Easy to imagine a solemn torch-lit procession. Chanting priests in robes and brass lamentation masks ready to prostrate themselves before their sinister god.

The temple facade. A titanic structure. Huge pillars. Twin bull colossi.

Lucy and Huang stood in the high temple doorway and peered into darkness. They cast long shadows across the flagstones.

They walked inside. They let their eyes adjust to the gloom.

A vast chamber. A vaulted roof. Eight gargantuan pillars inscribed with cryptic hieroglyphs and the outline of monstrous hybrid man-beasts.

Steps led to a raised sanctuary. A massive, snarling bull above the altar.

Lucy and Huang walked up the aisle of the cavernous, aeons-dead hall. Heavy boot-falls echoed and amplified.

They climbed time-worn steps to the altar. Lucy ran her hands over the stone. Black obsidian. Blood channels cut in the rock.

'Perhaps they sacrificed cattle,' said Huang.

'Could you coax a bull onto this table? No. Something a little more portable was laid on this altar and sliced.'

'I'd fight until my last breath.'

'Maybe they were a willing sacrifice. Maybe it was an honour. All dressed up in a fancy robe. Consecrated to the gods. They chewed a little opium and climbed on the slab feeling like a big shot.'

'Sick motherfuckers.'

Lucy shrugged.

'I've seen worse. I saw a guy walk up to a checkpoint and trigger a suicide vest. One of those volunteers from Saudi. A zealot pumped full of jihad. Big-arse smile on his face, ready for paradise. So eager to press the button he didn't take anyone with him. Threw his life away, just to scorch a little asphalt. I watched his head bounce fifty yards down the road. Fuck it. We're standing here with guns in our hands and knives in our belts. Humans haven't changed. Still driven by our savage gods.'

Lucy took out her radio.

'Advance team to *Bad Moon*, over?'

Gaunt's voice:

'*Go ahead.*'

'We have reached the objective. Get ready to roll. We'll call you in and pop smoke, over.'

'*Roger that.*'

*

Jabril sat with Amanda on the ledge.

'I spoke to your black friend,' said Jabril. 'He said you had killed many men.'

'Yeah.'

Amanda didn't take her eye from the sniper scope.

'You must see them close up, through your telescopic sight. See their faces, the sweat on their brows.'

'First time I popped a guy in the head, I didn't sleep for a week. We were stationed at a Forward Observation Base in As Salman. Yellow Nine. A makeshift fort in the middle of a shitty neighbourhood. We took mortar fire most days. I kept watch from a guard tower.

'A couple of rounds dropped in the vehicle yard one afternoon. We couldn't see the mortar crew. They were shielded by buildings. But I could see a young guy in the street holding a cellphone. He was talking to his militia buddies, supervising fire adjustment. He thought he was safe, thought we wouldn't shoot because he didn't have a gun in his hand. I centred my crosshairs on his forehead. Should have gone for a chest shot, centre-of-mass, just to be sure. But it was my first kill. I wanted to feel it. I wanted to do it right. And he looked up. Three hundred yards away, but I swear he saw me in the guard tower and looked me right in the eye. I blew his head apart. Neat drill hole through the cranium. Back of his skull flew off.

'The grunt sitting beside me in the sangar recorded it on his phone. Low-res bone and brain. Red pixel blur. He showed the whole platoon. That little phone clip turned me into the garrison rock star. I was high on adrenalin for a week. I got "One Shot, One Kill" tattooed on my shoulder. I got "Death From Afar" tattooed on my ass. Did it jailhouse-style. Lay on my bunk and got ink pricked beneath my skin with a hot needle. A week later, I crashed. Hit the booze. Popped a few pills. Couldn't sleep. Kept thinking about the dead guy. His parents, his kids.

'Second time was a little better. Same emotions. Euphoria then depression. But a little less intense, a little less drawn out. After that, killing a guy was like switching off a light. That's the sad truth. Once you cross the line, it's easy.'

Jabril lit a cigarette. He offered the pack to Amanda. She shook her head.

'How about you?' she asked. 'Ever killed a man?'

'With my own hands? No. I never have.'

'Your voice says different.'

Lucy:

'*The temple is clear. Meet us at the gate house. Let's find this fucking gold.*'

The Convoy

Fading light. A violet sky dusted with evening stars.

Lucy checked her watch.

'Looks like we'll be spending the night.'

Lucy and Huang walked between the vehicles of the burned-out convoy. Blackened hulks cast long shadows in the gathering gloom. The vehicles ticked and creaked as fierce noonday heat abated and the metal began to cool.

The whirlwind of flame that engulfed the trucks and Jeeps had long since died, but they could still smell the conflagration. The ghost-taint of melted rubber and scorched flesh.

They could see jumbled bone inside the vehicles. A clutter of skulls and ribs in the foot well of incinerated sedans.

They were both familiar with gasoline fires and the flesh-stink of street explosions.

During her time in the regular army Lucy had frequently been ordered to overcome panic and run towards the screaming mayhem of a recent car bomb. She was instructed to clear wounded and check for secondaries. She jostled against a tide of fleeing civilians, and headed towards the smoke and screams. Later, she joined fellow infantrymen on their hands and knees as they grid-searched street wreckage, ignoring dark and glossy pools of blood, severed hands and feet, as she searched for scraps of circuit board or lengths of wire that might betray the provenance of the suicide device.

Lucy checked the back of a troop truck. Jumbled bodies. Crisped flesh.

Charred banana clips scattered among bone.

'Most of these trucks were loaded with AK ammunition boxes. Shells must have cooked off in the fire. Popped like firecrackers. Spat bullets all over the place.'

'Fucking shitstorm.'

They looked beneath the truck. A body curled foetal, hands over its head.

'Could do with a drink,' muttered Lucy. 'A real one.'

'Could do with a fucking joint,' said Huang.

A couple of armoured personnel carriers, interiors scorched carbon-black.

A row of old impalas. Doors hung open. Seats burned down to springs.

A bunch of five-ton trucks, the ex-Soviet junk that comprised most of Saddam's hardware.

Lucy examined the hood of one of the trucks. The front of the vehicle had melted. The fender and grill reduced to a puddle of metal in the sand. The front of the engine block hung in drips.

'Someone threw thermite grenades.'

They walked down an avenue of junkyard wreckage. Their boots crunched on glass.

Lucy looked into the rear of an APC. Bench seats burned to metal frames.

Huang reached inside and lifted the lid of a wooden trunk with his rifle barrel. A melted Samsonite suitcase. Rolled prayer mats, Scorched Reeboks and bedding.

'Ever done a house clearance?' asked Huang. 'People's shit always looks small and pathetic after they are dead. The stuff they leave behind.'

Lucy pulled the long-range radio from her backpack. An ICOM wide-band hand-set the size of a brick. She extended the antenna.

'*Bad Moon*, do you copy over?'

Gaunt:

'*Go ahead.*'

'The objective site is clear. Bring in the choppers.'

'*Roger that.*'

They kept walking.

'Check it out,' said Huang.

The incinerated frame of a Land Rover Defender. Full off-road custom kit. Winch, snorkel exhaust, ram bars.

Lucy picked a licence plate from the sand.

'Fresh out of a Kuwait showroom.'

The tailgate hung open. The cargo compartment was bare.

Huang bent down. Broken sunglasses. He shook them free of sand. Oakleys.

'Want me to put Jabril in a headlock?' asked Huang. 'Find out what really happened?'

'I don't care what went down. Jabril is welcome to his secrets. I hate this damn country. I don't give a shit about the Iraqi people. I don't want to hear about their history, their fucked-up politics and feuds. I'm here to make money. I'm here for the gold. That's my only concern.'

They continued their search, weaving between burned-out cars.

Toon repositioned the SAW to give coverage of the convoy. He could see the distant figures of Lucy and Huang walking between the wrecked cars. Jabril and Amanda climbed the tower steps and stood beside him.

'You're damn sure none of your buddies are lying in wait?'

'How could anyone survive out here?' said Jabril.

'You said the ruins were haunted. Some of your men saw ghosts. Phantoms moving along the battlements at night.'

'Youngsters. Superstitious farm boys. They joined the army because it was a better life than herding goats. This battalion were supposedly elite Republican Guard but plenty of them could barely read and write. Some wore bone amulets to ward off the jinn that haunt the wilderness.'

'You believe any of that shit?'

Jabril shrugged.

'Can't help feeling we're not alone in this valley,' said Amanda. 'Lucy is right. There are eyes on us all the time.'

'Look around,' said Jabril. 'This is the deadest place on earth.'

Lucy knelt next to a Chrysler and examined bodywork. A door panel. She pushed her forefinger into a bullet hole.

'Big-arse holes. Fifty cal. Uniform direction of fire. Punctures on the left side of the vehicles, ragged exits on the right. Nice spray. Methodical. Each vehicle hosed down. I'm guessing the shooters took out trucks front and back. After that, everyone was trapped, boxed in. Easy meat. Soldiers took cover behind the cars but got cut to shit anyway. Fuel fires. Explosions. I reckon if we explored that valley wall we would find a couple of gun positions. A shitload of brass.'

'But why throw phosphorus grenades?' asked Huang. 'They killed everyone. The convoy was on fire. Why toss thermite? Lot of time and trouble. What did they want to burn?'

'Perhaps they wanted to cover their tracks. Wipe out forensics.'

'Maybe.'

Lucy kicked a pile of rags. Shreds of olive green camo clothing. Army boots baked crisp by the desert sun.

Jumbled bone. A skull rolled loose.

'Check it out.'

An empty can of gasoline. A Zippo held in a skeletal hand.

'Fucker burned himself alive. Maybe Jabril was telling the truth. Fear. Paranoia. Maybe they drove each other crazy.'

'It's getting dark,' said Amanda. 'Let's find the truck.'

They reached the rear of the convoy.

An armoured truck. It was boxed by automobiles.

She pressed the transmit button on her chest rig.

'Jabril? You there?'

'*Go ahead.*'

'I think I've found the gold.'

'*You should be looking at a big American armoured car. The kind they use for making cash and coin deliveries to banks. It was exported to Iraq before sanctions began.*'

Lucy jumped on the hood. She crouched. She spat on her hand, reached down behind heavy ram bars and rubbed the grille badge clean.

FORD.

It was a bank vault on wheels. A three-seat cab up front and a hardened steel cargo compartment. Two rear axles. The vault door was secured by combination locks.

'Looks like she got shot up pretty good. How much do you reckon this thing weighs?'

'*About fifteen tons. Twelve tons for the truck, three for the gold. It was hard to ship it across the desert. It continually sank in the sand. We had to attach chains and drag it with a couple of armoured personnel carriers.*'

'Toon. Got your binoculars?'

'*I can see you, boss.*'

'Reckon we can cut this fucker open?'

'*No problem. Chew through that door with our teeth if it comes down to it.*'

Toon stood at the guard tower parapet. He surveyed the convoy.

Lucy's voice:

'*Toon, get down here. Mandy. You too. We got to shift some of these cars.*'

'Two seconds, boss.'

He trained his binoculars on a troop bus.

'Thought I saw something.'

'*What did you see?*'

'Movement. Thought I saw movement. Corner of my eye. A flicker. Down there, among the cars. Can't pin it down.'

Toon rubbed his eyes. He scanned burned-out trucks, a couple of wrecked 4x4s.

'Sorry, boss. Trick of the light.'

'*All right. Ten-four. Stay sharp.*'

A furtive shadow. Something shifting in the burned-out bus.

'Shit. We got mail,' shouted Toon.

He cranked the charging handle of the SAW and let rip. Muzzle roar. The weapon kicked. Recoil made his flesh shiver. Smoking cartridge cases cascaded onto the flagstones, clink and chime. Bullets slammed into the troop transport at two hundred rounds per minute. The vehicle trembled and sparked as bullets pierced the body panels.

'*What have we got?*' shouted Lucy. '*Are we taking fire?*'

Toon grabbed his binoculars from the parapet ledge and scanned the bus. Dust and smoke slowly dispersed. Ragged bullet holes glowed dull red.

'*What the fuck is going on? Hostiles? Do we have hostiles? Come on, man. Talk to me.*'

He hooked a fresh box mag to the SAW. He clipped a belt into the breach and slapped the receiver closed.

'Standby. I'm going to take a look.'

Lucy and Huang took shelter behind wrecked vehicles. Machine-gun fire echoed round the valley walls. They could hear the punch and shriek of bullets ripping through steel bodywork.

Flashback: Sergeant Miller, lecturing Lucy and her platoon on Imber Live Firing Range, Salisbury. A dummy village used to simulate urban warfare.

'*If you ever find yourself in a street fight, don't be stupid enough to hide behind a car door. Sheet metal won't stop a crossbow bolt, let alone a high-velocity bullet. If you need to crouch behind a vehicle, get low and put the engine block between yourself and the shooter. Safe in your mother's arms.*'

The gunfire ceased. The echo died slow. Sudden silence.

'What's he doing?' shouted Huang.

Lucy looked over the buckled hood of a Lincoln. She saw the distant figure of Toon run from the guard tower. He was carrying the SAW. He ran to the convoy.

Lucy pressed transmit.

'Toon? What the fuck is going on?'

Breathless:

'*Something out here. Swear to God.*'

'Think he's lost it?' asked Huang.

Lucy sighed.

'Go look after him.'

Toon climbed aboard the incinerated bus. Rows of seats scorched down to springs. He walked down the centre aisle. Weak daylight shafted through empty windows and bullet holes that peppered the side panels and roof.

He wanted to find something. A snake. A dead vulture. Some kind of desert rodent. Proof he hadn't lost his mind.

A body at the back of the bus. A long-dead Iraqi soldier, charred and shrivelled, spine arched in a paroxysm of pain.

Amanda climbed aboard the bus.

'You okay?'

Toon shook his head.

'I saw something. For real.'

'Maybe the breeze.'

'There isn't a breeze.'

'Maybe a change in atmospheric pressure. Evening cool messing with your perspective. Sure as shit wasn't your friend on the back seat. He's been cooked down to charcoal.'

'You guys must think I'm some kind of burn-out case.'

'I think it's been a long fucking day and we could all use some rest.'

Huang stood in the bus doorway.

'Everything all right?'

'Yeah,' said Amanda. 'We're done here.'

*

'Okay,' said Lucy. 'First thing we have to do is clear some space. Give me a hand.'

Lucy took off her prairie coat. She unstrapped body armour. She stripped down to her Union flag T-shirt.

Huang shrugged off his flak jacket. *The Sisters of Mercy. Event Horizon tour.*

The truck was boxed by sedans.

'Let's see if we can roll these fuckers.'

Lucy and Huang each took a wheel arch. Amanda and Toon each grabbed a fender. They set the car rocking.

'One, two, three.'

They lifted and heaved in unison. Metal creaked and shrieked. The car rolled onto its roof. It shed doors, hood and hubcaps. It kicked up dust.

They rolled wreckage until the truck stood alone in open space.

Lucy uncapped her canteen and poured water over her head.

She examined the truck. It sat with wheels half buried in sand. It listed heavily to the right.

She looked up at the darkening sky. Evening stars. A full moon. Deep shadow pooled and coagulated throughout the convoy.

'We're running out of daylight. We need to get her stable before we can crack these doors. Let's see if we can get her running. I want to drive her to the citadel. Park her on flag-stones. Get some light on her and set to work.'

She checked the underside of the truck. Tandem axles. Mesh over the tailpipe. The complete drive chain – the engine, transmission and suspension gear – protected by galvanised steel plate tack-welded to the chassis.

She kicked the wheels.

'See that? She's got runflats. A big, solid rubber rim inside each tyre. Means you can drive on hubs, even if the tyres get blown out. Bust through a roadblock. Doesn't matter if a bunch of crooks throw a stinger strip across the road; take a shotgun to your wheels. Wouldn't even slow you down. You just keep on rolling. Fucking sweet. This baby is shopped like a tank.'

They tried the cab doors. Locked.

Huang unholstered his Glock and took aim at the handle.

'Don't bother,' said Lucy. 'You'd just catch the ricochet.'

One of the side windows was cracked.

'Ballistic polycarbon. Class One, but it's taken a shitload of hits.'

Lucy pounded the window with her rifle butt. The inch-thick slab of optical plastic split from the door seal and fell into the cabin.

Huang swung himself into the cab. He reached beneath the dash and popped the hood.

Lucy inspected the engine. She peeled off a glove and slapped dust from the motor. She checked filters. She checked injection lines. She checked starter cable.

'Can you hot-wire this thing?' shouted Huang.

'Watch me,' said Lucy.

She leant into the engine bay. She connected the coil at the back of the V12 engine to the positive terminal of the battery.

The dash lit up.

'Hey. Looking good.'

She reached beneath the battery into the fender well and tripped the starter solenoid.

Huang tore the cowling from the steering column. He spliced ignition cable.

Engine revved. The windshield wipers thrashed backwards and forwards, splashing sand. A single intact headlamp flickered and glowed steady.

'Sweet job.'

Lucy slammed the hood, and climbed in the cab. Huang let her take the wheel.

'And that, ladies and gentlemen, is how we do that.'

The truck was sunk in sand. Amanda and Huang chocked the wheels with trunk lids from nearby sedans.

'Okay. Let's get her rolling.'

Lucy revved the engine. She pumped the throttle, tried to rock the truck clear of deep ruts. The wheels span. Shredded tyre rubber whipped and tore.

Huang hung out the window and checked progress. He shouted encouragement.

'That's it. Keep going. Almost there.'

'Feels like I'm digging deeper.'

'Just keep going. An inch more, and you've got it.'

Huang jumped from the cab. He joined Amanda and Toon at the back of the truck. They pushed. They sweated. They strained. The armoured truck lurched free. They caught a faceful of grit.

A deep groan as the plated underside of the truck ground rock.

Lucy's voice over the radio:

'*How's it looking?*'

'You're doing okay.'

The truck pulled out of the convoy. It nudged the wreck of a Nissan aside. It lurched towards the citadel gate towers at a walking pace. Half a mile of lunar terrain. The engine laboured and revved. Toon and Amanda kicked rocks out the vehicle's path.

Huang turned back towards the convoy. His body armour and assault rifle were draped over the hood of an Impala.

A body sat in the driver's seat. A charred skeleton, fingers welded to wheel plastic. No hair. Empty sockets. Lips burnt away, giving the corpse a mirthless smile.

Huang turned his back on the carbonised corpse. He reclipped his belt. He clipped the holster strap round his thigh.

Behind him, the driver of the sedan began to move. The eyeless, grinning head slowly turned. Crisped skin cracked and flaked. Charred, skeletal hands flexed and tore from the steering wheel. The creature began to haul itself from the vehicle.

Huang rebuckled his armour. The rustle and rip of Velcro straps masked the grit-crunch of skeletal feet dragging through sand.

He slung his rifle. He unscrewed the cap of his canteen and prepared to swig.

Skittering stones. He swung round.

A tumorous figure, the colour of rot and dust. Something that used to be a man. Knotted metallic tendrils woven through flesh.

'Holy fucking Christ.'

The creature tensed, as if reacting to the sound of his voice. It lunged. Huang dropped his canteen, raised his rifle and fired full auto. The cadaverous figure was lifted from its feet, belly ripped open. The impact of high-velocity rounds threw it across a Cadillac hood. It fell in the dirt and lay still.

Huang crouched over the dead thing. Smoking gut wounds. A skeletal face, empty sockets, tight skin pulled back across the bones.

Lucy's voice:

'*What's going on? Who's shooting?*'

He hit the pressel switch on his webbing.

'Better get back here, boss. Something you need to see.'

The creature jerked to life. Rotted fingers seized Huang's shoulder. The broken creature gripped the collar of his body armour, dragged him down and sank teeth into his neck. Skin tore, blood bubbled and dripped. Huang screamed and tried to pull himself free.

He drew his Glock, pressed the weapon to the creature's stomach and pumped the trigger. Smoke. Muzzle flame. He emptied a full clip. The desiccated figure convulsed as bullets tore through its torso.

Huang tossed the gun. He pushed the creature to arm's length with his left hand. He unhooked a frag grenade with his right. He twisted the pin loose with his teeth. The safety lever flipped.

He punched the creature in the gut, driving the grenade wrist-deep into its belly. He heaved the rotted figure away with his feet, and rolled clear.

The creature staggered upright, flap of glistening muscle clenched between its teeth. Stretched out arms, like it was trying to find Huang by touch.

Huang covered his head.

Detonation.

He lay, curled foetal, pelted with grit, stones, and scraps of burning flesh.

The Barricade

Huang sat in the rear doorway of an armoured personnel carrier. He leant against the doorframe and rested his head against metal. He held a rag to his neck to staunch the flow of blood.

Lucy, Toon and Amanda crouched in front of him.

'Give yourself a morphine shot,' said Toon.

'No.'

'You're fucked up.'

'Let me rest a while.'

Amanda washed his neck with canteen water and dressed the wound.

'Sure you don't want a shot?'

'I'm okay.'

'How does it look?' asked Lucy, out of earshot.

'Deep,' said Amanda. 'He's lost a lot of blood.

Lucy walked between cars. Smoking fragments of flesh scattered in the dust.

She hooked blood-caked dog tags with the muzzle of her rifle. She examined them with gloved fingers.

'What have you got?' asked Amanda.

'Republican Guard.'

'Guess Jabril was wrong. Some of them made it.'

Lucy nudged a withered arm with her boot.

'Burnt. Mummified. This guy has been dead for weeks.'

'Huang says different.'

Lucy unsheathed the T-shaped push-knife she kept strapped to her webbing. She prodded the severed arm with the blade.

'Looks like something's embedded in his flesh.'

'Like what?'

'Wires. Tendrils. Fine thread knitted through muscle.'

'Shrapnel?'

'No. Something else.'

'Sooner we get out of here, the better.'

'Yeah,' murmured Lucy, sheathing her knife. 'I think you're right.'

The armoured truck was parked in the main courtyard of the citadel. Jabril circled the vehicle, inspecting bullet damage. He saw Lucy approach.

'These rear doors are your biggest challenge. The steel is three inches thick.'

Lucy grabbed the collar of his body armour and slammed him against the side of the truck. The impact shook free his prosthetic hook. It clattered on flagstones.

He tried to fend her off with his hand and stump.

'We just got jumped. Huang. Someone, something, just tried to rip out his throat.'

'Is he hurt? Is he bitten?'

Lucy shook Jabril. She knocked his head against the armoured hull of the truck.

'What happened out here, Jabril? What really went down?'

'You mustn't touch Huang. None of you. Tell your men. They must wear gloves each time they go near him.'

'Tell me. What happened here? The guy back there in the convoy. He looked like he had been dead for months. There's no way he should be running around.'

'You knew this place was poisoned. You all knew the risk in coming here.'

Lucy shook him.

'There was something in his skin. Wires, cables. Did he do that to himself?'

'No.'

'How many more of your buddies are wandering around?'

'I don't know.'

'Talk to me. What the fuck is going on?'

'I can't tell you.'

Lucy slapped his face.

'I promised you gold,' he said. 'There is gold in the truck. Just take it and leave.'

Lucy's crew crossed the courtyard. Huang supported by Amanda and Toon. He struggled to walk. He was pale and sweating.

'How's it going, boss?' asked Toon.

Lucy shook Jabril one last time.

'If we get hit by any more surprises I will seriously fuck you up.' She released her grip on Jabril's body armour. She turned to Toon. 'I'm going to get the truck under cover. Mandy: with me.'

Toon helped Huang across the courtyard and sat him in shade.

Jabril wedged the prosthetic hook back onto his wrist stump. He crossed the courtyard and sat on rubble beside Huang. He looked at the bloody dressing taped to the man's neck.

'I'm sorry,' said Jabril.

'The guy that jumped me. Swear to God, he was a living corpse. What the hell happened to him?'

Jabril looked down at his feet.

'I'm sorry. I'm so sorry.'

Lucy climbed in the cab. She gunned the engine. Puff of black diesel fumes. She eased the throttle. The vehicle inched forward.

She drove the truck through the citadel precincts. The central processional avenue cut a path through collapsed buildings and courtyards choked with debris.

The armoured car climbed the gentle gradient towards the entrance of the temple. The single intact headlamp projected a cone of light.

The truck passed between the two monstrous bull colossi and crawled into the darkness of the temple interior. The spluttering cough of the damaged motor echoed through the vaulted hall.

Lucy killed the engine. Amanda kicked open the cab door.

'The roof should hide us from over-flight,' said Lucy. She shone her flashlight into the shadows above them. Pillars supporting massive roof slabs. 'Our heat signature should be pretty well masked.'

They inspected the truck vault.

'Inch-thick cadmium steel. No windows, no gun ports. We could try C4, but it would be a waste of time. Take a hydrogen bomb to punch a hole. The door is the weak spot. Thinner plate, but it's sheathed in cobalt. Diamond drill wouldn't make a scratch. Hinges are recessed. Roof vents, but they won't give us any help.'

'Then I guess we do it the hard way.'

'Yeah. Check on the guys. I'll get to work.'

Gathering twilight. Bright stars. A red moon.

Toon crouched on the courtyard flagstones. He unzipped a side pocket of his backpack. A patty of C4 and detonators.

He pressed and punched the explosive into a crevice at the base of a high pillar near the citadel entrance.

He pushed a detonator deep into the clay. He backed away across the courtyard, unspooling command wire. He tied the wires to the terminals of a battery initiator. He crouched behind a massive stone block.

'Standby. Firing.'

The explosives blew with a gunshot crack. Puff of dust and stone chips. The pillar slowly toppled like a tree felled by an axe. Toon plugged his ears.

The pillar smashed across the courtyard flagstones with an infernal roar. Toon was pelted with rock shards.

He stood. Dust cleared. He brushed grit from his head

and shoulders. The shattered pillar formed a waist-high barrier across the citadel entrance. He set up the SAW and stacked boxes of ammunition.

Amanda joined him.

'Only way in and out of this place, said Toon. 'Anything comes prowling, I'll light the fucker up like the Fourth of July.'

Amanda flipped open the latches of her Hardigg rifle case. She pulled the SIMRAD night scope from its foam bed and clipped it to the picatinny rail of her rifle. A black lens the size of a saucer. She powered it up and flipped the cap. The view through her dayscope now boosted infra-red by a high-powered photocathode.

She lay out her mat, tipped the brim of her hat and took position. She unfolded the stubby legs of the rifle bipod and lay the weapon across a cylinder of fallen masonry.

The wrecked vehicles a quarter-mile distant were shadows in the gathering dusk. Viewed through the nightscope they became a strange luminescent landscape of sand-scoured, bullet-pocked metal. Hard to judge distance. The infra-red optics foreshortened perspective.

'Going to be a cold fucking night.'

Toon looked around at moonlit hieroglyphs gouged in every rock surface. Crude cuneiform letters. Men with the heads of dogs, bulls and snakes.

'I wasn't planning to sleep.'

Distant sound of rotors.

Toon stood at the centre of the courtyard, popped a signal flare and held it above his head.

The choppers circled the valley at two hundred feet. They hovered over the necropolis then settled into the courtyard. Toon tossed the flare. He and Amanda hid their faces from downwash and dazzling nose-lights.

The rotors slowly decelerated. Motor-whine died away.

Gaunt, Raphael and Voss climbed out of the choppers.

They unlaced bales of camouflage netting and threw them over the main rotors and tail boom. They tented the nets with poles, and pegged them down with stones. Gaunt sat in the *Talon* cockpit and checked avionics.

'How are we doing for fuel?' asked Raphael, looking round to make sure he was not overheard.

Gaunt checked a gauge.

'Burned almost half a tank. About a thousand pounds left. Should get us home okay as long as we don't make any detours.'

'Ready to do this?'

'Take care of this sorry crew? Heck, yeah. They aren't leaving here alive.'

He took a handset from his backpack. *ChemPro.* He examined the read-out.

'What's that?'

'Spectrum analyser. Scans for contamination. Chemical agents.'

'Anything?'

'Trace chlorine, way below the toxic threshold. Valley was doused with some kind of blistering agent, a long time ago.'

'So we should be okay, right?'

'Best if we don't hang around.'

Gaunt hid the unit as Lucy approached.

'Everything all right?' she asked.

'Gleaming.'

She climbed into the *Talon* cargo compartment. She released ropes and pulled back a cargo net. She balanced three folded tripod lamps on her shoulder.

'Need a hand with that?'

'I'm okay. Help man the perimeter.'

She hefted a heavy Vulcan battery with her free hand and headed back to the temple.

'Did you see the chink?' asked Raphael. 'See his neck? Said there were things, creatures, hiding out there in those fucked-up cars.'

'Yeah,' said Gaunt.

'You don't seem surprised.'

'Like I said. Best if we don't hang around.'

Gaunt and Raphael joined the barricade. They sat on flagstones, their backs to the toppled pillar.

Jabril slit open a foil soft-pack of Salems with his hook and offered cigarettes. Raphael lit with trembling hands.

'Place creeps me out,' said Raphael. He looked around at the deepening shadows of the extinct city. Moonlight outlined the megalithic ruins with gentle phosphorescence. 'Bad fucking hoodoo.'

'Don't wander off,' said Amanda. 'This place is a labyrinth. Cloisters. Courtyards. Avenues and alleys. If we hold this ground, we'll be safe until sunrise.'

'We got to wrap this shit up and get out of here,' said Toon. 'Hear what Huang said? Some kind of walking corpse.'

'He doesn't know what he saw.'

'That wound in his neck is pretty fucking real.'

Jabril savoured his cigarette.

'I made no secret this region was poisoned. The army tested munitions in the desert. Tethered cattle. Fired artillery shells packed with chemical and biological payloads. There were dark rumours that they also conducted human trials. Sacrificed some of their own troops to help refine the weapons. Here, in a sheltered valley, a place of cool shadows, a weaponised virus might lie dormant for decades waiting for a host. You need to collect your prize then leave here as quickly as you can.'

'Why the fuck did you pick this place to hide your shit?'

'Because no one in their right mind would come here.'

Lucy returned to *Talon*. She unstrapped a couple of aluminium planks from the bulkhead wall and wedged them against the cargo door frame. A ramp from the chopper to the ground.

She unlaced ropes and pulled a tarp aside. A quad bike.

She released the brakes. The bike rolled down the ramps into the courtyard. A Yamaha Grizzly in desert yellow. She hitched a trailer to the back of the bike and loaded up.

Gaunt leant against the chopper and watched her work.

'So what's in the truck?' he asked.

'You must have heard the others talk.'

'I want to hear it from you.'

'Gold. Three tons. You get a cut. Raphael gets paid out of your share.'

'So we fly back to Baghdad with the gold. Then what?'

'I know a guy in the Tenth Airwing. He'll take care of inspection paperwork. We stack the gold at the back of a couple of Conex containers. Label the boxes "engine parts" or some shit. Airlift to Turkey on a C130. Offload at Incirlik. Look for a buyer in Istanbul. We'll take a twenty-five, thirty percent hit when we convert to cash. I can live with that.'

Lucy straddled the bike. Key turn. She gunned the throttle and headed down the processional way towards the temple entrance.

Gaunt watched her drive towards white halogen light shafting from the temple doorway. He looked around, made sure he was unobserved.

He opened the *Bad Moon* pilot door and reached beneath the webbed seat. His daypack.

He discreetly checked the silenced Sig Sauer. He twisted the suppressor, made sure it was locked tight. He re-seated the mag. Chambered. Safety off. He peeled Velcro and tucked the pistol beneath his ballistic vest.

He touched the crucifix hung round his neck and said a silent prayer.

The vast temple hall. Cavernous dark. The armoured car ringed by tripod lamps, an oasis of light in the centre of deep shadow.

Lucy unloaded the quad bike. A portable generator: a four-stroke, forty-amp Cutmaster in a sound-suppressing case. A coil of cable, and the pistol-grip head of a plasma torch.

Shuffling feet and grunts of exertion echoed round the vaulted chamber.

She set the generator running and wired the cable.

She stripped down to her T-shirt. She strapped herself into a leather welder's jacket. She pulled on leather gauntlets and a welder's mask, visor raised.

She took a swig of water, fumbled the bottle cap with a gloved finger.

She stood at the rear doors of the truck. She dropped the face plate and pulled the trigger of the hand unit. A shrill hiss, loud despite earplugs. An impossibly fierce cutting flame, brighter than the sun. She pressed the flame to the truck door. Blue arc-light reflected in the smoked visor of her helmet. Metal began to bubble, blister and drip.

Amanda found Huang asleep in the shadow of a guard tower. He was sat on a pillar base, leaning against brickwork. He looked pale. His lips were tinged blue.

She plucked an iPod bead from his ear. Faint hiss of drums. Jay Z. '99 Problems'.

'Hey. Hey, you okay?'

Huang woke and rubbed his eyes.

'I feel fucked.'

She squirmed her hands into surgical gloves, and carefully peeled the bloody dressing from his neck. The bandage was red with blood, yellow with pus.

'How does it look?'

Amanda took a survival pack from the utility pocket of her trousers. Fishing line. Flint. Compass. Signal mirror.

Huang examined his neck wound in the mirror. A big, weeping bite. Veins surrounding the wound were inflamed. Infection creeping outward like tendrils.

'Least the fucker missed your jugular,' said Amanda.

'It's turning bad. Hurts to swallow. Hurts to talk. I can barely move my head.'

'Anything we can use in the WALK?'

'Yeah. You got to patch me up. I'll talk you through it.'

Huang's backpack. The Warrior Aid and Litter Kit. A folded stretcher and trauma gear. Amanda unzipped the pockets and ripped open sterile plastic packets with her teeth.

'Show me your neck.'

She swabbed the wound with Betadine solution and sprinkled QuikClot on the torn flesh. She threaded suture through a needle. Huang bit down on the nylon strap of his rifle as she stitched his flesh. She wadded the gouge with rolls of Kerlix dressing and taped them down.

'Done this before?'

'They made us practise on animals,' said Amanda. 'The survival course at sniper school. We each had to shoot a goat in the flank with our sidearm, then patch the wound. Good way to learn. Try to help a living thing while it screams and squirms and shits itself.'

'A good paramedic is a priest.'

'Anything you want to confess?' asked Amanda.

'It breaks my heart you were born gay.'

Huang took a hypodermic gun from the trauma kit. He loaded a tetracycline shot and fired into the crook of his elbow.

'You got morphine?' asked Amanda.

'Plenty. But I don't want to nod out. We need trigger men.'

The arc-flame burned a deep, circular groove in the truck door. Metal dripped like incandescent tears.

Lucy shut off the torch and lifted her visor. She pulled foam plugs from her ears. She jammed a screwdriver into the burn-groove and twisted like she was shucking an oyster. A circular chunk of steel plate flipped free and clattered on flagstones.

'You plan to cut through the door? That might take a while.'

Jabril stood in shadow, watching Lucy work.

'I'm going to cut a couple of chunks out of this cobalt layer so I can reach the steel beneath. Then I'm going to drill the locks.'

Lucy stripped out of her welder's smock. She was soaked in sweat. She drank a litre of Highland Spring and tossed the bottle. She emptied a second bottle over her head. She shook water from her hair.

'So I guess in a couple of hours we will know whether you are lying about the gold. My advice? If there is nothing beyond these doors but thin air, then you better take my gun and put a bullet in your head right now. The boys expect to fly home rich. They won't care to hear excuses.'

Lucy pulled on the leather welder's jacket. She pulled on gauntlets.

'There's food in the choppers,' she said. 'Feed the guys. Make yourself useful.'

She dropped her visor, triggered the plasma arc and began to cut.

Jabril split open a couple of MRE pouches. He distributed crackers and tube cheese.

'I'm not hungry,' said Toon.

'Eat,' said Amanda. 'You need salt.'

'If I eat, then I'll shit. And there is no fucking way I'm fumbling around in the dark trying to dig a straddle-trench. I'm not taking my hands off this fucking weapon until sunrise.'

Amanda scanned the convoy through her nightscope. The darkness of the moonlit valley boosted bright as day. Cross-hairs roved over buckled hoods, blown-out tyres, seats burned down to springs. The junkyard wreckage glowed with residual heat from the day.

A flicker of movement. Brief shadow beneath the fender of a truck.

'Reckon there are any snakes out here?' asked Toon.

'Coral snakes,' said Voss. He took a pouch of Red Man from his pocket and folded a wad of tobacco into his mouth. 'That's what you have to look out for in a desert. Venomous as a motherfucker.'

'Camel spiders. Ever seen one? Big as a dinner plate. Hate them.'

Amanda refocused her sight. A leering skull-face glimpsed between cars.

'Contact,' she shouted. She opened fire.

Toon swung the SAW and fired blind into the darkness. Huang and Raphael shouldered their rifles and let rip, full auto. Voss pumped his shotgun.

The gatehouse walls were lit by flickering muzzle-flare. Smoke and roar. Tracer rounds streaked across the valley floor, slamming into corroded hulks with a shower of sparks.

Huang took a 40mm pepper-pot grenade from his ammo pouch. Gold tip. High explosive. He slotted the shell into the barrel-launcher of his rifle and fired. Pop. Recoil. Vehicles flipped and burned.

Into The Vault

Lucy stood at the truck door, enveloped in smoke and the stink of hot metal. The brilliant needle-flame of the plasma arc blazed white. Cobalt liquefied and trickled like tears. Drips hit the granite flagstones between her boots and instantly solidified into a smooth mirror-sheet puddle.

She blinked sweat. Perspiration trickled down her back, her legs. She ignored the discomfort and concentrated on the incandescent flame slicing metal.

She completed a circular cut. A saucer disk of cobalt plate fell away from the door and clattered to the floor.

She shut off the plasma arc and threw it aside. She tore off her mask and jacket. She plucked foam plugs from her ears.

She poured water over her head and sluiced her eyes. She lifted the hem of her T-shirt and towelled her face.

Distant gunfire. She snatched her radio from the floor.

'Sitrep. What the fuck is going on, people?'

Toon strafed the convoy. The SAW ejected a steady stream of chain-links and smoking brass. The machine gun spat bullets at two hundred rounds a minute. Every fifth round was tracer. A needle-fine streak of light. The corroded hulks of the convoy shrieked and sang as bullets punched through metal and kicked up a storm of frag, dust and debris.

Amanda worked her rifle bolt. She fired at shadows.

Huang slapped a clip into his AR-15 and emptied it in a sustained four-second burst.

'Break contact,' shouted Amanda. 'Cease fire. Cease fucking fire.'

Sudden silence.

They crouched behind the rubble barricade, breathing cordite stink from the smouldering cartridges scattered at their feet.

Toon opened a box of ammo and clipped a fresh belt into the receiver of the SAW. He cranked the charging handle. He sipped mineral water. He splashed Highland Spring over the red-hot gun barrel. Water fizzed and steamed like spit on a hot plate.

Amanda loaded a fresh mag of .308 and scanned the wrecked convoy with her nightscope. Sedans peeled open by 40mm grenade detonations. Hot metal glowed luminescent green. Bullet holes burned like coals.

Movement at the back of the convoy. Something broken and skeletal dragging itself between trucks.

Amanda adjusted her grip on the rifle and lined up the shot. She whispered beneath her breath. First drill they taught her during basic, straight after they issued bedding and uniform:

'This is my rifle. There are many like it, but this one is mine. My rifle is my best friend. Without me, my rifle is nothing. Without my rifle, I am nothing . . .'

A snarling face, looking right at her. Cross-hairs centred at the bridge of its nose. Gun shot. Skull-burst. Cranium blown out. The thing flopped dead.

Lucy's voice over the radio:

'*Sitrep. What the fuck is going on, people?*'

Lucy and Amanda walked from the citadel. They crossed moonlit waste ground towards the convoy. Lucy shouldered her assault rifle. Amanda held her pistol in a double-grip.

'How many did you see?' asked Lucy.

'Three, hiding under trucks. Better watch out. Might be a bunch more.'

Lucy hit the pressel switch of her radio.

'Hey. Huang.'

'*Yeah, boss.*'

'Give us some light.'

A pyro streaked skyward. A star-shell launched from Huang's rifle. It burned brilliant white. It cast crazy, shifting shadows.

They walked between vehicles. A smouldering battle-space.

They shone flashlights into burned-out cars. Seat springs and steering columns, twisted and carbonised. They inspected the underside of each vehicle.

Amanda found a skeletal arm protruding from beneath a sedan.

'First body count.'

Lucy found a ribcage. She kicked it with her boot. Fragments of olive uniform smoked and burned.

'Got the second guy.'

Amanda found a third body slumped against the fender of a truck.

'Hey,' she shouted. 'Third guy. Back here.'

They stood over the body.

An Iraqi soldier, entry wound between his eyes. His uniform hung around him in folds. His skin dried out like jerky.

Lucy crouched. She trained her barrel light on his skeletal face.

'Something in his mouth.'

She unsheathed her push-knife, pressed the tip between yellow teeth and parted his jaws.

A mouthful of metal spines like needles.

'Christ.'

'Look at his hand,' said Amanda.

Fine needles protruded from dry flesh.

Lucy tapped a couple of spines with her knife.

'Looks metal, but it seems to be anchored in bone, like some kind of growth.'

'Radiation? Some kind of mutation? Weird-ass cancer?'

'Jabril has been talking about bio-weapons. Anthrax. Stuff like that. But half the armour-piercing shells fired in this war were tipped with depleted uranium. The desert is full of dust from old fuel rods. I don't know. Maybe these guys breathed it in.'

'Blood,' said Amanda. A crimson trickle from the bullet wound. It dripped from his chin. 'Guy looks like he has been dead a long while, but there was a beating heart, a functioning brain in that skull.'

Lucy wiped her knife on the dead man's jacket.

'Then I guess we did him a favour.'

Gaunt and Raphael watched from the barricade. The star-shell drifted to earth and burned out. They watched the distant light-cone of Lucy's torch move between vehicles.

Raphael spoke low, so no one could overhear.

'We have to think this through. Better if we don't hit them all at once.'

'Like I said, we wait until she opens the truck. They'll start loading gold onto the choppers. They'll split up, start moving around. We can take them one by one. They'll be dead before they realise anything is going down.'

'Cool.'

'Just hold back,' said Gaunt. 'Use your knife, if you can. Soon as they catch a glimpse of gold their discipline will fly to hell. They'll drop their guard. Start whooping and hollering. Big back-slapping frenzy. Whole thing will be over in seconds.'

Gaunt turned up the collar of his leather jacket. A cold night breeze sighed through the monumental ruins.

'We should spill some gas,' said Raphael. 'Burn the bodies.

Hard to imagine a forensic team out here, dusting for prints, but you never know.'

'Their sorry asses will not be missed.'

'Amen.'

Lucy beckoned Voss.

'Give me a hand with the drill.'

They each gripped a rope handle and hefted it from *Talon*, then dumped it in the quad trailer.

Lucy rode the bike back to the temple at a walking pace. Voss strode beside her, shotgun at the ready. He turned and walked backward every few paces, squinting into the moonlit warren of forecourts and collapsed buildings that lined the processional way.

Lucy drove into the temple and killed the engine.

The truck door. A ragged, circular cut next to each combination lock.

'I've burned through the first layer,' explained Lucy. 'Now we drill steel to access each lock drum.'

She prised open the wooden crate with a screwdriver. A DeWalt magnetic drill press wrapped in a blanket. She hooked it to the four-stroke generator. Green power light.

Lucy and Voss held the unit at head height and positioned it beside the upper combination lock. She engaged the magnets. Deep hum. Heavy clank as the drill clamped to the vault door.

Lucy locked the diamond drill bit in place with a hex key. She filled the coolant reservoir from a plastic gallon bottle.

'I'll stay with you,' said Voss. 'Too much weird shit going down. Someone ought to watch your back.'

'Thanks.'

Lucy pulled on gloves and goggles. She twisted foam plugs into her ears and wrapped her shemagh scarf over her mouth and nose.

She pressed Start. Slow rotation. She turned the head

wheel. The drill bit advanced and scoured steel. Metallic shriek. Coiled shavings. Mineral oil lubricant trickled down the vault door and pooled at her feet.

Huang collapsed. He was talking to Amanda. He swigged water and said:

'Maybe we should string a couple of grenades—'

Then he dropped his canteen. His eyes rolled upward and his mouth fell open. He toppled backwards onto the flagstones and began to shake. He arched his spine. His boots danced. He pissed his pants. He whined and drooled. Amanda held him down and tried to check his airway.

'Breathe. Come on. Breathe.'

He stopped trembling and lay still.

'Let's get you to the chopper.'

Toon helped lift Huang onto the stretcher. They laid him in *Talon*.

Amanda shone a Maglite in Huang's eyes. He blinked. Slow dilation. He turned his head.

'Just chill, all right?' said Amanda. 'Lie still. We'll get you home in no time.'

She jabbed him in the thigh with a morphine auto-injector pen, and watched him pass out.

'Go check the perimeter,' she told Toon. 'I don't trust Gaunt to watch our backs.'

She pulled on a fresh pair of gloves and peeled back the wad of dressing taped to Huang's neck. The wound had turned black. It stank of rotting flesh. Fine metal spines protruded from the putrid skin, like silver hairs. She took tweezers from the medical kit, pinched one of the spines and pulled.

'You can't help him.'

Jabril had quietly climbed in the chopper and sat on a bench seat.

'What is this shit?' asked Amanda.

'A disease. It's like rabies, in some respects. This sickness will progress. He will become demented and attack.'

Amanda redressed the wound. She loaded a fresh shot of tetracycline into the injector gun and fired it into Huang's thigh.

'How long has he got?'

'Not long.'

'We'll get him back to Baghdad,' said Amanda. 'Get him to the combat ICU. That's his best chance.'

'You should restrain him.'

'He's my friend.'

'It won't make any difference. A few hours from now he won't recognise your face. He will think of you as prey.'

'Watch him,' said Amanda. 'I'm going to check on Toon.'

She peeled off latex gloves and left.

Huang moaned. His eyelids fluttered.

Jabril reached beneath the bench. He pulled out a holdall. He opened a wholesale carton of Salems. A cloth package hidden behind packs of cigarettes. A Soviet frag grenade. The case was chipped and rusted.

He pulled the prosthetic hook from the stump of his forearm and pushed the grenade into the hollow cup. He twisted the prosthetic back on to his stump and buttoned his sleeve.

Huang coughed and arched his back.

'Don't fight,' murmured Jabril. 'It will be over soon.'

He sat back and contemplated the white light shafting from the distant temple entrance.

Gaunt and Raphael stripped *Bad Moon*. They tossed seat cushions, fire extinguishers, life vests and a raft.

'Unbolt the seat frames,' said Gaunt. 'Three tons of gold. We need space and lift.'

'These fucks won't be flying back with us. That's a shitload of weight we won't need to haul.'

Amanda's voice over the com channel:

'*Huang is pretty fucked up, boss. Not much I can do for him. We have to get him to a hospital. He needs specialist help.*'

Lucy's voice:

'*We're minutes away from the gold. We'll be airborne within the hour. Can he hold on?*'

'*Maybe. If his condition deteriorates any further, we'll need to haul ass no matter what.*'

Gaunt released the Velcro straps of his flak jacket and removed the silenced Sig tucked behind his chest plate. He rechecked the chamber, rechecked the mag.

'Follow my lead, all right?' he told Raphael. 'Be ready for my signal.'

Toon ripped the lid from MRE teriyaki and speared chicken with a plastic fork. He gagged. The food tasted of mildew.

He walked to the edge of the courtyard, spat the food and tossed the bowl into shadows. He uncapped his canteen and rinsed his mouth.

He saw a tall silhouette.

'Voss, baby. How's it going?' Toon rinsed his mouth again. 'Fucking rancid. Must be the heat. Got any of that Red Man? I need to clear the taste.'

The figure stepped forward and was lit by moonlight. Toon glimpsed wild hair and ripped clothes. He backed away and fumbled for the Maglite in his pocket. The beam lit a decayed, skeletal thing, reaching for him with clawed fingers.

Toon dropped the flashlight and drew his Glock. Six shots, centre-of-mass. The thing staggered backward, strobed by muzzle-flash. Chunks blown out of its belly and chest. It fell and lay still.

Amanda came running.

Toon picked up his torch. They stood over the body. A

withered skull face. A necrotic abomination, mouth open in a gaping yawn.

'Jesus fucking Christ,' muttered Amanda.

Strange metallic tendrils coiled through muscle and bone

The creature tried to sit. Broken spine. It rolled and tried to crawl, fingernails raking stone. Amanda and Toon backed away.

'Ever see anything like that?' asked Amanda.

'No. Never.'

The creature looked up and hissed.

Amanda stared into jet-black eyes. She felt herself appraised by a strange, implacably hostile intelligence.

'What the fuck are you?' she murmured.

Toon shot the malignant creature in the face. He fired until the mag was dry. He pulverised its head.

They fetched a jerry can of fuel from the chopper and slopped gasoline.

Amanda took a blue fifty-dinar note from her pocket. She lit the note and tossed it. The creature burst into flame. Flesh crisped and crackled. The skeletal corpse slowly curled foetal as it burned.

'It didn't come from the convoy,' said Toon. 'It came from behind us, from the citadel. It was hiding in the ruins. Could be plenty more.'

'We need a ring of light.'

Raphael and Gaunt grabbed boxes and benches thrown from the choppers and propped them in circle round both Hueys.

Toon and Amanda tore open a pack of cyalume sticks. They cracked the sticks and scattered them on flagstones. The chemical lights glowed blue, surrounding the helicopters in a ring of ethereal light.

Toon kept them covered.

They crouched by the choppers, weapons trained on deep shadows.

Raphael looked scared. Gaunt chewed gum.

Toon reached for the transmit button of his radio.

'Boss? Boss, do you copy? We got to get moving. We're starting to draw serious heat.'

Lucy leant against the drill as it cut steel with a shrill whine. The bit lurched forward as it broke through an air pocket within the vault door.

She shut off the drill and pulled foam beads from her ears.

'Okay,' she said. 'We've reached the locks.'

'Yeah?' said Voss.

'Smile. We're nearly done.'

She disengaged the magnets. She and Voss took the weight of the drill as it fell away from the truck door. They threw it aside.

'We pile the equipment and set it alight before we leave all right? Water bottles, food wrappers, everything we touched. You can bet other senior Ba'ath officials knew about this stash. Probably behind wire in some internment camp right now, but soon as they bust free they'll come looking for the gold. And then they'll come looking for us. Chase us down, if they can. They won't give up easy.'

Lucy opened a plastic case. A fibre-optic borescope in a foam bed.

She plugged the borescope into a Toughbook. She threaded the scope into the hole next to the upper combination lock. The probe slid down the narrow steel channel.

Camera view: the micro-lamp lit spiral drill-grooves, like the rifled barrel of a gun.

The wheel pack. The combination lock mechanism. Six titanium disks on a spindle.

Voss held the Toughbook. Lucy watched the screen and turned the dial. One by one the lock wheels aligned. Faint click as a bolt released.

Same procedure for the lower lock. She manipulated the combination drum. Clack of a retracting bolt.

She turned the crank handle and hauled the door wide.

She picked her TASC radio from the floor. She spoke into the throat-piece.

'Okay, folks. We're in.'

Double-Cross

The vault. Metal shelves braced against each wall. Black, high-impact boxes floor to roof.

Lucy climbed inside. She dragged a black box from a shelf. She dumped it on the steel plate floor. She flipped latches and threw open the lid. Gold jewellery. Watches, bracelets, pendants.

She dragged another box from a shelf. More jewellery.

She picked out a wedding band. Arab inscription. She threw it aside.

She pressed the transmit button on her webbing.

'Jabril, get the fuck up here.'

Jabril and Amanda came running. They entered the temple. Lucy jumped from the truck. She held up a fistful of jewellery.

'What the fuck is this shit?'

'Gold.'

'You said there would be bullion.'

'No. I didn't mention coins or ingots. I didn't say there would be a big stack of bars. I promised you gold. Three tons. And there it is.'

'Look.' Lucy held up a gleaming nugget. 'A tooth. An actual gold tooth.'

'Saddam killed thousands of men,' said Jabril. 'Tens of thousands. No point pushing a man wearing a Rolex into a mass grave.'

'We're not grave robbers.'

'You are mercenaries. You fight for money. Besides, if you

don't take this gold, sooner or later someone else will find it. If Peshmergas overcome their fear of this place they will discover this truck and use the gold to buy weapons. Blackmarket ordinance from Pakistan. Rifles, rockets, bombs. More of your countrymen will die.'

'Teeth. You sick fuck.'

Huang lay on a stretcher in the *Talon* cargo compartment.

'How are you feeling?' asked Toon.

'Fucking migraine. Eyes are messed up. Little squiggly lights, like fireflies.'

'Let's take a look at your neck.'

Toon wriggled on blue Nitrile gloves. He peeled surgical tape and gently removed the pus-stained dressing from Huang's neck.

Black, suppurating flesh. Strange metallic spines. He tried to hide his disgust.

Toon pinched one of the spines. He tried to pull it free. He pricked his forefinger.

'Shit.'

He examined his finger. He watched a bead of blood spread beneath the latex membrane.

He dabbed Betadine on to the neck wound. Huang hissed in pain. Toon taped a wad of gauze over rotting flesh.

'How's it looking?'

'Your neck looks pretty chewed up. Might need a graft. You'll have a bad-ass scar, but that's okay. Something to talk about in bars. Seriously. This baby could get you laid.'

'Yeah.'

'Or you could wear some kind of black silk scarf round your neck. Make it your trademark. You got to turn it around, kid. Put it to work.'

Huang looked down at his arm.

'Turning yellow. Frigging jaundice.'

'You're Korean, you dumb fuck. You were born yellow.'

Toon took a hypo pen from the map pocket of his ballistic vest and bit the cap. He jabbed Huang's thigh and pressed the plunger. Huang smiled, blissed out.

Toon stepped away from the chopper, made sure he was out of earshot. He pressed transmit.

'Boss. Do we have the gold?'

'*Yeah.*'

'We better load and get out of here. Huang is pretty fucked up. Smells like gangrene. We have to get him back to The Zone.'

'*We're stacking the quad. Tell Gaunt to get ready to fly.*'

Toon fired a fresh tetracycline shot into Huang's bicep. Huang winced and stirred.

'Rest. Don't fight the morphine. Roll with it.'

He peeled off latex gloves and patched his bleeding finger.

He gazed at the ruins. Moonlight cast chilly phosphorescence over the blocks and pillars, the oppressive towers and ramparts. Deep chiselled hieroglyphs bled shadow.

'You ain't dying in this God-awful place, kid. I promise you that.'

Toon called Raphael.

'Hey. Smiler. Help me strap him down.'

They strapped the stretcher to tether-rings in the aluminium floor of the Huey.

'There you go. Be flying for real soon enough.'

Raphael glanced at Gaunt. Gaunt gave a discreet nod of the head.

Raphael climbed out of the chopper and backed away, trying to act casual.

Outside, Gaunt adjusted his grip on the Sig and fought to control his heart rate. He was sweating, despite the cold night air.

Safety to Off.

Toon finished tightening belts. He balled a combat jacket and put it behind Huang's head as a pillow.

'You okay, kid?'

Huang gave a dreamy smiled and nodded.

'Get you home soon as we can. I'll give you another shot once we get in the air. You'll wake up in clean sheets.'

Toon jumped from the chopper.

'What's your top speed?' he asked. 'How soon can you get us back to Baghdad?'

'Afraid you won't be making the trip,' said Gaunt.

He brought the pistol from behind his back and aimed at Toon's face.

Toon looked down the silenced barrel of an automatic pistol. Astonishment quickly turned to dread. A shuddering exhalation. A strength-sapping wave of fear. He was a dead man.

'Do it, Ese,' urged Raphael.

Gaunt's hand trembled. He swallowed hard.

Toon locked eyes with Gaunt.

'Fuck you,' he whispered.

Gaunt shot him through the right eye. Compressed thud. A soft-nose NyTrilium hollow point. The low-penetration round mushroomed inside Toon's head and blew out the back of his skull like a shotgun blast.

Huang was spattered with blood, brain tissue and fragments of cranium.

'What the fuck?' he murmured, barely conscious. He tried to sit. He was held down by straps.

Toon toppled into the chopper cargo compartment. He lay across Huang's legs. He trembled. Last impulses from a shattered nervous system. His left hand twitched a couple of times like he was shaking out cramp, then he was still.

Gaunt looked round the nose of the chopper. He checked they were unobserved. He looked up the processional avenue to the temple entrance. Light shafted from within. No sign of Lucy or Voss.

'Help me shift the body,' said Gaunt.

They grabbed Toon's arms. They dragged him from the Huey doorway.

They hauled Toon to the pile of garbage thrown from the chopper. They threw him down. They covered him in a canvas sheet and a couple of discarded bench seats.

'We'll take them together. We'll wait until they return to the choppers. They'll start loading gold. I'll take Lucy. You take the Boer. Empty a full clip into the fucker. Make sure he is down for good.'

'Be a pleasure.'

'After that, we find Mandy and shut her down for good. Jabril hasn't got much fight in him. He won't be a problem.'

Raphael unslung his rifle and chambered a round. He walked back to the chopper.

Huang struggled to release the straps that held him lashed to the stretcher. He curled his wrist and thumbed open a flip-latch. The chest restraint slackened. He released the straps holding his waist and legs.

He drew his Glock as Raphael stepped into view. He struggled to focus. He struggled to aim.

He fired. The pistol kicked in his hand.

Raphael staggered backward. He dropped his rifle and sat down in the dirt. A big chunk of scalp missing. He reached up and touched brain.

Huang fired at Gaunt, blowing chips out of flagstones.

Gaunt ran for cover. He hid behind *Bad Moon*. He looked round the nose of the chopper, pistol held cocked and steady.

Raphael was on his knees collecting chunks of head. He fumbled like a drunk picking coins from a sidewalk. He blew sand from each fragment of scalp and stuffed them in his trouser pocket. He kept his left hand pressed to his shattered forehead to stop brain spilling out.

He saw Gaunt.

'Hey, Ese,' he mumbled. 'Think I might be hit.'

Gaunt edged forward. He could see Huang's boots at the lip of the cargo compartment.

The guy had fired seven shots. The Glock held fifteen rounds. Plenty left in the clip.

He crept further forward. He wanted to dispatch Huang with a quick, clean headshot.

Flicker of movement in the periphery of his vision. Lucy and Voss at the temple entrance. They stood in silhouette. He couldn't see their faces, but he could tell by their posture they were looking right at him.

Fleeting plan: maybe he could bluff it out. Tell them: '*Huang went crazy. He started shooting. Must have been delirious. I had to finish him off.*'

He was lit by the cabin lights of the chopper. They could see the pistol in his hand: smoke curling from the thick suppressor. An assassin's weapon.

Radio crackle. Huang shouting into the throat-mike of his TASC headset.

'*It was Gaunt. Fucking double-cross.*'

Gaunt fired at the silhouettes. Thud of suppressed gunshots. Smack of bullets hitting stone.

He snatched his backpack from the pilot cabin and ran.

He heard the crack of rifle-fire. Heavy shotgun roar. Flagstones and masonry erupted around him. Rock dust and stone chips. Double-nought buckshot and cupronickel penetrator rounds shattered brickwork.

He heard Lucy shouting to Voss:

'Don't hit the choppers.'

A bullet grazed Gaunt's ear. The shrill shriek of a high-velocity round streaking past his head. Burst eardrum. A shockwave like a hand slap. Reek of sulphur and cordite. He fell. He staggered to his feet and kept running. He swayed. He stumbled. Balance shot to hell.

He ran into darkness. He scrambled over titanic blocks of stone. Each boot-scuff betrayed his position and brought down a fresh volley from Lucy and Voss as they fired blind into shadow

He crossed a cloistered forecourt and threw himself behind a broken archway. He was sweating. His hands and face steamed in the cold night air.

Pop. Hiss. An illumination round streaked skyward and burned brilliant white as it drifted to earth. The rubble around him lit with shifting, sliding shadows.

He looked back towards the distant choppers. Lucy heading his way, pointing, shouting.

He shouldered his backpack and ran as bullets smacked into the wrecked cloister buildings. Whip and whine of incoming rounds. A bullet plucked at the sleeve of his leather jacket.

He sprinted down sand-choked colonnades and across courtyards, slowing to a walk as the sky-flare sputtered out leaving him in deep shadow, lost in primal ruins.

Raphael got to his feet. He staggered. He swayed. He turned to face Huang. He fumbled at his drop holster and drew his pistol.

Face-off. Huang and Raphael, pistols raised, each trying to focus.

Huang was pale and sweating. His lips were blue.

Blood trickled down Raphael's face. He wiped his eyes. He spat.

Huang pulled the trigger. Click. Jammed. He threw the pistol. It bounced off Raphael's shoulder.

Raphael struggled to aim his automatic. He tried to squeeze the trigger. The pistol slid through bloody fingers like wet soap and fell in the dirt alongside his rifle.

Raphael staggered to the chopper and fell against the fuselage. He slid along riveted aluminium to the pilot cabin and hauled himself inside. He flicked toggle switches. He wiped blood from his eyes. A gentle whine built to a scream as the rotor began to spin up.

*

Lucy and Voss stood among the citadel ruins. They surveyed a vista of moonlit rubble. Cloisters and courtyards. Jagged pillars. Half-fallen archways.

Amanda's voice over the radio:

'*What the hell is going on?*'

'We've got problems. I need you to guard the truck, all right? Look out for Jabril.'

'*Okay.*'

'If Gaunt comes calling, shoot him in the fucking face.'

'*Ten four.*'

Lucy turned to Voss.

'He won't go far,' said Lucy. 'We've got the gold. We've got the choppers. He's got no food or water. There's nowhere for him to run.'

'He's still armed. The little shit will pick us off if he gets the chance.'

'Let's get back to the temple. We can send Mandy out here with the nightscope. Should even the odds. Put her up one of the guard towers. One man among all this stone. He'll stand out like neon.'

'Tell her to knee-cap the fuck. Shoot him in the gut, or something. I want him to suffer.'

They heard the escalating whine of *Talon* preparing for dust-off.

'Damn. Raphael.'

'Motherfucker.'

They sprinted back towards the main courtyard.

Lucy ran towards the chopper. She was dazzled by light, blasted by a squalling dust storm. She glimpsed Raphael through cockpit glass. She waved her arms. She made cut-throat, shut-off gestures. She shouted to be heard over rising engine noise.

Escalating RPMs. Shredded netting wound round the rotor mast.

'Kill the fucking engine. You're losing the rotor.'

Raphael glimpsed Lucy. She was caught in the nose-light glare, battling to stay upright in typhoon wind. She was shouting. He couldn't hear words.

He pulled back the collective. He fumbled pitch control. The chopper rose and hovered.

He clawed blood from his eyes. The helicopter drifted backward as he tried to clear his vision. The tail rotor threatened to slice into the side of *Bad Moon* like the blade of a table saw.

Huang rolled out of the cargo compartment. He tumbled from the doorway and hooked a skid with his arm. He hung, legs swinging, then dropped onto flagstones.

The gearbox beneath the snarled rotor mast began to vent smoke. Alarms. Transmission pressure. BIM warning. Loss of hydraulic power.

Raphael blinked and shook his head. He tried to see straight. He tried to focus. He nudged the cyclic control with his knee and the chopper lurched forward, gathering speed.

Lucy threw herself to the ground. She covered her head. Dazzling light and cyclone wind as the Huey skimmed overhead. Rotor-wash tugged her clothes.

Chopper skids raked the flagstones, jetting sparks. Raphael cleared his vision, just as the helicopter slammed into the stump of a massive granite column.

Metal shriek. Explosion of glass. The chopper's nose crumpled, crushing Raphael's legs.

The Huey rolled on its side. The rotor blades sparked on flagstones then fragmented, strafing the compound with jagged shrapnel. The engine screamed high-revs then died. The broken knuckle of the rotor mast slowed to a stop.

Lucy could hear the glug of spilled liquid. Voss shone his flashlight. Fuel and hydraulic fluid washed across the paving slabs. Pungent stink of diesel.

The transmission assembly began to smoke and spark.

'Fuck. We could lose both choppers.'

Lucy searched through gear discarded from the Hueys. Bench seats and life preservers. She threw debris aside. She snatched up an extinguisher and ran back to *Talon*. She pulled the pin and directed a jet of foam into the main rotor housing.

She tossed the spent extinguisher.

Huang sat on flagstones. He looked down at his vest. A fine splatter of blood, bone chips and tufts of hair.

'Christ.'

Voss gave him a do-rag. He clumsily wiped Toon's blood from his arms and face.

A boot protruded from beneath a bundle of tarpaulin. Lucy hauled canvas from the body. Her torch lit Toon's pulped head. A glistening mess.

'Poor bastard,' said Voss. 'Cover him up. I can't look at him.'

She lay Toon's sweat towel over his shattered face. A dark stain spread across the fabric as blood soaked into the towel.

'We take him back,' said Lucy.

'Might be tricky,' said Voss. He gestured to *Bad Moon*.

Lucy shone her flashlight over the second Huey. A chunk of rotor had speared the windshield and shattered the centre console. Flight controls reduced to a mess of wire and circuit boards.

'Christ. Looks like we're walking home.'

Lucy examined the wrecked avionics.

'Might be fixable.'

'And who would fly it?'

'Gaunt.'

'Forget it, Bokkie. No way am I cutting a deal with that fuck. He dies, no matter what the cost.'

'You want to cross the desert on foot? It's big as Texas. Bigger. Anyone we meet is likely to be a Wahabi fuck itching to slit our damn throats. We'd never make it back to Baghdad. And what about Huang? He can barely walk twenty paces.

You want to carry him on your back? Leave him behind? Put a pistol in his hand as a mercy? We're all fucked unless we get airborne. We have to find Gaunt and cut a deal. See if he can fix this thing. I don't like it. It makes me sick. But we don't have a choice. He'll be hiding nearby. Skulking in the shadows. We'll get Mandy out here with the nightscope.'

Lucy hit the pressel switch on her webbing.

'Hey, babe.'

No reply.

'Come in, Mandy.'

No reply.

'Mandy, respond, over.'

No reply.

'Mandy, what the fuck is going on?'

Nothing but static hiss in Lucy's earpiece. She headed for light shafting from the temple entrance. She started to run.

Hostage

Amanda crouched at the back of the vault and nursed her broken nose. Blood and snot trickled between her fingers.

'I'm sorry,' said Jabril. He sat with his back to the door.

The door was wedged shut. A knife blade jammed between internal handles. Jabril's hook lay discarded on the plate floor. He held a rusted grenade in his left hand. He had pulled the pin with his teeth. If he released his grip the strike lever would flip and trigger the four-second fuse.

'I'm truly sorry,' he said. 'I didn't mean to hurt you.'

Amanda pulled Kleenex from her pocket. She blew. She spat.

'Jumped by a cripple.'

Amanda and Jabril had been stacking gold. They hefted boxes from the vault shelves and piled them on the flagstone floor of the temple, ready to be driven to the choppers.

Amanda had found a polymer trunk hidden at the back of the vault. Army green. Four foot long. She dragged it from behind a stack of boxes.

'Give that to me,' said Jabril

'What is it?'

She tugged at the padlock.

'Don't touch it.'

He pulled her away from the case. They fought. They threw each other against shelves. Boxes fell, split and spilled gold.

Jabril punched Amanda in the face. She thumped him in the gut and kicked him to the floor. She stood over him, knife in hand.

Jabril lay doubled up.

'Get up,' said Amanda. 'Get up, you fuck.'

Jabril rolled on his back. He had removed his prosthetic hook and extracted the grenade hidden inside. He gripped the ring between clenched teeth and pulled the pin. He held up the little green cylinder like it was a crucifix warding off a vampire. Stand-off.

'Let's just chill the fuck out, shall we?' said Amanda.

Jabril scrambled to his feet.

'Keep back.'

Jabril pulled the vault door closed, careful not to lose grip on the grenade.

'Give me your knife.'

'Fuck you,' said Amanda.

He held up the grenade.

'Really want to fight?'

Amanda reluctantly dropped her knife and kicked it towards Jabril.

The vault door had an internal handle in case a guard got shut inside. Jabril awkwardly tucked the grenade in his left armpit while he jammed the knife through the ring-latch, wedging the handle shut.

They sat facing each other. Jabril nursed his bruised belly. Amanda dabbed her nose.

'Give me the case,' said Jabril.

'Kiss my ass.'

Jabril's radio lay smashed in the corner of the vault. Amanda's TASC bundle lay on the plate floor. He snagged it with his foot and drew it close.

He held the grenade between his knees. He attached the earpiece and pressed transmit.

'Lucy? Lucy can you hear me?'

*

Lucy tugged on the vault door. Locked. Wedged shut from inside.

Faint voice from the earpiece hanging loose at her chest. Jabril.

'*Lucy? Lucy can you hear me?*'

Hiss and feedback. The radio signal degraded by the steel hull of the cash truck.

She hooked the receiver to her earlobe.

'What the fuck is going on?'

'*I didn't want this to happen.*'

'Where's Mandy? Is she in there?'

'*I need to talk to you.*'

'Open the fucking door, Jabril.'

'*You need to listen.*'

Lucy stood on the rear step-plate of the truck and tried to wrench the door open.

'Let me talk to Mandy.'

Brief pause. Amanda's voice:

'*Hey, babe.*'

'Are you all right?'

'*He's got a grenade.*'

'What does he want?'

'*No idea. You better talk to him.*'

Brief rustle as the radio was handed back to Jabril.

'Look,' said Lucy. 'I don't know what you want but I'm sure we can work it through. Just come on out. We can talk.'

'*Your friend. The oriental.*'

'His name is Huang.'

'*You must kill him. Kill him and burn the body.*'

Voss had half-carried the injured man up the processional avenue to the cavernous temple interior and sat him against one of the massive granite columns that supported the roof.

Lucy crouched next to Huang and checked him out. His eyes were closed. He appeared to be sleeping. She walked out of earshot.

'What the hell are you talking about?'

'*This valley is home to a pathogen so lethal, so virulent, it could wipe out entire cities. That's why I came back. To stamp out every last vestige of this virus. Your friend is infected. There is no treatment, no cure. He will slide slowly into dementia, then turn on you. He will attack. He will be driven by a feverish desire to bite, to penetrate, to invade. You've seen those soldiers out there. Those men used to be my friends. Now they are monsters. Better for Huang if he dies before the transformation is complete. Let him say his goodbyes then be at peace.*'

'I'll risk it.'

'*I understand. You want to get help. You want to fly your friend back to Baghdad and get medical attention. Dose him with anti-virals, antibiotics. It won't do any good. And you must understand the danger. If this pathogen reaches a major city nothing short of a nuclear strike would halt its progress. What is the name of that military hospital in the Green Zone?*'

'Twenty-eighth CASH.'

'*Picture it. All those people. Doctors, nurses, wounded soldiers lying in the corridor waiting for treatment. Huang thrashing, biting, spraying blood. It's a military trauma unit. They treat gunshots, blast wounds. They aren't equipped to quarantine a serious pathogen. The disease would soon be carried to NATO airbases in Europe and out into the world. Paris, London, New York, Tokyo. Millions would die.*'

'Well, that's certainly something to think about,' said Lucy. She removed her thumb from the transmit button clipped to her webbing and turned to Voss.

'We have to get in there and waste this fuck.'

'Forget it.'

'We could force the door. We've got a little C4. We could rig a breaching charge. And there are vents in the roof. I think there was a can of CS in one of the choppers. We could gas him out.'

'He has a grenade. We'd have to bust our way in and extract

Mandy in four, five seconds. Can't be done. We have to talk him out.'

'Go back to the choppers,' said Lucy. 'See what you can find. Don't leave weapons or ammo lying around. I don't want Gaunt re-armed.'

'How about you?'

'I'm going to cover those roof vents with my coat. Body heat will build up pretty quick. I want this guy to cook.'

Amanda lit a cigarette and placed it between Jabril's lips.

'Thanks. Sorry about the smoke.'

'Lucy and Huang go way back,' said Amanda. 'She's known him longer than me. She's shared a foxhole with the guy plenty of times. He's family. She's not going to blow his brains out, just on your say-so.'

'She'll kill him. She'll do it as a mercy. You've don't understand this disease. You can't imagine the horror. Your friend will rot before your eyes. And then he will attack. You saw those creatures out there in the valley. That is what he will become.'

'We can get him to Baghdad. Get him a doctor.'

Jabril shook his head.

'Too dangerous. If this virus reaches a major population centre the consequences are unimaginable. He must be shot in the head. And his body must be burned. Here, in this valley.'

'So how long are we stuck in this fucking truck?'

'Until Lucy listens to reason. You and your friends can take the gold and fly home. But Huang must stay behind.'

'What's in the case?'

Jabril held the grenade between his knees. He plucked the key from around his neck and threw it to Amanda. She released the padlock, flipped the hasps and opened the lid. Bundles of documents. NSA intercepts, eyes-only collations, embassy cables, Agency briefings. She leafed through papers. Photographs. Men chained to examination tables. Graphs and X-rays charted the course of infection.

'US intel,' she murmured. 'This shit gets deeper by the minute.'

Something else in the case. Two lengths of thick pipe lying in a foam bed. Rivets. Fins.

'A Hellfire missile. Stored in two sections. The lower part is the propulsion unit. A solid fuel rocket motor. The top part is the warhead. Laser optics in the nose. Payload compartment in the midsection.'

A glass cylinder lay alongside the two missile sections. It glowed blue.

Amanda reached for the cylinder.

'Don't touch it.'

'What is it?'

'The virus. Refined. Weaponised. That's why I brought you here. You and your friends. I needed your help to open the truck.'

'So what are you going to do with this stuff?'

'Burn it. Incinerate every last trace.'

Voss rode the quad bike back to the wrecked choppers.

The temperature continued to drop. Each exhalation produced broiling plumes of vapour.

He scanned the shadows. No movement. Lucy's voice:

'*You okay out there?*'

'Yeah.'

'*Grab what we need and head back. Don't hang around.*'

Voss inspected *Bad Moon* by flashlight. He checked the cab and the cargo compartment. He checked beneath the fuselage. He didn't want to get jumped. Gaunt was a coward. The man would spend many hours cowering in the dark and cold before he summoned the courage to come out of hiding and attack Lucy and her crew. But Jabril's undead battalion might drag themselves from the darkness any moment.

He examined smashed avionics. A fragment of *Talon* rotor had shattered the windshield and split the centre console like a blow from an axe. He brushed broken glass from dials and switches. He wrenched the chunk of broken rotor free and threw it aside. Frayed cable. A couple of snapped circuit boards.

Maybe Lucy was right. The Huey was antique. Perhaps the control systems were sufficiently basic a guy with pliers could fix her up. Splice wires and start her running. Perhaps Gaunt could repair the machine.

They would need to bottle their rage and cut a deal. Lure Gaunt with some bullshit plan. Tell him to fly east across the desert. They would pick a remote location far outside Baghdad city limits. Hover over secluded, rocky terrain at fifty feet and push the gold out the door. Mandy could rappel and guard the loot, ready for retrieval. The chopper would fly onward to the Green Zone. Set down near a crowd. Maybe land next to a hotel poolside, typhoon rotor-wash tipping loungers and parasols into the water. Or touch down at the airport in front of loading crews and sentries. Someplace public. Somewhere Gaunt felt safe to walk away with a duffel bag full of gold.

They would kill him anyway. Bullet in the back before he had time to unbuckle his harness. Leave him slumped in the pilot seat.

Voss climbed inside the cargo compartment of *Bad Moon* and ransacked it for ammo. A bag of grenades. Boxes of link for the SAW. Wooden cases of 5.56mm for the rifles.

He stacked munitions in the quad bike trailer, glancing at shadows for any sign of Gaunt.

He piled MRE pouches and bottled water.

He found his jacket and fingerless gloves beneath a seat. He put them on. He set down his shotgun for a moment and swung his arms to get warm.

He fetched the SAW from the barricade. He folded the bipod and released the belt. He loaded the weapon into the trailer.

Toon's body lay nearby, shrouded in a poncho. Voss hauled the limp body across the courtyard, leaving a dark streak of blood. He laid Toon in the trailer alongside food and ammunition. He didn't want to leave his friend lying in a pile of refuse.

Voss kept the dead man's head covered. He didn't want to see his shattered face.

He crossed the courtyard and examined the wrecked airframe of *Talon*. The helicopter had rolled almost onto its roof. He ducked into the cargo compartment and shone his torch over jumbled equipment. He found rifle mags and a couple of knives. He tucked them in his pocket. He found flashlight batteries, sun cream and crackers. He stacked them in the trailer next to Toon's corpse.

He checked the pilot cabin. The door was split from its hinges. He threw it aside.

Raphael hung upside down in the pilot seat, pinned by his crushed legs. His arms hung limp. Blood dripped from his fingers. Blood dripped from his split head.

Voss squeezed into the crushed cab.

He found an ICOM radio in a canvas pouch. He slung the strap over his shoulder.

He emptied mag pockets strapped to Raphael's vest. He took the machete from his belt. He took cigars and a lighter from the guy's shirt pocket.

Raphael opened his eyes.

'Help me,' he coughed. He struggled to move. He reached for Voss. 'Help me, Ese.'

Voss slapped his hand aside. He leaned close so he could whisper in Raphael's ear.

'*Fok jou.*'

He unsheathed his knife and drew the blade slowly across Raphael's throat, slitting his windpipe. Raphael's pig-squeal turned to a bubbling gurgle.

Voss sat back and watched the man choke and spasm.

Gouts of pulsing arterial blood washed over Raphael's face and spattered on the upturned roof. Blood steamed in the cold night air.

Amanda reached between shelves and touched the steel wall of the vault. Condensation trickled down cold metal. Body heat and breath.

Stifling humidity.

She closed her eyes. She breathed slow, tried to lower her heart rate. She sat perfectly still. Perspiration trickled down her temple. She let it run.

'They must have blocked the roof vents,' said Jabril. 'They are trying to drive up the temperature and force me out.'

Jabril spat the butt of his Salem onto the floor and stubbed it with a twist of his boot.

'Enough cigarettes, all right?' said Amanda. 'Hard enough to breathe.'

'I thought all American soldiers smoked. I heard they give you free cigarettes in Desert Storm.'

'I was in high school.'

'They say you are rich. Your friends. I overheard them talk. They say you are from California.'

'My parents are rich. They threw me out a long time ago. Probably dead.'

Amanda drained the dregs from her canteen. She licked the final drops from the neck of the bottle.

'Last of our water.'

Jabril shrugged.

The vault was lit by the beam of Amanda's Maglite. The torch lay on a shelf. The light flickered and dimmed. The warm, amber glow of a dying battery.

'So what now?'

'We wait for your friend to turn. It won't be long. He has already entered the final phase. He will become increasingly confused. He will experience irreparable brain damage. A series of small haemorrhages and lesions are slowly wiping his mind. Within a few hours the man you have known, the man you call your friend, will be totally erased. He will be a little more than a shell. An automaton. A creature with the intellect of a cockroach. His face will become slack and expressionless as the connective tissue beneath the skin slowly deteriorates. A tell-tale sign. We called it the Death Mask.'

'And what then?'

'Lucy will have no choice. He will turn homicidal. She will have to kill him, or be killed.'

'Then we should be there to help.'

Voss rode the quad bike back to the temple. He parked the quad across the wide doorway to make a barrier.

Lucy helped him lift Toon from the trailer, still wrapped in his poncho. They laid him on the steps of the altar. He looked like a sacrificial offering to the monstrous bull god looming from the shadows above them.

Voss sat next to his dead friend.

'Go tell the Spartans, passer-by, that here, obedient to their laws, we lie.'

'No law but his own,' said Lucy.

'Fuckin' A.'

'Raise a glass in the Riv,' said Lucy. 'Remember the good times. That's what he would want.'

'What about Jabril?'

'That vault must be oven-hot by now. He's got nothing to drink. Time is on our side.'

Voss checked his watch.

'It's going to be a long, cold night. I'll start a fire.'

He smashed wooden ammunition boxes and piled shards next to Huang. He split open a couple of rifle bullets and sprinkled gunpowder. He flicked his Zippo and touched off the powder. Fizzing, spitting flame. Wood started to smoulder and burn.

Huang woke. He huddled close to the fire and warmed his hands.

Voss unloaded the trailer.

'Couple of cases for the SAW. Plenty of rifle ammo. Not much for the Glocks.'

'Water?'

'Couple of days if we're careful.'

'Have to conserve as much as we can. Gaunt might be able to fix the chopper, but it's a long shot. Odds are, we'll be walking home.'

Voss gestured to Huang.

'What about him? Want to carry him across the desert on a stretcher?'

'If it comes down to it, yeah. Travel by night. I'm sure as shit not going to leave him here.'

'And what about the gold?'

'Hide it. Bury it. Maybe we can come back in a couple of months with fresh choppers. Or maybe we should just forget this nightmare ever happened.'

'That's our gold,' said Voss. 'We came here. We bled for it. It's ours.'

Lucy crouched next to Huang.

'How you doing, kid?'

Huang stared into the flames like he hadn't heard. Lucy clicked fingers in front of his face.

'Anything you need?'

'I'm all right,' he said.

His lips were blue.

'Got a stupid question for you.'

'Go for it,' said Lucy.

'My sister. What's her name?'

'Kim. She's called Kim.'

Huang nodded. Heavy eyelids. A dreamy smile. He stared into the flames once more and his face relaxed into a blank mask.

'Get some sleep,' said Lucy. She stroked his head. Strands of hair came away in her hand. She discreetly blew them from her fingers.

Voss found Amanda's sniper rifle propped against the rear step-plate of the truck. He crouched by the quad bike at the temple entrance. He checked the breech, then switched on the nightscope.

Acres of rubble glowed with residual day-heat.

Lucy knelt beside him.

'Stay frosty, all right? Any of those skeletal fucks come knocking, blow their heads off.'

'You got it,' said Voss.

'But we need Gaunt alive, yeah? Shoot to maim. Bring him down, but leave him breathing.'

Voss bit open a Balmoral and lit up.

'I'm going to douse some of these halogens,' said Lucy. 'No point sitting here back-lit like idiots.'

She pulled the plug on a couple of tripod lamps.

'Maybe you should get some rest,' said Lucy.

'Who would want to sleep in a place like this? Who would want to dream?'

Lucy took the ICOM handset from the quad trailer. She checked for a power light. She extended the antenna.

'You won't raise a thing,' said Voss. 'Too deep in the desert. Hasn't got range.'

'Worth a shot,' said Lucy.

'And even if you manage to summon a rescue party, the place will be crawling with marines. We'll fly home broke. You can kiss the gold goodbye.'

'Dude, listen to yourself. What about Huang? We have to get him to a hospital.'

She tuned to search-and-rescue. 40Mhz VHF. She pressed transmit.

'Mayday, mayday. This is fire support team Bravo Bravo Lima Two requesting urgent assistance, does anyone copy, over?'

No response.

'Mayday, mayday. This is Bravo Bravo Lima Two broadcasting on emergency four-zero, over.'

No response.

'Mayday, mayday. Does anyone copy this transmission?'

No sound but the hiss of a dead channel.

The Crypt

A rising wind blew through the citadel ruins. Dust devils whipped across courtyards and colonnades.

Gaunt crouched beside a toppled column. He zipped his leather jacket and turned up the collar. Too cold to stay in the open. He needed to find shelter.

He took off his right boot and examined the sole. A penetrator round had split the heel.

He looked across moonlit rubble. He could see movement in the far distance. A shadow sliding clumsily against a high wall. One of Jabril's monstrous legion drawn towards light shafting from the temple entrance.

Gaunt crossed himself. He shouldered his backpack and hurried deeper into the citadel precincts.

He sat on a granite slab. He pulled the sat phone from his backpack and extended the antenna.

Function switch on. 5kHz narrowband. He keyed the encryption code.

'Brimstone to Carnival, over.'

It took him twenty minutes to get a response.

Koell's voice:

'*Authenticate.*'

'Authentication is Oscar, Sierra, Yankee, Bravo.'

'*Go ahead, Brimstone.*'

'Requesting immediate exfil, over.'

'*Have you acquired the package?*'

'Negative.'

'*No case, no ride.*'

'Our transport is down. The choppers are out of action.'

'*How? What happened?*'

'An accident. A technical fault.'

'*You want to be a player? Stop bleating for help and do your damn job. Make shit happen. Find the case. Call me at oh-six-hundred.*'

The line went dead.

Gaunt tucked the phone into the side-pocket of his backpack. He pulled a steel cross from his shirt collar. Army issue, strung on a dog-tag ball-chain. He mumbled the Lord's Prayer.

He dug a hand-drawn map from his pocket, took bearings, and began to pick his way through the labyrinth of tumbled stone.

Voss crouched behind the quad bike, sniper rifle resting across the saddle. His eyelids drooped. His head nodded as he fought sleep.

'Hey.'

Lucy slapped his shoulder.

Voss shook himself awake and alert. He cracked knuckles and flexed to restore circulation. He rubbed his eyes. He took a pair of black-framed spectacles from a chest pouch, wiped the lenses on his sleeve and put them on.

'How long have you needed those?' asked Lucy.

'Got them last month. My eyes get tired. No big deal.'

He scanned the ruins through the SIMRAD nightscope. Half-collapsed buildings. Pillars and courtyards. Turrets and domes.

A flicker of movement. A shadow passing across stonework. One of Jabril's undead battalion. The stones of the citadel precincts glowed green with residual warmth, but the emaciated creature dragging itself through the avenues and arches had virtually no heat signature. It was an absence, a living shadow, a stumbling silhouette.

'Contact.'

'How many have we got?'

'Just one.'

He pressed his face to the cheek-piece of the rifle and centred the reticules. Cross-hairs zeroed on the creature's forehead. Slow-squeeze of the trigger. Four pounds of pressure. The whip-crack gunshot echoed through the citadel compound. The revenant's skull shattered like porcelain.

Voss worked the rifle bolt and chambered a fresh round.

Lucy sat with her back to the quad. She faced the temple interior. Ready to snatch up her assault rifle in there was any movement from the cash truck.

She dug inside a plastic bag.

'What's that?' asked Voss.

'Shit from Toon's pockets.'

A wallet with a few dollars and dinar. His passport. His provisional pass. A thumbed copy of *Soul on Ice*. A tobacco tin with medal ribbons and badges. Purple heart. Beirut. Combat Infantry. Jump wings.

'He left a bag back at the hotel,' said Voss. 'Socks and stuff. He always travelled light.'

Amanda wiped perspiration from her eyes. She took off her Stetson and fanned herself.

'Do you really want to die?'

Jabril shrugged.

Amanda had an open box of gold at her side. She raked her fingers through rings, bracelets and pendants.

'There's a ton of gold in these boxes,' said Amanda. 'Enough for everyone. You want to burn that missile, be my guest. Then why not head back to Baghdad with us and spend some money?'

Jabril shook his head.

'I don't deserve to live.'

'Why?'

'Many reasons, none of which I wish to share. I feel I have reached the end of a long, hard road.'

Jabril held the grenade between his knees and flexed cramp from his hand.

'How about you? Have you thought what you will do with the gold?'

'Retire,' said Amanda. 'Somewhere green.'

'With Lucy?'

'Yeah.'

'And your friends?'

'We've got unusual résumés. Played gun-for-hire on every continent. It's been fun. Twenty years on the bullet-end of war. But sooner or later you wake up old. We'll split the cash and head our separate ways. We've been family. But I guess it's over.'

Lucy's voice:

'*You guys all right?*'

Amanda picked up her radio and held the earpiece.

'We're okay. How's it going out there?'

'*Can't say much over an open channel.*'

'Okay.'

'*Can Jabril hear what I'm saying? Answer yes or no.*'

'No.'

'*Does he have any weapons other than the grenade?*'

'No.'

'*Can you take him? If it comes down to it, are you willing to try?*'

Amanda thought it over.

'Yes.'

'*Pass the radio to Jabril.*'

Amanda kicked the radio across the vault floor to Jabril.

'She wants to speak to you.'

He fumbled with the earpiece, careful not to lose his grip on the grenade.

'*How's it going, Jabril?*'

'I'm fine. How's your friend?'

'*Huang? Sinking fast.*'

'You know what needs to be done.'

'*Forget it.*'

'Tell him straight. He's dying. It will be slow and painful. Put a gun in his hand. Let him make the choice. He's your friend. Be honest with him.'

'*I'll give you water. You want water? You want to drink? Open the door a crack and I'll push through a Camelbak straw.*'

'And a gun barrel, no doubt.'

'*If you get thirsty, let me know.*'

Gaunt had received a pre-mission briefing from Koell. A summons to his luxury suite at the Rasheed.

Gaunt sat in a deep leather armchair and basked in a down-wash of cool air from a ceiling grille.

The room was littered with files, reconnaissance photographs and downlink screens.

Koell sat beside Gaunt and handed him a tumbler of scotch.

'Jabril wasn't the only person to walk out of that valley when the shit went down,' said Koell. 'There was another survivor. Doctor Ignatiev.'

Koell swivelled a laptop so Gaunt could see the screen. He clicked play. A squat Slavic guy sitting in an interrogation cell. His skin was burnt and peeling. The guy talked. No sound.

'The valley team got wiped out while I was taking care of business back in Baghdad. A couple of garbled distress calls then radio silence. A few days later I started to hear rumours. A white guy for sale in Mosul. Bedouin had found Ignatiev half dead in the desert. Figured he might fetch a good price. I flew to Mosul. We bartered. I bought him for forty thousand bucks.'

Koell handed Gaunt a reconnaissance picture of the citadel.

'Ignatiev found the crypt entrance among a bunch of

subsidiary buildings behind the main temple. It's the only underground structure. A deep catacomb with a vaulted ceiling. The crypt contains the bones of temple priests and their acolytes. Whenever the big guy died, the head priest, they carried him underground and laid him to rest. Then his pals drank some kind of poison draught and lay down beside him. Kept him company on his trip into the after-world.

'Jabril and his boys may have used the crypt as storage space. Plenty of sandstorms in that region. Extreme temperature fluctuations. The crypt would be safe and cool. Good shelter. When you arrive onsite, when you begin your search for the virus flask, it's the first place you should check.'

'Okay.'

'The trunk is green. No markings. About the size of a suitcase. It contains a thick document bundle, and the virus flask. We want both items. That is your mission. Your primary objective. You have forty-eight hours. After that, we pull the plug.'

The silence of the temple crypt was broken by the rasp of a stone lid hauled aside. A torch beam pierced the darkness.

Gaunt crept down worn stone steps. He swung his Maglite left and right, lit niches and plinths cluttered with bone.

He explored the crypt. He stooped beneath the low ceiling. Archways receded into impenetrable shadows. Strange hieroglyphs on walls and pillars. Hybrid blasphemies. Creatures with the bodies of men, the heads of eagles, alligators and bulls. Curling, sting-loaded scorpion tails.

There were calcite urns stacked around the base of each pillar. He shone his flashlight inside. Jumbled bone.

He examined a skull. Good teeth. A diet free from refined sugar.

Brown stains on the flagstone floor, criss-cross like tyre tread. The imprint of reed mats long since crumbled away.

Broken clay pots. Tiny skulls. Dogs and cats.

Something stank. New death. New decay.

His torch lit mummified bodies. Dead soldiers. Three Republican Guard in olive fatigues. They were sat facing a battery lamp that had long since burned out. Exit wounds in the top of each head. It looked like they passed round a Makarov pistol and, one-by-one, took a bullet in the mouth.

He unlaced his boots and compared sole-size with the dead men. He found a good match. Leather parade boots. They had been protected from leaking body fluid by a double layer of socks.

Gaunt tried them for size. He laced.

The dead guys wore gold jewellery. Drab uniforms decked out with pimp accessories. Rings. Bracelets. Neck chains.

Gaunt unclipped a gold Rolex with a black face. He wiped it clean. It still kept time. He threw his plastic Casio G-Shock aside and buckled the Rolex.

He checked the Makarov. No bullets.

He took stick deodorant from his backpack. He rubbed deodorant on a bandana, then tied it round his face bandit-style. The reek of decomposition masked by cloying perfume.

He searched pockets. The mummified faces grinned at him like they were sharing a private joke.

Coins. Prayer beads and a Koran. A couple of crappy penknives. No weapons, no ammo.

Gaunt kicked through smashed laptops, discarded clothes and food wrappers. He shone his flashlight into the deep shadow of the catacombs. No green trunk.

Gaunt rubbed his eyes. He felt tired. He felt out of his depth.

He found a blanket. He shook out dust and wrapped it round his shoulders like a shawl.

He sat on the worn steps of the crypt. He ejected the clip from his Sig and counted bullets. NyTrilium rounds. Blunt-ridged, like molars. Four left.

He sipped from his canteen.

He leaned against ancient brickwork and closed his eyes. He tried to sleep, despite the cold. Vapour curled from his mouth and nose like cigarette smoke.

A strange dream. His long-dead mother standing the other side of a crowded street. She shouted. She seemed desperate. He couldn't make out words.

Lucy's voice.

'*Gaunt? Gaunt can you hear me?*'

Gaunt jerked awake. He unzipped his leather jacket. His earpiece was hanging round his chest. He hooked it to his earlobe.

'Hello, Lucy.'

'*How are you doing out there?*'

'I'm walking on sunshine.'

'*Raphael is dead.* Talon *is destroyed.* Bad Moon *is damaged. I want to cut a deal. Repair the chopper and fly us home. We'll let you live.*'

'Is that right?'

'*Think about it. We have to get the Huey airborne. How do you feel about walking home? Several hundred miles of desert between us and Baghdad. Reckon you could make it on your own? Lucky if any of us get back alive.*'

'What if I can't fix the chopper?'

'*Then we're all fucked.*'

'You'd put a bullet in my head soon as we touch down. I'd be dead before the rotor stopped spinning.'

'*We'd find a spot outside the city limits. Put the gold out the door. After that, head for the Green Zone. You know that road outside the convention centre?*'

'Yeah.'

'*Set us down right there. Place is always crawling with traffic. There are CCTV cameras covering the entrance. Plenty of sentries. Land there and walk away. Take all the gold you can carry.*'

'Voss. Your girlfriend. They would track me down.'

'Then get the fuck out of Baghdad quick as you can. Yeah, they'll be gunning for revenge. But you would have a head start, if you are smart enough to use it.'

'What do your friends say?'

'They want to get out of here. They are prepared to be a little pragmatic.'

'Let me think it over.'

Jabril unhooked the earpiece from his ear.

'Your friends seem to be having problems. One of your helicopters is destroyed. The other is damaged. They blame Gaunt.'

Amanda wiped sweat from her face. She cracked her knuckles. She wiped her hands dry.

The flashlight dimmed a little further. The dying bulb threw out a warm ember glow.

Amanda yawned.

Jabril yawned in sympathy.

The instant his eyes squeezed shut Amanda snatched a handful of rings and watches, and hurled them at Jabril's face. His shocked flinch gave her the half-second she needed to throw herself forward and grip his left hand.

They rolled on the plate floor of the truck, scattering jewels, wrestling for the grenade. Amanda bent back Jabril's fingers and eased the grenade out of his hand. She gripped the grenade in both hands, fingers locked tight round the safety lever. She brought it down on Jabril's head like a rock. Repeated blows. She slammed his jaw. She cut open his forehead.

She removed the knife from the door mechanism, and kicked open the vault.

She jumped out. Cool air.

Lucy ran to the truck. They hugged and kissed.

Amanda held up the grenade.

'He's got the pin in his pocket.'

Voss dragged Jabril from the truck. Jabril lay on flagstones, holding his bleeding forehead. Voss kicked him in the back, the balls. Jabril curled foetal. He shook with each blow. He took the beating but didn't scream.

Amanda took the pin from Jabril's pocket, twisted it back into the grenade and set it down. She looked around.

'Where's Toon?' she asked.

'Toon and Raphael are dead. Both choppers are fucked. Gaunt is out there, in the ruins.'

'Holy fucking Christ.'

'Never trust a Christian,' said Voss. 'That's what my dad used to say. If you meet a guy with a cross round his neck, keep a firm hand on your wallet. Team Jesus. Think they are better than anyone else. Think they are a breed apart.'

'He wanted the gold?' asked Amanda.

'I guess. I'm not sure. I'm beginning to think the gold is a side-show. We're caught up in some nasty shit and I think it's about time we extricated ourselves.'

Voss dragged the metal case from the truck.

'What's in here?'

'Jabril's prize,' said Amanda. 'A Hellfire missile. It's loaded with some kind of bio-weapon.'

Voss opened the case. He examined the missile. He thumbed through documents and photographs.

'CIA black ops. You got serious friends, Jabril.'

Lucy lifted the glass cylinder from its foam bed. She held it up. It lit her face ethereal blue.

'It has to be destroyed,' croaked Jabril. 'The virus. The documents. The entire project has to be erased.'

Lucy lay the cylinder back in its foam bed.

'You've dropped us in some deep shit.'

'I'm sorry. I didn't mean to drag you into this mess.'

Voss threw the documents aside. He stood over the injured man.

'I think I've been fucked quite enough for one night, bokkie.

About time we regained the initiative.' He pressed the gun barrel to Jabril's forehead. 'I say we snuff the fucker right now. Save a little water.'

Jabril struggled to his feet.

'Wait,' he said. 'Please. Wait.'

'Fuck it,' said Lucy. 'Waste him.'

Voss racked the slide of his shotgun and took aim.

'Hold on,' said Amanda, pressing a tissue to her broken nose. 'Listen to what the guy has to say.'

'Why?' asked Lucy. 'Everything he told us so far has been lies. The man is a liability.'

'He can tell us about the virus.'

'It's fucked-up shit. That's all I need to know.'

'We need him. Both choppers are screwed. Odds are, we will be walking home. He managed it once before. He crossed the desert and survived. He could be our guide.'

Voss reluctantly lowered his shotgun.

'All right,' said Lucy. 'Tie him up.'

Voss lashed Jabril's left arm behind his back, tied his wrist to his belt. He put a rope round Jabril's neck like a dog-leash. He tethered him to a pillar near the campfire.

Lucy sat beside Jabril. He ran his tongue round his mouth and checked for missing teeth.

Lucy uncapped her canteen and held it to his mouth. He sipped. He sluiced and spat.

'It's going to be a long, cold night. So let's start over. Let's start from the beginning. Who are you, Jabril? What in God's name happened out here?'

Central Intelligence Agency

Directorate of Operations, Near East Division

FLASH CABLE - READ AND DESTROY

TO: Project Lead, D.Ops
FROM: R. Koell

08/23/05

21:18 AST

Colonel,

You requested I keep you apprised of significant developments in our attempts to retrieve the battle-strain from the contamination zone. Our man at the SPEKTR site reports the incursion team have encountered difficulties which have rendered their transport, two Bell UH-1 helicopters, non-operational. He has also been unable to locate and acquire the virus package.

11th Recon will not be able to resume Predator over-watch until first light, so we are unable to make an independent assessment of the situation. However I feel it prudent to put our assets in Sharjah on standby. The use of an expendable contract security team gives us the distance and deniability. Our man continues his survey of the site and I remain hopeful that the virus package can be recovered. However I also feel we need to be prepared to take significant steps should it become necessary to cleanse the site.

Next scheduled update: 05:30 AST.

Starfall

'How about a cigarette?'

Lucy put a lit Salem between Jabril's lips. He smoked a while, then spat the butt into the fire.

'Okay,' said Lucy. 'Start talking.'

I worked for the Office of Special Security under Uday Hussein. Ba'ath Party Intelligence, Directorate Four.

I worked out of Baghdad. We were based in Little Venice, the presidential compound next to the Tigris. The area that is now the Green Zone.

I was part of the weapons acquisition programme. I led a team of senior intelligence officers. Loyal men who spoke English, German, French. Our job, throughout the eighties and nineties, was to fly abroad and source materials for the biological and chemical weapons programme. We were called SEPP. The State Establishment for Pesticide Production. We used intermediaries. We bought precursor chemicals from Egypt, the Netherlands, Singapore. We bought steel fermentation tanks, centrifuges and reactor vessels from Japan and India. We sourced Anthrax, smallpox and yellow fever from labs in Moscow and North Korea. Samples were sent back to Baghdad sealed in a diplomatic pouch. The objective of the procurement programme was to develop chemical and biological weapons to be delivered by adapted SCUD and Badr missiles, and specially milled artillery shells.

Our work came to end during Desert Storm. All the major bio-warfare facilities were blasted flat by the American air force. A relentless barrage. Tomahawks. Incessant B52 strikes. The al-Salman facility south of Baghdad burned to the ground, ending our attempts to weaponise the plague. The al-Kindi bacteriological lab was levelled, destroying our stocks of Anthrax and Botulinum. The vaccine facility at al-Amoriyah was bombed, ending our attempts to refine typhoid, cholera and smallpox.

There was no serious attempt to restart the programme after the war. The country was in ruins, the army had been decimated. My greatest coup, in the latter years of the regime, was circumventing sanctions to procure a custom Lamborghini Uday had glimpsed on TV and decided he must possess at all costs.

The order came down a couple of years ago, days before the American invasion. It was a dark and desperate time. The US army was massed at our borders. We knew aerial bombardment would begin any day and the ministry buildings of Baghdad would be a primary target. Should we run? Should we abandon our posts and flee? Each man faced the same dilemma.

That is why I was astonished when the order came across my desk. Investigate an incident that occurred in the Western Desert near the border with Syria a decade earlier.

A strange craft had fallen to earth. It had not been recovered.

Why, in the dying days of the regime, would anyone consider it a priority to investigate this incident?

You have to understand that Iraq did not have a single state police. Saddam was too cunning to let a single agency become all-powerful. There were a series of rival intelligence agencies, some loyal to Uday, some loyal to Qsay. Everyone involved in the security apparatus understood they were pawns in a grand game of succession. There were no simple orders. A misjudged word or action could easily result in a show-trial and execution. We led a privileged life. But the price was constant fear.

Nevertheless, this order allowed me to flee Baghdad with the full sanction of the state. I was happy to comply.

I scoured records. I brought cart loads of paper from basement storage.

Ten years ago, military air traffic logged an unexplained radar hit over Al Anbar. An object passing from Syrian airspace at high altitude. A steep descent, at unbelievable velocity. Twenty-five times the speed of sound. At first it was assumed that a meteor had fallen to earth but examination of radar records revealed the object appeared to alter course and speed as it fell. There was a significant deceleration ten kilometres from impact, as if the object were trying to perform some kind of controlled landing.

A Mig pilot on night reconnaissance had glimpsed the unidentified object to his north as it crossed his flight-path. It was moving fast, burning bright. He described it as a shooting star. This took place in the early nineties. Our war with Iran had cooled to a stand-off. America and Russia were competing for regional domination. This entire sector was a cold-war buffer zone. Plenty of US *Blackbird* reconnaissance flights. I assumed some kind of spy plane had been forced to crash-land in the desert.

They sent out choppers the next morning. They were hampered by a fierce dust storm. When the storm cleared, no trace of the mysterious object could be found. Empty desert. No sign of wreckage. No crater.

We could expect little help from the locals.

Iraq is an artificial nation. Disparate tribes ruled by fear. Al-'Anbār governate was hostile territory. We could easily have been prey to Peshmerga guerrillas or Kurdish tribesmen, men with plenty of reason to hate Saddam and his attempts to secularise and unify the nation under his rule.

I requested thirty men. To my surprise I was assigned a full battalion and a truck-load of gold for bribe money.

We loaded excavation equipment and headed west down

the Fallujah highway. It was a relief to flee Baghdad. The city was already a ghost town. Anyone who could leave had already gone. Every shop locked and shuttered. Windows were criss-crossed with tape. Sandbags and anti-aircraft guns on each hotel roof. We were running ahead of the storm.

We drove out into the desert. Drove day and night. Miles of sun-baked highway. We had a grid reference, nothing more. A red cross in the middle of blank terrain.

We passed wretched villages. Hovels clustered around a well. It was a depressing sight. We had all risen from poverty. Every Iraqi, no matter how educated or powerful, can trace his recent ancestry to dirt-poor subsistence farmers trying to coax a few ears of corn from barren soil.

We left the road and drove into the dunes. A long, slow journey. Our trucks sank and stalled countless times. Slivers of frost-shattered rock punctured tyres.

We reached the contamination zone. We cut through the fence.

Some of the men did not want to proceed any further. There was no official record of the air-raid that saturated this stretch of desert in poison, but we had all heard rumours of the noxious chemicals that had wiped out the local population.

I urged the men to complete their mission. They had little alternative. Return to Baghdad and cower from bombs? Travel east to the Kuwaiti border and fight a futile war? None of us wished to die for Saddam. We feared him. We didn't love him.

We drove into the toxic wilderness.

We reached our objective. Map coordinates in the middle of nowhere. Featureless dunes. An ocean of sand. It seemed hopeless. Whatever plunged to earth had been swallowed without trace.

I radioed Baghdad. Heavy encryption. I explained the situation. Very little hope of locating the mysterious aircraft. But they insisted I continue my search.

We made camp. The men smoked and ate from cans. I walked among the dunes as evening fell.

I sat and reviewed radar records. Military traffic control in Baghdad tracked the object's descent. A long arc. A ballistic trajectory. A steepening dive as the UFO passed through Syrian air-space at hypersonic speed. The vehicle would have been subject to unimaginable G-force. It would have been seared by three-thousand-degree heat. Then, as it approached impact, the craft suddenly banked and levelled out, like a plane struggling to land. A further, sudden deceleration as the craft dropped out of radar coverage in a shallow dive and struck the ground.

I looked across the desert and tried to picture the moment of impact. The craft trailing drogue chutes, ripping through the dunes in an explosion of dust. It must have left a long trench and a trail of wreckage before coming to rest.

It must still be near the surface.

There was a village a few miles distant. Four adobe houses. Two cows. The place didn't have a name, didn't warrant a dot on the map.

The villagers were terrified. Soldiers in trucks. Mothers hid their children. Fathers lined up, expecting to beg for their lives.

Despite warnings, despite the terrible risk of disease and death, they had continued to live in the contaminated zone. They would rather watch their children grow sick and die than give up the only life they knew.

I gave them food. I explained we meant no harm. We sat and ate.

I gave them gold from the truck. You see, we had a strong-room in the presidential palace filled with jewellery taken from prisoners prior to torture and execution. Men would be seized from their homes. Stripped of their clothes, stripped of watches and rings. Our interrogation team would pull fingernails, burn genitals, until each prisoner confessed to imaginary crimes. That was my power. As a member of the OSS I could bestow fabulous wealth at whim or have a man executed on the spot.

I asked the villagers to describe the night, ten years ago, when something fell from the sky. One of the farmers said he saw the crash. He had walked a mile from the village in search of a lost goat. The sun had set. He climbed a boulder. He saw something in the sky, falling like a shooting star. The object grew larger. It was a fireball. He fell to his knees. He called on the mercy of God.

The thing passed overhead, so close intense heat scorched his face like sunburn. He glimpsed a strange craft, glowing like a hot coal.

I gave the man my notebook and pen. I asked him to draw what he saw that night. He drew a crude arrow. Some kind of delta-wing craft. He said it looked like a giant bat.

I asked the farmer to lead us to the spot he saw the crash. He refused. He was scared. He said the thing was a monster from hell. We should leave it undisturbed.

I bribed him with gold.

We walked from the village. He led us to a massive sandstone boulder protruding from the dunes. We climbed to the top.

'There,' he said, pointing south-west. 'It passed overhead and crashed in the distance.'

'How far?' I asked.

'Two miles, maybe three.'

We walked to the impact site. There was nothing to see. Featureless desert.

'You are sure this is the spot?'

The farmer refused to answer. The memory of the crash reduced him to whimpering terror. He ran back to the village. No amount of gold would induce him to help us further.

I gave the order to dig.

I immediately faced a near mutiny. The dunes presented

a double threat. Not only was sand likely to be contaminated with the residue of chemical warfare but, in his attempts to subdue local guerrillas, Saddam had ordered the region pounded by cluster-bombs and artillery fire. There was every chance we could unearth unexploded munitions.

My men simply wanted to hide from the war. They were Republican Guard, elite troops, chosen for their fanatical loyalty to Saddam. They had taken a solemn oath to lay down their lives at his command. But they were also realistic men concerned for the welfare of their wives and children back home. They had no interest in our Quixotic mission. They were happy to camp in the desert, listen to the war unfold over the BBC World Service, then return to Baghdad when the shooting had stopped. I could sympathise.

Four of the men tore the badges from their uniforms. They climbed in a Jeep, replaced the Iraqi pennant clipped to the radio antenna with a white rag of surrender and headed for their homes in Fallujah. I could have ordered them shot as they drove away but there was little point.

I explained to the remaining troops that American satellites and drones would be watching the highways. If they took to the road in a military convoy they might be targeted and bombed.

I also explained that whatever was taking place elsewhere in the world, I was still their commander and I intended to complete my mission.

They men could have mutinied, simply walked away, but they had lived in fear of Saddam's intelligence agencies all their lives. They were obedient as dogs.

I organised a grid search. We had brought Vallon mine-clearance metal detectors, sensitive enough to locate a bullet casing buried feet beneath the ground. We drove stakes into the desert to mark our path.

We must have covered acres of dunes. We trudged morning

until late afternoon, walking in a line. We swung the mine detectors in sequential, one-eighty arcs.

A detector sang out. A small hit at the edge of the search field. The soldiers gathered round as I crouched and brushed away sand.

A buckled scrap of metal little bigger than my palm. A lightweight alloy. Aluminium, or maybe zinc.

We continued our search. Two hours later we scored a big hit. An object six feet long. The men dug with spades. Then I crouched in the crater and probed the sand with my knife until I struck metal.

I ordered the men to stand at a safe distance. I brushed away sand with my hand, gradually exposing hydraulic rams, ropes of frayed cable, shreds of rubber. Thick tread. Fragments of a steel-ribbed tyre. We had discovered part of the undercarriage of an aircraft. The remains of a large double wheel attached to a hydraulic shock-absorber.

I took pictures. I had a soldier stand next to the wreckage for scale.

Minutes later we found more scraps of metal hidden beneath the dunes. Tubular titanium spars. Scraps of aluminium fairing. Black hexagonal blocks that appeared to be carbon-fibre heat tiles.

It quickly became apparent we had found the debris trench, the trail of wreckage left by this strange vehicle as it fell to earth and gouged into the sand.

The sun began to set. We slowly walked across the dunes in a wide line, sweeping the spade-heads of our metal detectors left and right. Then, in unison, our detectors began to sing. A rising chorus of clicks and whoops like whale song.

We surveyed the ground around us. A strong and constant signal. We had found the body of the craft. Whatever had fallen from the sky, years ago, was directly beneath our feet.

We drove stakes into the sand to chart the dimensions of

the object. An aerofoil shaped like a giant arrowhead. Sixty feet long, thirty feet wide.

I summoned the trucks and had them parked in a ring surrounding the crash site. I gave the men shovels and told them to dig.

They threw spadefuls of sand. I paced, and watched their progress. They dug for hours. Then they scraped metal. I jumped into the hole and pushed the soldiers aside.

I scooped with my hand and exposed a metal blade. Scorched hexagonal tiles, like snakeskin. I dug some more. I quickly realised we had exposed the tip of a big tailfin.

Night fell. We ran the truck engines. Head beams gave light while the men continued to excavate the craft.

Two teams. They dug for thirty-minute shifts. Downtime gave them a chance to smoke and rehydrate.

Midnight. The soldiers were exhausted. I ordered them to cease work. We ate, we drank. The night turned cold. We had no wood for fire. The men wrapped themselves in blankets, huddled together in the trucks and slept.

I pulled my blanket round my shoulders and stood at the edge of the crater. I couldn't sleep. I trained the beam of my flashlight on the strange tail fin.

According to records, the first radar trace of the craft had been detected high above the operating altitude of military or commercial jets. There seemed little doubt this vehicle had fallen from space. There was no insignia, no marking of any kind.

I stood staring up into the night sky for a long while, contemplating the stars.

Next morning, I ordered the men to continue excavating the spacecraft. I drove to the airbase at Samarra. I tried to requisition a heavy crane and a large flatbed truck. The commanding officer initially refused my request. His men had been ordered to the eastern front. But I gave him gold. He was grateful for the gift. The man was also from Saddam's home town of Tikrit. He had prospered during the long and bloody war with Iran. He had risen to the rank of general. He also ran a construction company and had been given lucrative building contracts. But the regime was about to fall and men like him would have to reinvent themselves. Burn their uniforms. Convince an occupying power they had taken no part in Ba'ath Party oppression. He probably had a strongbox somewhere in his home full of dinar bound with rubber bands. Kickbacks and blood money. Saddam's smiling face on every note stamped red, blue and green. All of it about to become worthless. A bag of jewellery and Krugerrands striped from the homes of purged party members could be an invaluable asset in the uncertain weeks and months ahead.

We returned back to the crash site. The craft was half exposed. A thick fuselage. Torn batwings. Scorched rocket-vents at the tail.

One of the men showed me a brittle shard of crystal. The craft had been so hot when it came to rest, years ago, that sand surrounding the airframe fused to glass, coating the entire surface like ice.

I radioed Baghdad. I told them what we had found. Then the strangest thing occurred. My immediate superior at the OSS was General Assad. I rarely spoke to anyone but him. But an hour after I contacted Baghdad and told them we had found an unusual vehicle buried in the sand, I received fresh instructions. I didn't recognise the voice. The man spoke Arabic. But he sounded American.

'*My name is Koell.*'

'What happened to General Assad?'

'*I'm in charge of this project. From now on, you talk to me.*'

He asked me to describe the craft in detail.

'*Is the hull intact? Tell me about structural damage. Is the cabin still sealed?*'

I told him the wings were badly damaged. The under-carriage was destroyed. The turbojet engine pods were burned out.

'*What about the crew compartment? Boot up your laptop. Send me pictures.*'

'My men are excavating the cockpit as we speak.'

'*I'm going to mail you a schematic of the craft.*'

I sat in the back of a truck with our communications gear. The file came through. I clicked print. Multiple views of the vehicle. Top and bottom. Front, side and back. It looked like a mini-shuttle. A sleek space fighter. The text was in Russian.

We continued the excavation. Koell demanded hourly bulletins.

We unearthed the snubbed nose of the vehicle. The side-hatch was still sealed. The cockpit glass was pitted and cracked but intact. We shone flashlights through the scorched glass but couldn't see inside.

I told Koell the shuttle had sustained considerable damage during re-entry and landing but the crew compartment appeared to be sealed. I asked how many occupants we could expect to find. He said he didn't know.

I drew up a plan. The vehicle was buried twenty feet beneath the surface. The sand was too unstable to allow a detailed inspection of the craft. Anyone who climbed into the crater risked being buried alive by shifting dunes. We needed to extract the craft and transport it to a sheltered, secure location where it could be examined in more detail.

I consulted our maps, and decided to exploit the rail network spread across the Western Desert like a web.

The railroad was built by European contractors during the nineteen eighties. The main phosphate production facility was in Akashat, linked to a processing plant at Al Qa'im, but there were satellite mining facilities dotted throughout the desert, all linked by rail. Organic phosphate compounds make good fertiliser, but can also act as a major precursor ingredient of chemical weapons such as Sarin and Tabun.

The railroad passed within two miles of the crash site. If

we could lift the wrecked vehicle onto a truck, and nurse it across the desert, we could load it onto a rail car.

I decided to bring the shuttle here, to the Valley of Tears.

There is an abandoned mine to the north of the valley, at the end of a deep ravine. A series of exploratory shafts and galleries. A sheltered, remote location. We could hide the craft in the tunnels. We could drape camouflage nets over any of our vehicles left in the open to mask them from aerial surveillance. The war would rage down south. Young men would squander their lives battling an invader they couldn't hope to defeat. But we would be safe. History would pass us by. We could work without interruption.

I radioed Samarra. I demanded the loan of winch gear, an additional crane truck and a flatbed rail car. An absurd request. The country was in chaos. Most people couldn't locate bread, let alone heavy-duty excavation equipment. Nevertheless, Koell told me the equipment would arrive in hours. I suppose, in a time of chaos, a man with briefcase full of US dollars can get anything he wants.

I asked Koell about the spacecraft.

I knew the Russians built their own shuttle. I saw it on television, years ago. It was called *Borun Snowstorm*. Pretty much identical to the American craft. It made a single, unmanned flight. Then the programme was cancelled. The vehicles were scraped. One of the decommissioned shuttles became a fairground attraction in Gorky Park.

The craft at the bottom of the crater was much smaller than a space shuttle. It was sleek, streamlined, little bigger than jet fighter. The wings were torn and blunted. Ailerons ripped away. Stripped heat tiles. Wing membranes peeled back revealing twisted titanium-alloy spars.

'What is it?' I asked Koell. 'This thing. This spacecraft. Where is it from?'

'*It's Russian,*' said Koell. '*A trans-orbital vehicle. Military prototype. They call it Spektr.*'

The Body

Lucy sat beside Jabril and fed him mouthfuls of cereal bar.

'Spektr.'

'That's right,' said Jabril.

'It's here, in this valley?'

'Yes. If you follow the railroad track across the valley floor it brings you to a mine.'

Voss joined them by the fire. He crouched, shook sand from the folds of a map, and spread it on flagstones. He and Lucy examined the terrain by flickering flame light.

'I've been mulling our options,' said Voss. 'Plenty of towns closer than Baghdad. If we walk out of here we could head north to Mosul. Or east to Ramadi or Fallujah.'

'Taliban strongholds. They would happily cut our throats.'

'We could jack a car soon as we reached habitation.'

'After a couple of days in the sun? We'd be in no state for a fire-fight. Our best bet is to head south-east for Baghdad. Turn ourselves in at a coalition checkpoint.'

'Some hard miles of desert.'

'Got any other ideas?'

'No.'

'You're a survivor,' said Lucy. 'A cockroach, just like me. You'll make it. You're not the quitting kind.'

'There has to be some way to summon help. How about we write a big SOS in the sand? Someone will see it. A satellite. A plane.'

'No guarantee,' said Lucy. 'We could sit here for days hoping for rescue, getting thirsty, getting weak, watching Huang die. I prefer to make my own luck. I'll try to raise Gaunt again on the radio in a while. Maybe I can reason with the guy. If he has any sense, he will cut a deal. He's marooned out here, just like us. But I reckon he's too scared to think straight. It'll be sunrise in a few hours. We should get our shit together. Be ready to head out at first light. We should carry water and basic weapons. Ditch everything else. How many bottles do we have left?'

'Enough to fill our canteens one more time.'

'All right.'

'What about the gold?' asked Voss.

'Fuck the gold.'

'It's ours. I'm not giving it up.'

'We hide it. Bury it. You want to come back here with some buddies and retrieve the stuff, be my guest. Me? I don't want to drive a Cadillac knowing I bought it with some poor bastard's gold teeth.'

'And Toon?'

'Yeah,' said Lucy. 'That's a bitch. The guy wouldn't want to be left in a godforsaken place like this. But what else can we do? We could load his body onto the quad, but it's only good for a few miles. What do we do after the fuel tank runs dry? We can't dump him in the sand. The man deserves a proper grave.'

'Yeah.'

'We bring Jabril along for the ride. He's an old fuck with one arm but he made it out this desert once before. Tougher than he looks.'

'I don't trust him,' said Voss.

'He's played out. No more surprises. Obedient as a puppy dog. Huang. That's the big question. We can't carry him on our backs. Sure as shit can't schlep a stretcher across five hundred miles of desert. But I'm not walking out on the guy. I'm not leaving him behind.'

Huang sat the other side of the campfire, staring into the flames. He was listening to his iPod.

Lucy lowered her voice.

'The guy is fading fast. He looks eighty years old. We'll stay. We'll keep him company the next few hours. But I reckon we'll be digging a second grave soon enough.'

Voss walked round the campfire and sat beside Huang.

'How you feeling?' asked Voss.

'Not so great,' said Huang. 'Think I'm running a fever.' His lips were blue.

Huang reached up and peeled the dressing from his neck.

'How does it look?'

Voss tried to hide his disgust at the rotting wound. Black flesh. Awful stench. Metallic spines protruded from the liquefying skin like needles.

'Not so great.'

'You've got to cut,' said Huang.

'What?'

'You've got to cut this shit out of me. Shoot me up with morphine. There's a scalpel in the WALK. Slice.'

'I'm not a surgeon.'

'You think I don't recognise the smell of gangrene? I'm dying. This is the only chance I've got. You have to cut down to clean tissue and plug the wound.'

'I can't.'

'I'm begging you, brother. I'll walk you through it.'

Voss walked to the temple entrance and talked it over with Lucy.

'The blood loss will kill him,' said Voss.

'We can't just stand around and let him rot. If his neck swells up any worse, he'll need a tracheotomy. I'll do it. Your eyes are too fucked for this kind of work.'

Lucy sat by Huang. She unzipped the medipac.

'Couple of scalpels in that plastic box,' said Huang. 'Bunch of Kerlix dressings. Pretty much all you'll need.'

He lay down on the flagstones.

Lucy uncapped a morphine hypo pen. She jabbed the pen

into Huang's bicep and pressed the plunger. She tossed the used hypodermic and checked her watch. Two minutes for the drug to take full effect.

She pulled on Nitrile gloves and tore a scalpel from its sterile pack.

'Wish we had some bourbon,' said Lucy, trying to steady her trembling hand. All set?'

Huang gave a woozy thumbs up.

Lucy leant forward, hesitated, then sliced into rotted neck flesh. Pus and blood. Unimaginable stink. She sawed. She trimmed a flap of flesh, did it quick and efficient like she was slicing roast chicken.

'Can I see it?' murmured Huang.

'The skin? No. You don't want to see it.'

Lucy threw the scrap of black, infected skin onto the fire. It spat, crisped and curled.

'Did you get it all? Did you dig out the infection?'

'Yeah,' she lied. The spines were buried so deep in Huang's neck they couldn't be excised without ripping open veins and arteries.

She packed fresh dressing round the bubbling wound and taped it down. Huang passed out.

'He's beyond help,' said Jabril, watching from the shadows.

'I didn't ask your fucking opinion.'

Lucy peeled gloves and tossed them on the fire. They shrivelled and melted.

She joined Voss and Amanda at the barricade.

Amanda crouched, sniper rifle resting across the quad saddle. She put her eye to the nightscope and scanned the ruins.

'How did it go?' asked Voss.

'I doubt he'll see the dawn.'

Voss tore open a fresh MRE meal pouch and distributed food. Lucy ate cold Thai chicken with a plastic fork. Voss ate cheese tortellini. Amanda ate crackers.

'Jabril says Huang will turn demented,' said Lucy. 'Better find some rope. Tie him up.'

'He couldn't hurt anyone right now, not even himself,' said Voss. 'If he becomes a problem, I'll deal with it.'

Voss walked across the cavernous temple hall and stood by the fire. He stripped to the waist. He washed himself with towelettes and applied fresh deodorant. He dressed.

'Want any food?'

'Yes,' said Jabril. 'Thank you.'

Voss unwrapped a meat patty and fed it to Jabril.

'What is it?'

'Pork.'

Jabril spat meat into the fire.

Voss checked the pockets of Jabril's discarded jacket. He found cigarettes. He lit and smoked.

'So how did you do it?' asked Voss. 'This desert. How did you make it out alive?'

Jabril smiled.

'You must have a reason to live. Something beyond yourself.'

'You wanted to save the world, is that right?'

'I'm worse than evil. I supervised unimaginable cruelty, ordered torture and execution, simply because it was my job. This is my chance to do something right.'

Voss unsheathed his knife and picked his teeth.

'How about you, Mr Voss?' asked Jabril. 'How badly do you want to live?'

Lucy sat on the altar steps beside Toon's body. He had been wrapped in a poncho shroud and lashed with rope. He looked ready for burial at sea.

She thumbed through his Eldridge Cleaver book. Some of the passages were underlined.

'*The price of hating other human beings is loving oneself less.*'

She wanted to ask Toon why he liked the book, why he carried it around.

A photograph pressed between the pages of the paperback. A gang photo taken in the Riv. Lucy, Toon and the team. Grinning, giving the finger, toasting the camera with beers.

She tucked the photo in her pocket.

'Sorry, dude,' she murmured. 'Let you down.'

Every commander's nightmare. The Big Fuck Up. Getting her men killed. She led Toon into the desert, promised him gold. Now he was dead, and she couldn't get his body home. Buried in alien soil a lifetime away from Tennessee.

Once they gate-crashed a party at the rooftop bar of the al-Rasheed. A pink sunset. She and Toon sipped Michelob and looked out over the city. Minarets and bombed-out ministries. Don McLean battled the call to prayer.

Conversation turned maudlin.

'If anything happens, don't leave me here,' said Toon. 'Not this shithole country. Get me back to the world.'

Lucy put her hand on the rope-lashed poncho.

'I'll miss you, pal.'

Toon's body moved. His back arched like he was stretching in his sleep.

'Hey,' shouted Lucy. 'Hey, he's alive.'

She unsheathed her knife and sawed through rope.

Amanda and Voss came running.

Lucy pulled the poncho aside.

'Fuck.'

She scrambled away from the twitching mess that used to be her friend.

They could see pulped brain tissue through the jagged hole in Toon's skull. Silver wires threaded through his brain like fine hair.

'When was he infected?' asked Voss. 'Was it Huang? Did Toon touch his neck?'

Lucy crouched and examined the gently stirring body.

‘Don’t get too close,’ said Amanda.

‘It’s more than a disease. It’s some kind of parasite. It’s woven through his whole nervous system. I don’t think it’s realised Toon is dead yet.’

Voss gently pulled Lucy aside. He racked his shotgun slide.

‘Sorry, bro.’

He vaporised Toon’s head. The blast echoed round the vaulted hall, dying like thunder.

He walked back to the temple entrance, shotgun over his shoulder.

‘Are you beginning to understand?’ shouted Jabril, his voice echoing through the vast temple. ‘This thing. This virus. It must be exterminated. It must never leave this valley.’

Lucy and Amanda pulled on leather gloves and rewrapped Toon’s headless body. They lashed rope.

‘Christ,’ muttered Amanda. ‘This shit is going to haunt my dreams.’

Fine silver tendrils protruded from the vertebrae stump of Toon’s neck. The tendrils slowly flexed and coiled, as if testing the air.

‘Some nasty, nasty shit.’

‘Never seen anything like it,’ said Lucy.

‘Poor fuck,’ said Amanda. ‘He deserved better. Way better. Promise me. If anything happens, if I get infected, finish me off. Do it quick and clean. I don’t want to end up like that. I don’t want to end up like Huang. I don’t want to walk around with weird shit growing out of my body. You’ve got to promise me.’

‘Let’s make sure it doesn’t come to it.’

They folded canvas over the smoking stump of Toon’s neck.

‘We’ve got to get out of here,’ said Amanda. ‘I don’t want to spend another hour in this place.’

‘We’ll pack our stuff and start walking at first light.’

They tied rope round Toon’s shrouded feet and hauled him through the temple.

Huang was conscious. He struggled to sit upright, clumsy like he was drunk.

'*Via con Dios*, buddy,' he shouted as he saw Toon's body hauled across flagstones. 'Be seeing you soon.'

Voss unblocked the temple doorway. He rolled the quad bike and trailer aside.

He watched as Toon was dragged past. He crossed himself.

Lucy paused. She nodded towards Huang.

'He's sinking fast. Tie him up, you hear?'

'Yeah,' sighed Voss. 'Yeah, I'm on it.'

Lucy and Amanda dragged Toon from the temple.

Lucy swung the barrel light of her assault rifle left and right, surveyed the sinister shadows of the citadel precincts. A steady night-wind moaned through the ancient ruins.

'This way.'

They hauled Toon's corpse through the moonlit necropolis. They dragged him past a colonnade of broken pillars.

'Here.'

A rubble-strewn courtyard. They lay Toon's shrouded body on flagstones.

Lucy hefted chunks of granite rubble and piled them on top of Toon's poncho until he was hidden beneath a cairn of jagged rocks.

Amanda kept watch. She paced the courtyard, kept a three-sixty scan of tumbled walls and dark doorways.

Lucy clapped stone dust from her hands. She wiped sweat from her face. Her skin steamed in the cold night air.

She placed Toon's dog tags on top of the cairn.

'We should go,' said Amanda.

Lucy crouched and laid a hand on the pile of stones.

'We'll come back for you, brother. We won't leave you out here. One day we'll come back and take you home.'

*

Voss found a coil of rope among the clutter of equipment in the quad trailer. He cut two long lengths.

He turned round. Huang was standing directly behind him.

Voss gripped his knife.

Huang stared at him a long while. His face was slack. Lips parted in a semi-snarl. A blank, dead-eyed stare like a shark.

He snapped awake.

'Going to tie me up?' he drawled, thoughts coming slow.

'Maybe.'

'Funny thing,' mumbled Huang. 'Sometimes I'm me, sometimes I'm something else.'

'Yeah?'

'This disease. It has its own thoughts, its own agenda.'

'Like what?'

'A lust for flesh. It wants to break out of here. This valley. It wants to reach the world.'

'I wish there was something I could do for you, kid.'

'Leave. You, Lucy, Mandy. Start walking, as soon as the sun breaks the horizon. Get the fuck out of here before it's too late.'

Huang unscrewed the cap of his canteen. He took a swig.

'Best if no one else drinks from this.'

He poured the remaining water onto the flagstone floor. He tossed the metal bottle into shadows.

Huang reached in his pocket.

'I want you to have this.'

He gave Voss a big folding knife.

'That's a damn good knife. Gerber. Strong.'

He pulled the Glock from his drop holster. He thumbed cartridges from the magazine. He gave Voss a fistful of bullets.

'Think you might need these more than me.'

Huang kept one round for himself. He held it up.

'True what they say. There's a bullet out there with your name on it. And here she is. The bullet that is going to kill me.'

He slotted the cartridge into the magazine. Loaded. Chambered.

'Small-town kid,' said Huang. 'Never thought I would find myself this far from home, dying under foreign skies. Fuck it. It's been a blast.'

Voss nodded.

'See you around,' said Huang.

'Take it easy, man.'

Huang walked out of the temple and was swallowed by night.

Lucy found Voss sitting by the campfire. The flames were dying. Nothing left to burn.

'Where's Huang?'

'Taking a long, long walk.'

Lucy nodded.

They sat round the fire a while.

'He'll be back,' said Jabril.

'He took a gun,' said Voss.

'He won't use it. Too far gone. The disease has the upper hand. He'll be back for you all.'

'You brought us here, you fuck,' said Voss. 'Lured us to this damned hell-hole. Toon. Huang. They'd be alive right now. We'd be propping the bar in the Riv, sipping a beer. Ought to slit your belly open.'

Voss lit a cigarette. He threw the pack to Lucy. She lit. She took a drag. She put the cigarette between Jabril's lips.

'All right. Tell me more about Spektr.'

Spektr

Lucy sat cross-legged. She field-stripped her assault rifle and cleaned the barrel with solvent. She fed a brass bore-punch into the barrel with sharp twists.

Jabril continued his story.

We continued to excavate the Spektr craft.

We tried to hold back the dunes with beams and boards. Two men were almost killed when props broke and they were engulfed by sand. We had to jump in the hole and dig them free with our hands. We dragged them to the surface spitting dirt and whooping for air.

Our men were farm boys with rifles. I forestalled further desertions by giving the men whisky and a fistful of gold each day. Rings, bracelets. There was nowhere to store their treasure so they wore jewellery as they dug. They looked absurd. They looked like pirates.

We cleared enough sand to loop heavy canvas slings beneath the craft. One at the tail, one at the nose. We coordinated both cranes by radio. The vehicle was slowly lifted from its grave, streaming sand.

The crane-trucks began a two-mile journey across the desert to the railroad line. The wrecked spacecraft hung suspended on a canvas cradle between them.

It took a day. We tried to steer the trucks towards firm ground, slowly weaved between the dunes. But the trucks sank every few feet. We had to dig with spades and ramp them free with planks. We crawled a few yards every hour.

We finally reached the railroad track late afternoon. Twin ribbons of steel snaking from the horizon. I powered up the radio. Koell said a locomotive would be with us by nightfall.

An hour later we glimpsed the gleam of a distant headlamp on the far horizon like an evening star. Faint blast of an air-horn. A locomotive pulling long, flatbed wagons.

The massive engine eased to a halt beside us with an explosive roar of air-brakes.

It took us a full hour to lower the spacecraft onto a flatbed wagon. I estimate Spektr weighed fifty or sixty tons. The wagon creaked as it took the load. The rails flexed. Sandstone shingle beneath the sleepers crackled like gunshots as rocks were crushed to powder.

We lashed nets over the orbiter as quickly as we could. We wanted to shield the craft from satellites and planes.

I sent men ahead of us in a jeep to make sure railroad switches were set for our journey to the valley.

I scanned the sky with binoculars. That's when I saw it. A distant speck to the west. A Predator reconnaissance drone. Ghost grey. Miles out. Circling like a vulture.

I told everyone to get moving.

We abandoned the crane trucks. Too heavy to salvage. We left them to sink into the sand.

Some of us rode an empty flatbed wagon. The rest followed in trucks and jeeps. The convoy kept pace with the locomotive for a while, lurching over dunes, then gradually fell back. They knew our destination. They would catch up.

The locomotive laboured to pull the heavy load. The five-thousand horse-power motor revved and growled. Drive wheels shrieked each time they lost traction and span.

The sun set. Rusted brakes and axles sparked beneath us, flickering red as if the infernal locomotive were riding on a wave of flame.

I sat crossed-legged on the rail truck. I radioed Koell. I

told him about the drone. He told me not to worry. From a distance, Spektr looked like a crashed Mig. Just another hulk. The battle for Iraq would be fought down south. No coalition image analyst would worry about handful of troops salvaging a wrecked plane.

There was nothing I could do. If the Americans dispatched an F15 or Apache Longbow, there would be no warning. We wouldn't hear engines. My world would wink out mid-breath, mid-thought, as TOW missiles slammed into the train ripping us to offal.

We reached the hills in the last dying light of day. The cliff carvings, the colossal sentinels, lit blood red. We stood and stared as the locomotive towed us between the two great figures and carried us into the darkness of the tunnel mouth.

Spektr was swallowed by shadow, ragged wings barely clearing the tunnel walls.

We were enveloped by a sudden cave-chill. Dancing flashlight beams illuminated the vaulted concrete of the tunnel roof as it passed overhead.

A brief mutiny. Three of our number, spooked by the tunnel darkness, became convinced we were travelling to our deaths. They wanted to head back to Baghdad. Uncouple Spektr at the first opportunity.

One of the men seized my lapels and screamed in my face. Called me a madman. I pushed him away and drew my side arm. I was sick with fear. For the first time in my life, I would have to kill a man face to face. Look him in the eye as I extinguished his life.

There was a gunshot. Muzzle-flare, like a camera flash. The man fell dead, shot through the heart.

Captain Hassim, my second in command, holstered his smoking pistol.

Blood trickled between wagon planks. We edged away from the body.

After a while, amplified engine noise felt like someone

drilling into my head. I tore some paper and plugged my ears.

We emerged from the tunnel and saw the citadel for the first time. I'm not an imaginative man. I'm not prone to fancies. But the jagged ramparts of this dead city made my skin crawl. It felt like someone was watching our approach. A sardonic, mocking intelligence old as humanity itself.

I radioed the driver. I told him not to stop until we reached the mine.

The train slowly crossed the valley floor. We stood in silence and contemplated the ancient citadel as it passed by.

The valley narrowed, and we found ourselves travelling slowly down a high ravine. Walls so tight and sheer the floor of the canyon would receive a few minutes of sunlight each day then lapse into twilight.

I looked up. A narrow strip of evening stars overhead.

The locomotive slowed to a stop. The engine cut off. Sudden silence.

'This is it,' radioed the driver. 'This is the mine.'

I jumped from the wagon and walked alongside the track.

At first it seemed we had a reached a dead end. The tight ravine terminated in a sheer cliff wall. But when I reached the front of the locomotive I saw a wide tunnel mouth arched by a concrete buttress. No mine buildings, no machinery. Just a tunnel bored in bedrock.

The railroad forked at the tunnel entrance. Multiple lengths of track headed into shadow.

I told the men to remain on board the train. I took a torch and explored the mine tunnel.

My flashlight beam played over ore wagons, box cars and carriages gathering dust. Abandoned rolling stock.

I followed the tracks into darkness.

The tunnel was two hundred yards long. It opened into a wide cavern. Archways led into darkness.

An object like a thick tree-trunk draped in heavy canvas

lay on the cavern floor. I dragged the tarpaulin aside. A Scud-B missile. The service panels had been removed. It had been gutted for parts. The guidance system was gone. The fuel tanks and turbopumps were crusted with leaked oxidiser and kerosene.

I wasn't remotely surprised to discover a neglected weapon. Iraq was a militarised state. Everything had a dual purpose. Every aspect of life, on some level, served Saddam's imperial ambition. Universities churned out intelligence officers. Car plants serviced tanks and milled bombs. I already knew that the mining industry had been structured to manufacture chemical weapons. The discovery that the rail network had been used to hide missile batteries in crude silos during Desert Storm was entirely unremarkable.

I gave orders. Check the Scud. Make sure the tanks were dry. Detach the warhead. Remove the impact and proximity fuses. Drag the payload out of the cavern. Roll the body of the missile aside.

I radioed the convoy. I asked for a situation report. They had lost two vehicles during their journey across the desert. A couple of APCs sank into the sand. They had been stripped of equipment and abandoned. The remaining vehicles were approaching the valley entrance.

I walked from the mine tunnel, along the length of the high ravine to the valley. Night had fallen. I flagged my flashlight back and forth as the convoy approached, kicking up a moonlit dust cloud.

The trucks and jeeps came to a halt. I suggested we camp in the citadel ruins. The men refused. Monumental walls, towers and ramparts lit by cold starlight. They declared they would rather die than go near the place. I was secretly relieved. The ruins filled me with an unaccountable dread.

I ordered the men to make camp. They unloaded equipment on a stretch of open ground. They covered their tents and vehicles in camouflage nets.

I returned to the mine tunnel. Four of my men had released lock bolts and removed the Scud nose cone. They improvised a sling from a couple of field jackets. They carried the warhead from the cavern and dumped it in a freight wagon.

The locomotive rumbled to life. It slowly advanced. The Spektr tail fin scraped the tunnel arch, bringing down a shower of rock chips and stone dust.

The driver made use of double track and points to uncouple the locomotive, back up, and shunt Spektr into the cavern.

I had the men set up battery lights against the cavern walls. The orbiter sat at the centre of the wide chamber, ringed by light.

I had the men bring tools. I was anxious to open the scorched space vehicle and find what lay inside.

My first task was to conduct a visual survey of the craft. I climbed a step ladder and examined the tail section. The rudder was broken. The main engine cones were crushed. There was a big gash in the hull. Quartz-fibre heat-tiles ripped away, steel skin peeled back revealing the engine bay and combustion chambers. I powered up a video camera and leant into the compartment. Zoom and pan. Orbital manoeuvre exhausts. Pipe work and clusters of spherical fuel tanks. Plenty of sand. Plenty of heat damage.

I told the men to carefully drill the tanks and purge any liquid propellant that might remain. The craft appeared to be in the same state as the Scud. Broken and depleted. Any volatile rocket fuel, liquid hydrogen or nitrogen-tetroxide, long since leeched away. But I didn't want to risk an explosion if we had to cut our way inside with oxyacetylene gear.

I knew there would likely be pyrotechnic charges bedded in the frame of the side hatch to enable an occupant to blow the door, but they were not accessible from outside and couldn't be disarmed.

I propped the ladder against the craft and climbed onto the hull. I walked from tail to cockpit.

I crouched and ran my hands over the heat tiles, tried to find a seam which might indicate some kind of payload bay, but it was sealed tight.

I climbed from the vehicle and filmed the belly of the craft. I filmed the keel in close-up. The ablative tiles that covered the keel like fish scales had been cooked by unimaginable heat. They had melted to a strange, petroleum sheen.

The nose of the orbiter hung over the edge of the wagon. I filmed the hydraulic stump of the nose gear.

Space debris often falls in this part of the world. Most Russian capsules re-enter the Earth's atmosphere over Egypt, passing over Iraq following a controlled trajectory that will allow them to touch down in the steppes of Kazakhstan. Radar records indicated Spektr followed a steep, ballistic trajectory. It suggested the craft was guided by an automated system struggling to control a vehicle in free-fall. Air-brakes unfolded and were instantly torn away. Ailerons extended to increase drag and shrivelled in fierce re-entry heat. As the craft blazed through the mesosphere any astronaut aboard would have been subjected to lethal G-force. If they were alive when Spektr left orbit, they were certainly dead by the time the vehicle broke the cloud-deck.

Spektr slowed two kilometres from impact. Maybe a drag chute had been released. Maybe braking rockets fired in the nose to decelerate the craft. The undercarriage deployed as part of a pre-programmed landing sequence. Then the super-hot vehicle ploughed into the desert and buried itself in the sand.

A lost Russian spacecraft. It should have been headline news. It should have mobilised armies.

And there was the orbiter itself. The very fact of its existence. The Russians built a couple of shuttle prototypes but didn't fly a single manned mission. The creation of the Spektr vehicle suggested a shadow space programme of astonishing ambition and sophistication had successfully eluded Western intelligence agencies.

I examined the crew access hatch. It was in the starboard side of the craft behind the cockpit. No obvious door release. Smooth heat tiles. No handle.

The hatch was circular. It was surrounded by a metal ridge. The metal had melted during the heat of re-entry and smeared in rivulets like candle wax. Some kind of docking collar. An umbilicus rim and capture latches. Spektr had not been alone in space. It had been tethered to a companion vehicle or high-orbit installation.

More questions than answers. I was anxious to open the hatch and explore the interior of the craft, but I received terse radio instructions that Spektr was to remain sealed until Koell himself was present. I was told to post sentries, make sure none of my men approached the vehicle.

Koell gave me desert coordinates. He ordered me to meet his plane.

The designated landing site was twenty miles from the valley entrance. A stretch of waste ground firm enough to be used as a crude airstrip.

My driver was asleep in a Jeep. I shook him awake.

We rode through the rail tunnel and into the desert. We parked in the middle of vast nothing. We created an improvised landing strip: drove flag-stakes into the ground and kicked aside rocks.

We waited. Dawn was breaking. I scanned the horizon with binoculars.

I was anxious to see the plane. If it was an Iraqi military flight, one of Saddam's ageing Ilyushins, then it had probably flown from Baghdad and I might still, at some level, be answerable to Saddam's command apparatus. If the plane was a modern, Western aircraft, then it would likely have originated from one of the Persian Gulf Emirates, south-west of Dubai. Clandestine hubs favoured by NSA and CIA black ops. Proof I had ceased to work for the Iraqi government and had a new paymaster, an intelligence entity that regarded this regional war as a trivial distraction from the pursuit of its own dark purpose.

It came from the east. The plane flew low. A dot that slowly resolved into the bulky silhouette of a turboprop freighter. A Fairchild Provider. Silver, with Red Cross markings. A CIA work-horse. The type of cargo-lift that flew resupply missions and defoliation runs in Vietnam.

The plane circled and swooped to land.

I crouched behind the Jeep alongside my driver and covered my ears. The back-wash of the plane threw out tornadoes of sand and grit.

Engine noise diminished to a drone. I stood and shook sand from my hair, slapped dust from my clothes. The plane taxied and came to a standstill.

A whine of hydraulics as the loading ramp descended, folded down like a castle drawbridge. Aircrew got out and checked tyres.

Two Land Rovers rolled out of the ribbed cargo bay. Brand new, fully equipped, sprayed desert drab.

The Land Rovers drew up to our Jeep. A man got out. I felt a cool wash of air-conditioning as he opened the door. He wore expensive hiking gear. I didn't recognise brand names but his boots and sunglasses were fresh out of the box.

He shook my hand.

'Koell.'

'Jabril.'

Cheerful, but distant. The kind of man that would maintain a pleasant smile as he drove a knife into your belly.

'Care to lead the way?'

We climbed in our Jeep and retraced our tyre tracks back towards the ravine.

I turned in my seat. Koell's Land Rover behind us. He smiled. He waved. His driver chewed gum and blanked us with wraparound shades.

Our little convoy kicked up a dust storm as it lurched across the dunes.

We drove into the rail tunnel. Engine roar amplified by tight tunnel walls. Bright lights behind us. Halogens mounted on the Land Rover grille, trained on our backs like searchlights.

We emerged into the valley. We shielded our eyes from sudden sun. We drove past the citadel and parked in front of our camp.

Koell and his men climbed from their Land Rovers. His team lit cigarettes. They talked among themselves. They spoke Russian.

'Who are these men?' I asked. 'I assumed you would bring Americans.'

He grinned.

'The nation-state is a rather antique concept, don't you think? These days we outsource our killing.'

Koell paid no attention to the extraordinary ruins on the other side of the valley floor.

'Show me Spektr.'

I led him through the narrow ravine. We walked beside the railroad. He didn't talk. He didn't look around. He strode towards the mine tunnel with unwavering focus.

We entered the mine. We walked the length of the wide passageway, past carriages and wagons, until we reached the cavern.

'Good God.'

Koell walked a full circuit of the Spektr craft. He was enraptured. He reached up and stroked heat tiles.

'*Pilotitruemyy Korabl-Perekhvatchik*,' he murmured.

'What does that mean?' I asked.

'The Manned Interceptor Spacecraft. A crude space fighter. The US had similar plans during the eighties, but they didn't progress further than a few balsa models.

'Spektr was just a rumour. A daydream. Brain-child of a

few old Soviet hard-liners who want to recapture the glory days of the Sputnik era and restore national pride. Nobody believed the Spektr project progressed further than a blueprint. Certainly never flew. But here she is.'

Koell unzipped his backpack and handed me a file. A heavy document bundle with a classified stamp on the cover. A grave miscalculation on his part. It didn't matter that I could speak three languages. He looked at a man like me, a bearded Iraqi in ill-fitting fatigues, and saw an ignorant camel-jockey. But I had worked for intelligence agencies my entire life. I knew, the moment he handed me confidential material, that I and my men would be killed once Koell no longer had a use for us. His thugs were outnumbered but they were hardened killers and I suspected they would prevail in a fire-fight.

I would be ready to flee at a moment's notice.

I spread my jacket, sat cross-legged on the cavern floor and thumbed through the dossier. Koell stood over me.

'What's this?'

A blurred monochrome shot. A gargantuan cylindrical object, like a grain silo, on a shrouded rail car.

'A Proton-K launcher outside the Baikonur cosmodrome in Kazakhstan. Back in the nineties, during the construction phase of the Mir space station, Western intelligence agencies monitored a parallel series of rocket launches conducted in great secrecy. Every single member of staff at the cosmodrome, from the most highly skilled technician to the lowliest railroad worker, would quit their post during these launch cycles and be replaced by a shadow team trained elsewhere. Each flight involved heavily encrypted telemetry traffic between the launch vehicle and mission control, Karlingrad. See that Proton booster? The bulge at the top? That's not a standard design for a Soyuz launch vehicle. There is something else inside, something unusual. Maybe Spektr. Perhaps, as the final stage of the Proton blasted free of the atmosphere, fairings were jettisoned and the orbiter drifted free. Fired into high orbit and completed its ascent.'

The next picture showed a ragged structure floating in deep darkness. Twisted antennae. Torn thermal blankets. Buckled solar panels like ripped sails.

'What's this?'

'Nobody knows. Some kind of deep-space installation parked in a graveyard orbit. The habitation modules are reminiscent of Mir, but the overall configuration is different. A big docking node. Substantial solar array.

'The installation was detected by NORAD a couple of years back. They were tracking space debris. They picked up something big, tumbling in high orbit. Mass of about three hundred tons. No attitude control, no active guidance, but it seems to retain some residual power. The station transmits a weird radio signal. A strange ticking sound, night and day. It never stops.'

'It's a wreck.'

'It's totally trashed. There seems to have been some kind of catastrophic event. Explosive decompression. A fire. A meteor strike. Who knows? The station is in free drift, about forty-thousand kilometres out. The habitation modules are little more than a loose aggregate of wreckage, surrounded by a debris field miles wide. Chunks of wreckage re-enter the atmosphere now and again. Most burn up. Some fall in the sea. Some hit land.

'I'm guessing Spektr was a supply vehicle. It's one of the few components to make it back to Earth intact. It must have been floating up there for years, drifting in a gradually decaying orbit. It re-entered the atmosphere. The gravity shift must have tripped some kind of inertial control in the cockpit. Tweaked some gyros. A bunch of automated guidance systems booted up. They triggered a retro-burn and tried to engineer a controlled descent.'

'But what was it for? This space station. Why was it built?'

'No one knows. Soviet military. Black ops. That much is obvious. Denied and disowned by subsequent Russian governments. I get the impression the construction of this installation was so secret, so compartmentalised, even the current Russian high command don't know fully understand why it was built. Some kind of microgravity lab, at a guess. Or maybe some kind of weapons platform. All the pieces that have fallen to Earth so far have shown traces of a strange pathogen, some kind of parasite.'

'Is that what this is about? You're chasing some kind of bio-weapon? You want to harvest the virus?'

Koell reached up and placed a hand on the airlock hatch.

'I suspect this spacecraft returned from space carrying a microscopic occupant,' he said. 'It's dormant but alive. And it's anxious to make our acquaintance.'

Resurrection

The temple entrance. Lucy knelt by the quad bike and watched the sky.

Stars winked out. Darkness spread from the east. The moon eclipsed by scudding cloud.

'What can you see?' asked Lucy.

Amanda surveyed the temple ruins through the SIMRAD scope. A rising wind blew dust across avenues and colonnades like drifting smoke.

'Visibility is dropping by the minute. Big-ass sandstorm heading our way. We better sit tight for the next couple of hours. It's going to get nasty.'

'Probably blow over by dawn,' said Lucy.

'We should be back in Baghdad right now,' said Voss. 'We should be popping champagne. '

'Yeah. Well. It went bad. Shit happens.'

'We have Jabril's virus. Some kind of doomsday weapon. Imagine how much that would fetch on the open market. Tens, hundreds of millions.'

'If we offered that shit to the Agency all we would get is a bullet in the base of the skull. They don't like loose ends.'

'I'm going after Gaunt,' said Amanda. 'The dumb fuck is out there somewhere. No food, no water. He's crouched behind a wall right now, pissing his pants. I'm going to bring him in. If he can't get the chopper in the air, we blow his fucking brains out.'

'He might have left the valley,' said Voss. 'He might be walking home.'

'I strung a wire between the guard towers this afternoon. Rigged a trip-flare. It hasn't popped. He's probably still here.'

Amanda checked her rifle chamber. She checked the magazine. She tied her hair in a ponytail and pulled sand goggles over her head.

'Wear this.' Voss handed her Toon's blue do-rag. She tied it over her face and mouth. She put on her Stetson and pulled the brim low.

Lucy gave her Raphael's machete. She tucked it in her belt.

'Sure you don't want me to come along?' asked Lucy.

'I've got night-vision. You haven't.'

Brief embrace.

'See you later, babe.'

Amanda headed into darkness.

Lucy buttoned her prairie coat to the neck and turned up the collar. She tied a shemagh scarf round her face.

'Where are you going?' asked Voss.

'The choppers. They each had an emergency radio. A UHF beacon. Probably fucked but I have to know for sure.'

'Be okay on your own?'

'Sit tight. Someone has to stay with Jabril. Easy on the trigger, okay? Don't shoot us coming back in.'

'Catch you later, boss.'

Gaunt stood at the foot of the crypt stairwell. He looked up. Furls of sand blown like squalling rain.

They used to call him Cherry Boy. No combat experience. The squad under his command treated him with contempt.

Sitting on the double bench seats of an oven-hot APC, jolting through the streets of Fallujah. Gaunt reiterated the mission.

'Ali Hassan. Possible links with Iranian intelligence. Wife. Five daughters. Standard knock and announce. We do not expect resistance.'

Private Larsen, blond, ex-quarterback, leaned forward and grabbed Gaunt by the neck of his ballistic vest.

'You just hang back and let us do our thing, all right, Lieutenant? You fuck up, you get any of us killed, I will personally frag your fucking ass, understand?'

A humiliating memory.

Gaunt twisted the West Point cadet ring round his finger.

Koell offered him meaning. The man was little more than a distorted, metallic sat-com voice, but he held the promise of world-shaping intrigue. He could lead Gaunt through the looking-glass into a clandestine realm.

It wasn't about the money.

Gaunt wanted to be a player. He needed to earn Koell's trust. Get on the Agency payroll. Maybe get hired for real. Be part of the fraternity. Two years at The Farm. Camp Peary, Virginia. Teach him how to run agents and handle covert communication. Teach him how to organise rolling surveillance, sabotage operations and targeted killings. He would finally belong.

He had to prove his worth. He had to find the virus.

He kissed the silver crucifix hung round his neck. He pulled on sand goggles.

He climbed from the crypt. Cold night wind. Swirling sand pricked his skin like needles. He switched on his Maglite. He narrowed the beam and trained it at the ground. He didn't want to betray his location.

He looked around. The moonlit ruins were fogged with broiling dust plumes. Citadel buildings were monstrous shadows glimpsed through a veil of driving sand.

He headed for the choppers. Maybe there was equipment he could salvage. Ammunition. Water.

He walked headlong into a blizzard of sand. His flashlight illuminated swirling particles. He cupped a hand over his mouth and nose.

The central courtyard. The wrecked helicopters.

His feet gummed down in a viscous substance like treacle. He crouched and sniffed. Kerosene mixed with sand.

The ghost shape of *Talon.* The smashed hulk of the chopper, lying on its side.

He checked the cargo compartment. He checked bags and wall-nets. Nothing. No water, no ammunition. The Huey had been stripped.

He checked the pilot cabin. His flashlight caught Raphael in its beam, hanging upside down like a carcass on an abattoir hook. Throat slit. Bled white.

He checked Raphael's pockets. The man was cold and stiff. His pockets had already been emptied. Nothing, not even cigars.

A scratching sound. Gaunt pulled the silenced Sig from behind his ballistic vest and turned round. One of Jabril's lost battalion stumbling across flagstones, dragging its feet through thick diesel slurry.

Gaunt aimed and fired. He blew out the creature's left eye. It slumped dead.

Three bullets left in the pistol.

He checked *Bad Moon.* Nothing of use in the cargo compartment.

He pulled open the cab door. He brushed windshield glass from the pilot seat and climbed inside. He flicked a couple of power switches. He flinched as the wrecked console popped and sparked. He shone his flashlight over the instrumentation panel. Trashed avionics. Frayed wires. Split circuit boards.

'Fuck.'

A dim light approaching across the courtyard. The cone of a torch beam glimpsed through swirling sand.

Gaunt quickly switched off his Maglite, slid from the pilot seat and ran from the chopper.

Amanda crept through the temple ruins. She kept her rifle raised, cheek pressed to the synthetic stock. Luminescent rubble. Swirling sand transformed to evil green mist.

A courtyard of statues. Loathsome mongrel creatures on

pedestals. Limbs and faces scoured to wind-worn stumps. Sinister deformities. Aborted, misshapen things. A pantheon of terrible gods arranged in a ring to observe whatever abominable rites had been conducted in their name.

Amanda walked through the forest of plinths and idols, sweeping her rifle left and right.

'This is my rifle,' she murmured. 'There are many like it, but this one is mine . . .'

Skull face. Black eyes. A walking cadaver. A skeletal soldier creeping between the broken statues like a giant arachnid.

Amanda backed away. She kept her rifle raised. The creature boosted ethereal green by the nightscope. A man locked halfway between life and death. Ragged uniform. Dog tags hung over a desiccated ribcage. Parchment skin stretched taut over bone. Flesh broken by metallic, cancerous knots.

The creature snarled and reached for her.

Yellow canine teeth.

She lowered her rifle. She pulled Raphael's machete from her belt. She swung, slammed the blade down, and split the creature's head in two. It fell twitching.

Amanda placed a foot on the soldier's chest. She jerked the machete free and wiped it clean on her trousers.

Boot prints on the sand-dusted flagstones. Chevron tread marks quickly blurring in the wind. Precise foot-falls. Not the drag and scuff of infected soldiers.

Gaunt.

She followed the boot prints, nightscope trained on ground. She crossed courtyards and colonnades.

The trail of fast-fading prints led her to the rear of the temple.

The crypt entrance. A slab pulled aside. Steps heading downwards into darkness.

She slung her rifle. She pulled one of the chopper signal flares from her pocket and struck the cap. It spat sparks, then fizzed crimson fire. She drew her pistol. She advanced down the ancient stone steps into deep shadow.

Gaunt crouched behind a broken pillar. He watched Lucy search the choppers. Sand swirled like smoke. He could see the dancing beam of her barrel-light, the silhouette of her prairie coat.

She examined each cab. Gaunt figured she was checking the chopper radios. Each bird had been equipped with UHF and VHF. Too deep in the desert to raise a signal.

He watched Lucy kneel and examine the emaciated body that lay beside *Talon*. She rolled the cadaver with her boot and examined the fresh head wound.

He saw her hand rise to the transmit button on her chest rig.

'*Gaunt? Gaunt, you out here?*' Lucy's voice over the radio. '*Can you hear me?*'

Gaunt turned his back on her, huddled to keep out of earshot.

'Yes, I can hear you.'

'*It's been a long, cold night. Better enjoy it while it lasts. Twelve hours' time the sun will be overhead and the desert will be a furnace.*'

'Yeah.'

'*So how about we fix up one these Hueys and get the fuck out of Dodge?*'

'Your friends will blow my brains out. I can't trust them.'

'*They'll keep their word.*'

'Voss? Your girlfriend? They won't let me live. They'll put a bullet in my head, whatever the cost.'

'*They'll do what I say.*'

'Wish I could believe you.'

'*I swear, if you fly us home, you get to walk away. We'll give you a full twenty-four hours to run. You could cover a lot of ground in a day. Get on a plane, put yourself halfway round the world.*'

'I'll let you into a secret, Lucy. The choppers are fucked. Both of them. They'll never fly again.'

Gaunt unhooked his earpiece. He raised his silenced pistol, held it steady with both hands. Lucy's silhouette obscured by a curtain of driving sand. He waited for a clear shot.

Lucy crouched in front of the wrecked chopper and scanned the courtyard around her. Nothing but gusting sand. Particles blurred in the beam of her barrel light like monsoon rain.

A figure in deep shadow. She raised the rifle to her shoulder.

'Gaunt? Hands above your fucking head.'

Nothing. Just the swirling sandstorm.

She hurried down the processional avenue back towards the temple.

She paused. Plenty of equipment piled beside the choppers. Tools. Arab phrase books. Salt tablets. Life rafts and dye markers in case the helos came down in water. Lucy didn't want to leave anything that might be of use to Gaunt.

She dropped the magazine from her rifle and slapped a fresh clip into the receiver. Armour piercing rounds replaced with red-tip tracer.

She raised her rifle. A momentary lull in the sandstorm. The twin hulks of the helicopters lit by weak moonlight.

A single shot aimed at *Talon*. The bullet streaked like a laser and punched through the aluminium fuselage in a burst of sparks.

Ignition. A wash of blue flame. Fire rippled across the fuel-soaked courtyard. The wrecked chopper quickly became a blazing pyre. Raphael was cooked, still strapped in the pilot seat. The ruptured fuel tank jetted fire like a plume of dragon's breath.

Flames reached *Bad Moon* and it too started to burn.

One week earlier. Koell's hotel suite.

Gaunt drained his whisky tumbler, held it out for fresh ice and a refill.

'I had a long and constructive chat with Doctor Ignatiev,' said Koell. 'He ran the Spektr project. I was the bagman, provided finance and logistic support. But Doctor Ignatiev and his crew were onsite calling the shots.

'Bio-Medical Unit 403. Ex-Vektor. Ex-Biopreperat. Fifteenth Directorate of the Soviet Army. They were based in an asylum. A mansion by the Moskva. Used to be owned by the Smirnoff vodka family. Got seized and turned into a sanatorium during the revolution.

'Ignatiev and his men had a basement lab during the eighties. Military project. The psycho-pharmacology of violence. They researched hypnosis, shock treatment, psycho-surgery, any means of exerting behavioural control. They'd get mental patients, dribblers, real headbangers. People sectioned for impulsive aggression. They would get them amped on speed and psychotropic drugs. Shoot them full of Phenobarbital then put them in a room together. Set cameras running while they tore each other apart. They were trying to create super-soldiers. Killing machines.

'We scooped Ignatiev and his boys from Moscow, years back. Now they work for us.

'Ignatiev oversaw the construction of the Spektr research laboratory. He used the phosphate mine tunnels. A logical choice. Safe from surveillance. Safe from sandstorms and extreme temperature fluctuation. That is where the virus flask is likely to be found. If it cannot be located at the citadel, if it isn't hidden in the crypt, you will find it in the lab.'

Gaunt shouldered his backpack. He picked his way through the citadel ruins. Courtyards and pillared avenues lit infernal red by the burning choppers.

A rising wind. Moonlight and flickering flame dimmed by swirling vortices of sand.

He drew his pistol. He checked darkened doorways. Nothing.

No sign of Lucy.

Gaunt hurried towards the guard towers that flanked the citadel entrance.

He reached the monumental propylaea gateway.

He paused as he passed between the two great towers.

He knelt. He brushed the ground with the loop-string of his compass. The string snagged an obstruction.

He crouched on his hands and knees. He switched on his Maglite. A strand of monofilament, thinner than a human hair. He traced the wisp of thread to a rock pile at the base of a guard tower. He gently lifted fist-sized lumps of rubble aside. Filament tied to the pin of a trip-flare.

Gaunt flicked open his knife and cut the wire.

He checked his map. He checked his compass. He aimed to strike north across the valley floor to the abandoned mine.

'*Watch your back. Those mine tunnels are likely to be crawling with infected soldiers. Could be hundreds of them down there.*'

A last glance at the citadel ruins. Domes and arches. Broken walls and toppled pillars. The ancient necropolis lit by rippling flame-light.

He headed out into the valley and was lost in swirling sand.

Voss lit a cigar. He blew a smoke ring. He could see the fuel fire from the temple entrance. The chopper airframes cooking in kerosene. A baleful red glow in the distance, a crimson smudge glimpsed through the sandstorm haze.

An approaching silhouette. He stepped back and raised his shotgun.

Muffled voice:

'It's me.'

Lucy climbed over the quad bike. She took off her goggles. She pulled the shemagh from her face. She shook sand from her coat.

She sipped from her canteen, swilled and spat.

'Mandy?'

'Still out there,' said Voss. 'She'll be all right. What's the deal with the choppers?'

'I burned them. Didn't want to leave anything Gaunt might find useful. The fuel tanks should blow any second. Thousand pounds of aviation fuel. Should be quite a bang.'

'Guess that's the last we'll hear from the guy.'

'He'll die out there among the ruins. Get ripped apart. Or go mad with thirst. Eat a bullet, if he has any sense. Fuck him.'

'When do you want to move out?

'Get your shit together. Anything you can carry on your back. We'll take turns riding the quad until it runs out of gas.'

'Want to wait for sunrise?'

'No. Soon as the wind starts to ease up, we should get going.'

Lucy tried her radio.

'Mandy, do you copy?'

No response.

'Atmospherics,' said Voss. 'The sandstorm. She'll be back soon.'

Lucy sat by the fire. She ripped Toon's Eldridge Cleaver paperback in half and threw it into the flames. She warmed her hands as paper curled and blackened.

'How about it, Jabril? Looks like we are walking home. Want to tag along?'

'No. The journey is hell.'

'You're sure? You want us to leave you behind?'

'Endless dunes. Nightmare heat. It drove me near insane. Wild hallucinations. I ate sand. I clawed my eyes. I screamed at God. I couldn't endure that torment a second time. I would rather die.'

'But you made it. You survived.'

'No. I died out there in that desert. It broke me.'

A sharp flash of light outside the temple, like a lightning strike. The darkness beyond the doorway lit by a wash of liquid fireball light.

A deep boom. A tremor ran through the temple floor. Campfire wood crumbled to ash, releasing a last puff of flame. Embers spiralled upward like fireflies.

'There go the choppers,' said Voss.

Amanda crouched beneath low vaulted archways. The flare in her hand fizzed and spat red fire. It filled the catacombs with a fine smoke haze and the stink of cordite.

She was deep within the crypt.

She found herself picking her way through a carpet of emaciated bodies.

Republican Guard. Olive uniforms shredded and burned by heavily calibre rounds. They'd been dead a long while. Fractured bones protruded from taut skin. No flies or maggots to consume their flesh. They had dried like jerky.

Broken bodies. Twisted, skeletal limbs. Rictus screams. Death-camp horror.

A tremor ran through the ancient edifice. A deep rumble. The vaulted ceiling shook. She heard the crack and grind of shifting stones. Trickles of dust from the brickwork above her head.

Amanda hit the transmit button on her chest rig.

'Lucy? What the fuck was that?'

No response.

'Lucy, can you hear me?'

Dead channel static. The signal from her TASC unit too weak to penetrate thick granite.

She unhooked the earpiece.

She continued her exploration of the vaulted catacombs. She ducked low. She raised the burning flare and squinted into deep shadow.

Clay pots jumbled with bone and funerary offerings.

Row upon row of squat pillars receding into gloom.

She examined the gargantuan cylindrical blocks that propped the roof. A sinister cosmology. Constellations and planetary movements. Celestial calendars plotting every equinox and eclipse.

Hieroglyphs etched into stonework. Serpentine, hybrid creatures. Phantasmagoric ranks of sculpted monsters that had stared into the subterranean dark, faces locked in a blank-eyed snarl, since the dawn of humanity.

Amanda reached out and touched granite cobra fangs. She shivered.

'Gaunt?' she shouted. Her voice echoed harsh, metallic. 'Gaunt, you down here?'

She listened for movement. At first she could hear nothing but the hiss of the burning flare, and the constant whine of battle tinnitus.

She became aware of a rasping, scratching sound. Something dragging itself over the granite slabs of the crypt floor.

A grinning abomination crawled out of the darkness. A wizened, mummified soldier, hauling useless legs.

It reached for her, tongue lolling like a strip of dried leather.

Amanda delivered a vicious kick that tore the creature's head from its shoulders and sent it bouncing into shadows like a football.

A hand gripped her ankle. She jerked her leg free and turned round. A second leering revenant. Amanda backed away. She drew her Glock and took aim.

Slow-seething movement on every side. Desiccated, crippled soldiers, dozens of them. Awful, mewing spastic things. Jabril's lost battalion, returning to life, crawling out of the dark.

Konstantin

Lucy sat by the campfire.

She sipped water. She held her canteen to Jabril's lips.

'All right,' she said. 'Finish your story. That spacecraft. Spektr. What did you find inside?'

Koell flew back to Baghdad. His final orders:

'Doctor Ignatiev has absolute authority. You are to follow his instructions without question.'

Ignatiev's men erected a bio-containment structure deep within the mine. A well-rehearsed procedure.

They carried equipment to the cavern. They set up lights and erected an aluminium scaffold over Spektr. They unrolled sheets of opaque polythene and pinned them in place. They glued seams with epoxy guns and sealed them with tape.

A geodesic dome.

They entered the tented enclosure dressed in white protective suits and gas masks. We watched them work. Ghost shapes behind plastic. They each had tanks of Clorox bleach strapped to their backs. They sprayed the interior of the bio-containment area. They drenched every surface, soaked the scaffold, the walls, the polythene floor. Then they soaked Spektr. We watched the blurred outline of the craft change colour. Dust washed away to expose white and black heat tiles.

They fired up a generator. We covered our mouths as bleach-mist was sucked from the containment dome by extractor fans and vented down the tunnel.

'You must pick a man,' said Ignatiev. 'Someone you trust.'

'Why?' I asked.

'Because you are going in. I want you to open Spektr.'

I summoned Captain Hassim. Hassim was a pleasant young soldier. We worked together in Baghdad. I sponsored his rise through the intelligence hierarchy. He supervised beatings at Abu Ghraib.

We were led to the cavern. We entered a polythene staging room next to the dome.

'Take off your clothes.'

We stripped. We stood naked in ultraviolet light to kill bacteria.

Ignatiev watched through the plastic sheet.

We stepped into white underwear ripped from sterile bags and zipped ourselves into green Tyvek suits. We pulled on rubber boots and taped the ankle seals. We wore two layers of blue Nitrile gloves beneath heavy rubber gauntlets. We taped the gauntlets at the wrist. I taped my empty sleeve round the stump of my arm.

Ignatiev had a radio. We each wore an earpiece and microphone.

'*Can you hear me?*' he asked. We gave a thumbs up.

We pulled on hoods. Each hood had a Lexan face-plate and an air hose at the back. We had electric filtration units clipped to our belts. Air pumped through charcoal filters. My headpiece was filled with the hiss of supply fans, and my own heavy breathing.

'*Open the box.*'

I popped latches. A video camera.

'*I want you to film the interior of the craft. You will be my eyes and ears.*'

Intelligence agencies always operate through proxies. They call it Resource Exploitation. Human chess. I have ordered the arrest and torture of countless men. Sat in my office and consigned prisoners to death as I sipped coffee. I never met my victims face-to-face. Never had to hear their screams, their pathetic pleas for mercy. They were numbers. Bruised and bleeding mug shots. I didn't sign execution orders. I took great care to commit nothing to paper. I gave files to my adjutant and requested 'stern measures'. Call it plausible deniability. Call it emotional distance, a coward taking refuge in euphemism.

Men like Ignatiev rarely get their hands dirty.

We walked from the staging area, down a sterile polythene umbilicus to the Spektr containment area. Our hazmat suits creaked and rustled.

We unzipped a plastic curtain and entered the dome.

My ears popped. Extractor fans kept the containment dome at negative pressure to prevent the back-flow of contaminated air. A sprinkler scaffold high above our heads fogged the atmosphere with a constant hydrogen peroxide mist. Lights glowed through opaque plastic sheets like weak sunlight.

The orbiter looked like a US space shuttle in miniature. Porcelain white. Black ablative bricks coated the nose, belly and aerofoil to help the fuselage withstand the white heat of re-entry.

We walked a circuit of the ship.

I reached up and stroked the pitted, seared hull of the craft. It was astonishing to think that the vehicle before me had voyaged beyond the earth. It had been exposed to the vacuum of space. The silicon dioxide tiles had been cratered by micro-meteoroids. They had been subject to absolute cold and the merciless gamma-blast of unfiltered solar radiation.

I was consumed by curiosity, desperate to climb inside the vessel and investigate. I wanted to know where it had been, what disaster had befallen the crew while in orbit.

We propped scaffold steps against the vehicle and climbed level with the hatch. We scanned the hull with a Geiger counter. Spektr had been floating in high orbit for more than a decade, baking in stellar radiation. The handset crackled triple background.

'There's a warning stencilled on the hatch tiles.'

'*English?*' asked Ignatiev.

'Yes. And Cyrillic.'

'*In case Spektr crashed outside Russian territory, I suppose.*'

ATTENTION
STEP ASIDE
THIS COVER MAY BE JETTISONED
PEOPLE INSIDE
HELP

'*There should be a small panel to the side of the hatch,*' said Ignatiev, over the radio. '*Can you see it? It looks like a heat tile, but it is held in place by screws.*'

'I've got it.'

'*Use the hex drill.*'

Hassim passed me a power drill. I unscrewed the titanium bolts and prised the tile free with the sliver-blade of a scalpel.

'*Describe what you see.*'

'Four sockets. A couple of nozzles. A couple of jacks.'

'*The port on the top left should let us test the internal atmosphere.*'

We took a gas spectrometer from a high-impact case. We plugged it into the hatch panel. We took a reading.

I tore off a strip of print-out.

'*Read it to me.*'

I recited numbers.

'*Lot of nitrogen. Lot of carbon dioxide. The air inside the ship is toxic but the seals are intact.*'

'How do we open the hatch?'

'*The access mechanism is identical to Progress capsules used to ferry astronauts to the International Space Station. Those jack plugs are for the benefit of the recovery crew. If, for any reason, the cosmonauts are incapacitated and unable to exit the craft, the rescue team can deliver a simple electrical pulse and trip the explosive bolts.'*

We piled sandbags against the hatch. We didn't want the heavy steel door to fly across the containment area and puncture the fabric of the bio-dome.

'*Are you ready?*' asked Ignatiev

Wire snaked from the sandbagged hatch, down the scaffold steps and across the polythene floor.

We crouched. I counted to three and touched frayed wires to the terminals of a twelve-volt battery. Sudden flame-flash and a shotgun roar. The sandbags absorbed the blast. The scorched hatch hung crooked.

I climbed the steps.

We dragged the hatch aside and lay it on the floor.

I held up the video camera and began to film.

A white-walled airlock, little bigger than a phone booth. The inner hatch was sealed. There was a pile of fabric on the floor. A space suit.

'*Switch on the camera. I want to see it all.*'

A big helmet with a gold visor. A big, quilted backpack. A heavy pressure suit in white canvas. The suit was in two sections. It seemed to seal at the waist. There were gauntlets with big lock-rings.

'*Must be an EVA suit. That confirms Spektr has an occupant. There are a stack of hermetic storage boxes in the containment area with you. Pack the suit and seal it up.*'

We packed the suit in a plastic trunk. We sealed the trunk with biohazard tape.

'*All right. Return to the airlock. My schematic says there is a mesh service plate in the floor.*'

'I see it.'

'*Grip the ring-latch. The plate should lift out.*'

'There's a socket inside. A five-pin, high-voltage connector.'

'*Spektr had a bank of chemical batteries but they will be long dead. If we run electricity from an external power source, we can get the ship's systems back online.*'

We unpacked a four-stroke generator and set the motor running. We ran cable up the scaffold steps to the airlock. I twisted the connector into the floor socket and there was an immediate power-up hum. Lights flickered and lit the airlock interior brilliant white.

'I've got a green panel light.'

'*The inner hatch is active. Open her up. Let's look inside.*'

I pressed the panel button and turned release handles. I pushed the inner hatch open.

'*Talk to me, Jabril. Describe what you can see.*'

I resumed filming.

'I'm entering a crew compartment. It's cramped. There are storage lockers. There is some kind of porthole at the back.'

Hassim shone a flashlight through black glass. The empty hold. Payload doors held shut by heavy piston actuators.

'The bay is empty,' I told Ignatiev. 'There is no cargo.'

A bank of winking red lights.

'I think I have found the life-support controls. Russian symbols. Might be CO^2 warnings. Depleted oxygen.'

'*There should be another floor plate directly beneath your feet.*'

'I see it.'

'*Open it up. Don't touch anything.*'

I lifted the plate aside.

A status panel flashed red, first in Cyrillic, then in English.

WARNING
DESTRUCT ARMED

'What in God's name is this?'

'*About thirty kilos of plastic explosive. The standard auto-destruct mechanism on all Soyuz and Progress flights, manned and unmanned. If a craft fails to deploy correctly, if there is a significant deviation from the launch flight-path, then Mission Control has the option to initiate a de-orbit burn and bring the vessel back into the atmosphere over the Pacific, east of the Mariana Islands. They wait until the vehicle descends to an altitude of about fifteen kilometres then transmit the self-destruct code.*'

'How do we defuse it?'

'*Press the amber button. Flip the toggle switch.*'

DESTRUCT DISARMED

'*Unplug the unit. There are grips either side of the console. The detonator and explosives should lift smoothly out. Get Hassim to help carry it from the vehicle.*'

We carried the auto-destruct unit from the airlock and set it down on the cavern floor.

'*Return to the crew compartment.*'

'Okay.'

'*There's a wall panel, secured by four lock-screws. Should be a voltage symbol on the panel.*'

'Got it.'

I unscrewed the bolts. A cavity. Clumps of cable.

'*The Saliut-5 data system. It captures telemetric and medical information for post-flight analysis. I'll talk you through the de-installation.*'

'It's gone.'

'*What do you mean?*'

'The entire unit has been removed. Someone cut through the wires.'

'*You're sure?*'

'There are data ribbons hanging out of the wall. They've been sawed with a knife.'

'*Chyort voz'mi,*' muttered Ignatiev.

'It seems someone was anxious to ensure Spektr kept her secrets.'

There was a long pause.

'Doctor? Doctor, can you hear me?'

'*Open the cockpit. It's time we saw who flew this thing.*'

The crew compartment was separated from the cockpit by a thick bulkhead.

I turned the release handles and pulled back the flight-deck hatch.

Darkness. The cabin lights had shorted out.

'Hassim. Give me some light.'

I crawled into the cramped flight deck and filmed. Hassim crouched by the doorway.

A single high-backed couch facing banks of instrumentation. Commsgear, telemetric read-outs, navigation management consoles and attitude controls. Row upon row of dials and toggle switches.

The flight-deck windows were smoked almost black by the heat of re-entry.

I crawled into the cockpit on my knees.

'*There should be six red switches. Centre panel, above the thrust levers.*'

'I see them.'

'*They isolate the main boosters. Flip them upward into the off position. I don't want some random command impulse to trigger the combustion chambers and blow us to pieces.*'

I put down the camera. I rested my stump on a deck plate for support and reached forward to flip the bank of switches.

'There's a pilot right next to me. He looks long dead.'

'*Any obvious signs of injury?*'

'No. His suit is intact.'

'*Film it.*'

The figure was strapped in the command couch. The couch was a foam and fibre-glass body-shell mounted on ram-jacks to absorb a heavy impact.

The cosmonaut wore a grey canvas pressure suit. His boots and gauntlets were attached by lock-rings. A hose anchored to his chest-plate was plugged into a wall-mounted oxygen supply.

'Give me more light.'

Hassim crawled into the compartment and held the torch above his head.

The dead cosmonaut had a silver rosary wrapped round his wrist.

'His helmet is sealed. I can't see his face.'

I kept filming.

A mission patch on his sleeve: the tricolour of the Russian Federation and a clenched fist. A name tape on his chest.

KONSTANTIN.

'*Can you move the pilot? Can you extract him from his seat?*'

'I'll try.'

'*Don't violate the integrity of his suit, understand? Don't release the lock-rings. Don't lift the visor.*'

I shut off the video camera and passed it to Hassim.

The cosmonaut was held in his seat by a five-point harness. I twisted the central clasp. The straps unlatched and fell free.

I turned a screw-ring, and released the oxygen umbilicus from his chest valve.

I shut off the light.

'Give me a hand.'

Hassim gripped the cosmonaut's ankles. I pushed my hand and stump beneath the pilot's armpits and supported his weight as we swung his body from the seat.

We manhandled the dead man from the cockpit, through the stowage area and out the airlock.

'*Put him in the sarcophagus.*'

I pulled a polythene sheath from a long box. A steel coffin with a big biohazard symbol etched into the metal and a porthole in the lid.

We laid the cosmonaut inside the steel container, still in his pressure suit, and folded his arms across his chest. We sealed the lid.

We entered the decon cycle. We scrubbed our suits with bleach, hosed down under a shower head, then stood bathed in ultraviolet light.

We towelled and dressed.

'We shall rest,' said Ignatiev. 'Rehydrate. Get something to eat. We begin the autopsy in an hour.'

We walked from the tunnel mouth, down the narrow ravine and back to the camp.

Morning light.

The men had set up generators and draped camouflage nets. A semi-permanent township. Dormitory tents with canvas cots.

I watched them dig defensive trenches and fill sandbags. They pulled on armoured gloves and rolled out concertina wire.

Elite troops, Saddam's praetorian guard, prepping eighty-gallon fuel drums for use as latrine buckets. The air was full of dust.

Ignatiev's team had their own tent. I saw trunks of communication equipment hooked to a big mesh tripod dish pegged into the sand, angled to face the western sky. Some kind of uplink.

I sat with Ignatiev and Hassim. We drank sweet tea and smoked cigarettes.

'How long have you known Koell?'

'Long enough,' said Ignatiev. He didn't look me in the eye.

He took the kettle from the primer stove and poured water. I stole a glance at his wristwatch. Raketa. A red star on the dial. A communist relic.

The doctor was an exile. A man without a state. Modern Russia overrun by gangsters and oligarchs. Statues of Lenin torn down and consigned to the scrap yard. Skyline transfigured by glass mega-structures and corporate signage. He could never go home. The proletarian state he knew from his childhood didn't exist any more.

'You work for the Americans?'

'I work for myself.'

Ignatiev stood and walked away. It fed my conviction I was due a bullet in the head soon as my use was at an end.

I should have run. Picked my moment. Walked from the camp, climbed the valley wall and fled into the desert. But I was fascinated by Spektr. I wanted to examine the Russian cosmonaut. I wanted to confront this strange disease.

We returned to the tunnel mouth. Ignatiev joined us in the staging area.

We zipped biohazard suits. We sluiced our overboots in trays of caustic soda and lye. Then we pulled back a polythene curtain and entered the containment dome.

Hassim unfolded the legs of a plastic table and sprayed the surface with Envirochem.

We released latches. We lifted the cosmonaut from his silver sarcophagus and laid him on the table. Ignatiev told me to hold the video camera and film.

Slow pan. I surveyed the suit head to toe. Ignatiev took still photographs from every angle.

'Who was this man?' I asked.

'Hard to be sure. We have background information concerning a group of young men that passed through Soviet flight school in the eighties. I think he might be Vasily Konstantin. Born in Riga. Joined the air force. Trained at Akhtubinsk. Test pilot, second class. Seconded to the Yuri Gagarin cosmonaut school, Star City. He was part of the civilian space programme for a while, then dropped off the map. Declared dead three years later. No details. "Deceased" stamped on the cover of his personnel file. He was posthumously awarded Hero of the Russian Federation.'

'Do you think he had a family?'

'I imagine his parents buried a coffin full of rocks. They've been laying flowers on an empty grave, while Konstantin slowly orbited the Earth. Let's get him out of his suit.'

Ignatiev unscrewed retaining bolts and unlatched the gauntlet lock-ring.

'My God,' said Hassim, as the glove slid clear.

I'm not a religious man, but I murmured a prayer.

'*Bismillah ar rahman ar rahim*.'

Mummified fingers. Strange metallic ropes and tendrils woven into flesh.

'Film it,' said Ignatiev. 'Film it all.'

I held the video camera while they cut the cosmonaut free. They sliced through the canvas oversuit with trauma shears. They couldn't release the helmet lock-ring, so they cut through neck fabric and lifted the helmet clear.

'In the name of God the merciful,' muttered Hassim..

'Keep filming.'

An emaciated skull. Dried skin taut like leather. Sharp metal spines bristled from his mouth, his eyes.

Ignatiev pushed me aside. He leaned forward and examined the spines.

'What happened to him?' I asked. 'What in God's name happened to him?'

'I wish I knew.'

'But your people created this monstrosity. The Soviet military.'

'You assume this is the work of man.'

'What are you suggesting?'

Ignatiev didn't reply. He took more pictures.

Hassim and Ignatiev continued to strip the astronaut. They cut away the temperature regulated undersuit. Stretch fabric webbed with heating pipes.

They peeled away electrodes planted on the cosmonaut's chest and abdomen to monitor bio-function.

Hassim held the cosmonaut's head while Ignatiev peeled away the grey communications skull-cap with forceps. A scalp rippled and knotted with tumorous metallic growths.

Hassim winced. He pulled off the outer glove of his suit

and examined his forefinger. A smear of blood beneath blue Nitrile rubber.

'What happened?' asked Ignatiev.

'Nothing. I'm all right. I just pricked my finger.'

Ignatiev opened a plastic case. He loaded a vial of liquid into an injector gun.

'Show me your hand.'

Hassim held out his hand. Ignatiev gripped his wrist, twisted his arm and locked him in a half-nelson.

He fired the hypodermic through the bicep of the Hassim's bio-suit.

Hassim pulled himself away. He clutched his arm.

'What did you do?' he asked, looking at the spent injector gun in Ignatiev's hand.

He stumbled and fell to his knees.

'You bastard.'

He toppled face forward onto the polythene floor and passed out.

Ignatiev pulled off the technician's hood and checked his pupils for dilation.

'Let's get him in quarantine. Get him out of this suit. Rig some restraints. I want multiple cameras. Regular biopsies. Minute-by-minute analysis.'

'He's got some kind of infection?' I asked. 'We have anti-biotics. Antivirals. We should set up an intravenous drip.'

'Koell showed you pictures of the installation drifting in deep space?'

'Yes.'

'It is breaking up. Piece by piece. Spektr isn't the first chunk of debris to fall to Earth. The station is locked in a slow-decaying polar orbit. Fragments have re-entered the atmosphere over Mongolia, Latvia, Greenland. I visited a crash site myself. China, near the border with Kyrgyzstan. A four-day journey. I made the last sixty miles on horseback. The villagers showed me pictures. A spherical object, big as a van, burned black by the heat of re-entry. It fell one night like a shooting star. Dug a fifty-foot crater in a rice paddy. The crash was quickly followed by the outbreak of a strange and terrible disease. By the time I arrived at the impact site with my team, there was nothing left to see. The local militia had incinerated the infected bodies. They had pushed the module down the shaft of an abandoned coal mine and used dynamite to bury it beneath a cascade of rubble.

'But now we have Spektr. This is our chance to observe the pathology of this illness first-hand.'

'Will Hassim die? Can he be saved?'

'There is nothing I can do for him.'

'He's my friend. He's a good man.'

'The virus is already replicating in his bloodstream, attacking sheath-fibres in his brain and spinal column. The process is irreversible.'

'Dear God.'

'I'm sorry. But he's not your friend any more. He is Test Subject Number One.'

Battalion

Huang wandered through the temple precincts, gun in hand, looking for a good place to die.

The moon was eclipsed by cloud. The night wind brought a rising sandstorm. He took a Maglite from his pocket and switched full-beam.

Movement up ahead. One of Jabril's undead legion sliding along a temple wall. Spines and tumours erupting from rotting flesh. The mutant creature ignored Huang and kept walking.

I'm not a target, thought Huang. *They know I'm infected. They know I'm one of them. Must be the smell. They sniff out fresh meat. I have taken on their signature stench of disease and death.*

He found shelter. Some kind of subsidiary chapel built against the high perimeter wall. The little chamber was intact. The walls and roof had withstood squalling desert cyclones for countless aeons.

His flashlight lit a small dais with a scorpion chiselled on the front. An altar dedicated to a minor god.

He reclined on the step. He switched off his torch and sat in darkness. He listened to the mournful whisper of the breeze outside.

Huang always knew he would die young. A gut conviction, ever since he was a kid. He carried a tarot deck in his back-pack. Each time he shuffled, he drew the death card.

He always pictured a soldier's homecoming. Sent back to Greenville, Michigan, in a coffin. Unloaded from a C-17

Globemaster, folded flag and dress-blue photograph on the lid. White-gloved reservists firing a blank fusillade as his casket got lowered into the ground.

He held the Glock. He stroked the rough polymer grip with his thumb. His whole life – boyhood, adolescence, college and army years – concluding in this godforsaken necropolis, miles from home. His body would not be discovered for decades, possibly centuries. Nothing but a pile of dried bones picked over by men from some science-fiction future, so augmented by cybernetics and gene manipulation they were no longer homo-sapien. They would see rotted teeth plugged with amalgam, an old break in his leg crudely pinned with titanium screws. They would think him impossibly primitive, some kind of troglodyte.

Or maybe his body would never be discovered. His bones would crumble to dust. He would merge with the desert. Meld with an ocean of silica.

He arched his back. Sudden indescribable pain as if his spine were white-hot metal. The disease, the strange parasite boring into his central nervous system.

He crouched on all fours in the dark. He ran his hands over the flagstones, trying to find his flashlight, trying to find his gun. He sobbed. He wept blood. He shook his head, tried to clear his thoughts.

'My name is . . . My name is . . .'

He couldn't remember his name. Mind slipping away.

A last, random memory:

The sweet smell of cut grass.

Huang crawled towards the chamber doorway. He hauled himself to his feet. Scudding cloud. Brief moonlight.

The thing that used to be Huang roared into the rising storm.

'Did you hear that?' asked Voss. He stood at the temple entrance, staring into swirling sand.

'What?'

'Sounded like a scream.'

'Man or a woman?'

'Not sure.'

Lucy pressed transmit.

'Mandy? Mandy, can you hear me?'

No response.

'I heard something a couple of minutes ago,' said Voss. 'Over the comms. Sounded like her voice. I couldn't make out words. The signal was breaking up. Might be atmospherics.'

Flickering light. The remaining arcs were dying. Softening to an amber glow as the batteries ran dry.

'What about the gold?' asked Voss.

'Hide it, I guess.'

'Where?'

'Let's ask Jabril.'

Lucy crouched next to the extinct campfire.

'Hey. Jabril. You know a lot about this place. Where should we hide the gold?'

'Just leave. Forget the gold. Take all the water you can carry and walk out of this valley. Right now.'

'Two of my boys died today. I won't let it be for nothing.'

Jabril sighed.

'There's a crypt beneath this temple. A deep catacomb.'

'Where's the entrance?'

'There are steps out there, among the ruins.'

'I don't want to head outside with those fucks running around.'

'I heard a rumour there was a second entrance. Here, in the temple.'

'Yeah?'

'A slab by the altar. I'm not sure which one.'

Lucy and Voss walked across the vast hall to the altar. Lucy crouched and brushed sand from granite flagstones. One of the slabs had been etched with astrological symbols. Constellations. Planet and stars.

Lucy stood and stamped her boot. Hollow thud.

'Bingo,' said Voss.

'Maybe Jabril is right,' she said. 'We should just grab our shit and go.'

'I'm not leaving the gold,' said Voss. 'It's ours. We earned it. We stash it and come back with fresh choppers. We don't leave it out in the open so the next fuck that wanders through this valley can fill his pockets.'

They fetched a tyre iron from the truck.

They crouched. They hammered the crowbar between flagstones and levered the granite slab from its bed. They strained to push the slab aside. Grind of heavy stone.

Lucy shone her barrel light into the dark aperture. Ancient steps descended into subterranean darkness.

A vaulted catacomb. Grotesque hieroglyphs. Pillars and archways.

'Doubt anyone will go looking down there, among the bones.'

Voss carried a box of gold from the armoured truck. He set it down on the flagstones and flipped the lid. He pawed through the jewellery. He selected a gold signet ring and twisted it on to his finger.

He held out a silver watch. The face was ringed with diamonds.

'Rolex.'

Lucy shook her head.

'I don't want a souvenir. I just want to get out of this fucking hell-hole.'

Voss clipped the watch to her wrist.

'We might as well get something out of the trip, right?'

Footfalls. Something scrambling up the crypt steps.

Lucy stood over the crypt entrance and trained her barrel light down into the subterranean gloom.

Amanda, dazzled, shielding her eyes from the beam.

'Mandy. You okay?'

Amanda scrambled clear of the crypt. She dropped to her knees and tried to slide the heavy lid across to seal the crypt entrance.

'Help me, for God's sake.'

Lucy glimpsed a jostling crowd of rotted soldiers crawling from the dark recesses of the crypt. Grasping, stumbling gangrenous things dragging themselves up the steps. Charred, ragged uniforms. Bloody, dirt-caked hands. Slavering moans and death-rattle hisses.

'Jesus fucking Christ.'

Voss joined Amanda as she struggled to shift the flagstone slab and plug the crypt entrance.

Lucy switched full auto and emptied a clip down into the advancing army. She swept the assault rifle left and right. Stuttering muzzle flash. Chests ripped open. Shattered ribs. Torn flesh and burning uniforms.

The mummified battalion continued to advance.

Lucy ejected the magazine and slapped a fresh clip into her rifle. She cranked the charging handle. Disciplined fire. Snarling faces shattered by green-tip penetrator rounds. Brain-burst exit wounds. Stink of gunsmoke and burned hair.

She threw down her weapon and joined Amanda and Voss as they struggled to push the heavy flagstone lid back in place.

Jabril kicked at the ashes of the campfire. The noose round his neck pulled taut as he stretched out his leg.

He pushed aside charcoal fragments of ammo crates. Something clinked. Something metal. A scorched bullet case. An empty 5.56mm cartridge. He snagged it with the heel of his boot. He raked it, clinking and clattering across the flagstones, towards him.

Jabril's left arm was twisted behind his back and bound to his belt by a plastic tuff-tie. The stump of his right arm hung free.

He pawed at the cartridge with the stump of his forearm and pushed the brass shell case behind his back. He picked it up with his left hand, and used the crimped neck of the cartridge to saw at the vinyl cuff. The serrated brass began to scratch and score plastic.

A distant clatter. He looked towards the temple entrance. The rotted figure of a Republican Guard clumsily stepped over the quad bike. It stumbled and fell to the temple floor. The ghoul looked up, saw Jabril and slowly leered.

The granite lid rasped across the flagstones and settled over the crypt aperture with a dull thud.

They could hear the muffled slap and scratch of hands scrabbling at the flagstone lid from below.

'Jesus,' said Lucy. 'How many of those fuckers are down there?'

'They can't lift that thing, can they?' asked Voss.

The lid trembled and shifted.

'Oh fuck.'

Lucy and Amanda threw themselves onto the slab and held it down. It began to rise, despite their combined bodyweight.

'Get me something to pin this damn thing,' shouted Lucy.

Voss looked around. He grabbed boxes of gold stacked beside the truck and piled them onto the slab.

Lucy drew her pistol, reached around the slab and fired blind down into the crypt. She shot the magazine dry.

More boxes. Accumulating weight slowly forced the slab downward. A snarling, squirming skull-face crushed flat. Bone-crackle and pulped brain. Fingers sliced through. The lid settled in place.

A distant shout from Jabril:

'Over here.'

Three Republic Guards lumbered towards Jabril as he lay bound and helpless. He kicked the dead campfire, scattered charred sticks in a feeble attempt to trip the shambling creatures.

Amanda dropped to one knee and shouldered her rifle.

Gunshot. A soldier reeled like he took a blow to the face. He fell forward, a smoking void in the back of his head.

She worked the bolt.

Gunshot. Second soldier shot through his open mouth. He choked and toppled backwards into the extinct campfire.

Voss fired his shotgun. The blast slammed into the third soldier's belly like a heavy gut punch and sent him skidding across the flagstone floor.

Voss walked towards the prone soldier. He racked the shotgun slide. He spat tobacco.

The soldier struggled to sit up. Entrails slid from his belly wound in gelatinous knots. Voss shot him in the face.

Lucy flicked open her knife and cut Jabril free.

'No more fucking around,' she said. 'It's time we got the hell out of here.'

The creature that used to be Huang prowled through the desolate precincts of the necropolis. He couldn't see the main temple building, but he could smell it up ahead. Heartbeats like an earth tremor. Lucy and her crew. Their blood, sweat and fear.

He stumbled through rubble-strewn courtyards. He scrambled across tumbled masonry. Skin torn by jagged stone. Bleeding hands, bleeding knees. He felt no pain. He was drawn inexorably towards the sweet scent of fresh meat.

Jabril's battalion. They squirmed from every dark doorway and crevice like agitated ants pouring from a nest. Clawing hands and snapping skeletal faces. They emerged from shadows into the swirling dust storm.

Huang walked alongside infected soldiers. Tattered uniforms. Taut, cankerous flesh. Brief moonlight revealed the stumbling, shambling horde as they groped through the megalithic ruins towards the temple entrance. A wraith army.

Distant gunfire.

He crossed a pillared avenue.

The sudden whine and slap of bullets hitting granite. Tracer rounds streaked out of the dust storm. Soldiers toppled and fell dead.

Huang grabbed the soldier next to him. He used him as a shield. Shotgun hits like sledgehammer blows.

Huang threw the smouldering, headless body aside, and took cover behind a pillar. He pressed his face against the stone. Residual instinct. Conditioned response. A faint memory of Ranger school summoned by a crippled, cockroach brain.

Soldiers cut down around him. Clean headshots. Shattered skulls.

Bodies toppled and slumped.

Huang crept closer to the temple entrance. A slithering, belly crawl. He could see light shafting from the interior. A weak glow through swirling dust.

Silhouettes. Three figures crouched behind a quad bike.

Steady gunfire. Bodies littered the causeway in front of the temple entrance, lay sprawled at the feet of the great stone colossi that flanked the doorway. Uniforms shot to smouldering rags. Bloody exit wounds.

Huang inched closer. One of the figures wore a hat. A big straw Stetson. A girl. The faint echo of emotion, an unrequited yearning.

More gunfire. Soldiers span and fell. Dumb, lumbering targets. No pain. No fear. Limbs shot away. Skulls smashed. No screams. Just the grunt of impact, the gurgling sigh of a dying breath.

Voss took a pouch of Red Man from his pocket and folded a wad of tobacco into his mouth.

He slotted fresh double-nought shells into the breech of his shotgun. He racked the slide.

More figures stumbling out of the storm. He took calm, careful aim. He let them get close before decapitating each soldier with a jet of buckshot.

Bodies piled up. Advancing soldiers stumbled over dead comrades. Voss spat tobacco, took aim and cut them down.

'They walk right into it,' he said. 'No sense. No fear. They line up to get cut down.'

'They are insects,' said Jabril. 'Lobotomised. Individually they don't count for much. But they mass. And they are relentless. There are hundreds of them, and they will keep coming until you have used up every bullet and have nothing to throw at them but rocks. They won't quit. They won't retreat. They have a single, all-consuming purpose. To tear into your flesh.'

Amanda leant her rifle across the saddle of the quad bike. The ruins beyond the temple boosted luminescent green by her nightscope. Pale pillars and jagged walls. Bodies sprawled on flagstones.

More soldiers shambled out of the darkness. Dust furled round them like smoke. Living cadavers. Slack, desiccated faces. Stench carried on the wind. The reek of decomposition.

She lined up kill-shots, soft entry points, reticules centred on jet-black eyes.

Gunshot. Skull-burst.

She worked the bolt.

Gunshot. Shattered jaw.

The magazine ran dry. She slapped a fresh clip of .308 into the receiver. She folded a fresh stick of gum into her mouth.

'Enemy left. Bunch massing by that archway,' she said.

'Save your ammo,' said Voss. 'Let me deal with it.'

Voss set aside his smoking shotgun. He slung the strap of the SAW over his shoulder and locked a fresh belt of ammunition into the receiver.

'Give me some light.'

Amanda threw cyalumes into the darkness beyond the temple entrance. The scattered sticks glowed ectoplasmic blue.

Six soldiers lumbering out of the dust storm into the pool of strange, chemical light.

Voss braced his legs, gripped the heavy machine gun and shot from the hip. Jack-hammer roar. Muzzle-flame. Two hundred rounds per minute. Cartridge cases cascaded from the weapon, chimed and skittered across the flagstones. His arms trembled as he fought to control the machine gun.

The soldiers were torn open. Legs scythed at the knee. Arms torn from their sockets. Smashed ribs. Fractured spines. They were thrown backwards by the impact of heavy calibre rounds.

Two of the soldiers tried to struggle to their feet. Their olive uniforms were bullet-scorched and burning. A fresh sweep of the gun. Heads smashed open. Skull shards. Pulped brain tissue. They fell dead and twitching.

Lucy ignored the muzzle-roar and gun smoke. She shook out daypacks and grabbed stuff they would need for their journey across the desert.

She decanted mineral water into canteens and Camelbaks. She ripped open MRE pouches. She tossed plastic meal pots. She kept dried fruit.

She divided the remaining ammunition. She checked her pockets, made sure she had her map and compass.

'Everybody suit up,' she said. 'We'll lay suppressing fire with the SAW, then make a break for it. You too, Jabril. You're coming with us. No argument. I'm going to get you home.'

She offered Jabril a pistol.

He smiled and shook his head.

'I'll make a deal with you all.'

'Talk later, all right? Your old pals have sniffed out fresh meat. If we stay here much longer we'll get overrun.'

Jabril pointed to the metal trunk lying in the quad trailer, half hidden by Toon's flak jacket.

'Let me have the missile case. The documents. The virus. Give them to me, and I will show you a way home.'

Voss let rip another stream of machine-gun fire.

'There's a way out of here?' shouted Lucy.

'The freight train. We used it to haul Spektr. It's still here. Maybe you can get it started. Ride it across the desert.'

'Where is it?'

'I'll show you. In return for the case. Give me the missile, and I will get you home alive.

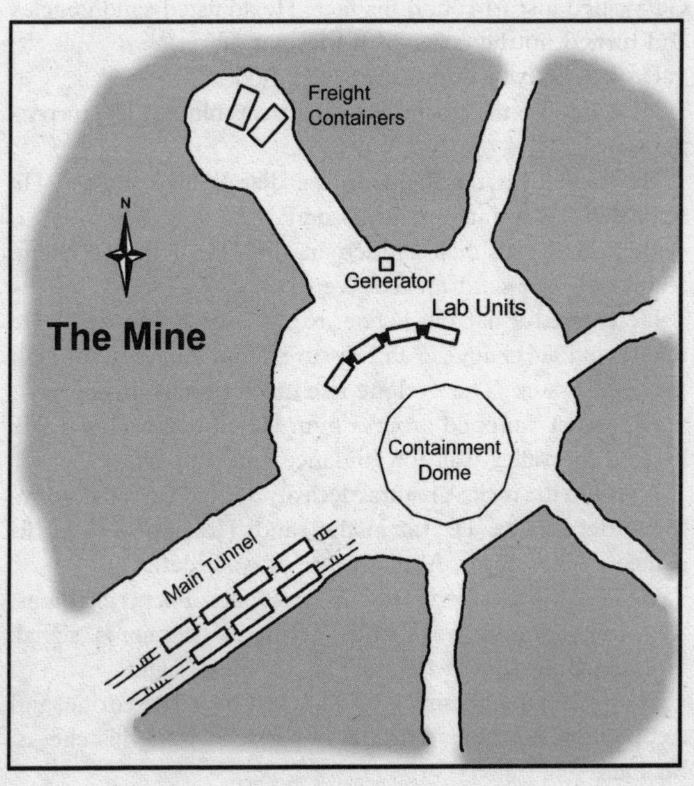
Freight
Containers
N
Generator
Lab Units
The Mine
Containment
Dome
Main Tunnel

Containment One

Gaunt tied a scarf round his face. He adjusted sand goggles and turned up the collar of his leather jacket.

He was halfway across the valley floor.

He leant into the storm. Sand particles blurred like torrential rain.

He trained his flashlight on the dial of his compass. He struggled onward, alone in the dark.

He found rails half hidden in dirt. He followed them, stumbling over sand-dusted sleepers.

He entered a narrow ravine. Rough, sandstone walls. He felt the sudden change in air pressure. Wind funnelled through the tight fissure. The cyclone risen to a jet-scream.

His jacket whipped around him. He zipped it closed. He hugged the valley wall for guidance and support.

A split in the rock. A natural declivity. He hid from the storm.

A brief respite. He sat in the sand. He sipped from his canteen. Half empty. About a litre of water left.

He took the sat phone from his backpack. Flickering digits. The unit scanned wavebands, trying to acquire a signal. Nothing. Too deep in the ravine. No line-of-sight.

He packed the comms gear, knocked back Dexedrine, and stepped out into the storm. Sand particles stung his cheeks, his hands.

He followed the rails. He felt like he had walked for miles.

The track abruptly terminated in a jumble of wooden beams and sacking. He surveyed the obstruction by flashlight. A blocked tunnel. High and wide.

He pulled planks aside. He rolled an empty oil drum. He shone his flashlight into the cave mouth and let his eyes adjusted to the dark.

A ragged tunnel blasted through bedrock. Wooden props at twenty-foot intervals. Railroad track receded into shadow.

He walked inside. Wind noise dropped to a low moan. He pulled down his scarf, unzipped his jacket and took off his sand goggles. He shook dust from his ears.

Twin railroad track. His boots crunched on shingle. Footfalls echoed from the high tunnel walls.

The passageway was cold as a meat locker. Skin-prickle chill. His breath fogged the air in front of him.

A glint up ahead. A scintillating, multifaceted jewel, like a giant arachnid eye. The lens glass of a hooded lamp high on the snout of a massive diesel locomotive.

A plough-blade welded to the front of the motor house. Gaunt grabbed handrails and hauled himself up onto the nose platform of the locomotive.

He used a narrow walkway to shuffle the length of the engine. Rust-streaked service panels and intake fans. A wide engine/alternator compartment. He leant over the railing and inspected wheels, pistons and brake shoes. The vehicle seemed to be intact.

He reached the cab. The slide door was locked. He rubbed dust from the glass and shone his flashlight inside. The control panels were undamaged.

A body on the floor of the cab. He could see a boot, a spent cartridge, a mummified hand holding a pistol.

He ran his hand over bodywork. Rock dust. He looked up. A web of cracks in the sandstone roof. Heavy wooden props straining to hold back imminent tunnel collapse.

Gaunt climbed from the cab. He shone his torch further down the passage. The locomotive had been unhitched from wagons and coupled to two ornate Pullman carriages that had clearly been housed in the tunnel for decades. Wood panels. Cream livery. Dust and blistered lacquer.

He climbed a door ladder and shone his flashlight through glass fogged with dust.

An office. Brass light fixtures. Exquisite marquetry panels. A grand desk. High-backed Queen Anne chairs. Furniture centred on a heroic portrait of Saddam in full generalissimo braids.

The second carriage was a dining car.

Gaunt jumped from the coach and walked deeper into the rail tunnel. He walked past box cars, ore wagons, flatbed trucks.

He approached the cavern. The beam of his flashlight was too weak to penetrate the vast space. He could make out the curve of rock walls. The depths of the cavern were lost in shadow.

The grit-crunch of his footfalls echoed round the cave.

He glimpsed the opaque plastic of the containment dome. Something white inside. Something huge.

He kept walking.

His flashlight lit the riveted silver hulls of the lab containers.

Four metal bio-medical units. Gleaming chrome, like old-time Airstream trailers. They were lined in a row, nose to tail. Bolted together to form a single, long hermetic environment.

A mobile bio-weapons lab. Swiss made. Shipped from Europe. Dispatched to the valley the moment Koell stroked the Spektr heat tiles, and saw for himself that the vehicle was solid and real.

The lab docked at Qatar. Each unit loaded onto a flatbed railcar and draped with tarp. The lab was towed across Syria surfing a wave of bribe money. US dollars clearing the route, switching every junction, turning every light green. A tight brick of currency changed hands at a border checkpoint. Guards pulled barriers aside and let the locomotive pass unrecorded into Iraq's Western Desert.

Gaunt examined the lab door. He stroked metal. A steel hatch, like the bulkhead door of a ship.

One week earlier.

Koell's hotel suite. Gaunt sipped his third whisky and watched interrogation footage on a laptop.

Ignatiev, tied to an office chair. Raw brickwork. A battery lamp hung from a roof girder. Probably a basement room in one of the bombed-out ministry buildings by the banks of the Tigris.

Koell was off-screen.

'Do you comprehend the scope of this endeavour?' asked Koell. 'The time, the money, I've spent chasing Spektr? I had to oversee this entire recovery project in the middle of a fucking war. Can you grasp the scale of the undertaking?'

'You weren't there,' said Ignatiev. 'You weren't on site. You were safe in Baghdad. This is the most destructive disease I've ever seen. Forget Marburg. Forget Ebola. This isn't some jungle bug that will make your gums bleed for a couple of days. This thing is lethal and spreads like wildfire. No cure. No vaccine. There were two hundred men in that valley. Once the infection got loose, it took twelve hours to wipe out the entire battalion. You have to believe me. This disease cannot be weaponised. It cannot be effectively contained. Eradication. That's the only sane course of action.'

'I've dedicated years of my life to this project. I scoured Moscow. I kicked down the doors of shitty apartment buildings and put the thumbscrews on every old communist fuck that worked out of Star City. I've bled Special Projects dry chasing this piece of space junk. Called in every favour. I'm out on a limb. I've got to produce results.

'I know all about you, Doc. The things you've done. I've seen pictures. The asylum. You didn't have a qualm when you sliced up those inmates. Drilled their skulls. Too late in the day to grow a fucking conscience.'

'You have to listen to me. Try to understand. This virus. This parasite. It's like nothing on earth. It's monstrous. I can't even begin to describe it.

'The structure is crystalline. Almost metallic. Maybe it's synthetic. A chimera virus, an artificial construct. Nanobots or recombinant DNA manipulation gone horribly wrong. Or maybe it is something else.'

'Like what?'

'It's not a sudden mutation. It's a complex form of life. Highly evolved. Supremely adaptive.'

'What are you saying?'

'It's not from Earth.'

'Listen to yourself,' said Koell. 'You had a simple job: locate the virus; bring it back. That's all you had to do. '

'I don't care what happens to me. You can go to hell.'

'Tell me about the lab.'

'Fuck you.'

Koell stepped into view. Shirtsleeves and a butcher's apron. He held a pair of pliers. He hunched over Ignatiev, back to the camera.

A long scream.

Koell stepped away. Ignatiev drooled blood. A front incisor missing.

'The lab. Is it intact?'

Ignatiev coughed and spat. A weird smile. The knowledge he was minutes from death manifest as a strange euphoria.

'Maybe. I don't know.'

'I'm going to send a retrieval team. A bunch of mercenaries. One of my guys will attempt to secure the virus. So tell him what he needs to know. Talk him through it. How do we get into Lab One? How is it secured?'

'There is a keypad and swipe-slot, but it won't work. The lab is in lock-down. I triggered a contamination alert.

The doors sealed tight. None of the access codes will register. You'll have to cut your way inside. Each unit is a double steel shell. Might take a while.'

'The labs,' asked Koell. 'What will we find inside?'

Ignatiev spat more blood.

'The main power will be off. The labs will be in sleep mode. Essential systems only. Chloride storage batteries will provide a trickle of AC power to keep the freezers operational. You will need to restart the grid. It's easy enough. There's a fuse box as you enter Lab One. On your left, at head height. One of those lightning bolt high-voltage stickers on the lid. There is a single breaker inside. You will be able to run at full power for about seventy-two hours before you need to fire up the generator to recharge.'

'Tell me about Lab One.'

'We used the first unit as a necropsy room. Specimens were brought for dissection and analysis. That was where most of our work took place once the human field tests began.'

Gaunt examined the lab door. A steel hatch, like the bulkhead door of a ship.

He opened his backpack. He loaded a cartridge into a caulking gun. Demex 400. An extrudable demolition charge used by SWAT breach teams. It oozed from the nozzle like toothpaste. He ran a stripe of explosive down the door seal. He coated the keypad and lock mechanism.

He pressed a detonator into the putty and ran firing cable.

He backed out the cavern, walked down the rail tunnel spooling det cord.

He crouched. He stripped insulation with his teeth.

He touched the wires to a nine-volt battery.

White light.

The blast echoed round the tunnel like thunder.

Gaunt walked back to the cavern. His flashlight beam

shafted through smoke and swirling dust. He examined the lab. The door hung open, twisted and burned.

He kissed the crucifix hung round his neck. He cranked the handles and pulled the heavy hatch open. Darkness within. Intense cold. Counters and lockers.

The fuse box. Locked. He smashed it open with the butt of his pistol. Breaker to on. Faint hum. Overhead strip lights flickered to life.

Gaunt switched off his flashlight.

He was in some kind of vestibule, sealed from the rest of lab by a glass partition.

A warning stencilled on the glass:

DANGER
HOT AGENT

BIOHAZARD
LEVEL ONE

Contamination alert. A roof beacon washed the room in crimson light.

Gaunt unzipped his jacket and released his body armour. He piled them in the corner.

Breathing equipment hung in a locker. He punched out glass, unhooked an M50 gas mask and pulled it over his face. A pig-snout respirator with twin filters. He tightened straps.

He tugged a pair of Nitrile gloves from a wall dispenser and wriggled them on.

He shouldered his backpack, pulled back the glass partition and entered the lab. The air-handling system created a compressed hush, like the pressurised cabin of a transatlantic jet.

He stood over a zinc autopsy slab. Sluice channel. Plug hole.

The gas mask reflected in mirror-metal. Black rubber. Smoked glass, like the empty eye sockets of a skull.

A freezer. The digital read-out said -70.

Gaunt pulled the latch. The door popped with a hiss. A cascade of broiling nitrogen-smoke. Frosted jars.

Gaunt brushed away ice crystals. Body parts preserved in formaldehyde. Fingers. Teeth. An ear. A scrap of scalp.

Ignatiev lolled in the office chair. He was unconscious. Blood and spit drooled from his mouth.

Koell stepped into camera range carrying a hypodermic. He gave Ignatiev a shot in the arm. The man gasped and jerked awake.

Ignatiev looked around. He sobbed. Dragged from oblivion to endure more pain.

'Tell me about the human trials,' asked Koell.

'Hassim was our first test subject. He was kept restrained in the Spektr containment area while we waited for the lab units to arrive. We told him help was on its way. A hospital train. There would be fresh diagnostic equipment to help track the spread of the disease, fresh drugs to treat the infection. I didn't have the courage to tell him the truth. The locomotive was hauling a pathology lab on wheels. The lab units contained nothing that might conceivably cure his condition. Even as we soothed him, held water to his lips and pressed ice-packs to his forehead, we were planning his dissection.

'We did our best for him. Dosed him with broad-spectrum antibiotics. Tetracycline, streptomycin, ciprofloxacin. Administered shock-doses of antiserum. Tried to lower his fever, clear the pneumonia fogging his lungs. But nothing halted his slow slide into psychotic dementia. He asked me the time of day, kept asking over and over like his mind got jammed in some weird repetitive cycle.

'Sometimes he was lucid. He was calm. He prayed. But then his prayers would dissolve to gibberish and obscenity. He spat and swore as we injected him with morphine.

'He slowly began to choke. His throat became obstructed by fine hairs that seemed to grow deep within his lungs. We gave him a tracheotomy.

'He languished in a coma. Intracellular breakdown. Clots forming in his liver and kidneys. Gastrointestinal bleeding. His breathing was laboured and shallow. His mouth slowly filled with metal spines, slowly forcing his jaws apart.

'Strange needles bristled from his flesh. His skin was mottled by blotches and ulcerated lesions. The virus attacked his ocular cavities. Burst blood vessels turned his eyes near black. Liquid metal leaked from his tear ducts.

'He lay comatose for several hours. We took blood and saliva. We took liver biopsies and lung cell cultures. We drained spinal fluid. We drilled his skull and took brain tissue.

'He woke. He roared, and snarled and tore at his restraints. Hassim had gone, and a monster had taken his place. I made the decision to end his suffering. I administered Demerol. It should have been a lethal dose. It should have paralysed his heart and lungs. But he arched his back and continued to fight.

'I powered up the surgical drill, slotted it through the hole in his forehead and bored deep into his brain. He convulsed and died. Perhaps I should have preserved his brain intact. But I wanted to end his torment. Besides, subsequent human trials would allow us to study the precise manner this strange disease attacked the spine and brain stem.

'The train arrived. It slid into the valley like a silver snake. Four lab units resting on flatbed wagons. I had the lab cars shunted into the tunnel. Jabril paid the Syrian crew with fistfuls of gold.

'We used a crane truck to swing the lab units from the rail cars and set them down in the cavern beside the bio-dome.

'The labs were well equipped, but I decided it would be inappropriate to perform a full autopsy of the dead cosmonaut. He needed to be shipped back to a proper research facility for extensive examination. I ordered Konstantin sealed in his triple-lined steel coffin and stored in Lab Four, the virus vault, ready for transport to a more appropriate site.

'Hassim was a popular soldier. Jabril explained his absence to the men. He told them Hassim had died of septicaemia as a result of a cut sustained while exploring Spektr. It was a plausibly mundane account of his death.

'We held a funeral. Buried a body bag full of rocks. Said solemn prayers over an empty grave. Gave him a soldier's headstone: a rifle staked in the ground, helmet balanced on top. Later that night, when the men were singing and drinking, we began the dissection. Hassim would indeed get a funeral. When the autopsy was complete, when his body had been stripped of useful tissue. He would be little more than a jumble of bones, cartilage and hair. His eviscerated remains would be dumped in a deep pit and smothered in lime.'

'Tell me about the dissection.'

'We examined tissue removed from his cerebral cortex and spine. The structure and molecular composition of this pathogen is unlike anything I have ever seen. Forget the usual viral proteins. I'm not even sure it would class as a virus at all. This is a complex organism. The structure is almost crystalline. An ordered lattice. High-tensile strength yet it maintains a constant viscosity. It is a lethally efficient parasite. Swift dendritic growth. It commandeers flesh and bone for its own sinister purpose. Once the fibrous viral strands have penetrated the nervous system, fused with the cytoplasm of host cells, they immediately begin to interfere with neurotransmission.'

'What are you saying? The brain is damaged? Victims can't think straight? Or are you saying the mind is actually rewired?'

'I'm saying Hassim died long before his heart stopped beating. He was eaten from within. The insect intelligence that looked out from behind his eyes as he spat, snarled and pulled at his restraints – it wasn't him. Some other creature inhabited his body. I don't understand this organism. I don't know where it is from. I don't know what it wants. But it is implacably hostile.'

'What about a vaccine? An antidote? Is there any way to reverse the infection?'

'You can't inoculate against this malignancy, any more than you can inoculate against a shark attack.'

'Plants? Animals?'

'We tried to infect dogs. They quickly died. This organism seems to prefer a human host.'

'Could you put a name to it?'

'We called it Mystery Pathogen One. EmPath for short.'

'How long can a person live once they become infected?'

'Irreversible brain damage within a matter of hours. The body itself can last many weeks. Metabolism slows almost to a standstill. Low heart rate. Low respiration. They exist, almost in a state of suspended animation, until they sense the presence of a fresh host. Then they are galvanised to action.'

'Tell me about the human trials.'

'Your man in Baghdad supplied us with test subjects.'

'General Nassar?'

'He sent us a truck load of Shi'ite deserters. I believe his emissary received a kilo of gold in exchange for each man.'

'How many expendables?'

'An initial batch of twenty. We conducted medical examinations. The men had clearly been kept in poor conditions for many months. Two of the prisoners were suffering from tuberculosis. I decided they were inappropriate experimental subjects. I had them terminated. The rest were given yellow jumpsuits and housed in a couple of Conex shipping containers. Each man had a number and blood group tattooed on the back of their left hand. It made them easy to identify, and spared us the need to use names. We dug incinerator pits, ready to receive human remains.'

'How did the soldiers react? The men you assigned to guard the prisoners?'

'The Republican Guard were the creation of a totalitarian state. Supposedly praetorian troops, but utterly docile. We had their absolute obedience.'

'And your Russian colleagues?'

'They knew what to do. When time came to shut down the operation, when our mission was complete, all Iraqis on site were to be exterminated. We would wait until evening. Give the men food and alcohol. Let them sit round campfires and drink themselves into a stupor. Then the Russians would take position with .50 calibre machine guns. It would be quick, thorough. There was some talk that we might keep a work party alive. A few men to help hide bodies from aerial surveillance by dumping them among the citadel ruins.'

'Tell me about the weapon.'

'This is madness. There can be no "tactical" use of this weapon. It cannot be contained.'

'Did you complete the weapon? I have to know.'

'Please.'

'Just finish your story. Then you can die.'

'We built a production line. We propagated amplified cultures. Human flesh suspended in amino acids and calf foetus serum. The virus cultures were harvested, freeze-dried and milled. Then they were micro-encapsulated in a polymer coat.'

'Is it viable? As a weaponised agent?'

'It's the perfect battle strain. Supremely resilient. It can easily survive blast dissemination as the payload of an artillery shell, cluster bomb or missile warhead. It is impervious to sunlight, and most chemical counter-measures. We refined a single litre. That was the results of our efforts. Particulates held in suspension, four microns in diameter. Fine enough to enter the upper respiratory tract. We loaded the warhead reservoir. Air-burst over any major city would be devastating. A slow-settling cloud of infection. Odourless. Invisible. Commuters would be coughing blood within minutes. Mass panic, mass casualties. Victims would soon turn savage. The streets would become a war zone. Men, women, children. Ripping throats. Gouging flesh. Picture it. New York, Los Angeles, quickly turned into a living hell. The government would have to respond within minutes if they were to have any hope of containing the situation. The only effective response, the only hope of halting the spread of infection once it began to vector, would be a nuclear strike.'

'You built it? You armed the prototype?'

'God help me, yes.'

'So where is it? Where is the warhead?'

'I don't know.'

'Tell me.'

'I swear I don't know.'

The Ravine

Lucy flipped latches and opened the missile case. She examined the glass cylinder. The liquid glowed sickly blue.

'We've got frag grenades. Why not blow the damn thing to scrap metal?'

'The liquid is a polymer resin,' explained Jabril. 'The pathogen itself is held in suspension. Little particles, like the flakes of a snow globe. You can't see them, but they are there. Fine as dust. The liquid was synthesised to protect the virus against blast decompression. There would be no use detonating a bio-weapon if the very act of firing the burst charge destroyed the payload.'

'I guess.'

'If you throw a couple of fragmentation grenades inside this case you will simply spread the pathogen and contaminate this entire valley. You would die. Anyone who subsequently entered this ravine would die. And sooner or later the disease would be carried back to a major population centre and trigger a pandemic.'

'So what do we do?'

'We take it to the mine. There are explosives. High-yield demolition charges. Enough to incinerate the pathogen and simultaneously bury it beneath a million tons of rock.'

What about the soldiers, out there among the ruins? Each one of them is incubating this parasite.'

'The soldiers are slowly dying. A few months from now they will be dust and bone. Military scientists may visit the valley, but they will find nothing to harvest.'

Jabril took the cylinder from her hand and held it up.

'This is the prize. The virus in its refined, weaponised form. More powerful, more devastating, than a hydrogen bomb. That is why it must be destroyed.'

'All right. Let's go.'

They loaded the missile case onto the back of the quad bike. Voss straddled the bike and gunned the engine.

They secured sand goggles, chambered their weapons and headed into the storm.

They emerged from the temple, observed with sardonic detachment by the titanic twin colossi that flanked the entrance.

Voss drove slowly down the processional avenue towards the gates of the citadel. Lucy, Amanda and Jabril jogged by his side. The head-beam of the bike lit driving dust particles.

Night-wind. A gusting sandstorm.

Slack, desiccated figures loomed out of the megalithic ruins. Lucy and Amanda stopped, shouldered their rifles and delivered efficient headshots. They stood over the fallen men, boots planted on their skulls, and delivered second point-blank kill-shots.

They ran through the citadel precincts.

Hands reached from the swirling storm and wrestled Jabril to the ground. A skeletal revenant crouched over the fallen man and tried to rip out his throat. Jabril struggled to fend off snapping jaws.

Lucy shot the soldier in the chest. He reeled like he took a gut punch. He fell. He tried to sit. She jammed the gun barrel beneath his chin. Burst of gristle and bone.

Lucy helped Jabril to his feet.

Movement all around them. Prowling silhouettes. A wraith army.

'Let's go,' said Lucy. 'We'll be all right as long as we keep moving.'

'Hold on.'

Amanda pointed into the darkness.

'Thought I saw someone, standing watch.'

She took a couple of steps forward.

A momentary lull in the storm. A distant figure stood among broken columns. They glimpsed coyote fatigues.

'Is it Gaunt?' asked Lucy.

'I think it's Huang,' said Amanda.

Lucy pulled Amanda by the arm.

'We better go.'

They continued down the processional avenue. They were dimly aware, by the monstrous shadows looming above them, that they were approaching the twin guard towers of the temple entrance.

'Wait.'

Amanda shouldered her rifle, took a Maglite from her pocket and checked the ground.

A wisp of monofilament.

'The trip flare. It's been cut.'

'Gaunt?'

'Who else?'

Voss revved the Yamaha quad. He swerved around pillar rubble lying across the entranceway, and drove through the massive propylon gateway.

They left smooth flagstones and headed across the rough terrain of the valley floor. The bike kicked up sand and grit. It lurched over the rock-strewn, lunar waste.

'Least we are leaving those fuckers behind,' said Lucy.

'No,' said Jabril. 'They will follow us. We can outrun them for a while. But they will keep coming. They won't deviate. They won't rest. If we hurry, we can buy time.'

They jogged. It had been a long time since basic training. Lucy settled her breathing. She found her own pace.

Jabril puffed and panted. Each inhalation sucked a mouthful of sandstorm. He spat dust.

'You okay?'

'Yes.'

'Want to ride the bike?'

'No.'

'What is this? Some kind of victory lap? You want to feel the blood pumping one last time?'

'Something like that.'

'The wind is dropping,' said Amanda.

'Fuckin' A,' said Voss.

'I don't know how those infected soldiers track their prey,' said Jabril. 'Maybe it is smell. Maybe it is some sixth sense. But they will come after us fast and strong once the storm has cleared. We need to get you aboard the locomotive and out of here.'

Camp wreckage. Collapsed pup tents. Canvas cots.

'This was your bivouac?' asked Lucy. 'You and the Republican Guard?'

'For a while. Then the men moved into the mine tunnels. The passageways were cool and free of dust. They left the tents standing.'

Amanda snagged tent fabric with the barrel of her rifle and pulled it from the sand. Ragged scorch holes.

'Looks like fucking Swiss cheese.'

'What happened that night?' asked Lucy.

'A long story.'

'Tell me anyway.'

'We kept infected men penned in a freight container deep within the mine. They broke free. It was night. Most Republican Guard were in the tunnels. Either asleep, or carousing in one of the side-gallery recreation halls. They drink, smoked hashish, jeered American action movies. Next thing they knew, the creatures were among them, ripping and tearing. It was chaos.

'Our Russian overseers, Ignatiev's thugs, initiated a pre-arranged plan. Maybe Ignatiev gave the eradication order. Maybe they acted on their own initiative.

'They ran from the mine. They took heavy machine guns from a truck and stationed them at the head of the ravine, near the old tented camp.

'Men fled down the narrow ravine, thinking it was a route to safety. They ran into a firing squad.

'Soldiers begged for their lives. Gun positions cut them down with a stream of heavy .50 calibre bullets.

'It was a bloodbath. Streaking tracer rounds. Broken bodies.

'Many of the Russians were overwhelmed. Weight of numbers. They swung their machine guns left and right, scythed panicking troops, but were overrun by injured and desperate men. Some of Ignatiev's goons were beaten to death with bare fists.

'Hand-to-hand combat. Knives and rocks. I was spared. I crawled over a carpet of bodies. I crawled between the burning trucks of the convoy. I was smeared in blood and soot. I was lucky. It was night, it was chaos. I escaped the ravine and climbed the valley wall.

'I turned and watched from high crags. Moonlit slaughter. Screams and moans.

'Some of the men escaped the carnage and reached vehicles parked in front of the citadel. Ignatiev's goons followed them. They strafed the convoy and threw grenades. A succession of fuel fires incinerated trucks and sedans.

'The surviving Russians walked among bodies, pistols drawn, and executed wounded men.'

Lucy kicked scattered mess tins. She raked through sand and unearthed a fistful of cartridge cases. She dug. She found a boot. Half-buried razor wire.

'How many men died? In total?'

'Nearly two hundred.'

'But they were shot,' said Lucy. 'They weren't bitten. They weren't infected. Ignatiev and his men gunned them down.'

'Any pathologist will tell you human limbs respond to electrical stimuli many hours after the heart has stopped beating. The central nervous system retains a residual charge. Some of these soldiers, perhaps the majority, were bitten, scratched and infected before they died. The pathogen got to work. Even after they were clinically dead, after respiration had ceased and brain activity dropped to near zero, their cadavers provided a rich environment for this strange disease to replicate and spread. As long as the medulla oblongata wasn't destroyed, as long as the central cortex of the brain remained viable, the bodies could still provide a vehicle for infection. Bodies lay buried in sand, curled in burned-out cars, dumped in piles beneath the temple. But the pathogen continued to spread through still-warm flesh. '

'But they were dead. They were actually dead.'

'I use terms like "virus", "disease" and "pathogen", because it is the only language I have to describe this entity. But this life form is more than a string of dumb RNA. This is a highly adaptive parasite. It uses each body as a chassis. A dumb host. The human cadaver is a shell it can hijack and pilot as it pursues its single, unshakable purpose: to spread and replicate. You saw what happened to your friend. Toon. He was dead. No pulse, no breath. But he came back.'

Amanda took off her Stetson and looked up at the stars.

'Where do you think it came from?'

'Maybe the Russians were experimenting with nanobots or gene manipulation. Recombinant DNA. Something that required zero gravity and the isolating vacuum of space. But I doubt it. The Soviet Union was a mess. Their submarines sank. Their nuclear reactors blew up. The population lived on turnips. Their army was large and secretive, but incapable of producing something of this level of sophistication.'

'What then?'

'The cosmonauts on that space station were drifting in a deep orbit far from Earth, way beyond commercial space lanes. Perhaps something found them, out there, alone in the dark. Something found its way aboard and made a home.'

'What are you saying?'

'This virus is a crystalline structure, like metal or glass. Some kind of amorphous alloy. It's an entirely new order of life.'

'The parasite is alien?'

'I don't know. But I hope you begin to understand what is at stake. This virus is the equal of humanity. It is so lethal, so efficient, it would spread across the globe in a matter of days. Infection escalating at an exponential rate. It would be unstoppable. Mankind doomed within hours of first contact.'

They entered the ravine. The moon shone high overhead. They walked along the track. Voss rode the quad. Motor noise echoed off high canyon walls.

A glint.

Lucy stooped. A scrap of foil in the sand. She turned it over in gloved fingers. A blister strip of pills. Dexedrine. UCB Pharma: an American brand.

'Gaunt must be running ahead of us.'

They reached the tunnel entrance. A high arch in a rock face, blocked with a jumble of planks, beams and sacking.

'The mine,' said Jabril. 'This tunnel leads to a central cavern.'

'And Spektr?'

'Yes.'

Lucy stepped over planks. She shone her flashlight into the dark.

'It's down there,' said Jabril. 'The locomotive. It's parked in the tunnel, about a hundred yards in.'

Lucy turned to Amanda and Voss.

'You two stay here. Cover our backs.'

A wide, high tunnel. Double rails. A rubble conveyor corroded to scrap.

Lucy inspected the fissured, limestone walls. Steel crossbars and chock-jacks reinforced slabs of rock that threatened to slough from the roof.

She raked her fingers across the wall. She held a limestone shard between her fingers and crumbled it to powder.

'This shit could collapse any moment. I'm frightened to cough.'

Jabril led her deeper into the tunnel. Boots crunched on ballast. He held a blue cyalume above his head.

'Cold as a tomb,' muttered Lucy, buttoning her coat. 'Hey. Jabril. Let me ask you something. That story you told us in your prison cell. All bullshit, yeah?'

'Every word.'

'So how did you lose your arm?'

He ignored the question.

'Here she is.'

A massive locomotive. Lucy shone her barrel light over the rust-streaked prow.

'Jesus. Big as a fucking battleship. Looks like it has been to hell and back.'

'It weighs about two hundred and fifty tons.'

'What are these passenger cars?'

'Relics,' said Jabril. 'Saddam ordered a replica of the *Orient Express*. He wanted to travel the country in style. Too afraid to use it, of course. Too frightened of assassination. A couple of carriages must have been dumped in this tunnel years ago. Been here way longer than the engine. Left to rot.'

'The train. Will it run?'

'Why not? It's been sitting in this tunnel gathering dust. It hasn't been exposed to the weather. It looks undamaged. The batteries might need a charge. Otherwise it is ready to go.'

Lucy clasped grab-rails and hauled herself up the side of the great locomotive to the walkway. She held out a hand and helped Jabril climb the ladder.

She tried the cab door. Locked. She chambered her Glock.

'Stand back,' she told Jabril.

She shielded her eyes. She blew out the lock. The gunshot echoed round the tunnel walls.

She drew back the slide door and entered the cab.

A cursory glance at the circuit breaker panel and engineer's console.

A dead man on the plate floor. Lucy crouched beside him.

'Syrian rail crew,' said Jabril.

Desiccated. Mummified. The man wore a boiler suit. The folds of the suit deflated round skeletal limbs.

A neat bullet hole in his temple. Muzzle burn. An old Makarov pistol in his hand.

Lucy ejected the magazine and checked the corroded weapon. The slide was jammed rigid.

'Locked himself inside and blew his brains out,' murmured Lucy. 'Can't blame the guy. Guess he wanted to stay dead.'

Amanda and Voss stood at the tunnel mouth. Voss hauled planks aside to allow the quad bike to drive into the tunnel.

Amanda raised her rifle. She scanned the high ravine behind them with her nightscope.

'Contact?' asked Voss.

'Nothing yet.'

They pulled planks and beams back in place, barricading themselves inside the mine entrance.

Amanda unfolded the bipod of her rifle and rested it on jumbled planks.

Voss took the SAW from the quad trailer. He clipped a fresh belt into the receiver and laid it on an oil drum.

'Those fucks from the citadel will be heading our way sooner or later,' said Amanda. 'They move slow, but they are on their way. That locomotive better work. If we have to retrace our steps, it will be the fight of our lives.'

Containment Four

Gaunt entered the second containment. Overhead strobes flashed a red contamination warning.

Mirrored steel counters. Toppled swivel chairs. Milling machines. A centrifuge. An electron microscope.

Gaunt pictured men at work. Test tubes and Petri dishes. Technicians in white hazmat suits, arms thrust inside the thick handling gloves of hermetic containment boxes. The intellectual myopia of virologists struggling to solve the practical problems of encapsulation and dispersal, wilfully blind to the monstrous doomsday weapon they were helping to create.

He crouched and checked smashed computer shells. Hard drives ripped out. Ring binders stripped of notes.

Somebody wanted to obliterate all trace of research. They systematically stripped the lab before the contamination alert locked it tight.

Splintered glassware, culture dishes and fermentation vials, crunched underfoot.

He opened a freezer door. Ice smoke. Body parts preserved in storage jars.

He took a jar from a shelf. A section of spine.

Another jar on the shelf. A severed head floating in formaldehyde. A young man, eyes half open, lips parted, quizzical expression.

Eyelids flickered. Jaw twitch.

Gaunt jumped back. He dropped the jar in his hand. Glass

smashed. Formaldehyde splashed his boots. The vertebrae lay on the plate floor and slowly curled.

More laptop interrogation footage.

Koell jolted Ignatiev awake with a second shot in the arm.

'Just kill me.'

'Earn it.'

'I've told you everything.'

'Tell me about the refinement process. You brought infected specimens to the necropsy room. You cut them up. What then? How did you amplify the virus?'

'Naturally, the primary purpose of the human field trials was to assess the pathology of the parasitic illness, to chart speed of infection, latency period, resistance to antibiotics. The usual tests that would be performed on any emerging pathogen. We also wanted to refine the disease. We wanted to capture the strongest, most lethal concentration we could distil. The best way to achieve that goal was to incubate the virus in a living host.'

'You've done this before?'

'Yes. During my time at Vektor. We were working with Ebola. Our acquisition team had secured samples during a virulent outbreak in the Republic of Congo. They were nominally UNHCO personnel on site to coordinate emergency relief, but in reality they were senior members of Biopreperat.

'Swabs were sent to Moscow in a diplomatic pouch and we began to culture the virus in our level-four lab in the basement of the Koltsovo Health Institute, Siberia. We conducted exposure trials on guinea pigs and rats.

'One of our support technicians, a young man named Karpov, was accidentally exposed to the virus while fixing the air-filtration system. He was working on a wall vent in one of the containment labs. He was tired. He was careless. He punctured his glove with a screwdriver as he opened an exhaust filter and cut open his hand. He quickly fell ill. We did what we could. Made every effort to treat the man. We had antiserum flown from the Ministry of Defence in Zagorsk. We dosed him with ribavirin and interferon. But his condition deteriorated.

'He lasted two weeks. The disease liquefied his internal organs. He bled from his eyes, nipples, anus. We gave him transfusions, tried to keep enough blood in his veins to maintain circulation.

'Escalating brain damage. A PhD in virology reduced to an imbecile. We kept him in a chemically induced coma, partly for his comfort, but mostly to silence his idiot grunts and moans.

'The moment he was dead, his body was transported to our necropsy room. We harvested as much as we could. The samples of virus we drew from his lungs and liver were far more virulent than the original Congo strain. The process of incubating the disease in a live human host had somehow refined the pathogen and made it more aggressive.

'Karpov's body was soaked in chloramine and sealed in a steel box. I attended the funeral. As soon as the priest had finished his oration, a truck reversed to the graveside and smothered the coffin in concrete.'

'We stopped work on the Congo strain of the virus the next day. We immediately began to study and weaponise the samples taken from Karpov. The new strain was named Ebola-K, in honour of its host. It was one of the most lethal pathogens we had in our vault.

'The samples should have been destroyed. If Vektor complied with subsequent arms limitation treaties, their vast bank of bio-weapons would have been consigned to the furnace. But somehow I doubt it. I suspect Ebola-K remains in deep storage, frozen in nitrogen, waiting for the day it becomes tactically advantageous to decimate an enemy population.

'That is the process we set in motion in the Western Desert. Human amplification.

'We requisitioned twenty prisoners and kept them penned in a couple of freight containers deep within the mine. We planned to infect each man and watch the virus progress to full term. Then, when their blood and internal organs were rich with the viral load, we would dissect their bodies in an attempt to isolate and refine the pathogen.

'The second containment would act as our factory floor. The virus could be freeze dried and milled to a powder. Then each particle could be electrostatically coated with a polymer shell that would protect it from the degrading effects of sunlight and extreme temperature fluctuation.'

'Can this parasite sustain life outside a human?'

'No. It will always seek out a host.'

'How does our man get inside Lab Three?' asked Koell.

'There's no point trying to shoot your way through the door. It's inch-thick steel and ballistic glass.'

'Key code?'

'Automatically locked out the moment the contamination alert was tripped. Your man will need to bypass the mechanism entirely.'

The third containment. A steel door with a porthole.

DANGER
HOT AGENT

BIOHAZARD
LEVEL THREE

Gaunt took a Bosch drill from his backpack. Compact, like an electric toothbrush.

He drilled out the lock panel. He levered the keypad. He stripped wires and shorted the mechanism. Crack. Spark. Magnetic bolts disengaged. He cranked handles and pulled the door open.

Blast of hot, humid air.

Glowing storage vats like fish tanks. Incubators. Gaunt wiped condensation. Arms. A torso. Sections of spine.

Sweat collected inside Gaunt's gas mask. He shook his head, blinked perspiration from his eyes.

'Lab Three was our main incubation chamber. There are tanks. Vats. Human body parts suspended in a rich growth medium. Synthetic plasmas. We called them milk shakes.'

'And the result?'

'You can't farm this material. It will not thrive under artificial conditions. It will only exist in symbiosis with a living, thinking host.'

'How many test subjects did you use for the terminal trials?'

'All of them. Then we ordered twenty more.'

'There will be no come-backs for the programme?'

'We infected every prisoner with this disease. They must be long dead by now. The soldiers that escorted them from southern internment camps were given plates of food, and shot in the back of the head as they ate. Thousands of young men were killed in this war. A generation wiped out. Entire platoons missing in action, shovelled into mass graves in some god-forsaken corner of the desert. The men that died in that valley will never be traced.'

'It all went as planned?'

'At first the prisoners were docile. They were kept corralled in freight containers. Bare enclosures with a single shit-bucket. The containers had been carried into the mine by crane truck and dumped at the end of a wide tunnel.

'We subjected the prisoners to long hours of darkness, then sudden blinding light. We played rock music and white noise. Petty torments to keep them disoriented.

'We gave them basic food and water. The men assumed they were being kept for some kind of work detail. It was not uncommon for deserters and criminals to be used for hazardous operations such as mine clearance or the deactivation of unstable munitions.

'Once we were done with Hassim we selected our next test subject.

'I asked Jabril, the Iraqi intelligence officer running the camp, to make the selection. He made all our selections. He seemed to enjoy the process.

'We had welded bars at the entrance of each freight container. He would stand in front of these makeshift pens and observe the prisoners, enjoy the power of life and death. It was as if he was visiting a seafood restaurant and choosing a lobster from a tank.

'Number eight. I don't know his name. He was the first to be chosen. We escorted him to Lab One. He began to struggle and shout as he entered the lab and saw the necropsy table and surgical instruments laid out. The sound of his screams echoed down nearby tunnels. His companions heard the commotion.

'It took six men to drag him to the table and strap him down. We introduced the parasite into his bloodstream by subcutaneous injection and monitored the spread of infection.

'After that, we adopted a different routine each time we removed a test subject from the cells. We discovered, among the clutter of cuffs, chains and other prison equipment Jabril had requested from his contacts in the secret police, that we had been supplied with a tranquilliser pole. A crude spear with a hypodermic at the end. The kind of device zookeepers push through the bars of a cage to sedate a dangerous animal.

It enabled us to drug our chosen subject with a Thorazine and Largactil cocktail, and remove him from their freight container cell with very little resistance. The doped prisoner would then be cuffed. We would pull a hood over his head. Our subjects were semi-conscious. Docile, but responsive to commands. Much easier to manage.'

'The men in the cells. Did they try to break out?'

'There was a minor rebellion. Jabril had been instructed to select a fresh test subject. The guards sedated his chosen candidate. When they unchained the pen, nine prisoners rushed the guards. The prisoners were beaten back with rifle butts.

'Jabril later became concerned that the prisoners might begin to whisper between the bars, appeal for help from the younger, more impressionable guards. He assigned older men to watch over the cells, thuggish brutes who regarded the prisoners with boredom and contempt.

'We checked the empty shipping containers before the second consignment of prisoners arrived. We discovered the previous group had scratched messages warning future inmates that they were condemned men and should seek any means of escape. Jabril ordered the messages be gouged until they were unreadable.

'I did my best to accommodate Jabril. I let him indulge his sadistic inclinations. I felt a profound distaste for the man but he was useful. He was a senior member of the Iraqi intelligence service. The men followed his orders without question. Even though we heard radio reports that Baghdad had fallen and Saddam had been overthrown, he still commanded fear. And the prisoners were abattoir cattle. They were selected to die. Specimens to be euthanised, then dissected. If we had begun to interact with them, cared for their welfare, it might have proved . . . counter-productive.

'Jabril fell in love with his role as overseer. Theoretically, he was responsible for the upkeep of the entire camp, for marshalling the troops, mounting patrols, and manning a defensive perimeter. He was tasked with making sure latrine and cooking facilities were maintained. But I always knew where to find him, day or night. He would be standing in front of the prisoner pens, enjoying their fear. He would pace in plain view and sip from a glass of water as they lay parched and hungry. He would visit them at night and drag a tin bowl across the bars, to rob them of sleep.

'Once, I saw him drunk. It was late at night. The men were bivouacked in the tunnels, eating, drinking, playing back-gammon. I heard shouts from a remote passageway. Jabril was standing in front of the condemned men. His shirt was off. He was waving an empty bottle, dancing to music only he could hear. I asked what he was doing. He recited those Oppenheimer lines from the *Bhagavad Gita*. "I am become Death, the destroyer of worlds . . ."

'He told the prisoners about the experiments, told them what lay in store once they were selected for treatment. He described the disease. He described the process of dissection. He described the lime pits that would receive their remains, the acid stench of slow-dissolving body fat. I had a couple of my men drag him away. I slapped his face and told him to sober up.'

'The experiments. Were there any variation in symptoms? Are some men more susceptible than others? Did anyone show signs of natural resistance?'

'This parasite is a killing machine. It's not flu. It's not salmonella. I use terminology like "virus" and "disease" because I don't know how else to characterise this damn thing. But it is a whole new species. A new and lethal order of life that hasn't existed on earth before. Antibodies can't repel this pathogen any more than they can ward off a bullet. None of our test subjects showed the slightest sign of resist-ance. They all quickly succumbed. Drug treatment had no effect. This disease is a death sentence. There is no reprieve.'

'Your swipe card. Will it grant access to the fourth containment?'

'It will get you into the final lab unit. But it won't open the virus vault.'

Gaunt approached the entrance to Lab Four.

EXTREME DANGER
HOT AGENT

FULL
BIOHAZARD
PROTOCOL

Gaunt took a laminated swipe card from his pocket. Doctor Ignatiev's Slavic face beneath the plastic glaze.

He entered the key code and swiped the card. He opened the heavy door and stepped through.

He found himself in a glass airlock cubicle.

A large Chemturion bio-suit and hood hung on a wall hook.

He peeled off his gasmask and stripped out of his clothes. He pulled on surgical scrubs. He stepped into the heavy white hazmat suit and sealed the zipper seam. The suit had an integral hood and Lexan visor. Boots and gloves secured with lock-rings.

He hit open. The glass partition slid back.

He lumbered like an astronaut. Heavy footfalls.

He entered a steel enclosure. Mirror-metal walls like a bank vault. No chairs, no counters. An empty space. A constant contamination alert lit the room red.

Gaunt put his backpack on the floor, his movements made slow and deliberate by the cumbersome suit. He plugged the yellow coiled air hose into a wall socket. He fumbled. Thick gloves like mittens.

An abrupt hiss. His ears popped as pressure within the suit increased. Rubber crackled as it inflated and ballooned around him. Stale air replaced by fresh.

A metal coffin in the middle of the vault floor. Konstantin, the dead cosmonaut, sealed in a triple-lined casket.

Gaunt knelt beside the coffin. The sarcophagus lid was secured by latches, wing nuts and a rubber seal. He looked through the porthole. An eyeless, mummified face stared back at him. Skin stretched like leather. Lips pulled back in a snarl. Blond stubble. A web of strange metal knots and tendrils woven into dried flesh. Metallic fibres bristling from the man's mouth, nose and eye sockets. Brain colonised and eaten away.

'What about the virus vault?' asked Koell.

'A large freezer. Bomb-proof. Independent power source.'

'Who had access to the vault?'

'I did,' said Ignatiev.

'Jabril?'

'No. Certainly not. I wouldn't let him near the fourth containment. The more I spoke with the man, the more I became convinced he was unhinged. His universe had come to an end. He had been part of Saddam's security apparatus his entire adult life. His role had provided money and status. Now, with the fall of the regime, he had no identity. He was desperate for direction and meaning. And he found himself confronted by something alien, something stranger than he could possibly imagine. He was enthralled. His fascination had a religious intensity. I felt he had become dangerous.

'Technicians, including myself, already had reservations about the Spektr project. The more we studied the pathogen, the more we became convinced it could not be safely contained. My colleagues were dedicated biochemists. Men of science, not prone to fancy. Yet we began to speculate that the parasite possessed some glimmer of sentience, a strange insect cunning. Some nights, as I lay in my bunk, I convinced myself the infected body parts racked in jars in our freezers contained some kind of hive mind, possessed by a single harmonious purpose: to reach out beyond this valley and infect a major population centre. I began to fear and hate the thing I saw writhing and blossoming each day; the sinister cellscape beneath the lens of my microscope. Metallic fibres as they branched and spread, slowly infiltrating human nerve cells. I began to suspect, during long hours I spent alone in the lab, that we under-estimated this organism. Maybe it was studying us.

'It seemed Jabril experienced a similar epiphany. He understood the destructive potential of EmPath. He was intoxicated by the holocaust the parasite could unleash. I ordered that Jabril be watched. I told Karl, one of our Russian goons, to observe him and report erratic behaviour. When the time came, when Jabril was of no further use, he was to be shot in the back of the head and thrown into the lime pit. Until then, he was vital to the operation of the camp. Troops followed his commands without question. But he continued to drink heavily. I judged he was becoming a liability. He was simply too curious. He was fascinated by the virus.'

'Tell me about the Hellfire. Is it intact?'

Ignatiev's voice, tired, defeated: 'It's still sealed in the case, ready to fly.'

'Good.'

'What was the target site?' asked Ignatiev. 'If we delivered the virus, what would you have done with it?'

Long pause.

'The target was a UN refugee centre outside Mosul,' said Koell. 'Inmates call it "New Medina". Fifteen thousand displaced families in a tent city. No good to anyone. No good to themselves. Blast dispersal. We would wait for optimum wind conditions. Late evening, as the air settles and cools. The missile would be launched from a drone and tracked via GPS. We would detonate at five hundred feet, directly over the Red Cross inoculation clinic at the centre of the camp. Thirty acres of tents arranged in a rigid street-grid. A perfect environment to test the efficacy of the weapon.'

'You sick motherfuckers.'

'We would have men on site. Have them pose as volunteer doctors from Saudi Red Crescent. They would wear bio-suits and film the outbreak. Take blood samples, track the speed of infection. When they judged the test had run its course, when the pandemic began to threaten their personal safety, they would drive from the camp and steps would be taken to contain the situation.'

'You couldn't halt the spread of infection,' said Ignatiev. 'The virus would quickly pass beyond the camp and out into the world.'

'We would drop a massive fuel bomb. It would erase the entire camp in a moment of cleansing fire.'

'You're a fool. An absolute fool. I'm happy to die. I mean it. I consider myself blessed. You can't comprehend the horror you will unleash. You'll turn the surface of this planet into hell. I don't want to see it. I don't want to be alive when it happens.'

'Is that it? Nothing left to tell?'

'Kill me. Please. I've talked long enough. I've told you everything I know. Just kill me. Let me sleep.'

'But what about the freezer? How do we release the lock?'

'It is a simple biometric mechanism.'

'All right.'

'If you truly want to serve your country, you will destroy every trace of this virus.'

'Fuck America. A single litre is enough to switch off the human race. No one has ever had that kind of power, held it in their hand.'

'You're out of your fucking mind.'

Koell walked into camera shot. He held a hypodermic gun. He fired the gun into Ignatiev's bicep.

'Damn you,' murmured Ignatiev. His eyelids drooped, his head sank to his chest and his breathing slowed to a halt.

The recording came to an end.

Koell leant forward and closed the laptop. He refilled Gaunt's whisky tumbler for the fourth time.

'Are you clear?' asked Koell. 'You know what you have to do?'

'Yeah. I got it.'

Gaunt stood before the virus vault. A steel freezer.

CAUTION
LIVE BIOLOGICAL AGENTS

He typed the entry key. He swiped the card.

Ocular scan required

He reached into his backpack. An eyeball floating in a small jar. Pale iris and a tuft of optic nerve.

He held the eyeball to the L-1 Ident iris scan. A brief wash of red laser-light.

Thank you, Doctor Ignatiev.
You are clear to enter.

Hum and clack. Bolts retracted. Gaunt unlatched the door and hauled it open. Icy exhalation. A torrent of nitrogen fog cascaded from the freezer, washed across the floor and engulfed his boots. Skin-prickle chill.

The fog slowly cleared.

An empty shelf. No case. No missile. The warhead was gone.

The Catacombs

'Let's find the generator,' said Voss. 'Let's get the lights on.'

Jabril led him deep into the tunnel. Voss pulled a flare from his pocket. He struck the cap. Splutter and fizz. Crimson fire. Limestone walls lit blood red.

'How does it feel to be back?' asked Voss.

'I dream about this place every night,' said Jabril. 'Awful nightmares. It almost feels like coming home.'

'Yeah?'

'It's difficult to explain. Some events, some places, are so terrible they become an indelible part of you.'

The cavern.

Voss checked the lab units.

A scorched hatch hung open and crooked.

'Someone blew their way inside,' said Jabril. 'Some kind of breaching charge. Very recent. I can still smell the cordite.'

'Gaunt. Better watch our backs.'

Voss stepped inside the lab.

He kicked at the Chemturion suit crumpled on the floor.

He examined the polished zinc of the necropsy slab. Cuff restraints. IV stand. Examination lights. A camera tripod.

Surgical instruments laid out on a metal table. He picked up stainless steel pliers.

'Bone rongeurs,' explained Jabril. 'For splitting skulls.'

Voss snorted in disgust. He threw the rongeurs onto the necropsy slab. Harsh clatter.

'We should leave,' said Jabril. 'We shouldn't be in here. It's too dangerous. We have no protective clothing.'

They left the lab.

They approached the high, opaque plastic dome of the bio-containment structure.

'Is this Spektr?' asked Voss.

'It's safe. The craft itself is not contaminated.'

Voss slung his shotgun. He unsheathed his knife and slit plastic. He ducked through the polythene curtain, and held the flare above his head.

The orbital craft rested on a flatbed rail car.

Voss walked a slow circuit of the vehicle. He ducked beneath the ragged Delta wing. He reached up and stroked thermal tiles discoloured by the unimaginable heat of hypersonic re-entry.

'This thing actually flew through space,' he murmured. 'Left the Earth and came back again.'

Jabril contemplated the shadows of the open airlock.

'Pandora's box. We should have left this craft in the desert. It would have been buried forever.'

Lucy climbed the ladder to the locomotive walkway. She entered the cab.

She rolled the dead engineer with her foot. No signs of infection.

She checked the pockets of the engineer's boiler suit. Cigarettes. Prayer beads. A key.

She dragged the body out onto the walkway. She lifted the desiccated corpse over the guard rails and threw it onto the track.

She returned to the cab. The engineer's console. Red brake handle. Big throttle. Key slot.

She inserted the key and turned the ignition.

Nothing. No instrumentation lights, no engine noise. She looked around the cab for breakers, any kind of power switch.

A brief flutter of panic and despair, crushed before it began.

RSM Miller, her platoon sergeant, laid it out for her, the day she applied for the Fourteen Intelligence Company.

'*The difference between regular army and special forces is simply the ability to maintain composure. To think straight in situations of extreme peril. Special recon training is a constant live-fire exercise. Endless boot camp endurance tasks while bullets whizz past your head. I've been out to that dummy village they built on Salisbury Plain. So many cartridge cases lying around, they crunch underfoot like gravel. The instructors will teach you to think through a haze of adrenalin and exhaustion. They'll teach you to survive.*'

Lucy swigged from her canteen. She rubbed her eyes.

The locomotive wouldn't fire up. Maybe the ignition battery was dead. Must be some way to check available current.

She began a methodical survey of the cab.

Jabril left Voss in the cavern.

'I want to find my old room, collect some of my things.'

He wandered down a low passageway. His blue cyalume lit chiselled walls, timber props and roof beams.

A faded door sign.

Dynamite Store.

Jabril pushed open the rough wooden door. A small cell. A windowless cave.

A canvas cot, a table, a trunk. A wash table and mirror.

His old room.

Jabril sat on the bunk. He lay the cyalume on the blanket. The chemical stick lit the room cold blue.

He dragged the trunk towards the cot. Leather. Louis Vuitton. A relic of his previous life.

He unbuckled straps and popped latches.

Books and neatly folded clothes. He searched among his possessions. He found a gold cigarette case and a Ronson lighter.

He lay on the cot and smoked a Turkish cigarette. He cried a little, then sat up and wiped tears.

He flicked away the cigarette.

He took a folded shirt from the trunk. Crisp white. He unrolled a black silk tie. Socks. Silk underwear. Polished brogues.

He unzipped a suit carrier, and laid a white linen suit on the cot. He smoothed creases. He brushed away lint.

Voss explored the cavern. He found a 24 KvA trailer generator parked in a wall niche. Power for the cavern floodlights.

He filled the tank from a jerry can, turned the ignition and set the generator running. Cough and splutter. A puff of diesel smoke. Output needles twitched.

A ring of light towers flickered and glowed steady. The cavern was lit brilliant white. Spektr floodlit beneath its polythene dome.

A voice echoed round the cavern.

'*How's it going?*'

Gaunt. Quiet, mocking.

Voss crouched. He fumbled at a chest pocket. He put on his glasses. He scanned the cavern. No movement. No sign of Gaunt.

'*Reckon you can get that locomotive working?*'

Voss pressed himself against the rough sandstone of the cavern wall.

'*So, after all this blood and anguish, Lucy wants to send you home empty handed? How do you feel about it? You've seen your friends die. All for nothing.*'

Voss gripped the shotgun. Multiple tunnel mouths. Gaunt's voice reverberated round the cavern.

'*That bomb. That warhead. Do you have any idea how much it is worth? Forget the gold. Boxes of watches and rings, pawned for a fraction of their value. You didn't want a few dollars in your hand. You weren't looking for another paycheque. You flew out here with bigger dreams in your head. Lucy promised you a fortune. You were going to lie on a beach for the rest of your life, umbrella drink in your hand. Help me get the warhead back to Baghdad. I swear, you will never work another day in your life.'*

'Come on out,' said Voss. 'Let's talk it over.'

'*Think about it. What's waiting for you back home? Do you even have a home? Half your life in jail. Zonderwater. Krugersdorp. You're old. This is your last roll of the dice.*'

'Gaan fok jouself.'

'*I killed your friend. So what? I won't apologise for pursuing my self-interest. Neither should you. I want to be rich. I want to matter. I want to prove the world wrong. I'm sure you know what that is like. To always be bottom of the pile, the back of the queue. Well, this is it. Your one and only chance to change your life.*'

Voss circled the cavern. He checked the entrance of each passageway, shotgun at his shoulder. No sign of Gaunt.

'*The virus cylinder. It's small enough to slip in your pocket. Small enough to carry home. And it will buy anything you ever wanted.*'

'What would you want in return?'

'*Fifty-fifty split.*'

'I'd be waiting for a double-cross.'

'*That's why I would play straight.*'

Voss thought it over. He rubbed tired eyes.

'*So what do you say?*' prompted Gaunt. '*Tell me you are interested. That's all I need to hear. Tell me we have something to talk over.*'

'Yeah,' Voss heard himself say. 'Yeah, I'm interested.'

Lucy walked to the mine tunnel entrance. Amanda crouched behind the plank barricade, rifle at her shoulder. Weak dawn light.

'We had our first customer,' said Amanda.

Lucy squinted into the gloom. A body on the track.

'When did he show up?' asked Lucy.

'He came round the corner ten minutes ago.'

Voss joined them.

'They'll eat through our ammo, pretty quick if they attack en masse,' he said. 'How many did Jabril say were out there?'

'His battalion was under-strength. He reckons about two hundred men.'

'I've got a few boxes of .308,' said Amanda. 'A good stack of mags for the rifles, a few for the Glocks. But sooner or later we would shoot dry and get overrun.'

'What about the locomotive?' asked Voss. 'What's the deal? Can it roll or what?'

'Yeah,' said Lucy. 'Given time, I reckon she'll move.'

'We need to set a deadline. If you can't get it running in the next couple of hours, we walk out of here.'

'All right.'

'That guy has a pistol,' said Amanda.

She refocused her night scope. The reticules of her optics zeroed on the dead guy two hundred yards distant. An officer sprawled across the track, right quadrant of his head blown open. Amanda focused on the leather holster strapped to his hip. An automatic pistol.

'He's got mag pouches clipped to his belt.'

'Want to go get them?' asked Lucy. 'We could seriously use the ammo.'

'Let's do it quick.'

The night scope flashed a battery warning. Amanda unclipped it from her rifle and threw it in the quad trailer.

She handed the rifle to Voss.

'Get going,' he told her. 'Get out there, before any more of those fucks show up. I'll keep you covered.'

They climbed over the beams and drums that blocked the track.

Lucy looked up. Stars fading into a pale blue sky.

'Come on. Let's get this done.'

They ran along the railroad track. They crouched and checked the body.

The corpse bristled with strange malignancies. Face gone, frontal lobes blasted away. Misfiring synapses deep within his shattered cerebral cortex set his foot twitching like he was grooving to a tune only he could hear. Whatever residual spark of life remained with his shattered head would quickly be extinguished when the sun reached its zenith and exposed brain tissue shrivelled dry.

A Russian Makarov pistol. Amanda tried to pull back the slide. The weapon was corroded solid.

'Fucked up. This baby need a bucket of solvent and a couple of days' work.'

'Keep the ammo. We might find a good one.'

Lucy stuffed magazines into her pocket. Old Soviet calibre. Incompatible with Glocks.

'This guy has a full canteen,' said Amanda.

'No good. He might have drunk from it.'

Lucy patted pockets.

'Prayer beads and a hipflask. A man of contradictions.'

'I don't get why they haven't hit us yet,' said Amanda, looking towards the canyon entrance. 'I thought they would be all over us by now.'

Voss spat tobacco. He crouched by the quad, rifle laid across crooked planks.

Amanda's M40. He adjusted his grip, his hand and shoulder too big for her custom-moulded McMillan stock.

He squinted through the sniper scope and watched the distant figures of Lucy and Amanda search and strip the body.

He sat back and rubbed his eyes.

He looked at the quad trailer next to him. The missile case.

He glanced back down the mine tunnel. The massive

locomotive beneath a string of arc lights. Ore wagons and flatbed railcars. Train tracks receding to a distant cavern.

No sign of Jabril.

Voss flipped latches and lifted the lid. He gazed down at the virus cylinder, mesmerised by the ethereal blue glow.

TOP SECRET SPECIAL HANDLING NO FORM

Central Intelligence Agency
Directorate of Operations, Near East Division

Doc ID: 575JJUJF
Page 01/1

08/22/05

MEMORANDUM TO: Project Lead, D.Ops
SUBJECT: Spektr

Colonel,

11th Recon confirm their Predator drone has been launched and has entered the Western Desert. We should resume eyes-on-target surveillance of Valley 403 within the hour.

We will re-establish contact with our man at the SPEKTR site shortly, and seek confirmation that the virus package has been acquired.

If our man is unable to provide assurance that the package has been retrieved, if Predator surveillance reveals further evidence of hostile activity within the contamination zone, we may be forced to accept that re-activation of the SPEKTR site will not be possible.

Our assets at Sharjah continue their preparations. We have received clearance for over-flight from QTAC. The plane has been registered as a shipment of urgent medical supplies. The SUNRAY device is loaded and ready to deploy.

The aircrew are on standby. They are prepared to initiate CLEANSWEEP on my command.

R. Koell
Field Officer
CA Special Proj, Baghdad

PE4-A

Lucy returned to the train.

She shuffled along the narrow locomotive walkway. She opened service panels with a large hex key.

The train was a diesel/electric hybrid. A massive turbo-charged V-12 powering an adjacent generator the size of a Volkswagen.

She shone her flashlight round the tight engine compartment. Cables and pipe-work intact. No obvious signs of damage.

She vaulted the walkway rail and jumped down to the track. She shone her barrel light beneath the locomotive. Leaf springs. Brake shoes. Traction motors. No leaks, no damage.

She grasped grab-irons and hauled herself back up to the walkway. She returned to the cab. She sat in the driver's seat: a leather bar-stool patched with duct tape.

A small brass plaque screwed to the console.

Montreal Locomotive Works.

The engine had, in a previous life, been owned by the Canadian Pacific Railway.

She looked over the console once more and tried to decipher the controls. Dials. Switches. A red brake handle. A directional selector. An eight-speed throttle. None of the controls would respond.

She paced the cab and examined wall boxes. High-voltage warning zags. Locked. She hammered them open with her rifle stock.

STARTER CIRCUIT

She cranked a lever to On. She flicked banks of breaker switches, turned every light green.

The cabin overhead bulb lit up. The filament emitted a weak, flickering glow like candle flame.

She tried the ignition. A jolt ran through the locomotive, a cough like the engine engaged but immediately cut out.

A winking red light.

BATTERY WARNING

Lucy snatched keys from a wall hook and jumped from the cab.

Jabril wiped dust from the washstand mirror. He was stripped to the waist.

He poured a bottle of mineral water into a tin bowl. He unzipped a wash bag. He stripped naked and soaped himself down. He rubbed shampoo into his hair until it frothed, then emptied the basin over his head.

He towelled himself dry with his army jacket and threw it in the corner.

He tested the battery of an electric shaver. He scoured away grey stubble. He combed. He dabbed cologne onto his neck.

He buttoned a pristine white shirt. He turned up his collar, draped a black silk tie round his neck and tied the knot one-handed. He shrugged on his suit, tied shoes and tucked a silk handkerchief into the breast pocket.

White linen. In a dirt-poor country where most people were a couple of generations clear of camel-trading Bedouin, his white suit screamed status. A guy who spent his life behind a desk. A guy who gave orders. A guy that didn't break sweat. He could walk down any street. Nobody would mess with him.

He took another Turkish cigarette from his gold case and lit it with the click of his lighter. He checked the magazine of his compact Makarov pistol and tucked it in his waistband.

He pulled a second Louis Vuitton suitcase from beneath his cot and flipped latches.

Blocks wrapped in wax paper. PE4-A, Portuguese high-grade plastic explosive.

A box of detonators.

Hundred-metre rolls of twin-flex phone cable.

He unwrapped a slab of explosive. He slapped it against the washstand mirror, kneaded it against the glass. He mashed a detonator into the clay and spliced cable.

He backed out of the room and down the corridor, spooling cable as he walked.

A storeroom.

He kicked open the rough wooden door. Document boxes.

Jabril kicked over the boxes. Forms and files. Digital video tape and CDs. Hard disks and flash drives.

Paper spilled across the floor. Records of terminal trials: observation notes, temperature graphs, X-rays.

Black and white photographs showed a series of anguished, naked men tied to the necropsy table, and the frame-by-frame progress of infection.

Jabril slapped a patty of explosive against a ceiling beam and ran cable.

There were jerry cans in the corner of the room. He uncapped a can and pushed it over. Gasoline gulped from the nozzle and soaked paper.

He backed out the room, running command wire.

The holding pens. Two freight containers sitting at the end of a tunnel. The container doors had been removed and replaced by welded bars. Crude jail cells.

Jabril instinctively covered his mouth and nose with the hooked stump of his arm. The tunnel used to smell of faeces. Most soldiers wouldn't approach the place unless they were ordered to pull sentry duty. If they were forced to stand guard, they would plug their noses with toilet tissue sprayed with deodorant. Some of the prisoners lost bowel control each time a removal team arrived to extract a fresh victim. The men would huddle in shadows at the back of the container. They would piss and soil themselves.

Jabril would make the selection. The team would drag the semi-conscious man clear while his companions were kept at bay with Taser batons.

The inmate would be marched to the cavern labs, thrashing as he saw the zinc table and nylon restraints waiting to receive him.

'*Cameras running.*'

A lab tech would tightened wrist, ankle and chest straps, tug buckles and checked for slack.

'*He's secure. Go ahead.*'

That long, despairing shriek as the prisoner lifted his head, watched a needle prick the skin of his forearm and deliver its lethal load.

Jabril had spent his working life in Baghdad instigating torture and executions. He would work his way through a prisoner list as he sipped his mid-morning coffee. Part of the daily routine, like glancing through the sheaf of anonymous denunciations that arrived by mail each morning.

He leafed through intelligence reports and circled names. His subordinates understood the code. A cross meant arrest and detainment. A circle meant interrogation. A red tick meant death. He didn't have to give a direct order. The words never passed his lips. He didn't have to hear the screams. He didn't have to smell the sweat, piss and blood of the torture cells.

But the Spektr project gave him the direct power of life

and death. He stood in front of the prisoner pens every couple of days, surveyed the snivelling men and made his choice. He would point out his chosen victim, watch them cower from his pointed finger like he was aiming a gun. It was intoxicating. God-like potency. A heart-galloping thrill, like illicit sex.

Jabril stood by the bars and stared into the dark cave-mouth of the empty freight containers. He could still hear the ghost-screams, feel the old flutter of excitement.

He set the suitcase down. He popped latches. He slapped explosive against timber wall props and pushed detonators into the putty. He twisted together frayed copper strands and ran cable.

Voss climbed a ladder to the locomotive walkway. He entered the cab.

'How's it going?'

'Wish we could get hold of Gaunt. Break fingers until he showed us how to crank up this fucking thing.'

'Think he knows how to run it?' asked Voss.

'How did he know about the mine? The lab? Someone gave him a detailed brief. They might have told him about the train.'

Voss didn't reply.

Lucy crouched and pulled a battered ring binder from a shelf beneath the engineer's console. She flipped pages.

'This baby is some kind of diesel/electric hybrid. I've got juice to the driver's desk, but I'm getting some kind of power warning.'

'I checked the track,' said Voss. 'The switch-rails are set to put her in a parallel siding.'

'So fix it.'

Voss jumped from the cab. He walked the track in front of the locomotive. He examined the rail switch. Mechanical operation. No hydraulic actuators, no electrics. A tall lever next to a rail junction. He threw his bodyweight against the lever. It wouldn't shift.

He headed down the tunnel. He searched for something he could use as a sledgehammer.

A couple of flatbed freight wagons. He pulled bundles of tarpaulin aside. Rotted planks. Chains. Yellowed al-Ba'ath newsprint. A heavy, rusted wrench.

Voss hefted the wrench.

He became aware of a distant figure in the periphery of his vision. A man stood at the end of the tunnel, back-lit by cavern arc lights. Hunched, simian. He was staring at Voss.

Voss stood back from the wagon to get a clear view. He glimpsed a red boiler suit as the figure ducked into shadow.

'Gaunt? Gaunt, is that you?' His voice echoed and died.

Voss walked deeper into the tunnel, boots crunching on shingle. He crouched and peered beneath a row of ore hoppers. He glimpsed bloody, bare feet and the legs of a tattered red boiler suit.

An infected soldier.

'Here I am, you raghead fuck. You want meat, come get it.'

He glimpsed a horribly distorted face watching him from behind a wagon. Flaking flesh. Strange, tumorous eruptions.

'Come on. What are you waiting for?'

The face ducked out of sight. Sound of clumsy, running feet.

Voss threw down the wrench, drew his sidearm and ran between ore trucks in pursuit.

Jabril entered Lab One. He wriggled his hand into a surgical glove, and tugged at the latex cuff with his teeth.

He took a gas mask from a wall hook and pulled it on.

He unlatched the refrigerator. A cascade of nitrogen fog. Storage jars. Body parts held in sub-zero stasis.

He propped the door open. He wrenched the power cable

from the back of the freezer. The temperature read-out blanked. Cooling fans slowed and died.

He dumped the suitcase on the necropsy table.

He stroked the mirrored metal. He contemplated the wrist and ankle straps, the drain hole at the foot of the table to help sluice blood.

He had supervised the murder of forty men. Stood outside the lab units and relished muffled screams as the men were strapped down and forcibly injected.

He was both horrified and aroused by the memory.

The freezer storage jars were already starting to defrost. Water dripped and pooled on the plate floor of the lab.

He slapped explosive against the side of the freezer and wired det cable.

Jabril mashed a nub of explosive onto the roof panel above the table. He pressed a blasting cap into the putty and strung detonator wire.

He stepped through the doorway into Lab Two.

Cultivation equipment laid out on steel counters. A bio-weapon production line. Microscopes. Centrifuges. Fermentation reactors.

Glass crunched beneath the leather soles of his Oxford brogues. Broken flasks. Culture dishes.

The growth chamber. Legs, spines and lungs suspended in frosted vats. Each body part floated in a thick serum of amino acids and bovine placental tissue. Metallic tendrils erupted from flesh and bone as if reaching out, seeking a fresh host to invade.

Jabril slapped explosive against the glass. Submerged body parts shivered and twitched.

He wired detonators.

Lab four.

He crouched, span wing nuts and flipped latches. He opened the steel sarcophagus. Konstantin, laid out like Tutankhamen, arms folded across his chest.

Jabril moulded a fist-sized nub of C4, wired a blasting cab, and wedged the explosive between the dead astronaut's fingers.

He left the lab units and crossed the cavern.

The bio-dome. Spektr, under arc lights.

A stack of chemical drums. Skull stickers streaked with corrosion. Jabril rolled yellow drums of peptone, ethylene and paraformaldehyde, and stacked them beneath Spektr.

He tore nubs of plastic explosive and mashed them onto each drum lid with the heel of his palm. He took a fresh reel of cable from the case and ran det cord.

A flicker of movement. A figure outside the opaque plastic of the containment dome.

A red boiler suit brushed against polythene. Jabril crouched behind the drums and drew his pistol. He watched the blurred figure stumble the perimeter of the containment dome, hands sliding and squeaking across taut plastic.

He heard the echo of dragging footfalls as the figure shuffled down a passage, away from the cavern.

Jabril slowly climbed to his feet and continued to rig the bomb.

Subject Nine

Lucy walked deep into the tunnel. She passed a row of flatbed cars and ore hoppers.

She found a small locomotive. A small diesel engine hitched to mine wagons, paintwork streaked with corrosion.

The engine cowling had been removed, and the motor stripped for parts.

Maybe the starter battery was still in place. Maybe it still held a charge.

She ran a quick circuit of the locomotive, rifle raised. All clear.

She climbed the ladder and pulled open the cab door. Trashed controls. Smashed dials and frayed cable.

Another mummified corpse. An engineer in a boiler suit. He was crouched prostrate, face to the floor like he was kneeling in prayer.

She prodded the dead man with the barrel of her rifle. The desiccated cadaver toppled over. The yellow wooden handle of a screwdriver wedged in his eye socket. The guy had knelt on the plate floor of the cab, positioned the screwdriver, then drove his head down onto the spike.

Must have been hell. That final night when infected prisoners broke loose and ran riot. Troops mown down by terrified Russian overseers. Young men blowing their brains out, slitting their throats, hugging grenades, anything preferable to joining the mindless mutant legion.

Lucy jumped from the cab and surveyed the exterior of the locomotive. She searched for a battery compartment.

A big metal box on the rear footplate between buffers. Padlocked. She shot the lock and kicked open the lid. A big Exide 32-volt power cell. Four times the size of a standard car battery.

Faint crunch of shingle.

She jumped from the locomotive and crouched on the track. She peered beneath wagons. She glimpsed the legs of a red boiler suit.

Jabril knelt beneath Spektr and continued to wire yellow drums of formaldehyde and ethylene.

His companion had returned. A shambling figure in a red boiler suit. A crimson ghost shape glimpsed through opaque plastic. The figure circled the perimeter of the containment tent. Bloody handprints on polythene.

'I'm sorry, my friend,' murmured Jabril. 'I'm so sorry. It will be over soon.'

Jabril recognised the tall, thin figure in the boiler suit. Corporal Haq.

Haq and his twin brother Abdul tried to flee the valley one night. They wanted to reach Fallujah, make sure their mother had survived the war.

They blacked their faces with boot polish and ran from the mine. They managed to evade Russian sentries at the head of the ravine and climb the moonlit valley walls.

Abdul triggered an anti-personnel mine halfway up the slope and was blown to flesh-scraps and blood-vapour. The blast drew searchlights and soldiers. They found Haq cradling his brother's leg.

They dragged Haq back to the mine. They shaved his head and dressed him in a boiler suit. They sprayed a big nine on his back and pushed him into a holding pen.

Jabril brought him water.

'Come to gloat?' asked Haq.

Jabril passed a bottle of mineral water between the bars. Haq took a sip and threw the bottle to fellow prisoners cowering at the back of the freight container.

'I'll talk to Ignatiev. Do what I can.'

'If you really wanted to help, you would pass me a gun.'

'They will never let you escape.'

'I don't plan to escape.'

'Just hold on. Let me argue your case.'

'Listen to yourself. You are a major in the Mukhabarat. You should be the authority here. Not these foreigners.'

'Our world has changed.'

'You think it will be any different for you? Sooner or later, you will find yourself behind these bars.'

Jabril held up his hook.

'They want young men, in good health.'

'Then you will simply be executed.'

'You think I don't know what Ignatiev has in store? None of us will leave this place alive.'

Later that night Jabril visited the lime pit. A trench dug in the valley floor near the citadel. Stacked lime sacks. A mass grave.

The pit held a mound of eviscerated bodies caked in white powder. Strong stench of acid decay.

He shielded his mouth and nose with his sleeve.

Arms. Legs. Exposed ribcages. The eviscerated bodies twitched and stirred as they slowly dissolved into caustic lime slurry.

Lucy hit the pressel switch on her chest plate.

'Mandy. I need you back here.'

Amanda jogged down the tunnel.

'Babe?'

'Over here,' shouted Lucy.

Amanda climbed onto the rear plate of the freight locomotive.

'Give me a hand with this thing,' said Lucy.

They unscrewed terminals and struggled to lift the massive battery from its box compartment. They lowered it down to the track. They pulled on gloves, each grabbed a handle and carried the power cell down the tunnel, muscles straining.

'Voss says there are infected guys running round the mine,' said Amanda.

'No wonder the fucks from the citadel didn't follow us,' said Lucy, panting with effort. 'There's something else in here. Something worse.'

'We better find Jabril and warn him. He might get jumped.'

Jabril crept down a passageway lit by bulbs screwed to roof beams.

He stalked the figure in a red boiler suit. The suit had a big fifteen sprayed on the back. The revenant's bald head was punctured by a crust of metallic tumours, like a rippled steel skull-cap.

The creature stopped. It sniffed the air.

It turned. It saw Jabril and snarled.

Jabril put a bullet between the creature's eyes. Gun-roar echoed down the passageway.

The prisoner fell against the tunnel wall and slid to the ground.

Another creature watched from shadows at the end of the passageway. Jabril raised his pistol and took aim, hook-arm steadying the gun. A bald, emaciated mutant thing. Number nine sprayed on the breast of the boiler suit.

Haq.

Jabril hesitated, and lowered his pistol. The figure ducked out of sight.

The moment Jabril discovered the full extent of the Spektr project, he decided to destroy every piece of equipment in the valley. Obliterate it all.

Ignatiev often talked about Phase Three. He mentioned it to technician colleagues while Jabril was in earshot, disregarded his presence like he was a pet or a piece of equipment.

Jabril put it together:

Phase One. Locate Spektr and acquire virus.

Phase Two. Weaponise pathogen.

Phase Three?

Weeks ago, Jabril had seen a heavy impact-proof case locked in the ammunition store. He had a key to the store. He visited the storeroom late one night and opened the trunk.

A Hellfire II missile on a foam bed.

The missile was dove grey. About three feet long, aluminium shell thick as drainpipe. Lockheed Martin batch stamp. Fins at the rear and neck. The nose cone, with its glass laser-optic lens, had been detached. The payload compartment, the copper fragmentation sleeve, was empty.

Koell intended to test his bio-weapon. As soon as Ignatiev delivered the weaponised virus, he would pick a significant population centre and fire the missile from a drone. The missile would arm itself in flight. When it reached a specific GPS coordinate, a preset grid ref and altitude, the ground targeting crew would send the destruct signal and the missile would detonate mid-air, releasing its lethal payload.

'Imagine a battalion of these infected creatures,' he once heard Ignatiev say. 'Imagine the destructive potential. A formidable fighting force. Men devoid of pity, impervious to pain and fatigue.'

Koell and Ignatiev. A shared insanity.

Jabril played it cool. Business as usual. He ran the camp. He supervised prisoners caged in their pens.

Phase Three of Koell's programme would take very little manpower. He would have no further use for Iraqi troops. He would wait for word Ignatiev had concluded his research and was ready to break camp. Then he would radio the order to eliminate non-essential personnel.

Friday night. The Iraqi battalion has been promised downtime. Ignatiev's team secured a stereo, a bunch of CDs and a case of vodka. The deep galleries of the mine were soon filled with of raucous music and laughter.

The Russians stayed sober.

This is it, thought Jabril. *Extermination day. At the height of the revelry, when the troops are drunk and euphoric, the Russians will break out heavy machine guns and mow them down.*

He hurried to his cell. He stripped out of his white suit, pulled on combat gear and tucked a pistol into his belt.

He emptied clothes from his Louis Vuitton suitcase onto the floor, carried the case to the munitions store and filled it with patties of explosive and detonators.

He stashed the suitcase beneath his bunk and headed for the lab units.

The cavern was still and silent.

Faint music echoed from distant tunnels.

Jabril had memorised the door code. He let himself into Lab One. He filled a garbage bag with paperwork. He smashed open a couple of computers and levered hard drives from their bed.

He moved on to Lab Two. He swept documentation into a bag.

'What the hell are you doing?'

One of Ignatiev's techs, wearing a lab coat.

Jabril snatched a flask from a shelf and smashed it over the man's head. The technician fell to the floor, face peppered with blood and glass. Jabril stamped on the man's throat and left him to choke. He collected the garbage bags as the technician writhed and turned blue.

Jabril dumped the garbage bags in the munitions store. Hid them in empty document boxes. He planned to wire explosives to the wall timbers and incinerate all trace of the Spektr project.

A klaxon. A rising air-raid wail. Someone had found the dead technician.

Jabril stepped into the corridor. A guard shouted something in Russian. Jabril shot him through the heart and ran.

No time to rig the demolition charges. He headed for the main tunnel.

A quick detour. The prisoner pens. A chance to create additional chaos to aid his escape.

Eight infected men awaiting dissection. Flesh blotched with strange mutations. Red boiler suits matted with blood and pus. Ignatiev preparing to harvest samples on an industrial scale.

Jabril shot padlocks, released chains and threw open the cage doors of the freight containers. He ran down the tunnel. He looked back. He saw infected men emerge from their steel dungeons and sniff the air.

He kept running.

The main tunnel. Milling soldiers, confused and bewildered, half dressed and half drunk. The klaxon echoed round the walls.

Jabril pushed through the crowd. He had minutes to escape the mine and flee the ravine before Ignatiev's Russian henchmen organised themselves and began their eradication drill.

Screams. A glimpse of red boiler suits. Blood and tearing flesh. Panic swept through the crowd. The soldiers ran for the tunnel entrance.

Jabril ran down the ravine, swept along by fleeing Republican Guards.

Heavy machine gun fire. The man next to Jabril was lifted into the air by the impact of heavy .50 cal rounds, and hit the ground dead.

Jabril kept running. Men cut down around him. He was pelted with rock splinters and stone dust. He was splashed with blood.

The fleeing men reached the open valley. They ran for vehicles parked in front of the citadel. The convoy of trucks and cars a mile distant, shrouded in camouflage nets.

Jabril reached the convoy. More gunfire. Door panels shrieked and sparked as a .50 cal tracer punched holes. Jabril hit the ground and played dead. Wounded men screamed and died in the dust around him.

Fuel fires. Cars flipped and burned. Nylon camouflage nets smoked and shrivelled.

Jabril belly-crawled to the convoy. He rolled beneath a bus. The chassis above his head shook as heavy rounds rocked the vehicle. Smashed window glass hit the dirt.

He looked out from beneath the bus. Burning sedans. Burning men.

He glimpsed lab techs through smoke and flickering flame. They were loading the missile case into the rear of the cash truck. They sealed the door. They headed for the cab, and were jumped by figures in red boiler suits. Inhuman strength. An armed ripped off. A face peeled away.

A soldier squirmed beneath the bus and crawled hand over hand towards Jabril.

'Help me.'

Bite marks. Strips of skin torn from the man's face.

Jabril tugged the Makarov from his waistband and shot the soldier through the eye.

He rolled from beneath the bus and scrambled to his feet. Burning cars. Streaking tracer rounds.

He ran for the valley wall, screened from the Russian shooters by a curtain of smoke and flame.

He scrambled up the rock slope, hand and hook raking scree.

He hid among boulders. Faint screams and gunshots from the valley below.

He watched Russian goons machine gun terrified Iraqi troops. Republican Guards drew sidearms and fired back. A slow, unfolding bloodbath. The valley quickly turned into a corpse field.

He saw red boiler suits among the crowd. The infected prisoners shrugged off bullet strikes. They gouged and ripped. A flesh-frenzy. Russian gunmen over-powered and pulled apart.

The infected berserkers ran among burning cars and trucks. They punched out windshields and dragged drivers from their vehicles. Throats torn from wounded soldiers as they lay helpless in the sand.

Jabril turned away and climbed the ravine, the clatter of stones merging with faint screams from the valley below.

Gaunt sat in the darkness of a remote side tunnel. He crouched on the floor, back to the wall, head resting against cool stone.

A muffled beep from his pocket. The sat phone. Incoming call.

Koell's voice:

'*Carnival to Brimstone, over.*'

'Go ahead, Carnival.'

Gaunt wondered, briefly, how a sat-phone signal was able to reach deep within the mine. They must be using the Predator to boost the signal. Dawn had broken. The drone was back in the air, circling the valley. The UAV operators were probably sitting in a van at the edge of the desert, tweaking a joystick, monitoring the data flow, relaying encrypted transmissions via the drone's EISS telemetry package. A military surveillance crew leased by the hour as part of some inter-departmental exchange. And despite it all, the digitisation, cryptographic algorithm and satellite bounce, Gaunt could hear the intimate acoustic of Koell's hotel room. The compressed hush. The faint hum of air-con.

'*Authenticate.*'

'Authentication is Oscar, Sierra, Yankee, Bravo.'

'*So what's the situation?*'

'I have the package.'

'*You have the package? Confirm: you have the package in your possession.*'

'Yeah.'

'*You have the actual cylinder?*'

'Yeah.'

'*Read me the serial number.*'

'Say again?'

'*I need proof. There is a serial number stamped on the steel cap of the cylinder. Read it to me.*'

'I don't have the cylinder actually in my hand. But I know where it is. It's secure. I can get it.'

'*You can get it.*'

'Swear to God. I'll have it within the hour.'

The line went dead.

'Hello? Carnival? Koell?'

He checked the sat-phone display.

TRANSMISSION TERMINATED

'Shit.'

Voss sat at the mine entrance. He leant Amanda's rifle across planks and checked the narrow ravine ahead. He turned and checked the tunnel behind him. Spooked by shadows on every side.

He folded a fresh wad of tobacco into his mouth.

Gaunt's voice:

'*Voss? Can you hear me?*'

Voss adjusted his earpiece. He'd retuned the selector so he and Gaunt could speak via a closed channel.

'*Voss? Are you there?*'

'Yeah.'

'*Ready to do this?*'

'I guess.'

'*We can't wait around any longer. Soon as they fire up that locomotive, we make our move.*'

'No harm comes to Lucy and Amanda. I mean it. They don't get hurt. If they won't play ball, we leave them behind. Alive. Pull any rough stuff, I'll blow your head clean off your fucking shoulders.'

'*We've got serious issues. If Jabril's battalion attack en masse, you'll get overrun.*'

Voss spat tobacco.

'I can hold them off. And those fucks in the tunnels.'

'*That's the least of our problems. There's a Predator drone. It's been watching us. Eye-in-the-sky. Watching us the whole time.*'

'What are you saying?'

'*I'm saying we've got three or four hours to get out of this valley before it lights up and we get cooked like brisket.*'

'Christ.'

'*Let's get aboard that train and get out of here. Let's go get rich.*'

Juggernaut

The mess hall. A wide, low cave.

Toppled tables. Broken chairs. Relics of that final night when drunken revelry turned to panic as sirens wailed, infected prisoners broke loose, and mine tunnels became bloody mayhem.

Voss walked between the upturned tables, pistol drawn. Empty vodka bottles rolled and clinked.

'Come on out.'

Gaunt stepped from shadows.

'Put your fucking hands where I can see them.'

'We're on the same team.'

'Put down the bag and show me your fucking hands.'

Gaunt set down his backpack and stood, hands raised.

Voss jammed the Glock beneath Gaunt's chin and patted him down. He checked jacket pockets. He confiscated the silenced Sig and a knife.

He lashed Gaunt's wrists with plastic tuff-ties. He pushed him towards a chair.

'Sit.'

'We have a common interest,' said Gaunt. 'I'm not your enemy. I'm here to help.'

Voss didn't bother to respond. He pulled a table upright. He dumped the backpack on the table and searched inside.

Caulk explosive. A couple of flares. A sat phone.

'Who's on the other end of this phone? CIA?'

'Give or take.'

'How about you? Are you Agency?'

'I'm a contractor.'

'Lay it out for me. The whole thing.'

'Covert ops,' said Gaunt. 'They spent a lot of time and money locating the Spektr crash site. Invested a shitload more cash to bring the virus to a weaponised form. Then all hell broke loose. Their team got wiped out.'

'What about us?'

'Guinea pigs. They sent you into the contamination zone to see if you would survive, to see if the virus could be retrieved.'

'Don't they have their own guys? Couldn't they use Delta?'

'Does this look like an officially sanctioned operation to you? Congressional oversight, all that shit? This is deep black. Strictly back-channel assets. A small bunch of ambitious guys. They've overreached themselves, and now they are trying to clean up.'

'But they'll pay?' asked Voss. 'If we deliver the virus, they'll pay?'

'Dollars or roubles. Langley, Russian intelligence, China. Who gives a shit? Someone will make us rich.'

'So call him up. This guy.'

'His name is Koell.'

'Get him to send a chopper.'

'He's written us off. He's pulled the plug. Right now, it's sun-up, and aerial surveillance is showing him a fuck-ton of bodies and a couple of wrecked choppers.'

'He's going to call down some kind of airstrike? You're sure?'

'The plane is probably in the air right now. If we are going to ride that locomotive out of here, I suggest we get going.'

The battery compartment. A steel box bolted to the under-skirt of the locomotive.

Lucy smashed the padlock with the butt of her rifle. She unclipped the dead battery. Amanda helped drag it from the compartment and dump it on the tunnel floor.

They pushed the fresh Exide battery into the vacant space and attached bulldog terminals.

They climbed in the cab. Lucy checked the driver's console. Battery indicator lit green.

'That's it,' said Lucy. 'We're in business. Let's grab some water and ammo, and get the fuck out of here.'

They ran to the tunnel entrance. No sign of Voss.

Lucy hit the pressel switch on her radio.

'Voss? Where the fuck are you?'

No response.

'Voss. Come on, man. Time to go.'

No reply.

They filled a backpack with ammunition, water and a couple of MRE pouches.

Lucy slung the backpack. Amanda carried the SAW.

They headed back to the train. They climbed aboard one of the umber and cream carriages hitched to the locomotive.

Amanda checked out the interior of the coach.

'Christ.'

Cobwebbed grandeur. Elegant Queen Anne furniture. Panelled walls inlaid with marquetry foliage. Brass fixtures.

Tunnel light shafted through the windows and lit swirling dust.

Amanda brushed sand from a heavy mahogany desk. She looked through a door into the adjoining carriage. A banquette table and chairs.

'What is this?' asked Amanda. 'Some kind of palace on wheels?'

'Pretty much.'

Voss climbed into the carriage.

'Where's Jabril?' asked Amanda.

'Haven't seen him.'

'Go look. We're about to leave. See if he still wants to die in this fucking mine.'

'I brought a gift.'

Voss hauled Gaunt up into the carriage.

He kicked Gaunt's legs from under him. The man fell to his knees. He turned to look at Voss.

'What the fuck are you doing? We had a deal.'

'The guy says we are on a clock,' said Voss. 'Says they are going to sterilise the whole fucking area.'

He took Gaunt's Thuraya sat phone from his pocket and passed it to Lucy. She examined it.

She stood over Gaunt and kicked him in the gut. He rolled foetal on a Persian rug.

'What was your mission?'

'Check out the valley,' he gasped. 'Assess the current level of contamination. Retrieve the virus, if possible.'

'And now?'

'Mission failed. They'll fry the entire valley.'

'What are we talking about? F16s? B52 strike?'

'A massive thermobaric bomb, big as a bus. It's called a Sentinel. Blast area wide as a tactical nuke. It'll airburst over the valley, incinerate everything in a two-mile radius. Burn like the sun. Turn sand to glass.'

'Fuck,' muttered Amanda.

'The over-pressure will break every bone in your body. Then the heat will turn you to ash.'

'I get the picture. How long have we got?'

'At a guess, the plane is already in the air, en route from the Emirates. Probably took off at sunrise. Four or five hours' flight time. We don't have long.'

Lucy held up the sat phone.

'Call your boss. Cancel the raid.'

Gaunt shook his head.

'He won't listen to me.'

Lucy threw the phone onto a table. She turned to Voss.

'He said you made a deal.'

Voss fetched the missile case from the quad. He set it down on the carriage floor.

'The virus,' said Voss. 'You said it yourself. We're old. Used up. This is our last war. We can get a few dollars for the gold. But the virus is our true meal ticket. We can make a trade. Put ourselves on easy street.'

Lucy drew her pistol. She dug the barrel into Gaunt's ear.

'What about Toon? Fucker shot him in the head.'

'Toon was my best friend,' said Voss. 'He'd walk through hell for any one of us. If he were here right now, he would take the deal. He'd want us to walk away rich. End our run ahead of the game.'

'Jabril says this shit has to be destroyed. I think he's right.'

Lucy crouched and flipped hasps. She lifted the case lid. She took the glass virus cylinder from its foam bed, her face lit blue.

'Think about it,' said Voss. 'Want to spend the rest of your life living out of a bag? One fucked up warzone after another? That litre of liquid is worth millions. Tens of millions. We could have a whole new life. Go where we want, be what we want. All we have to do is deliver that shit to Baghdad.'

Lucy stroked the glass.

'This is the United States government we're talking about,' said Voss. 'The good guys. They just want to study this bug in a lab somewhere. They wouldn't use it. They don't want to wipe out cities. Shit, for all we know they might tweak this stuff and cure cancer.'

She shook her head.

'I don't trust governments. I've seen too many good men die for no reason.'

She replaced the cylinder and closed the case.

'We burn it.'

Voss drew his pistol and pointed it at Lucy.

'I can't let you do it, boss. I just can't.'

Lucy slowly got to her feet.

'Hold on, Voss. Take a moment. Think it through.'

'I'm taking the virus. You can come with me, or stay behind.'

Amanda raised her rifle. Voss shot her in the thigh. She fell to the floor, clutching her leg, hand already wet with blood.

'Throw down your shit,' he said. 'Come on. Both of you. Throw down.'

'What the hell are you doing?'

'We've finally got our hands on a big score. I'm not going to let you put a match to it.'

Knives and guns clattered on the floorboards.

Lucy's assault rifle lay across a table. Her hand twitched like she was itching to snatch it up.

Voss took aim at Amanda's head.

'Try it. I'll drill your girlfriend through the eyes.'

Amanda limped along the tunnel track. She held Lucy for support.

'We'll be all right, babe,' murmured Lucy. 'Just have to keep it together.'

'Keep moving,' said Voss.

They passed ore trucks and box cars.

Gaunt walked beside Voss. His hands were still tied.

'You going to cut me loose?'

'I might.'

'Don't get any ideas,' warned Gaunt. 'I know how to start the locomotive. Without me, you're going nowhere.'

Voss prodded Lucy in the back with his gun barrel.

'Over there. By the wall.'

A timber prop thick as a telegraph pole supporting a roof beam.

Lucy and Amanda embraced the prop. Voss lashed their wrists with plastic cuffs.

The tunnel lights flickered and dimmed for a moment. The generator running dry.

'How many times have I saved your life?' asked Lucy, challenging Voss to make eye contact. 'Think about it. How many times?'

He checked her cuffs.

'Sorry, boss. I don't want to die poor.'

Gunshot. The whine and spark of a pistol round hitting an ore truck.

Gaunt and Voss took cover behind a box car.

Lucy and Amanda crouched at the foot of the roof beam and tried to cover their heads.

Jabril shot from deep within the cavern. Voss returned fire. Gunshots echoed through the tunnel. Bullet strikes punched deep into the brittle limestone roof, bringing down dust and rock chunks. A ricochet smacked the tunnel prop, showering Lucy with splinters. She gnawed the tuff-tie binding her wrist, tried to bite through the plastic.

Voss sprayed random fire. He and Gaunt ran for the locomotive.

Lucy waited until the sound of their footfalls diminished to silence.

'Jabril,' she shouted. 'Over here.'

Lucy craned to look at Amanda's wounded leg. Camo fabric and desert boot wet with blood.

'How you doing?' she asked.

'Not so great,' said Amanda. Her face was chalk white.

'It's not an arterial bleed, but we've got to patch that hole.'

Distant engine splutter from the locomotive. Tunnel echo. The diesel engine turning over, trying to engage.

'There goes our ride.'

The locomotive cab. Gaunt held out his hands.

'Come on. Cut me the fuck loose.'

'Just drive the damn train.'

Gaunt studied dials. He tapped a gauge.

'The fuel tank is nearly dry.'

'Then what's the fucking point?'

'I talked it over with Koell. This train was my way out of the valley if the choppers went down. He said there was a fuel truck, out there in the convoy. Locomotive-grade diesel.'

'It probably got blown to shit. Nothing but scrap iron.'

'I saw a couple of intact trucks among the wrecks. We have to check. We have to know for sure. Come on. Don't pussy out on me now. Koell might be ready to pull the plug on this operation, but he can still tap a massive black budget. You want twenty, thirty million in unmarked bills? He wouldn't give a shit. Wouldn't catch his breath. He's been chasing this virus for a decade. Probably dreams about it each night. If we show up in Baghdad with the virus, he'll cut a deal, no question. We'll show him a phone picture, whet his appetite. Make the exchange in the underground garage at the Al-Rasheed. Think about it. A holdall full of cash. Seat on a military flight back to Vandenberg. Like that idea? Couple of days from now, we could be in California. Palm trees. Beaches. Girls. More money than you can spend. We just have to keep our balls and get through the next few hours. Find the truck and pump some gas.'

The tunnel lights flickered.

'The generator,' said Gaunt. 'Must be running out of gas.'

'Get us rolling.'

'Come on, man. Cut me loose.'

Voss flipped open his lock-knife, sliced the cuffs and pushed Gaunt towards the breaker panel.

'Get to work.'

Gaunt opened the panel. A red switch. ENGINE PRIME.

Fuel pumps engaged.

Injectors loaded.

Batteries to START. A thud. A second thud. The great engine cylinders fired and warmed up. A rumble to a roar.

'Yeah, baby,' shouted Gaunt. The overhead cabin light burned bright. The console lit up.

A black fog of diesel fumes started to fill the cab.

'Close the fucking door.'

Gaunt sat at the driver's console. He released the automatic brake. He pushed the throttle from Idle to Run. Amp needles twitched and rose. He released the second, independent brake. He pushed the throttle forward. Shriek of seized metal starting to shift and turn. The locomotive jerked. Black fumes belched from side exhausts. Carriages slammed and began to roll.

Voss reached across the control desk and flicked HEADLAMP. A fierce cone of light stabbed from the nose of the locomotive, illuminating the tunnel mouth, the beams and planks lying across the track.

'Hold on.'

The locomotive bulldozed through the barrier. Splintered planks. Tumbling oil drums.

The engine rolled from the tunnel into daylight. A corroded behemoth. A two-hundred-and-fifty-ton dust-streaked juggernaut.

A soldier standing on the track. Mown down, broken by the plough and crushed to pulp beneath steel wheels.

The locomotive wound its way through the tight canyon, saurian diesel roar amplified by the high walls of the ravine.

'You have to retrieve the virus,' said Jabril. He flicked open his pocket knife. He cut Lucy and Amanda's wrist ties. 'That's your responsibility. Your lives are a secondary consideration. You understand, yes? It must be destroyed at all costs.'

'What about you?'

Jabril shook his head.

'Too old. Too tired. This is your fight now.'

Lucy checked him out. He looked exhausted. He looked used up.

Amanda tied a bandana round her wounded thigh.

Lucy held the flashlight while Jabril lashed patties of plastic explosive to the roof support with duct tape. He ran twin flex cable. He pressed blasting caps into the putty. He wired the detonators to a white box.

CASTLEKEEP.

'An automatic garage door mechanism,' he explained. 'Our acquisition team had five thousand shipped from China before the war began. We knew we couldn't defeat the Americans by conventional means. We were prepared for a guerrilla war.' He held up an infra-red key fob. 'They are the perfect IED trigger.'

He twisted copper strands, wired the garage door mechanism to a fourteen-volt motorcycle battery.

'That's it. Firing circuit complete.'

They ran for the tunnel mouth.

They reached the tunnel entrance. Scattered planks and beams. A skeletal creature broken and limbless on the track.

Jabril helped unhitched the quad bike and set it upright. Lucy straddled the bike and gunned the engine. Amanda rode pillion.

Jabril gave Lucy his pistol. He pulled Raphael's machete from the upturned trailer and gave it to Amanda.

'Go on,' he said. 'Get out of here.'

Tyres spat dirt as the bike pulled away.

A figure in a red boiler suit lurking between box cars.

'Hey,' shouted Jabril. His voice echoed down the mine tunnel. 'Hey, over here.'

Jabril jumped on a flatbed wagon. He took a flare from his pocket and struck the cap. It fizzed purple.

'Hey. You there.'

Two figures shuffled from shadow and moved towards him.

'Yes. That's right.'

Jabril ran the length of three rail cars, then jumped down to the track.

'Come on. That's right.'

He backed deeper into tunnel darkness. The foul, rotting creatures stumbled in pursuit.

Jabril threw down the flare. It spluttered at his feet.

He took the key fob detonator from his pocket.

'Come on, you poor bastards,' he murmured wearily. 'I think we all deserve a little sleep.'

The infected men shambled towards him, arms outstretched.

Jabril psyched himself to press the button.

'Let's bring this nightmare to a close.'

It should have been a moment of epiphany. His last seconds on earth. Last sights, last sounds. Last thoughts, last memories. But Jabril was tired and just wanted to die.

Teeth sank into his neck. Jabril dropped the fob and twisted free. He turned. Haq, chewing a mouthful of flesh.

Jabril sank to his knees clutching the pulsing wound in his neck. Blood bubbled between his fingers. A spreading, glistening stain across the shoulder of his linen suit.

He was seized by grasping hands. He kicked the jostling creatures. Nails tore his suit, dug into his flesh. One of the infected prisoners broke teeth as he gnawed the hook at the end of Jabril's right arm.

Jabril shook himself free. He raked rail-shingle as he scrabbled for the fob. He snagged the keyring with his prosthetic hook.

He gripped the fob in the bloody fingers of his left hand.

He pressed the button.

Charges blew deep in the tunnels. Timber props instantly reduced to whirling splinters. Passageways filled with fire, rock-dust and tumbling rubble.

Spilt paperwork in the ammunition store instantly crisped and carbonised by inferno heat.

Drums of ethylene and formaldehyde stacked beneath Spektr burst and filled the cavern with fire. The orbiter was briefly lifted from its rail-car bed as if it were performing a vertical take-off, borne upward by a wave of flame.

The polythene bio-dome shrivelled. The scaffold frame collapsed.

The lab units were ripped apart by a series of vicious internal blasts, and crushed flat by a thousand tons of falling rock.

The main tunnel collapsed, ore wagons and box cars pulverised by an avalanche of limestone.

Jabril, and the soldiers that tore at his flesh, winked out of existence in a millisecond of concussive heat.

Fuel

Gaunt pulled back the throttle and hit the brake. The train slowed to a halt. The motor shuddered and died. They felt the shunt and clank of carriages jolting to a stop behind them.

They were at the mouth of the ravine, the point where the high canyon walls opened out into the wide valley basin.

Voss stood on the locomotive walkway. He watched a broiling wave of smoke and rock-dust sweep down the tight ravine towards him.

He stepped inside the cab and closed the slide door. The train was engulfed in a thick dust cloud. Nothing beyond the windows but swirling vapour.

'Jabril pressed the button,' said Voss. 'Guess he was trying to bring the canyon down on us or something.'

'So your friends are gone,' said Gaunt. 'Just you and me now.'

The swirling dust slowly dissipated, sunlight slowly filtering into the cab as the haze began to clear.

Gaunt took binoculars from his backpack and scanned the valley through the side window of the cab. He surveyed the burned-out convoy, and the austere ruins of the citadel.

'I don't like it,' said Voss. 'Plenty of those fuckers out there. Chilled, for the time being, but it won't take much to get them riled. A hornets' nest, just waiting to be stirred.'

'You want to walk through open desert in fifty-degree heat? Fuck that. Jabril made it, but he got lucky. We can ride this thing home. All we have to do is get some gas in the tank.'

Faint radio crackle. Voss took the sat phone from his backpack. He adjusted volume.

American voice:

'*Roger that, Angel Flight. We have your TAC visual. Holding at nineteen thousand feet.*'

'Who are they?' asked Voss.

'Encrypted frequency. Must be the plane. We can eavesdrop on their radio traffic. They're requesting clearance to over-fly the US carrier group in the Gulf of Oman, as they move up the Saudi coast.'

'Sure you can't talk sense into them?'

'These agency guys don't give a shit. They follow orders. We're expendable assets. Hired guns. They've got no use for us. They won't hesitate to drop the bomb. Probably relish the chance. Prove to their boss they are ideologically pure. True believers, loyal to the cause.'

'I have to try,' said Voss. He pressed transmit.

'Incoming plane, do you copy, over? Angel Flight can you hear me?'

No response.

'Forget it,' said Gaunt. 'They won't answer.'

'Angel Flight, this is fire support team Bravo Bravo Lima Two. There are men on the ground. Do you copy, over? Do not bomb this site. There are men on the ground requesting urgent assistance. We require immediate evacuation. Please respond.'

No response.

'How much time do we have left?'

'Two, three hours tops,' said Gaunt. 'They fly fucked-up old freighters, make a few runs, then sell them to a wrecker's yard. Junkers. The kind of planes that won't attract attention on the taxiway of a third-world airfield. Russian cargo lifters. Old twin-prop Providers. They'll fly slow up the Saudi coast then swing through southern Iraq. I'd say we have a two-hour window to fuel the train. After that we haul ass, on foot if necessary. Hang around any longer, and we burn.'

They left the cab. They vaulted the rear knuckle coupling of the locomotive to the Pullman carriage behind.

The cobwebbed grandeur of Saddam's salon. Their boots kicked up billowing clouds of dust from a Persian rug.

Voss emptied Lucy's backpack on an antique desk, mahogany cracked and warped by dry desert air.

Grenades and magazines.

Gaunt slapped a fresh thirty-round clip into the receiver well of an assault rifle and stuffed mags in his jacket pockets.

Voss slotted shells into his shotgun and racked the slide. He looked out the window.

'All right. Let's go.'

Voss kicked open the carriage door. They jumped from the train and ran towards the convoy.

They jogged across open ground. They walked among wrecked vehicles, weapons raised, sweeping left and right.

'Should be big,' said Gaunt. 'A ten wheeler.'

Voss checked his watch. He rubbed dust from the glass with a dirty thumb. Seven thirty. They had been in the desert less than twenty-four hours. It felt like a decade.

They picked their way through the avenue of burned-out vehicles. Crumpled sedans, trackless APCs, troop trucks burned down to a skeletal chassis.

Boots crunched on windshield glass. Blackened bones snapped like twigs.

Voss came to a sudden halt.

'What the fuck is this shit?'

He backed away from a scorched bus. The bus lay bedded in sand. Arms clawed and clutched from beneath the vehicle. Hands scrabbled and slapped the bodywork. Soldiers must have crawled underneath the bus during the fire-fight and got crushed as tyres burst and the vehicle settled into the dust. They succumbed to infection as they lay pinned beneath the ten-ton hulk. Entombed, halfway between life and death.

He unhooked a grenade from his webbing.

'Don't,' said Gaunt. 'Leave them. We haven't got time.'

They found the fuel truck between two shattered APCs. A heavy Russian Kraz in desert yellow. There was a boom arm at the top of the tank. A thick transfer hose terminated in a heavy coupling.

Voss checked the storage tank. Bullet holes high in the tank. Oil in the sand.

'Lucky this thing didn't blow sky-high. A single tracer hit would have been Game Over.'

He touched drip-streaks and sniffed his fingers. Diesel.

'Sure this isn't JP-8?'

Gaunt shook his head.

'Locomotive grade. It took a tank of gas to get the locomotive to this valley. It will take another tank to get her home. That's why they brought a reserve.'

Voss rapped the hull with his knuckles. A dull thud.

'She's three-quarters full. Intact below the bullet holes.'

Gaunt checked out the cab. It was burned out. Seats scorched down to springs. Dash-plastic hanging in petrified drips.

The hood had blown off. The engine was shot to hell.

'It's fucked,' said Voss. 'It'll never move.'

'Hold on. Let's think this through.'

The quad raced down the narrow ravine. Lucy drove parallel with the track. The bike bucked over rough terrain. They drove through a haze of rock dust, slow-settling powder ejected by the collapsed mine tunnel.

Amanda slapped Lucy on the back. Lucy stopped the bike.

'I got to patch my leg.'

Amanda lay on the ground. Lucy patched her leg with Kerlix dressing and gave her a shot of morphine.

'Like it?'

'Love it.'

'We have to get out of this fucking valley,' said Lucy. 'We have to get deep in that rail tunnel. I mean real deep. Shelter from the blast wave and heat.'

'How long do you think we have?'

'Couple of hours, tops. We better burn rubber.'

'I don't think I can make it,' said Amanda.

'Don't even start with that shit.'

'What if my leg gives out? How am I going to make it across the fucking desert? Are you going to carry me on your back?'

'If that's what it takes. I'll get you home, babe. I lost everything. Toon. Huang. Voss. I'm not losing you.

A Republican Guard stumbled along the track towards them, skin laced with metallic tendrils.

'Give me the machete,' said Lucy.

She approached the soldier.

An officer. Red beret and epaulettes. An AK strapped to his back. His flesh oozed metal.

He snarled. He reached for Lucy's throat. She stood her ground as he stumbled towards her. She hacked off his arm. He fell to his knees. She lopped through his neck.

Lucy stood over the body.

'I expected more of these fuckers. Guess they must have returned to the citadel. Hibernating, or something.'

She unhitched the rifle. A Tabuk, with a folding stock. The crude AK47 clone manufactured for the Iraqi army. She worked the bolt. A poor action, but the weapon would fire.

She took magazines from pouches strapped to the dead man's chest.

'Want to give me the pistol?' asked Amanda.

'Later,' said Lucy. She worried Amanda might blow her brains out rather than become a fatal burden.

They climbed on the quad and set off. The four-stroke engine echoed round tight canyon walls.

They turned a bend in the ravine. Lucy brought the bike to a halt. The train was parked up ahead.

'Why did they stop?' asked Amanda. 'Out of fuel already?'

They got off the bike. Lucy chambered the AK. They crept along the valley wall. Lucy kept her rifle trained on empty carriage windows.

'Give me a fucking gun,' said Amanda.

Lucy tossed the Makarov pistol.

They crept the length of the train. They reached the locomotive. Lucy climbed the ladder. She pulled Amanda up onto the walkway.

They flanked the cab door. Lucy pushed the slide door with her foot and ducked inside, rifle raised.

Empty.

'They took the key. We can't start her up.'

Lucy helped Amanda jump the coupling to the carriage.

Rifles, but no magazines.

Amanda kicked an empty backpack.

'Looks like they took most of the ammo.'

She slumped in a chair and massaged her wounded leg.

'How much morphine have we got?'

'Couple more shots,' said Lucy. 'Better save them. If that wound gets infected, you'll be hurting for real.'

'I could use a fucking drink.'

Lucy offered her canteen.

'A real drink. A beer. Can't stop thinking about it. Ice cold. Condensation running down the glass.'

Amanda flicked open her lock-knife and cut the crusted dressing from her leg. She unzipped Huang's trauma kit. She unrolled fresh gauze round her thigh, and lashed the dressing in place with a combat tourniquet.

'How's it looking?' asked Lucy.

'A little fresh blood. Not much. It'll be okay, long as it doesn't get infected.'

Amanda popped codeine from a blister strip and knocked them back with canteen water.

'Take it easy with that shit, all right?

Lucy kicked open the missile case.

The Hellfire guidance cone. The solid-fuel rocket motor. A vacant scoop of foam where the virus cylinder used to sit.

'Gaunt took the virus. He must be carrying it with him.'

She wiped grime from a window and focused binoculars.

'What can you see?' asked Amanda. She fanned her Stetson.

A couple of half-rotted soldiers stumbled and crawled from the ancient necropolis. They emerged from the great propylon gateway and dragged themselves across the valley floor towards the column of wrecked vehicles.

'Two infected guys. They seem to be converging on the convoy.

She surveyed the burned-out trucks and cars.

'There. I see them.'

'Gaunt?'

'And Voss.'

Gaunt and Voss arguing, gesticulating.

'They're checking out some kind of fuel truck.'

'Voss is mine, all right?' said Amanda. 'I want to see the look on his face when I pull the trigger.'

The Bomb

Three hundred miles from target.

The plane. A silver Fairchild Provider. A twin-prop freighter in Red Cross livery.

'*Angel Flight, you are leaving our air. Maintain two-eight-five, at fifteen thousand. Good luck.*'

'Roger that, QTAC Centre. Maintaining two-eight-five at fifteen thousand. Have a good day.'

Jakub took off his headphones. He wiped sweat from his neck and brow with a do-rag. He checked heading and altitude.

Jakub: a fat guy in a Motörhead shirt.

He looked out the cockpit window. The blur of the starboard propeller. Baghdad to their north. A bombed-out sprawl. Minarets and shanty squalor.

A thread of black smoke rose from the old quarter. A car bomb or garbage fire.

'Fucking shithole. Giant fucking latrine. Dust and donkey turds. You know, I bet half the wars round here would stop in an instant if they got some decent TV channels. All they have is those fucking brain-rot Egyptian soaps. Nothing in their lives. No hope. No booze. No nothing. Bunch of rabid junkyard dogs, ripping out each other's throats.'

Tomasz checked the map. A big stretch of yellow. The Western Desert. No towns, no topographical features. A straight run to the target.

Tomasz: a big guy with a moustache. Swastikas and Aryan Nation tatts down both arms.

Both men were ex-GROM. Polish 'thunderbolt' special forces. Recruited by the CIA seven years ago. Training and indoctrination at the US Army School of the Americas, Fort Benning. Seven years' billet in downtown Columbus. Part of a language immersion programme. Taught to speak American, think American. They were currently on retainer contracts running covert ops for the Office of Technical Services. Prisoner transports. Rendition flights. Hooded, hog-tied detainees flown to black interrogation centres in Eastern Europe and North Africa.

Tomasz checked his watch.

'How long to the objective?'

'Hour. Hour and a half, maybe. Return journey will be quicker. Should gain about thirty knots, once we've dumped the payload.'

There was a sat-com unit bolted to the flight control panel. A hi-tec addition to antique gauges and dials.

A faint voice:

'*Incoming plane, do you copy, over? Angel Flight can you hear me?*'

Jakub put on headphones. He adjusted volume.

'*Angel Flight, do you copy, over?*'

'There they go again,' said Jakub.

'Same guy?'

'No. He sounds South African. He's using our channel, our encryption key. He must be for real.'

'*Angel Flight, this is fire support team Bravo Bravo Lima Two. There are men on the ground. Do you copy, over? Do not bomb this site. There are men on the ground requesting urgent assistance. We require immediate evacuation. Please respond.*'

'Maybe we should radio Koell,' said Jakub. 'Let him know there are people on site.'

'He won't give a shit.'

'I think we should talk to him.'

'Don't be weak. You've got your orders. Just sit tight and fly the plane.'

'I don't like it,' muttered Jakub. 'Doesn't seem right.'

Tomasz unbuckled his harness.

'I'm going to check on our passenger.'

He ducked through the cabin door. He climbed down a short steel ladder into the hold. A wide cargo space ribbed with girders. A couple of overhead bulbs.

He blinked, tried to adjust to windowless cave-dark.

A huge object, a cylinder big as a van, beneath a canvas shroud.

Tomasz swayed, like a sailor crossing a deck in high seas. He untied rope and began to pull back the tarp.

'Time to do your thing, baby.'

A giant thermobaric device. Twelve tons of high explosive.

White paint on black metal:

UNCHAINED MELODY

Tomasz patted the steel hull of the bomb.

'Let's make sweet music.'

Republican Guard. A button-popping fat guy with no arms. He fell, and struggled to his feet. He wove between burned-out sedans.

Voss shouldered his shotgun and braced his legs.

'*Gaan fok jouself*,' murmured Voss, as he lined up the shot.

The fat guy's head exploded. Brain-splash. He toppled to the ground, half his head ripped away. His legs pedalled like he was still trying to walk. He churned circles in the dirt.

Gaunt checked his watch. He kicked the burned hubs of the fuel truck.

'She's got to be towed. Hitched to something big, and dragged to the locomotive.'

Voss pointed at the sky.

'What the fuck is that?'

A distant, dove-grey plane circling like a vulture.

'It's the drone I told you about. Koell's eye in the sky. We're being surveilled. Watching us the whole time we've been out here.'

Voss took off his jacket and waved it back and forth.

'What the hell are you doing?' asked Gaunt. 'Koell isn't going to send the cavalry. He's going to tape your death and post it online.'

Gaunt looked towards the Predator and flipped the bird.

'Get that in infra-red, you fuck.'

Lucy stood at the carriage window and watched the drone through binoculars. The ghost-grey airframe of a UAV.

Rolls-Royce turbofan tail engine. Eyeless, bulbous head. The Predator slow-circled the valley at high altitude.

'You think it's been up there this whole time?' asked Amanda. 'How long can those things stay airborne? Think it's been shadowing us this past couple of days?'

'Maybe.'

'How much do you reckon it cost? A thing like that?'

'Three-, four-million-dollar optics package. Doesn't take much to run. Guy in a pilot van toggling a joystick, watching a screen.'

'Shoot it.'

'Too far out. Might as well throw rocks at the bastard.'

Lucy lowered her binoculars and turned her attention back to the truck. She adjusted focus.

'Come on, guys,' murmured Lucy. 'Get your shit together. Move the damn truck.'

Gaunt opened the tool compartment above the rear fender. He found yellow canvas tow straps wound in a coil.

'All right. Here's the plan,' said Gaunt. 'We fire up the cash truck. Drive it from the temple. Use it to tow the tanker.'

They jogged across sand towards the citadel entrance. They passed between the twin gate towers. The burned-out choppers still smouldered in the central courtyard. The air was still bitter with the taint of burnt plastic.

They passed titanic ruins. Sinister silence. Domes, arches, colonnades. Courtyards and avenues half-choked with sand.

They entered the shadow of the baleful colossi that flanked the temple entrance.

The vast temple interior. Cool darkness.

A gangrenous soldier shambled from the shadows. A frail, mummified creature. Skin like leather. Dendritic growths woven through flesh. Clothes hung in blood-smeared strips.

He had no eyes. He stumbled. He bumped pillars. He advanced like he was tracking their scent. The soldier was barely alive, but still compelled to rip and tear. An unquenchable thirst for flesh. That final thought dying slow, like campfire embers.

Gaunt kicked the creature. It stumbled and fell. He stamped on his head. Skull burst. He scuffed his boot on flagstones like he was scraping dog shit.'Come on.'

They ran to the truck.

Voss reached into the fender well beneath the battery and tripped the starter solenoid.

Ignition. Engine roar echoed round the vaulted interior of the temple. The single, intact head lamp flickered and glowed steady. The beam shafted through swirling dust motes.

Half-dead soldiers lay sprawled over altar steps beneath the great, contemptuous bull god. They turned towards the sudden radiance, stirred slow and clumsy like they were waking from a long sleep.

'Damn,' said Voss. 'Let's go.'

They ran to the cab. They reversed away from the altar, swung round, and headed for daylight shafting through the temple doorway

A soldier crawled up the processional ramp to the temple entrance. Legs sheared at the thigh. Bone and ragged flesh. Tumorous tendrils trailed from each stump. He paused at the temple threshold, reached out like he was trying to grasp the approaching head beam. Tyres crushed his torso as the armoured truck rolled over his body and out into sunlight. His ribs crunched beneath the wheels. His skull crackled and splintered like glass ground under a heavy boot.

The truck rolled down the temple ramp. Two rotted soldiers reached for the vehicle, arms outstretched. They were smashed by ram bars, pulped beneath the wheels.

The cash truck rode over smooth flagstones, through

ceremonial precincts and out the citadel gateway. It bounced over rock-strewn dirt.

'Quarter of a tank,' said Gaunt, checking the dash gauge. 'If we can't get the loco running, we use the truck to get out the valley. Throw some water and ammo in the back. Should help us cross a few miles of desert before we have to get out and walk.'

They reached the convoy. Gaunt revved and rammed the column of vehicles. He bulldozed a passage between cars. Body panels shrieked. Doors ripped free. A Subaru tipped and rolled.

They pulled up in front of the fuel truck. They lashed tow straps.

'You got to walk me back to the train,' said Gaunt. 'Keep the fuckers off my back while I drive.'

Gaunt gunned the throttle. The armoured car crept forward. The tow strap slapped taut and creaked at full tension. High revs. Gaunt pumped the throttle and rocked the fuel truck free.

Voss stood guard. He climbed on the hood of a burned-out Lincoln. A row of automobiles, toe to tail. He jumped roof to roof. He kept pace with the lurching fuel truck as it rolled forward.

He climbed across the blistered hull of an APC. A soldier squirmed from a turret hatch, face a mask of knotted malignancies. Voss delivered a vicious kick to the head. Neck snap. The creature fell limp and slid back into darkness.

More grasping hands emerging from gaping hatchways, scrabbling like spiders. Snapping skull faces.

Voss pulled the pin from a frag grenade and dropped it into the dark interior of the APC. He heard it clang and clatter. He jumped clear.

Muffled blast. A jet of smoke from every vent and hatch. The hull resonated like a gong. The sound echoed round the high valley walls, and died slow.

*

'How you doing?' asked Lucy.

'All right,' said Amanda. She massaged her leg. 'Riding the codeine wave.'

The sun high over the valley walls. Merciless, lacerating light. The carriage was starting to bake.

They watched the trucks lurch across wasteland towards the locomotive. They could hear the distant engine rev and labour. The vehicles kicked up a high dust plume.

Amanda looked up at the drone.

'They must know there are people alive down here. Someone in Baghdad is watching us close-up. Examining every hair follicle and skin pore. Toying with us, like a kid frying ants with a magnifying glass.'

'They want us dead. We are a loose end. This whole operation is a bleed they want to tie off and cauterise. Soon as we get back to Baghdad, we switch to fake ID. Destroy dog tags, credit cards, anything with our names. Collect our shit from the Rasheed, then vanish.'

'Damn,' said Amanda. 'Check it out. The citadel.'

Lucy raised her binoculars. She focused. Half-dead soldiers were staggering and crawling from the citadel gate. A wraith army, relentlessly dragging themselves across sun-blasted terrain.

'Christ. Jabril's battalion, coming out to play. Looks like they heard the trucks. Fifty, maybe sixty men. They're heading this way. Moving slow, but they'll hit us soon enough.'

'How many rounds do we have?'

'Five or six in the AK. Half a clip in the pistol.'

'Let Gaunt and Voss hook up the fuel line,' said Amanda. 'We'll pump some gas and get the hell out of here.'

Hook-Up

Faint radio crackle. The sat phone lay on a table.

'*Roger that. Climb and level at one-eight-zero. Heading hold.*'

Lucy picked up the handset.

'Must be locked on a secure channel,' said Amanda.

'Hello? Hello? Can you hear us? This is Lucy Whyte. There are British and American citizens at your target site. Do you copy?'

No response.

'There are wounded personnel at your target site requesting urgent evacuation, over.'

No response.

'Hello? Incoming plane, do you copy?'

'Reckon they can hear us?' asked Amanda.

'Yeah.'

'Unbelievable. They're going to kill us. They know we are here. They're going to drop the bomb anyway.'

'It's a pay cheque.'

Lucy shielded her eyes from the sun. She watched the vehicles two hundred yards distant, slowly lurching over lunar terrain, kicking up a high dust plume. She could hear the cash truck strain and grind.

She could see Gaunt in the cab, hunched over the wheel. Voss walking beside the bank truck, ghost-white with dust. He turned and delivered an efficient headshot to soldiers following the gouge-trench left by the damaged tanker.

Lucy hooked the TASC earpiece to her lobe.

'How's it going, Voss?'

'*Jesus. Lucy.*'

He tried to work out her position. He checked out the locomotive and scanned the valley walls.

'Bet you thought we got buried with Jabril.'

'*It wasn't personal, boss.*'

'Open ground. I could drop you in a heartbeat. I've got you in my sights right now.'

No response.

'Well? Don't you want to live?'

'*What do you want me to say, bokkie?*'

'Help us get out of this valley, and maybe I will let you live. Can Gaunt hear us? Is he wearing his wire?'

'*No.*'

'The moment you guys hook up the fuel line, we whack him.'

'*We need Gaunt to drive the locomotive. We need him alive.*'

'Fuck him. We'll figure out the controls.'

Lucy pulled the earpiece from her ear.

'You want to let Voss off the hook?' asked Amanda. 'After what he did to us?'

'Let's get out the valley. After that, if you still want to snuff the guy, be my guest.'

The vehicles reached the locomotive. Voss checked out the carriage windows, trying to work out if Lucy and Amanda were hidden inside.

Gaunt jumped from the cab.

Voss climbed an iron ladder to the tanker roof. He swung the boom arm towards the locomotive. Six-inch transfer hose swung like an elephant's trunk.

Gaunt grabbed the hose and pulled it to the walkway. He pulled a ring-latch and lifted a section of grating. He unscrewed the heavy fuel cap. He grabbed the swinging hose. Male to female. Twist to engage. Flip cam locks to clamp the coupling in position.

Voss crouched on the tanker roof and examined the pump. A 14V Dynavolt battery. An electric compressor in a mesh safety cage. He checked connections and flipped a power switch. Green light. The pump began to hum. The fuel pipe trembled. He leant forward and put his ear to the pipe. Gulp and gush.

'We're in business. She's fuelling.'

Voss descended the ladder. Gaunt jumped from the locomotive. They faced each other.

Gaunt gestured towards the convoy. They could see creatures, twisted by strange cankerous growths, weaving between burned-out vehicles.

'Think we can hold them off?' asked Gaunt.

'Smart fire. Clean medulla shots. Let's not waste a single bullet.'

'Okay.'

Gaunt fetched a backpack full of ammo from the truck cab.

'Better get ourselves a fire position.'

He headed for the carriage. Voss held back.

Gaunt reached up and gripped the door handle.

'What's up with you?'

'Nothing,' said Voss.

Gaunt took the locomotive ignition key from his pocket and held it up.

'Don't forget. You still need me. You want to get home? You want to get rich? Then you need me alive.'

Gaunt pulled open the carriage door and hauled himself up into the carriage. Gunshot. Windows momentarily lit by muzzle flare like a camera flash. Gaunt was hurled from the coach. He rolled in the dust.

Lucy and Amanda climbed from the carriage. Smoke curled from the barrel of Lucy's AK.

Gaunt was shot in the hip, just beneath the hem of his flak jacket. He crawled, dragging his injured leg, blood soaking into the sand. He gripped the side of the carriage and slowly pulled himself upright.

Lucy picked up the locomotive key and put it in her pocket. She hoisted Gaunt's backpack from where it lay and slung it over one shoulder. She raised the AK and took aim.

Gaunt popped an ammo pouch on his chest rig and held the virus cylinder above his head.

'You want to shoot? Want to crack this baby open, see what happens?'

He backed away, sliding along the side of the carriage, dragging his injured leg.

'Back up. Back the fuck up.'

Lucy lowered the gun.

'You've got nowhere to go, Gaunt. This place is going to burn.'

Gaunt began to limp away across the sand, still holding the virus cylinder.

Amanda took a couple of steps but Lucy held her back.

'Leave him,' said Lucy. 'Better this way. Let him piss in fear as the bomb drops.'

'What about the virus?'

'Let the firestorm do its job.'

They watched Gaunt reach the valley wall. Dripping sweat, dripping blood, dragging his useless leg.

'How long can he last?' asked Amanda.

Lucy shrugged.

'I've seen Talib last a whole day with their guts hanging out.'

Gaunt struggled to climb. A slow scramble. Behind him a cadaverous soldier clawed upward in slow pursuit. Fingers raked dirt. Boots gouged loose an avalanche of scree.

'Tempted to shoot him as mercy.'

'No,' said Lucy. 'He brought this on himself.'

A skeletal hand locked round Gaunt's ankle. He screamed. A thin, girlish wail. He tried to kick himself free.

The creature gripped his legs. It dug fingers and teeth into the wound at his hip, like it was drawn by the scent of blood.

Gaunt pounded the revenant's head with a rock. He was too weak to shatter the creature's skull.

They rolled down the slope in a stone-chip landslide. The soldier pinned Gaunt's chest and tore at his shoulder and neck.

'Adios, fucker,' murmured Lucy. She turned away, ignored the shrill screams that echoed round the valley wall.

She turned to Voss. 'How long will it take to fill the tank?' she asked.

'Couple of hours. She's pumping at thirty-five, maybe forty gallons a minute.'

'We don't have much time. We pump for one hour, then unhitch and haul arse no matter what. She'll get us part the way home. Get us halfway across the desert if we are lucky. After that, we walk.'

'All right,' said Voss.

'You want to live? Then earn it. Get up on that carriage roof and give us cover fire. Let's hold off these fucks as long as we can.'

Voss shouldered an assault rifle and climbed an iron ladder to the coach roof. He sat cross-legged on hot sheet-metal.

'Watch your fire,' shouted Lucy. 'If you put tracer in that fuel tank, you'll blow us all to hell.'

Voss lowered the brim of his baseball cap to shield his eyes from the merciless sun. He hooked his radio earpiece to his ear.

'Bastards are massing. They're moving out the citadel, heading this way. Looks like we stirred the hornets' nest.'

Lucy's voice:

'I guess we sit tight long as we can, then get the hell out of here.'

'We should leave. Right now. I got a bird's-eye view where I'm sitting. Dozens of the fuckers moving through that convoy. Won't take them long to cross open ground and reach us.'

'*We've got to keep our nerve. Every minute that pump is running we put more fuel in the tank and get closer to home.*'

Voss swigged from his canteen. He took off his baseball cap and wiped sweat from his brow.

'Christ. Bastard fucking place.'

Lucy upturned Gaunt's backpack. Ammunition spilt across the floor. Pistol clips and rifle magazines.

'Back in business,' said Amanda.

They slid knives into belt sheaths. They slotted fresh magazines into their Glocks, and dropped them into hip holsters. They tucked STANAG clips into ammunition pouches strapped to their chest-rigs. They slapped mags into their carbines, racked the charging handles and each chambered a round.

'Like it?'

'Love it.'

They smashed out windows. They set up fire positions.

Amanda shunted an ornate Queen Anne table beneath the window and laid out the SAW.

Lucy pulled a couple of chairs to the window. She sat and rested her rifle on the sill. She stacked STANAG clips on the chair beside her.

They took aim at the convoy, waited for incoming soldiers, waited for a clear shot.

Radio crackle. The sat phone lying on a nearby table. The winking red light of an open channel.

'. . . *Roger, Papa One. Maintain at sixteen* . . .'

Lucy pulled a map from her pocket and shook it open.

'Papa One. That's the QTAC call sign for Baghdad International.'

'Shit,' said Amanda. 'I didn't think they had reached the coast.'

'Puts them about three hundred miles south-east of here,' said Lucy. 'A cargo plane, hauling a heavy load. Flying between one-fifty, two hundred knots. A straight run across the desert. I reckon they'll be overhead in ninety minutes.'

'Be lucky to live that long,' said Amanda. She looked towards the convoy. Soldiers, dozens of them, weaving between cars.

Lucy focused her binoculars. Soldiers slithered from the turret hatches of APCs, crawled from beneath trucks, tumbled from the trunks of wrecked sedans.

'We're starting to pull a serious crowd.'

Movement from waste ground in front of the convoy. The sand crust began to ripple and bulge. Skeletal hands broke from the dirt. Dozens of naked, half-dissected creatures squirmed upward into daylight.

'My God,' murmured Lucy. 'Must be some kind of mass grave.'

The vivisected soldiers climbed to their feet, trailing shroud-sheets. Skin half-melted by caustic lime. Their chest cavities were wired open. Their scalps were peeled back. Their skulls were drilled.

The skeletal army began to stagger and crawl towards the locomotive.

'Jesus fucking Christ,' murmured Amanda.

Lucy aimed her rifle. Amanda pressed the butt of the SAW to her shoulder. They both opened fire. Muzzle roar and flame.

The Bomb

One hundred miles from target.

Tomasz descended the cockpit ladder to the cargo bay.

Ribbed girders. The bullet-pocked skin of the plane patched like the sail fabric of an old ship.

The exterior fuselage still bore the insignia of 302 Tactical Airlift Wing. Paint had been scoured from the side door, but the aluminium retained a shadow impression like a fading tattoo. A relic of the plane's glory years. Fresh out the Fairchild plant, shipped to Bien Hoa to fly defoliation missions along the banks of the Mekong. Skimming the treeline, taking small-arm dings as it vented Agent Orange into the jungle canopy.

This would be the plane's last mission. As soon as the Provider returned to the staging base at Sharjah it would be issued with a fresh tail number and fresh registration. It would be flown to Thailand or the Philippines. It would be discreetly gutted and scrapped. Or maybe parked, strung with speakers and lights, and finish its days as a beach bar.

Unchained Melody.

A big, black cylinder. Riveted plate, like a ship's boiler.

Tomasz used a wrench to unscrew lock-nuts and remove a side panel.

He flicked a couple of toggle switches. *Batt Test.* Green power light.

He pulled a high-impact Peli case from beneath a bench seat. Four rods packed in foam. The fuses. High-explosive cores.

He removed safety caps and slotted each of the igniters into the primer panel. He screwed them in place. Quadruple failsafe: baro switch, radar proximity, hydrostatic pressure, interval timer. A button above each fuse. *Test.* He got green Go lights from each arming circuit.

He adjusted the mechanical altimeter. Set for airburst at nine hundred feet.

He took three brown envelopes from the lid pocket of the case, and tore them open. Three numbered keys. He inserted the keys into the fire panel. PALs. Permissive Action Links. Three safing lock-outs to prevented premature detonation of the weapon.

A final visual inspection of the drogue chutes packed in a canvas sling at the nose of the bomb. Rip-cord clipped to a hundred-metre tether.

He returned to the cockpit.

'All set?' asked Jakub.

'Flick the switch and we are ready to rock and roll.'

A voice from the sat com. A woman. Tired, desperate.

'*Hello? Hello? Can you hear us? This is Lucy Whyte. There are British and American citizens at your target site. Do you copy?*'

'I don't like it,' said Jakub. 'She's English. No fucking camel jockey, that's for sure.'

'*There are wounded personnel at your target site requesting urgent evacuation, over.*'

'Mercs,' said Tomasz. 'Stateless scum blocking a lawful military target.'

'*Hello? Incoming plane, do you copy?*'

'Put it from your mind. Fly straight and do your fucking job.'

Fallback

Lucy dropped the spent clip from her rifle and slapped home a fresh magazine. She gulped from her canteen. She poured water over her head.

Two soldiers, a hundred yards distant. She fired. She missed.

'Fuck.'

She wiped sweat from her eyes. She took aim and fired again.

Amanda clipped a fresh ammunition belt into the smoking breach of the SAW and slammed the receiver closed.

The window was framed by a shredded, muzzle-scorched velvet curtain. She tore it loose and stamped out embers.

'Got any more Codeine?' she asked.

Lucy passed her a foil blister-strip.

Amanda knocked back a pill. She swigged mineral water and sprayed a mouthful over the SAW barrel. Droplets steamed and fizzled, like spit on a hot plate.

She chewed balls of paper, moulded them into plugs and twisted them into her ears.

She gripped the SAW. Burst fire. She trembled with fierce recoil.

A line of advancing soldiers hurled backward by heavy .50 cal rounds. Five men, chests ripped open, spines broken, heads split.

Some lay dead, clothes burning. Some struggled to stand. They trailed viscera. They dragged useless legs.

A second sweep of machine-gunfire shattered skulls and reduced the soldiers to rags and splintered, bloody bone.

Amanda pulled off Nomex gloves and wrapped surgical tape round her red-raw trigger finger.

A thud. She pulled the plugs from her ears. A second thud.

'Shit. They're hitting us from all sides. I think they're under the train.'

A cadaverous figure gripped the sill and tried to pull himself inside. Skull face. Gleaming chrome erupting through flesh.

Amanda unsheathed the knife from her webbing and stabbed the deformed soldier through the eye. She twisted the blade. The creature released its grip, toppled backward and fell dead in the dirt.

Voss crouched on the carriage roof. Steady fire. The killing ground between the convoy and locomotive littered with bodies like a battlefield.

He exhausted six mags of tungsten carbide penetrators. He shook cramp from his trigger hand. He flexed his shoulder.

Skeletal creatures stumbled between burned-out vehicles. Seething movement.

Lucy's voice:

'*Swarming like bugs.*'

A couple of soldiers crawled along the Pullman roof towards Voss.

'Chrome motherfuckers flanked us. Circled our fire avenue and reached the train. Still got some residual smarts.'

He took aim. Neat headshots. The skeletal creatures fell dead, slid from the carriage roof and landed in the dirt.

'Time to get radical.'

He climbed down the ladder and jumped to the ground. He opened the carriage door and climbed inside.

'How you doing?' he asked.

'Sweet,' said Amanda. 'Don't worry about us.'

Voss snatched a bandolier of rifle grenades. He slung the belt over his shoulder: 40mm pepper-pot rounds in leather loops, like elephantine shotgun shells.

He jumped from the carriage. He ran across open ground towards the convoy.

Lucy and Amanda on over-watch. Soldiers lumbered towards Voss. They cut them down. Skull-shattering impacts.

Voss pushed a grenade from a belt loop. Gold tip, high explosive. He slotted the grenade into the breach of the launcher slung beneath his rifle and snapped it shut.

Voss aimed the launcher and fired. Thud. Whistle-whine. Rotted troops blasted to fragments. It rained rocks and scraps of flesh.

He advanced. He stepped over cratered ground and smoking limbs. He could see soldiers massing among the wrecked vehicles of the convoy.

Voss grew up in Bloemfontein. A dilapidated house. A pile of wrecked furniture in the backyard. 'Put a match to it,' his father said. Voss slopped gasoline and threw a burning rag. Rats streamed from the woodpile as smashed cupboards and chairs started to smoke and burn.

He thought of rats as he watched rotted soldiers swarm and teem among burned-out vehicles.

He slotted a fresh grenade into the launcher and fired. Thud. Streak of efflux. Thunderous concussion. Eruption of sand and smoke. Trucks rolled. Sedans flipped and burned.

Amanda fed a fresh belt into the SAW. She locked the receiver closed.

'This is it. Last chain. Two hundred rounds, then she's done.'

'Make them count,' said Lucy.

Two half-dissolved Republican Guard stumbled towards Voss. Skin hung in strips. They tried to flank him from the right as he fragged the convoy. Amanda cut them down. The SAW spat brass. The soldiers were ripped apart.

Nearby sound of smashing glass. Amanda pulled plugs from her ears.

'Shit. They hit us from the rear. They got in.'

She opened the connecting door to the second carriage. The dining car. A banquet table. Upturned chairs. Cobwebbed dereliction.

A rotted figure squirmed through a broken window. He hauled himself over the sill, shredding clothes and flesh on jagged shards.

More soldiers crowding outside the coach. Hands slapped glass. Windows cracked and broke.

Amanda grabbed the SAW. She slung the strap over her shoulder and lifted the weapon. She stood in the doorway of the dining car.

The man-thing fell to the floor of the coach. He struggled to his feet. His right arm was a mess of metallic spines.

He saw Amanda and hissed.

She braced her legs and pulled the trigger. The heavy machine gun ejected a stream of links and smoking brass. The soldier burst apart. He was hurled backward. He hit wall panels and slid to the floor. Another burst from the gun obliterated his head.

Windows shattered. Three Republican Guard began to haul themselves into the carriage. Amanda opened fire. The creatures were pulverised and flung from the train.

The SAW ran dry. Amanda unhitched the strap and dropped the smoking weapon at her feet. She unholstered her Glock and backed out the carriage. The floor was carpeted with spent shell casings. Her boots kicked scorched brass.

'Did you get them?' shouted Lucy.

'There will be more,' said Amanda. 'We can't cover both carriages. We have to barricade the doorway.'

Amanda tipped the mahogany desk onto its side and pushed it to block the connecting door.

Lucy fired from the window. Soldiers approached across open ground from the east. Headshots. They fell dead.

She flexed cramp from her trigger hand. She slapped a fresh mag into her rifle.

'Give me a hand,' shouted Amanda. She pushed a heavy bureau towards the carriage doorway.

Lucy lay down her rifle, threw her bodyweight against the bureau and helped shunt it against the barricade.

Voss continued to frag the convoy. Trucks and jeeps blown apart. Flame and eruptions of dust. Scattered doors, trunk lids, seat springs and axles. Each detonation followed by the lazy thrum of whirling shrapnel.

Republican Guard converged from all sides. Voss oblivious as encroaching soldiers threatened to flank his position.

Lucy and Amanda gave cover fire. A succession of clean headshots.

Dead man's click. The mag run dry. Lucy ejected the clip. Nothing in the ammo pouches strapped to her vest. She took a fresh magazine from the backpack.

She shouted into her radio.

'Voss. Hey, Voss.' No response. 'Voss. Arsehole. Pull back. We're running dry.'

His earpiece hung loose.

'What's he doing?' said Amanda. 'Fucking idiot. He's going get ripped apart.'

'Keep him covered,' said Lucy. 'Do the best you can.'

She slapped the mag into her rifle and cranked the charging handle. She took aim and fired.

Voss watched a group of Republican Guard push open the rear door of an APC and emerge from darkness. He took aim and fired a grenade into the interior of the vehicle. Flame jetted from every vent and hatchway. The soldiers were ejected from the APC, reduced to burning, scattered limbs.

He checked the bandolier slung over his shoulder. No more frag grenades. He retreated from the convoy, backed slowly towards the carriage. He loaded a red-tip flare into the grenade launcher.

Three skeletal figures heading his way. He aimed and fired. The middle soldier staggered like he took a gut punch, flare imbedded in his thorax. Ignition. A jet of red, magnesium fire. Ragged uniforms caught alight. All three soldiers burning like they had been doused in gasoline. They fell to their knees. Pillars of fire. They collapsed, flesh slow-cooking with a blue flame.

Voss slotted a fresh illume into the launcher. He snapped the receiver closed.

Two men weaved between convoy wreckage, fused like conjoined twins. They must have lain pinned beneath a truck, or curled in the trunk of a sedan, as the parasitic infection took hold. Metallic carcinomas erupted from flesh and melded the two Republican Guards together.

Voss took aim.

A hand grabbed his ankle. He looked down. A rotted figure slowly pulled itself from the dirt, streaming sub-surface sand. A horrible, sightless thing, vomited half-dissolved from the ground. Flesh scoured by lime, skin sloughed in strips.

Voss stumbled backward and fell. He tried to jerk his leg free. The ghoul bared its teeth. Voss struggled to aim his rifle.

A second half-dissolved creature broke through the sand-crust behind Voss. A skeletal hand closed over his face.

Voss gagged. His head was wrenched back. Stink of advanced decomposition. He tried to squirm free and screamed as teeth sank into his calf.

He tore his head from grasping claws. Clumps of hair ripped out at the root. He looked down at the rotted revenant that gripped his leg. The creature drooled blood. It spat flesh. Voss fired the grenade launcher. The illume punched through the creature's mouth and wedged in its throat. Voss rolled clear as the creature's head exploded in a brilliant sunburst of red fire.

*

Lucy dragged Voss aboard the carriage and slammed the door. She swept empty mags from a chair. He sat, face white with shock.

Lucy unsheathed her knife. She sliced open his pant leg. She examined the wound. A deep bite mark.

She turned to Amanda.

'Pass me Gaunt's jacket.'

'Why?'

'We're out of surgical dressing.'

'Fuck him.'

'Come on. Give me the fucking jacket.'

Amanda reluctantly lifted the jacket from the back of a chair and handed it to Lucy.

Lucy ripped out the nylon liner and cut it into strips. She pulled on latex gloves, took Raphael's Zippo from her pocket and held her knife blade in the flame.

'Bite your rifle strap.'

'Didn't do Huang any good. This shit is a death sentence.'

'Do it anyway.'

Voss unclipped the rifle strap and bit down. Lucy propped his leg on a chair.

'Hold him still.'

Amanda gripped his leg.

'Hope this hurts, motherfucker,' said Amanda.

Voss closed his eyes and balled his hands into fists.

Lucy sliced flesh with the hot knife. Voss screamed and arched his back. Amanda fought to keep hold of his leg.

Lucy carved out the bite mark. She grabbed the gobbet of flesh with a gloved hand and threw it out the window. It fell in the dirt. Infected soldiers crouched and fought over the scrap of muscle.

Lucy padded the wound with a couple of tampons and bound it with satin strips.

She took a morphine syrette from her pocket. She popped the cap, jabbed the needle in Voss's thigh, and squeezed.

'What the hell are you doing?' protested Amanda. 'Wasting our last fucking shots on this guy?'

'Check the window. Keep us covered.'

'Crappy day,' panted Voss.

'We acted quick,' said Lucy. 'Maybe we stopped the infection.'

Voss shook his head.

'We both know the score.'

'Well, as long as you can pull a trigger, I don't give a shit.'

A cadaverous soldier began to climb through the window. Amanda raised her rifle and pulled the trigger. Dry click. She swung it like a club. The plastic stock cracked the creature's skull.

She checked the magazine.

'That's it. I'm out.'

She threw the rifle aside. She grabbed the machete and hacked at the sill. Fingers flew.

'Beaucoup hostiles. Time to unhitch and roll.'

Transmission crackle.

Lucy picked up the sat phone.

'*Roger that, Carnival. Holding at fifteen thousand. Heading two-nine-five. Approximately twenty minutes from target . . .*'

'Let's get the fuck out of here.'

Voss

Lucy opened the carriage door and was immediately beaten back. The malignant army massed at the doorway reached for her, tearing at her legs and ankles, trying to haul themselves into the carriage. A seething mass of rotted flesh. Awful stench.

'Cover me,' she shouted to Amanda. 'I've got to shut off the fuel pump.'

Lucy fired into the crowd. Headshots. She jumped from the carriage and found herself surrounded by a jostling horde of grotesquely mutated soldiers. Metal dripped from suppurating wounds like they were bleeding chrome.

They lunged. A circle of grasping hands. She switched full auto. She opened fire, and swung her rifle in a sweeping arc at head height. The crowd scythed by bullets. A rolling wave of skull fragments and brain tissue.

She ran for the fuel truck. Her path blocked by a cadaverous soldier. She cracked his skull with the butt of her rifle. He fell. She stamped on his head.

She reached the ladder. She slung her rifle and started to climb. Skeletal hands seized her feet and dragged her down. She thrashed and fought as she was dragged beneath the truck. She lay beneath the chassis, kicking at snapping, snarling mouths. Two soldiers clawed at her legs. She couldn't release her rifle strap. She drew her pistol and fired between her feet.

Lucy rolled clear of the truck. Emaciated figures stood over her. Blood-caked hands reached down.

Gunfire from the carriage. Headshots. Three mutations fell dead. They slumped across Lucy and pinned her to the ground.

She squirmed free of stinking bodies. She grabbed her rifle from the dirt and ran for the carriage. Amanda leaned from the coach and held out her hand. She hauled Lucy aboard and slammed the door.

Lucy checked herself over. She patted down, looked for blood and torn clothing.

'Think I'm okay. Didn't make it to the pump.'

She climbed to her feet. She slapped sand from her rifle.

Fists pounded the side of the carriage. A steady drumming like heavy rain. They heard fingernails gouge the lacquered livery.

'We have to unhook that fuel line,' said Amanda. 'Someone has to get on top of that tanker and hit the Off button. If we pull away while the truck is hooked up and pumping gas we'll be incinerated.'

'Go ahead,' said Lucy, pointing at the carriage door. 'Be my guest.'

The barricade blocking the doorway to the adjoining carriage began to tremble under heavy blows. The shriek and rasp of shifting furniture. The desk obstructing the door began to slide.

'Bunch of them in the next coach,' said Voss. 'Must have piled through the windows.'

Lucy got to her feet. Voss stood unsteadily by her side.

'Got any shotgun shells?'

Voss slotted five shells into the receiver of his Ithaca pump.

'Last few.'

'Let's put them to good use.'

Lucy unhooked a frag grenade from her webbing. She pulled the pin.

'Okay. On my mark.'

She gave the nod.

Amanda and Voss put their shoulders to the upturned desk and bureau and shunted them aside.

Three soldiers stumbled through the doorway and fell to

their knees. Voss stepped forward, racked his shotgun slide and blew their heads apart.

Lucy looked through the doorway. Soldiers massing in the dining car, squirming through broken windows.

She released the safety lever of the grenade and tossed it to the far end of the carriage. The grenade bounced beneath the banquette table and rolled between rotted, dirt-caked combat boots.

'Down,' shouted Lucy. They threw themselves away from the doorway and covered their heads.

A muffled boom. Dust and flame.

They got to their feet. Carnage glimpsed through blue smoke-haze. The banquette table and chair blasted to fragments and draped in viscera.

A soldier lay among smashed furniture, struggling to move.

'Leave him,' said Lucy. 'We don't have time for this shit.'

Amanda ignored her. She kicked through wreckage, swung her machete and split the creature's head with a single hacking blow.

They rebuilt the barricade. They shunted furniture against the doorway. They threw headless bodies from the train.

Soldiers climbed through the windows. Amanda delivered precise headshots with her Glock.

Voss fired his shotgun dry. He threw it down and picked up his rifle.

Sound of splintering wood. Amanda pulled a rotted Persian rug aside. A fist punched upward through the centre of the floor, shattering hard-wood planks. Clawed hands tugged at broken floorboards to widen the hole. A snarling, skeletal thing began to squirm through the aperture. It saw Amanda and hissed. She decapitated the soldier with her machete. The severed head rolled across the floor. She grabbed its hair and threw it from the window.

Lucy overturned a heavy table and slammed it across the

hole. She threw the missile case on top of the up-turned table for added weight.

'Use the grenades,' she shouted.

They unhooked frag grenades from their webbing and pulled pins.

'Keep them clear of the fuel truck. All right. Count of three. One. Two. Three.'

They hurled grenades from the carriage windows. They crouched and covered their heads.

One of the ghouls looked down as a grenade rolled in the sand at his feet, his expressionless face clouded by a moment of memory and doubt.

Eruption of dust and flesh fragments. Body parts littered the sand. Flesh and bone trampled by boots as comrades pushed forward to hammered the side of the coach.

The carriage was filled with blue combustion smoke and the bitter taint of chemical ignition.

Sat-com handset:

'*Angel Flight to Carnival, over.*'

'*Go ahead.*'

'*Approaching target.*'

'*Roger that.*'

'We got to roll,' shouted Amanda. 'Forget the fuel line. Just rip it loose and take our chances. We're out of ammo. We're out of time. We have to go.'

Lucy distributed the remaining mags. Amanda kicked among spent cartridges on the carriage floor, searched for bullets ejected during gun jams.

They loaded their weapons.

'That's it. Last rounds. All I got left. Make them count. Let's retake the loco, and get moving.'

Voss shook out a couple of ammo pouches. A single 40mm grenade fell from a pouch and rolled across mahogany. Gold tip. High explosive. He put in his pocket.

'Lucy. Mandy. It's been a privilege.'

He pushed the carriage door wide. He shielded his eyes from fierce sunlight. A horde of rotted creatures jostled for him. They reached and clawed his legs.

'What the fuck are you doing?' shouted Lucy.

Voss shouldered his rifle and emptied his mag full auto. He dropped the spent clip and slapped a fresh magazine into the receiver.

He jumped from the carriage doorway. A carpet of bodies. Horribly deformed soldiers closed in on all sides. He raised his rifle and lay a sweeping arc of fire in a four-second burst. Chests ripped open. Republican Guard hurled backwards, sent reeling.

He hitched the empty weapon over his shoulder and drew his Glock. He edged towards the fuel truck, delivering swift headshots as snarling, mutated creatures lunged for him.

He shot the weapon dry, then used the butt as a bludgeon. Hammer blows. He cracked skulls.

A soldier tore at his face, ripped skin above his eyebrow. Voss delivered a vicious head-butt. The creature staggered backward.

He threw the pistol aside, drew his knife and punched it through the revenant's eye socket. It toppled backward, knife jammed in its head.

Voss gripped the ladder and climbed. Fingers clawed his legs. Teeth sank into his calf and ankle, tearing fabric, tearing flesh. He yelled in pain and anger. He kicked himself free.

'Motherfuckers.'

He rolled onto the tanker roof. He hit the red Off button with his fist. The steady hum of the fuel pump died away.

He stood. Lucy leant out of the carriage window.

'Don't do it.'

'Good luck, bokkie.'

Voss limped the length of the tanker. He jumped to the adjoining bank truck. He slid through the side window into the cab.

His face was torn. Blood trickled into his eyes. He wiped with the cuff of his sleeve.

He cranked the handle and raised the side window, shutting out snarling faces and scrabbling hands.

He caught his breath. Monstrous creatures surrounded the truck. They massed, snarling and hissing. They pressed themselves to the glass. They smeared spit and pus.

Voss sat in pristine silence, no sound but his own panting breath.

He reached beneath the steering column and sparked ignition cables. Tortured grind. The engine engaged and growled to life.

The cash truck jerked forward. Tow straps sprang taut. The tanker shifted, lurched and began to roll.

The fuel transfer line ripped from the locomotive coupling.

The trucks laboured to cross waste ground. They gouged deep ruts in the dirt. The vehicles jolted and lurched. The disconnected fuel line dragged in the sand.

The engine coughed and stalled. Voss tried to restart the bank truck. The engine turned over, but didn't engage.

He checked a cracked side mirror. He was a quarter of a mile from the train. A crowd of rotted Republican Guard had turned from the besieged carriages. They limped and stumbled towards the trucks.

Monstrous skeletal, creatures surrounded the cab. Voss sat calmly in the driver's seat as hands, deformed grotesquely, slapped and clawed the ballistic glass around him.

A figure pushed through the crowd. Khaki camouflage gear streaked with blood and grime. A *Sisters of Mercy* tour shirt bulged tight over erupting carcinomas. Huang. His face was swollen and distended. Arms bristled with metallic spines.

Huang climbed onto the hood of the cash truck. He snarled and tried to punch through the windshield. He shattered his hand. He kept punching. Blood spattered the glass.

Voss cranked down the cab's side window and squirmed

out. Grasping hands tore at his clothes and rifle strap. He pulled himself free.

He climbed onto the cab. He walked across the roof.

He leapt and landed awkwardly on the hood of the fuel truck. Hands clawed for him. He climbed onto the Kraz cab, then walked the length of the fuel tank.

'Come on, fuckers,' he shouted.

He looked down at grasping, jostling soldiers surrounding the tanker. They reached up for him.

Voss wiped blood from his eyes with the back of his hand. He took a pouch of Red Man from his pocket and folded tobacco into his mouth.

A skeletal abomination gripped the ladder and began to haul itself rung over rung. Voss waited until the creature reached the tanker roof. He delivered a jaw-breaking kick to the head.

'*Fok jou.*'

The soldier drooled teeth and toppled into the crowd.

Voss stamped on the green Start button of the fuel pump. The segmented transfer line convulsed and gulped diesel. Gasoline bubbled from the pipe, washed into the sand, soaked booted feet, turned the ground beneath the truck into a viscous quagmire.

Huang scaled the fuel truck. He climbed from the heavy fender onto the hood. He climbed the cab to the storage tank.

He stood facing Voss. A simian crouch, like he was preparing to attack.

'How's it going?' asked Voss. He slotted the high-explosive round into the grenade launcher. He snapped the breach closed.

Huang emitted a low, stuttering snarl.

'Yeah,' said Voss. 'Me too.'

He took a last look around at the world.

'Been a long fucking day.'

He pointed the rifle between his feet and fired into the tanker hull. The world winked out.

The Bomb

Fifty miles from target

The cargo hold. Fuselage reverberating with the steady drone of Pratt and Whitney turboprops.

Tomasz conducted a last visual inspection of the bomb. He stroked riveted metal.

He checked the delivery frame. The massive thermobaric device sat on a scaffold bed. When the moment came to deploy, Jakub would pull back the joystick. The C123 would tilt and lift, Unchained Melody would be carried to the rear cargo door on greased runners and ejected from the plane. A hundred yards of tether would quickly play out and trip the drogue chutes. Jakub would bank the plane hard left and climb. Thirty seconds to fly clear before the primary barometric fuse initiated a Hiroshima-sized detonation wave, an expanding bubble of over-pressure that would smash the plane from the sky.

Tomasz checked the trigger panel.

Isolators to Off.

Master Safety to Off.

He slotted a final key into the primer console and switched from Safe to Enable. Amber indicators winked red. Weapon armed. The bomb began an insistent warning beep.

Tomasz replaced the cover panel and span lock nuts.

He cranked a wall lever. Whine of hydraulics. Typhoon roar as the loading ramp at the rear of the plane began to open. He gripped a wall strap for support. He saw blue sky. He saw desert, thousands of feet below.

He returned to the co-pilot seat.

'Final confirmation?' he asked.

'Koell says green light.'

'All right, then. Hot to trot, baby.'

He opened his backpack. Thermos flask. Cheetos. *Hustler.* He took out a video camera. He checked for charge and removed the lens cap.

'What's that for?' asked Jakub.

'Koell wants pictures. Says he wants to see the valley burn. Says he's got to see it for himself. Jerk off over it, or something.'

'What about the drone?'

'Probably long gone. Landed, defuelled, broken down, trucked back to base. Koell doesn't want those recon guys sitting in their downlink van, taping the big bang and mailing it to their buddies. Strictly eyes only.'

Tomasz unfolded the map. Blank desert. Empty grid. Rippling contour lines indicated northern hills. A crude red X marked the target site.

'How far are we from the objective?'

'About twenty-six miles,' said Jakub. 'Making good time.'

Tomasz looked out the cockpit at the hogback ridge of hills slowly emerging from the haze up ahead. A barren, biblical landscape.

'There she is. Valley four-oh-three.'

'What's that?' asked Jakub. A black smudge rising into the sky. 'Smoke? There's a smoke plume rising from the valley. Something is burning.'

'Be burning for real in a couple of minutes.'

'I can't do it, bro,' said Jakub.' There are people down there. Yanks, Brits, whatever. Our guys. White hats. We should give them time to get clear.'

'Don't fuck around. This is it. This is the bomb run. Just fly straight and hit the tail release. That's all you have to do.'

'I can't. I can't do it.'

'Shit, let me have control. Film, all right? Take the camera and film.'

Tomasz buckled and took the joystick. He checked airspeed and altitude. He pulled back the collective. He reduced thrust. The plane began a steady deceleration, a steady descent.

A woman's voice from the sat com. She sounded tired and desperate.

'*Angel Flight, do you copy, over? Angel Flight, do you read?* . . .'

Tomasz took the handset from its charge shoe. He hit the off switch and threw it behind him. The unit clattered on the deck.

'Okay. Here we go. Descending to five thousand. Eighty knots. Love from above, baby. This is going to be a big one. This is going to light up the fucking sky.'

Countdown

'We've got to get to the engine,' said Lucy.' This is turning into the fucking Alamo.'

They unchained the door at the head of the carriage. Amanda pulled the door wide. Two Republican Guard tumbled into the coach. Lucy shouldered her rifle and fired. Neat drill holes between the eyes. The back of their heads blew apart. She kicked the bodies aside.

Lucy jumped the knuckle-coupling and landed on the rear platform of the locomotive. Soldiers jostled, reached up for her.

A rotted infantryman gripped the guard rail and began to haul himself up onto the platform. Lucy delivered a vicious kick to his head. He toppled from the train.

More soldiers crowded round the coupling. Lucy delivered headshots.

'Jump,' she shouted.

Amanda jumped. She landed, screamed, and clutched her injured leg. Lucy helped Amanda limp along the narrow walkway.

Lucy knelt and capped the fuel tank.

A skeletal revenant sat on the locomotive roof above the slide door, crouched like a vulture. He leaned down. He leered and hissed. Lucy shot him through the mouth. A streak of red tracer. His jaw flew off. The back of his skull blew out in a shower of sparks. He hung dead.

Lucy grabbed the lifeless man by the collar and threw him from the train.

The cab slide door was open. A rotted infantryman inside, lurking in shadow. Amanda split his head with the machete. They dragged him from the cab and toppled him over the walkway guard rail.

Soldiers climbed up onto the walkway. Lucy delivered swift headshots. The rifle clicked dry.

'I'm out.'

She tossed the weapon.

They sealed themselves inside the cab. More soldiers on the walkway. Lucy struggled to hold the slide door closed. Bloody hands slapped and pawed glass.

Lucy squinted through the blood-spattered window. Black smoke rose from the mangled, smoking chassis of the fuel truck. A distant dot approaching from the south, cresting the valley ridge. Something big. Something silver. An incoming plane. A heavy twin-prop cargo lifter.

She was overcome by a strength-sapping wave of failure. She led her guys into the desert. Promised them gold. They died, one by one, in this god-forsaken shithole. Couldn't even get her boys home alive.

'We're fucked.'

Amanda stood at the engine's console.

A cadaverous figure crouched on the hood of the locomotive. He stared through the windshield, spat and snarled. He punched plate glass until his hand was a bloody pulp.

Amanda tried to put the sound from her mind. The thump and smear of knuckles mashed against the windshield. The muffled mewing of Republican Guards out on the walkway, clawing at windows, hungry for flesh.

She struggled to clear her head and concentrate on the control panel in front of her. She tried to decipher the ignition sequence.

She checked the breaker panel. Every circuit switch set to On. Rows of green lights.

You're going to die, said an insidious voice in her head. *You are about to be consumed by searing fire. These are your last moments. Watching your hands flick switches and turn dials.*

Fuck that shit, said a counter-voice. *Don't give into bullshit fatalism. Fight to live.*

She felt drunk with exhaustion. She rubbed her eyes. She checked controls.

Brake released.

Reverser to Forward.

Throttle from Idle to Run 1.

Roar of turbocharged motive power. A jolt. The locomotive began to inch forward.

Throttle to Run 2.

Amp needles jumped. The engine began to accelerate. Gathering speed.

Amanda sagged and fell. She examined her leg. Fresh blood bubbled through the surgical dressing. She dug in her chest pouch for the last morphine syrette.

Lucy struggled to keep the cab door closed. Monstrously malformed soldiers massed on the walkway outside. She kicked open a tool box and used a wrench to jam the latch.

She looked out the window. She craned to see the sky.

She took the sat phone from her pocket.

'Angel Flight. Incoming plane, do you copy? There are people on the ground. Do not drop the bomb. Please, do not drop the bomb. There are British and American personnel in need of rescue, do you copy, over?'

Amanda struggled to her feet. She limped across the cab and stood by Lucy's side. They wiped dust from the glass, and watched the incoming plane reduce speed, reduce altitude. The cargo ramp was extended.

'Angel Flight, do you copy? Can you hear me? Come on, guys.'

The plane climbed and banked.

'Thank God,' said Amanda. 'They called off the drop.'

Something black fell from the tail of the plane. A cylinder, big as a van. Three candy-stripe drogue chutes unfurled and blossomed.

The bomb began a slow descent into the valley.

Lucy put her arm round Amanda.

'Sorry, babe. I'm so sorry.'

Detonation

The Fairchild banked hard starboard. Turboprops laboured to carry the plane clear of the blast field.

The thermobaric device drifted for twenty-three seconds. The point of release calculated to bring the device over the citadel complex.

Soldiers lay among the ruins. Too decomposed, too far gone to move. Sprawled among the ancient rubble, struggling to look up at the strange object floating in the clear blue sky.

Nine hundred feet. The bomb directly above the high roof of the temple.

The altimeter fuse sent the detonation impulse.

Airburst.

The high explosive core of the device split the bomb case and triggered the main charge. Ten tons of H6. A potent mix of RDX plastic explosive and aluminium powder.

Blinding light. A cataclysmic sunburst over the temple complex. A radiant shock wave expanding at eight thousand feet per second.

Crushing blast pressure flattened the temple. The roof instantly pulverised. Slabs of granite tumbled into the vast hall. Pillars sheared and fell. The sinister altar-god smashed by a wave of fire.

The temple floor collapsed. Subterranean chambers flooded with flame. Boxes of gold liquefied by ten-thousand-degree heat. Catacombs buried beneath countless tons of rubble.

The temple facade crumbled in a cascade of tumbling

blocks. Monstrous hieroglyphs instantly obliterated. Sardonic stone colossi imploding in an avalanche of granite rubble.

The blast spread through the citadel precincts. A tsunami of flame rushed down colonnades and processional avenues. Pillars and arches smashed and scattered like building blocks. Flagstones seared black. Walls and domes shattered to stone chips. Ramparts and gate towers punched flat.

The infernal energy wave washed across open ground. Sand melted to glass by the stellar heat of detonation.

The wrecked vehicles of the convoy tossed like toys, punctured by bullet-velocity rock shards. Tumbling chassis swept in a maelstrom of debris.

A horde of Republican Guard, caught on sun-blasted terrain halfway between the citadel and the locomotive, turned and snarled at the oncoming firestorm. They were enveloped in a supersonic wall of flame. Suppurating flesh seared from their bones in a moment of blow-torch heat.

The nova-blast of detonation sucked air like a hurricane. Gouts of sand drawn upward into the blast cloud. Republican Guard snatched skyward like they were raptured into heaven.

The concussive wave tore across the valley floor in a furious cyclone of fire.

The train entered the rail tunnel, just as the blast wave hit.

Departure

The tunnel. Sudden darkness and screaming engine noise. The cab lit by a single bulb.

An inspection hatch at the back of the cab hung ajar. Lucy and Amanda threw themselves inside the engine bay and slammed the door.

Impact.

Flame rushed down the tunnel like floodwater and engulfed the train. The pressure wave blew out the remaining windows and filled the cab with fire

Lucy and Amanda lay beside the massive generator. Lucy spread her prairie coat over them both as flames jetted through intake fans in the locomotive roof.

The blast was so loud, so overwhelming, it became a strange kind of silence.

Lucy pulled back her smouldering prairie coat. She looked around the tight engine bay. The smoke-filled compartment dimly lit by winking function lights. The power plant hummed with motive power.

'You all right?'

'Yeah,' said Amanda.

They got to their feet and kicked open the engine compartment door.

The interior of the cab was burned black. The foam padding of the engineer's chair spewed smoke. A melted mineral water bottle lay fused with the deck plate. The sat phone was reduced to scattered circuit boards.

Amanda checked the controls. The console was dusted with broken dial glass.

Wind-roar. Tunnel darkness beyond the windows.

'Mean old beast. She's fucked up, but she'll keep trucking.'

Lucy checked the locomotive controls. A tool box propped on the cut-out brake. The throttle roped to Run 2.

The cab reverberated with a deep turbo rumble.

She checked the map.

'We should pass out of the tunnel in a few minutes. Then it's a straight run across the desert.'

Amanda leaned against the cab wall. She slid to the floor and sat, head in her hands. Lucy uncapped her canteen and helped Amanda drain it dry.

The cab slide door was half open. An incinerated Republican Guard wedged in the aperture. Skin and muscle burned with a flickering blue flame. Stink of cooking flesh.

Lucy wrenched the door fully opened and kicked the body from the train.

'I'll be back soon.'

'Where are you going?' asked Amanda.

'To make sure we aren't hauling any passengers.'

Lucy inched along the walkway to the rear platform of the locomotive, coat whipped by the fierce airstream.

The carriages behind the locomotive were burning. Flame rippled across the coachwork like liquid. Tunnel concrete lit blood red as it streamed past.

Lucy jumped the knuckle coupling and stumbled through the carriage doorway.

Gaunt was waiting for her. He lolled in a blackened chair, legs stretched out. He was stripped to the waist. He was badly burned. His arms were blistered and weeping. Half his face was red-raw, hair seared away. Deep wounds at his hip, shoulder and neck. Metallic spines bristled through flesh and fabric.

'Jesus,' said Lucy. 'I watched you die.'

Gaunt smiled.

'Not dead. Transfigured.'

He held up the virus cylinder. The glass had cracked, frosted opaque by a fine web of fissures. The cylinder glowed ethereal blue.

'Behold, I am alive for evermore, and have the keys of hell and of death.' Flame licked at the window frames. The wreckage of Saddam's salon lit flickering orange. Thick smoke rose between floorboards. The interior of the carriage seared carbon-black. Delicate marquetry panels destroyed by blow-torch heat.

'Give me the virus,' said Lucy. 'The money is no good to you now.'

'Been taking it up the ass my whole damn life. Used. Shut out. Maybe I don't want to be the good guy. Maybe I want some fucking payback.'

'You're dying. But you could make a difference. Destroy the virus. Save the entire human race. No one will remember your name. But you could do something heroic. Vindicate your life.'

Gaunt thought it over. He stared into the blue glowing liquid.

'Yeah. I'm dying. But I'll live long enough to make it back to Baghdad. All I have to do is make it through the doors of the conference centre. Smuggle the cylinder under my jacket. Delegates of fifty nations carving up reconstruction contracts. Smash the flask on the chamber floor and the virus will spread round the globe in hours.'

'Scream *Allahu Akbar* as you do it?'

'New York. Moscow. Tokyo. Panic in the streets. The world wiped clean in a matter of weeks. A silent earth. Peaceful. Pure.'

'You're out of your fucking mind.'

Gaunt got to his feet. He placed the virus cylinder on the floor.

'Don't you want to be part of a new breed?'

Lucy grabbed a broken chair and threw at Gaunt. He snatched it out the air and dashed it against the wall.

Lucy unsheathed her bayonet and lunged. She aimed for his neck. Gaunt deflected the blow. The knife imbedded in the carriage wall.

He punched Lucy in the face.

She reeled. Blood sprayed from her nose.

She drove her fist into Gaunt's chest, delivered a death-blow that should have stopped his heart. He snarled and kicked her across the carriage. She skidded across the floor and slammed into the wall.

Lucy tried to clear her head. She crouched against the carriage wall. She blinked, struggled to clear her vision. The floor beneath her smouldered, hot to the touch.

Gaunt tugged the knife from the wall. He examined the blade, his blurred reflection. The strange disease had begun to transform his senses. The interior of the carriage danced with weak luminescence from the virus cylinder.

Lucy crouched in the corner of the carriage, panting with fear.

He smiled. He stood over Lucy. He grabbed her by the collar, pulled her upright and pinned her to the wall.

He wondered how best to kill her. He decided to drive the knife through her eye. He positioned the knife tip and braced to strike.

Lucy had a broken chair leg in her hand. She jammed the jagged shaft into his hip wound. He grunted. She twisted the chair leg. Pus and blood bubbled from blackened, infected flesh. He cried in pain and released his grip. He staggered backwards and pulled the wooden shaft from the wound.

Lucy threw all her weight into a throat punch. Her fist slammed into his neck. He staggered backward, clutching his throat, gagging and gulping. He toppled, scattering cartridge cases as he hit the floor.

Gaunt lay in the middle of the carriage. He arched his back as he tried to draw air through a crushed larynx.

Lucy picked Voss's shotgun from the floor. She stood over Gaunt. She gripped the barrel of the weapon and lifted it over her head.

He bared his teeth, like he was trying to say 'fuck you' but couldn't find the breath.

'Go to hell.'

She brought the shotgun down in a sweeping arc. The impact split his face and shattered his skull. She pounded his head with the butt. She pulped his brain.

Fire spread through the carriage. Burning roof panels curled and fell, setting carpets ablaze.

The virus cylinder rolled across smouldering floorboards. Blue liquid wept from hairline cracks in the glass. Lucy kicked the cylinder into flames.

She flipped latches on the missile case. The disassembled Hellfire. She took the solid-fuel rocket motor from its foam bed. A grey cylinder with fins, a batch-plate and NO LIFT stencil. She hurled it across the carriage. The rear section of the missile clattered and came to rest beside Gaunt's body. It began to smoke and cook.

Lucy ran from the carriage.

She jumped the coupling to the rear platform of the locomotive. Darkness lit by flickering flames. Stonework and concrete buttresses blurred past.

She lay face-down on steel deck plate, and seized the release lever of the carriage coupling. She gripped it and wrenched with all her strength. Rust-shriek. The lever snapped up, the knuckle-coupling unclenched and the carriage released. Pneumatic brake hose ruptured and whipped compressed air. A loop of power cable pulled taut, sparked, and broke.

Lucy stood on the rear platform of the locomotive. She watched the blazing carriage decelerate and recede. Tunnel walls lit by flickering flame-light. Mahogany coachwork consumed by fire.

Lucy hurried to reach the cab and shelter from the coming blast.

The Western Hills. High crags and rubble. Bleak and barren, like the surface of Mars.

Twin colossi flanked the rail tunnel entrance. Gargantuan Akkadian kings carved at the dawn of humanity. Austere, blank-eyed sentinels staring out across the desert.

The dull thud of detonation. A jet of flame from the tunnel mouth. The locomotive burst from the portal riding a wave of fire, like it was tearing out of hell.

The engine charged headlong into the desert. The scorched and scoured juggernaut jetted black diesel fumes. Bodywork burned carbon black. Windows blown out. Nose lamp shattered. Access doors buckled and ripped away.

The locomotive ploughed through dunes, tore down a track that stretched across desolate terrain and merged with rippling heat-haze at the distant horizon.

Amanda sat slumped in the engineer's chair. She gazed out the smashed windshield at high sun and open desert. She drowsed, nodding out, pale and sick.

Lucy put a hand on her shoulder.

'You okay?'

'The sun is getting high,' said Amanda. 'No water. We're going to get cooked in here.'

'We'll find some shade.'

'How long will it take to cross this fucking desert?'

'At this speed? Ten or twelve hours, if the fuel holds out.'

'Christ.'

'We'll make it, babe. We'll make it.'

Cleansweep

IBN Sina Hospital, Baghdad.

Lucy lay in her hospital bed. She struggled to stay conscious. Her mind was fogged by Amytal.

Street noise from an open window.

The crackle and squeak of bio-suit rubber as Colonel Drew loaded a hypodermic gun.

'Are you going to kill me?' she murmured.

'Taking care of loose ends,' he said, voice muffled by his face plate. 'It's nothing personal.'

Lucy let her arm droop over the side of the mattress. She snagged the wrist strap of her Rolex on the metal bed-frame and discreetly released the clasp. She shook the metal bracelet down her hand and gripped it like a knuckle-duster.

Drew leant over her.

'Try to relax. It will be quick. It won't hurt.'

He picked up her right arm. He positioned the needle, ready to prick skin.

Lucy punched his faceplate with an armoured fist. Lexan cracked. His nose broke against the visor. He spritzed the safety glass with blood and spit.

She rolled off the bed and pinned Drew to the tiled floor. She sat on his chest. She could see herself reflected in the crack visor. A wide-eyed crazy woman.

She pulled off his hood. Another blow to the head. The diamond bezel of her Rolex cut open his cheek. He coughed blood and spat a tooth.

She shook off the wristwatch and threw it aside. She snatched up the hypodermic gun.

'Please,' croaked Drew.

'Fuck you.'

Lucy punched the needle into his right eye and pulled the trigger. Gas-cartridge hiss. His eye inflated and burst, spilling clear liquid.

He convulsed. He arched his back. Blood leaked from his nose and ears.

Lucy stood back. Drew gripped her bare ankle. She jerked her leg free.

She watched him thrash and slowly die.

She patted him down, slid her hands over the heavy rubber in case he had a holstered pistol beneath his suit.

Nothing.

Her clothes lay in a heap in the corner. She bent and picked them up. Amytal head rush. She swayed like a drunk.

The clothes had been cut from her body, reduced to rags.

Her prairie coat was still in one piece. She threw it over her shoulder.

She stepped into the corridor, bare feet padding silently on floor tiles. She stumbled down the passageway, leaning against the wall for support.

Amanda lay in her hospital bed, drowsed with morphine.

Koell stood at a side table, loading a hypodermic gun. She listened to the creak of his Tyvek hazmat suit. She was lulled by the electric hum of his backpack respirator. Air sucked through charcoal virus filters.

'Don't kill me,' she murmured.

He stood over the bed. He lifted her arm and positioned the hypo gun.

'I read your MI profile. Spoilt little rich girl. Trust-fund junkie. All that promise. All that potential. The person you could have been.'

He lifted her arm and positioned the hypo gun.

'You and your friends. No country. No code. No high ideal. Nothing but the tawdry pursuit of money. And look where it got you. A miserable death. Utterly alone.'

Lucy's voice:

'Hey, Koell.'

Koell turned. The base of a drip stand struck him in the face. His rubber overboots slipped on the tiled floor and he fell on his back. A second blow smashed the hazmat faceplate.

Lucy threw Amanda a hospital gown and her Stetson.

'Let's get out of here.'

Lucy sat on Koell's chest. She tore off his hood, grabbed the hypodermic gun from the floor and jabbed the needle into his neck.

'Don't,' he whispered. 'Please. Don't.'

'Where did you suit up? You and the other guy.'

'What?'

'Your clothes. Where are your clothes?'

The underground parking level of the Al Rasheed.

Koell's Lincoln Navigator sat in shadow. Koell at the wheel, Lucy by his side. She kept him covered with the Sig P226 she found in the glove box.

Lucy wore Colonel Drew's oversized fatigues. Koell wore Lucy's ripped trousers, her laceless boots.

'You won't get far,' said Koell.

'Shut the fuck up. Keep your hands on the wheel.'

They watched Amanda check out their battered, shot-up Suburban. She wore Koell's shirt, slacks and brogues.

She peered through cracked windows. She crouched and checked beneath the vehicle. She climbed in, dropped keys from the sun visor, and gunned the engine.

Thumbs up.

'Okay,' said Lucy. 'Get out.'

They climbed out of the Navigator. Lucy could see the red dot of an active CCTV camera in corner shadows. She hid the pistol in her jacket pocket.

'Act casual.'

They crossed the empty parking structure. Footfalls echoed in the cavernous space.

Koell limped.

'Walk properly.'

'Boots are about six sizes too small.'

'Walk.'

They reached the Suburban.

'Get in.'

Amanda shifted seats. Koell took the wheel. Lucy got in the rear.

'Drive.'

'Where are we headed?

'Across town. QRF Indigo. The Canadian staging base on Route Irish.'

'Why?'

'Just drive the fucking car.'

They pulled out, and took the up-ramp into blinding sunlight.

The old quarter. Trash fires, feral dogs. Suspicious locals watched the Suburban speed past.

Lucy unzipped a holdall on the back seat. Fresh clothes. She changed. She strapped on a tac vest. She clipped a black nylon belt and dropped a HK 9mm into the drop holster.

She threw her dog tags from the window.

Koell watched her in the rear-view.

'You and your girlfriend were going to skip out on your buddies. Was that the plan all along? Load the gold and run?'

Lucy examined the crumpled gang photo. Lucy, Amanda, Toon, Huang and Voss. Hanging out in the Riv, laughing, toasting the camera.

'None of your damned business.'

They pulled over. Lucy and Amanda switched seats. Koell drove while Lucy kept him covered. Amanda sat on the back seat and dressed.

'Why Indigo?' asked Koell. 'What do you think the Canucks are going to do for you?'

'We're going to hitch a ride on a supply flight back to Germany.'

She opened the glove box and shook out an envelope. Canadian passports. A wad of dollars. Bribe money had secured an amendment of provisional records. A handful of key strokes summoned two freelance journalists into existence. New names, birth dates, press accreditation and social insurance numbers.

'We'll be leaving our old names behind.'

'And what about me?' said Koell.

'Pull over.'

'Here?'

'Stop the fucking car.'

Koell pulled the battered SUV to the side of the road. He parked outside a bombed-out restaurant. He shut off the engine. The chill blast of air-conditioning dwindled and died.

He anxiously looked around. A deserted street. Shanty squalor.

'Why here?'

'Shut up.'

Lucy took plastic tuff-ties and lashed Koell's wrists to the wheel.

'What are you doing?'

Koell started to sweat.

'Don't worry,' said Lucy. 'I'm not going to hurt you.'

Amanda climbed out and shouldered the holdall.

'Don't,' said Koell. 'Don't leave me here.'

Lucy reached round the steering column and turned the ignition key to ACC.

'Relax, said Lucy. 'Listen to some music.'

She turned Cypress Hill up full volume and climbed out of the car.

'Let's go,' she said.

A last glance at Koell.

'Please,' he mouthed through the windshield.

Lucy and Amanda hurried down the deserted street, 'Ain't Going Out Like That' blasting from the battered Suburban. The song mingling with the mournful, city-wide call to prayer.

Koell struggled to snaps the cuffs. Deafening, jackhammer bass-beat.

He twisted his hands, stretched his fingers to reach the ignition. Plastic cut deep into his wrists.

He kicked off a boot, raised his foot and tried to press the CD off switch with his toe.

A beat-up Mercedes pulled to the kerb behind the Suburban. Koell checked the rear-view. Five Iraqis in track-suits got out the car. One of them carried an AK and yammered into a cellphone. The group lit cigarettes.

Koell leant down and butted the door handle until he engaged central locking.

The men circled the Suburban.

Stubble. Cruel eyes. Local militia.

The lead guy hammered at the cracked side window with the butt of his AK. Cracked ballistic glass began to bow inward.

Koell sobbed with fear. He tried to chew his way through the plastic cuffs.

The window broke. Koell closed his eyes and whimpered as a clawing hand reached inside and popped locks.

They cut Koell's restraints and hauled him from the SUV. He clung to the wheel. He clung to his seat.

'No,' he sobbed, as they prised his fingers free and dragged him from the vehicle.

He lay in the street. He lost bladder control.

'I'm important,' he croaked. 'I'm worth money.'

The leader crouched beside Koell. He smelled of cigarettes and talc.

'You should not have come here, my friend.'

Lucy and Amanda ran down the deserted street. They could see sangar gun towers above the roof tops. A maple pennant hung from an antenna.

Garbage in the road. A stinking sewer trench. Locked doors and shuttered windows, like the locals were braced for a storm.

Amanda sagged with exhaustion.

'Come on. Keep moving,' said Lucy

She wrapped her arm round Amanda's waist and helped her run.

They turned a corner. The QRF compound up ahead. High walls and guard towers. Entrance gate flanked by Hesco barriers and concrete bollards.

The gates pulled back. An armoured patrol rolled out in a haze of dust and diesel. Two Humvees and a Stryker eight-wheeled APC setting out on some kind of snatch operation.

Lucy blocked the street and flagged her arms. The vehicles braked. The turret .50 cal on the lead Humvee swivelled and took aim.

Troops ran from the APC. They took cover behind the lead Humvee, assault rifles trained on Lucy and Amanda.

Loud-hailer:

'*Stay where you are.*'

Lucy tossed the pistol. Amanda dropped the bag.

They stood, hands raised.

'We're civilians,' shouted Lucy.

'*Take off the coat. Lose the hat. Lift your shirts.*'

Lucy shrugged off her prairie coat. Amanda threw her

Stetson aside. They lifted their shirts and turned full circle. No suicide vest.

Lucy held up passports.

'We are Canadian citizens. We got carjacked. My friend is hurt. She's been shot in the leg. She needs medical attention.'

'*Kneel. Keep your hands where we can see them.*'

They knelt, hands on heads.

Amanda sagged with exhaustion.

'It's all right, baby,' murmured Lucy. 'We made it. We made it home.'

TOP SECRET **SPECIAL HANDLING** NO FORM

Central Intelligence Agency

Directorate of Operations, Near East Division

Doc ID: 58h
Page 01/1

10/25/05

Partial transcript of hostage video released by an unknown Sadrist/Shia insurgent group thought to be linked to the Mahdi Army. Digital footage is poor quality, but appears to show Field Officer Robert Koell. Koell is wearing a red boiler suit. He is clean shaven. He has a dirt mark or bruise on his right temple. He sits in front of a white sheet backdrop and reads a prepared statement to camera. He speaks in a monotone. He appears disoriented, possibly sedated.

'. . . The New Crusades have exposed the ugly face of the infidel West and its apostate agents in our Islamic region. This pact is led by the empire of evil and criminality, America. Their criminality has manifested itself in atrocities committed against our Islamic peoples in Iraq, Afghanistan and Palestine . . .

'. . . We swear by Allah the Magnificent, who raised the sky without pillars, that neither America nor those who live in America shall have peace until all infidel armies have left the land of Muhammad, peace and prayers of Allah be upon him . . .'

BURN NOTICE IMMEDIATE ACTION

Central Intelligence Agency
Office of Director, Washington DC, 20506

Doc ID: 67bd
Page 01/1

12/19/05

MEMORANDUM TO: Special Adviser, Office of Director
SUBJECT: Spektr

Sir,

We have concluded the sterilisation of the Spektr station in Baghdad. All cryptographic coms equipment has been secured and all relevant documentation shipped red-bag to Andrews Airforce Base aboard our Suisse GeoTech Gulfstream.

Staff stationed at the staging base Sharjah have been ordered to stand down and relocate.

The body of Colonel Drew has been repatriated. The standard KIA notice has been issued to his family.

Officer Robert Koell remains officially MIA while we await identification of the headless body found by scavengers in a refrigerator at the garbage dump in Kasrah Waatash, a residential area northeast of Baghdad. However the West Point cadet ring recovered by our informant suggests the remains are indeed those of Robert Koell.

The Spektr project may be regarded as closed.

J.Lawrence
Senior Regional Coord.
Office of Director, Qatar Station

PRESENT DAY

Eyewitnesses report fireball in night sky

—Spokane Daily Record

A fireball lit up the sky last night, prompting panic calls to emergency services across the county.

Eyewitnesses described a blinding white light passing above the clouds, accompanied by a high whistling sound.

The dash camera of a police car involved in a traffic stop near Airway Heights caught blurred images of a flickering white light that, for a few moments, lit the sky bright as day.

Trentwood Police Dept, Spokane, released the recording of a call from gas station attendant Dwayne Mothersbaugh, who took a series of pictures of a white fireball passing behind trees.

DM: *Some kind of meteor. It's burning. It's moving fast. And there's a whistling sound, like a plane in a steep dive. Can you hear it? If I hold up my phone, can you hear the noise? It's high. Hard to judge, but I think it's high altitude. A fireball moving unbelievably fast. Seems to be coming down quick. It's big, whatever it is. Big like a passenger jet. It's passed behind trees.*

DISPATCHER: *Sir, am I to understand a civilian airliner has crashed into the woods?*

DM: *No. I mean I don't know. It didn't look like a plane. It was big. The object was big. I couldn't make out detail. It was like a comet, a big ball of fire.*

DISPATCHER: *Has there been an explosion? Can you see flames?*

DM: *I heard a bang. Could be a sonic boom. It came down north, over towards Green Bluff. I can't see flames.*

Police are reluctant to discuss the matter further, but we understand an aerial survey of woodland near Green Bluff conducted by helicopter at first light located what appeared to be a large impact crater and small brushfires.

A police spokesperson refused to discuss rumours the impact site contained an item of scorched space debris. However, unconfirmed eyewitness accounts describe a large cylinder, possibly a fuel tank, at the bottom of the crater. Press speculate the wreckage might by the third-stage booster of a military rocket or the habitation module of a Soyuz spacecraft.

We understand an exclusion zone has been declared around the site.

'Federal authorities have advised local law enforcement not to approach the impact site at this time,' said a PD spokesperson. 'A specialist military recovery team has been dispatched and will be on site within twenty-four hours.'

Laure Pernette, lead scientist at the Orbital Debris Programme Office attached to the Johnson Space Centre, confirmed that NASA has, for several weeks, been tracking a large debris field caught in a decaying orbit.

'Mass and alignment suggest the wreckage of an orbital installation akin to Mir or Skylab. This loose aggregation of debris is beginning to re-enter the atmosphere. We are currently liaising with our counterparts in the Russian Space Agency to see if this object is a relic of their Soyuz programme.'

Items of space detritus, such as rocket boosters and redundant satellites, frequently re-enter the Earth's atmosphere. These objects usually reach velocities twenty times the speed of sound and burn up during re-entry. Those objects that survive the ablation of uncontrolled descent usually fall into the ocean or land in remote, unpopulated areas.

The Johnson Space Centre currently tracks over twelve thousand substantial astral objects using radar arrays in Goldstone, California and Arecibo, Puerto Rico.

'We estimate several more large items from this debris field may re-enter the Earth's atmosphere in the coming days and weeks,' said Pernette. 'Data supplied by NORAD suggests a series of re-entries over North America and the Atlantic. We understand wreckage may also be scattered over Northern Europe and the Arctic Circle.

'The Federal Aviation Authority has issued a bulletin to US pilots warning a potential debris hazard may exist for the next couple of weeks. Our international partners have also been informed and are taking appropriate steps.

'I understand some news agencies are attempting to link the impact on Sunday night with a series of emergency admissions to the trauma department of Providence Medical Centre. We do not believe these two situations are in any way connected.

'We certainly advise the public not to approach anything they believe may be an item of space wreckage. Some older communications satellites were powered by plutonium power cells. Booster rockets that have fallen to earth may still contain carcinogenic traces of hydrazine propellant. However, we understand the current CDC level-four quarantine at Providence relates to a viral pandemic alert described as a 'contagious haemorrhagic pathogen', and is therefore very unlikely to be associated with the wreckage that fell in remote woodland near Green Bluff.

'There will be further re-entries in the coming weeks. We look forward to a spectacular light show.

There is no reason to be alarmed.'

Acknowledgements

Illustrations by Noel Baker.

I would like to thank Charles Walker at United Agents and Oliver Johnson at Hodder.

Five years have passed. Five years in which the plague has spread across the world leaving only tiny enclaves of survivors . . .

OUTPOST

They took the job to escape the world.
They didn't expect the world to end.

Kasker Rampart: a derelict refinery platform moored in the Arctic Ocean. A skeleton crew of fifteen fight boredom and despair as they wait for a relief ship to take them home.

But the world beyond their frozen wasteland has gone to hell. Cities lie ravaged by a global pandemic. One by one TV channels die, replaced by silent wavebands.

The Rampart crew are marooned. They must survive the long Arctic winter, then make their way home alone. They battle starvation and hypothermia, unaware that the deadly contagion that has devastated the world is heading their way . . .

HODDER